TIMEWRAITH
THE IMMORTALITY TRIALS TRILOGY
BOOK TWO

MADISON NICOLE

MN BOOKS LLC

Editing: K.F. Starfell

Proofreading: K.F. Starfell

Cover Art: Amanda Hawkins, Eternal Geekery

Sensitivity Read: Cruella G.

This book is for 18+

❀ Created with Vellum

To those that fight every single day to be seen, heard, understood and loved.

Before you read...

This book contains themes of fetishization, self-harm, suicidal ideation, completed suicided by a parent (not heavily described), death of a parent (past), loved one in a coma, torture, blood, gore, violence, misogyny, mind control, alcohol consumption, death of animals (no pets), animal cruelty, bullying, addiction, depression, anxiety, choking, stabbing, manipulation, sexual content, explicit language, physical abuse, mental abuse, emotional abuse, kidnapping, murder, abandonment, manipulation of the dead, colonialism and other adult themes. This book is intended for mature audiences and reader discretion is advised. If you have any concerns about the contents of this book feel free to email the author, Madison Nicole, at info@madisonnicolebooks.com. Your mental health matters.

Additionally, this book was originally published in 2022. I have made changes and updates to the manuscript as I have grown and evolved as an author. You may notice small changes from your previous read if you enjoyed the original version. Don't worry, I have kept all the fun, spice, and suspense, just polished it up. Happy reading!

ONE

GREER

Darkness surrounded me.

I wriggled my heavy, sore body back and forth but found little movement. I was lying on what I assumed was a bed. My hands and feet were shackled, just like they had been before when I had completely lost my shit.

Fuck.

I should have been scared. Except I had locked my fear out in my catastrophic explosion of emotional energy earlier. I shut it down to survive whatever would come next.

It felt like I was a puppet on a string with all my limbs tied up. Like I was being shoved forward, violently, and aggressively to do the bidding of a demented puppeteer.

I blinked, thinking of how long I had stayed curled up on the king's throne room floor.

Minutes?

Hours?

Days?

It didn't matter. The roaring of emotions that had drowned me and burned through my throat were still there, but they had settled into a dull ache in every part of my body instead of a relentless pounding through my blood.

My body still felt... *different*. Like it had been pulled apart and put back together with more energy and matter than I had before. My skin felt too tight, and everything was foreign, like my soul had been put into something else. Something that was no longer mine.

Maybe I would just continue to lie here and wither away. The idea oddly brought a grim smile to my lips until I realized that my body was now immortal. Which meant there was no chance of me dying now. Death would not greet me like an old friend anymore. It had abandoned me, too.

I was always worried I would end up like my mother, with so much pain coursing through me that the only possible way for it to end was by my own hand. I almost had.

But right now, I thought I finally understood.

The gods were cruel. Xael said she had tried to save us, and the other gods had turned her magic deadly. It had driven my mom to take her own life. And, right now, the choice wasn't mine to make anymore, but if I could, I was worried I would. That I would rather die than be forced into destroying the mortal realm. To destroy the people I loved. It was a price I would gladly pay if it meant these immortals would leave my friends alone.

An ache started to blossom in my chest, thinking about how my biggest fear had been that I would turn to death, and, at this present moment, I would welcome it with open arms. If my mother's pain matched my own, I could finally understand why it would seem like the best option. An end to the relentless torment of what I knew to be the time magic would be welcomed instead of inciting fear and chaos like it used to.

Funny, how for so long I fought my own trauma, only to have it cemented into my bones. Before, I had the option to rid myself of it, and now it was ingrained in my soul and my cells. Time was no longer something that I had to worry about. I had it now without limitations. My life and power were unironically filled with nothing but fucking time.

I frowned. How was I just supposed to live with this? Even though I might feel like dying, and maybe I even wanted to... I couldn't. I had no choice anymore. I had to live with this darkness suffocating me alive, like the living dead. And that was now going to be used against me while other people tried to manipulate and use me for their own agenda.

My emotions felt like they were at war with one another. The dull ache of hopelessness and anxiety had been a companion for so long, and now it was supposed to bring me power. Power that would be manipulated to hurt humans and others. And I was supposed to like it? To be happy about it and rejoice in its splendor? I didn't know how to reconcile with all of this. All that had occurred still felt like an out-of-body experience. Like at any point, I might wake up with the familiar cloud of depression over a body that had been its home for the last two and a half decades.

But I knew I wouldn't. That version of myself no longer existed. That version had been allowed to die for this new Greer to rise.

I was honestly fucking terrified.

I wanted to claw at my skin and scream until my voice gave way to whispers and squeaks. But those feelings were not a luxury I could indulge right now.

So, I pushed all that shit away. They were a non-option for my new immortality, and I hadn't wept in front of those bastards to give up. I would use the sorrow and fire in my body to give them all what they deserved.

A searing bright light burst in front of me. I closed my eyes in an effort to scurry back into the darkness that I was becoming so accustomed to.

"You're awake," a familiar voice said with some relief.

I kept my eyes squeezed shut because I didn't want to look at his face. Another wave of emotions, so painful and powerful, was building from my belly and was threatening to erupt uncontrollably. But I forced it down. Locked it up tight with the rest of my turmoil.

With my eyes closed, I could hear him moving about the room, which was now disgustingly bright. The smart thing would be opening my eyes, taking in my surroundings, and formulating a plan. Except I was too damn weary to fight right now and too raw to face what was right in front of me.

Soon. But right now, I wanted to shut everything out a little longer.

Seeing Kyra might break me again. I wasn't ready. I honestly didn't know if I would ever be. My heart was already scattered across that throne room with my grief and agony—the pieces, unlikely to find each other perfectly again.

"Go away," I said, barely recognizing my own voice. It was dry, raspy, and desperate. Sore from screaming and crying as the immortals delighted in my pain.

"Greer, please look at me," he quietly pleaded.

I could *feel* him right next to what I still assumed was the bed.

I took three deep breaths and told myself I would only need five seconds of bravery to start this conversation. It reminded me of Nova, and my heart squeezed inside of me. What would happen to my friends? Lux? Waverly? Even moody Sutton?

Shit.

I flung my eyes open, and the light burned my vision.

I swallowed hard and let my eyes adjust while Kyra came into view. His beautiful, dark hair was long and tousled, while his ruby irises looked vacant. Dark circles hung under his eyes, and he looked exhausted.

Like he was filled with pain and despair.

My heart pounded at the sight of him, and I silently cursed it, telling it to get its shit together because he had betrayed us.

But godsdamnit, he was still beautiful, and my heart nearly fractured again. His eyes poured into mine. I whipped my head back and forth and saw that I was indeed on a large bed with black silk sheets and my hands and feet wrapped in metal manacles. It seemed like the more I moved, the tighter the damn things got. Pain shooting up my arms and sending agony through my fingertips.

The room was plain and dark, with a vanity off to one side and two doors on the other side of me. There was a table next to the bed, and Kyra was sitting in a chair next to me with a cup of water.

It was plain. Dark and bleak like everything else. Like my whole godsdamn life.

Someone had changed my clothes into a plain shirt and leggings. I tried to sit up, but the cuffs gave me another zing of torture. Wincing, I huffed out a frustrated sigh. I directed my attention back to Kyra and narrowed my gaze at him.

"I'm looking at you. What do you want?" I said, trying to put venom in my words, but it wasn't working very well. They fell flat and were laced with anguish.

Hopelessness wound its way into my blood, but it didn't feel familiar anymore. Instead, I wanted to scream at it and tell it this feeling was useless now. Because it didn't matter how I felt. There was no way out of this hellhole.

Hurt flashed across his features, and his cheekbones looked sharper as if he hadn't eaten much in the last few days.

His spine was rigid, as his eyes swept back and forth through the room like he was looking for something lurking in the shadows, even though there wasn't a damn place anyone could be hiding in this simple bedroom.

His eyes landed back on me, and a surge of emotions

slammed into my stomach once again, but I dug my fingernails into my palms to draw the emotional pain away.

"I'm not supposed to touch you," he said carefully. There were silver cuffs on his wrists that looked like mine, but without chains. Dark red angry burns swirled around his hands and forearms, snaking up to where his long-sleeved shirt was shoved to his elbows.

Kyra had also been chained in the throne room, and he had thrashed around with his fire to try to free himself, but it didn't work. These cuffs were made of something that couldn't be touched by magic. But his burns looked fresh, like they had just happened moments ago. Was he hurting constantly, too?

I stifled the sob that threatened to escape from me at the thought of Kyra being hurt or tortured. I loved him, and even though he betrayed me, I didn't want him injured. My soul felt like a gaping wound, too fresh to be exposed to what the world had to offer, but there wasn't any choice in the matter. We were both collateral damage to a bigger picture.

"But I can give you this water," he said slowly, as if he were calculating each word.

Carefully, he moved towards me and tipped the water cup to my lips. I swallowed greedily, draining the whole cup. Kyra didn't take his eyes off me as he pulled away, and the cup automatically refilled itself.

"Do you want any more?" he asked softly, like I would break into a million pieces right then and there.

I could have. Gods, I wanted to. But I wouldn't.

I drank three more cups and tried to sit up once again, getting tired of feeling like a child.

"Why can't I sit up?" I growled.

"Father, please, allow her to sit up," he said politely through gritted teeth, not taking his gaze off me. His eyes flashed black.

It was so quick I almost missed it, but then they settled back into their scarlet hue.

There was a change in the air like a quick static shock, and less tension on my restraints. I gingerly sat up and wiggled my way to the back of the bed toward the iron bars that served as my headboard and anchor.

Kyra was swift and careful not to touch me as he adjusted the pillows behind me. I held my breath as his warmth pulsed inches from my body. My belly erupted in butterflies, followed by a sharp pang in my heart.

It was like my body reacted before my mind could tell it that we were *extremely* pissed off at him and hurt. I was being torn in two from just his proximity.

"Why?" I whispered, with Kyra still hovering close.

He moved so our eyes were inches away, and I bit my lower lip to avoid reaching out and kissing him. The urge was so strong, yet I knew it would be painful—impossible even.

His eyes flicked to my mouth, then jumped back and forth across the room, still waiting for something to pop out. His body was stiff, and I could practically hear the fire in his veins. His posture relaxed, and he opened his mouth to speak when darkness fell in the room again. I couldn't help it. I called out for him.

"Kyra!" I screamed.

I lunged forward with my chains, and I briefly felt my arms wrap around him, and tingles ran across my skin for a split second. He screamed my name in agony, and I was blasted back with a heat wave and slammed back into the metal bars behind me, my chains growing rigid again.

Light burst through the room again, and he was gone—like he had never been there in the first place.

I started to panic then because I wondered if my new powers made it impossible for people to touch me, and my whole body shook, but tears wouldn't come. Why had Ky screamed? Were they hurting him? I squeezed my eyes shut and ground my teeth together.

I didn't understand any of this.

I needed to talk to Kyra even though it was beyond painful. I wanted to soothe his burns and feel his arms and his lips despite the gaping hole of his betrayal.

How fucking confusing were all these emotions swirling around inside me?

I screamed out again, feeling frustrated and overwhelmed.

Invisible vines tangled and slithered around my limbs, and I gasped. The essence of time wrapped around me like a living, breathing entity.

My powers.

I was a timewraith.

I needed to figure out what that meant and how to wield my powers. I needed to understand what was happening to me and what had happened to Kyra. I needed to start planning on how I was going to get out of there and stop the gods from taking over the mortal realm.

"Please don't hurt him," I whispered the words before I even realized they were out of my mouth.

"Oh, little wraith, your feelings for my son are quite unexpected," Riordan purred.

I whipped my head looking for where he could be, but there was nothing.

"Right here," he whispered into my ear, and I nearly jumped out of the bed, but the chains kept me firmly in place. I screamed at his proximity. One moment, his voice was haunting me, and the next, his body was right next to my bed.

"Gods, why are you here?!" I seethed, scooting away from him as he walked to the end of my bed and pulled a chair over.

His features were sharper than the last time I saw him. As if his godly form was more on display. Riordan was massive. Tall and broad, olive skin, and a hard jaw. His dark hair was tied back, and he wore plain clothes as if he didn't have a damn care in the world.

"The more you struggle, the tighter they will become. If it cuts you so deeply that your hand breaks or you lose circulation, you could lose your hand. Don't worry, it will grow back, but the process is... excruciating." Riordan smirked and nodded at my manacles.

"Good to know," I said, swallowing and trying to sit up as much as possible.

"See, your cuffs were designed to hurt you and break you. Kyra's were simply meant to keep his damn firepower under control. However, we know that love makes us reckless, so until he learns, he will burn from them." His eyes drilled into mine, and a shiver worked its way up my spine.

"I will not break." My voice was feeble, but the words made it out regardless. My body may have been shaking, but I would not be made into something I was not. These people had already taken too much for me. I would not let them take any more.

"Oh, you will. I will make sure of it."

Riordan's scarlet eyes flashed black, and I screamed. My wrists were on fire. One that scorched my skin and traveled across the entirety of my body. I thrashed and writhed, trying to escape the pain that seemed invisible to my eye but could be felt in every fiber of my being.

"Have a good evening, wraith." Those were Riordan's last words as he left me sobbing in my bed.

The pain eventually subsided, but my body spasmed from the aftershocks of the effects. No physical burns perturbed my skin; rather, it was like a heat in my veins that wouldn't go away.

I swear there was a chuckle inside my head just before the lull and pull of sleep, my body finally giving out. Was it safe to even rest here? It didn't matter. I would welcome the reprieve anyway.

↤

"Greer, my child."

I sat up. The chains were gone, but their marks were there, and all the torture they had caused me still hung heavy in my bones. I had been lying on the ground like I had been asleep, except the person hovering close by wasn't Ky.

It was Xael.

She looked exactly as she did last time.

Like me, except sharper.

Is that how I looked now? As an immortal with her powers? Would I even recognize myself anymore?

I shuddered and glanced at the angry bruises on her wrists, ankles, and neck poking out from her billowing white gown.

"Xael," I said, finding my voice wasn't as raspy and raw as before.

In fact, it sounded downright normal. My body felt great, even if the memories of pain lingered.

Instead of darkness, everything was light.

We were in a brightly lit meadow with a small pond off to the right.

It was picture-perfect with wildflowers bursting from the ground in a smattering of colors, and a clear blue sky welcomed my eyes with a bright shining sun.

Xael transformed from hovering above me to sitting beside me and facing the small glassy pond. She wore faded, ripped jeans, no shoes, and a simple white T-shirt. Her red hair was tied back in a long ponytail. She looked almost normal, like I had before.

"I thought this might make you feel more comfortable." She gestured to her clothes and the world around us.

"*Where are we?*" *I asked, looking down to see I was in the leggings and shirt I had fallen asleep in.*

"*You are sleeping in the infernal realm right now. This is the best way I can reach you.*"

She reached over to grab my hand, and I stared down at it. It was nearly identical to mine. It was like sitting next to my long-lost twin.

"*You were there when I turned immortal,*" *I said, not knowing what else to say.*

"*Yes, now that your body and mind have fully accepted immortality and my power, our connection is stronger. I can communicate with you much more easily. We are linked. And I will not abandon you,*" *she said. Her green eyes with that same rim of blue flaring with light stared into my heart.*

"*I'm scared,*" *I whispered, looking down at our hands again.*

There was a slight breeze that carried the smell of sunshine and grass.

I wanted to bask in this warmth and never leave; it felt safer here. Like everything else was a dream, and this was what was normal and real. I didn't want to go back to the infernal realm. I didn't want to go back to feeling pain and emptiness that was now a permanent part of who I was.

If I stayed here, maybe I could forget the trials. The immortality. The power. Kyra.

"*I know, child. And it seems easier now to wish those things away. I wish it could have been different. I wish I could have taken the burden. Instead, I hurt so many of you,*" *Xael said, her voice pained and rough. A tear started to slide down her cheek.*

"*You can read my thoughts?*" *I asked, trying to figure out if I should be comforted by that or not.*

"*We are connected. I am always with you, inside here and here.*" *She tapped her head and heart. "Greer, whenever you sleep, I will be here. I am going to show you how to wield your power, how to fight against the gods, and I will tell you how this all came to be. The curse they used to weave throughout my magic did so much damage. There are some things that I do not know, but I will help you in every way I can." She smiled painfully at me.*

I nodded, knowing that I would need her help. I would need her to find answers to understand how to survive this.

"You must have many questions. I will do my best with all of them." Xael gazed over the glassy pond and gave my hand a little squeeze.

"I do, but is it okay if, just this once, we just sit?" I whispered. "There are too many things right now, and I don't know where to start. I'm overwhelmed and scared. Betrayed and hurt. I just want to enjoy this place today, and next time I'll be ready."

I wanted to enjoy this feeling for a few moments longer before the image fractured into a million pieces like the rest of my life.

"Yes, my child. I will be here every time sleep takes you. I will not abandon you. But I must warn you, they will try to break you. They will use Kyra against you, and you against him. I know your heart hurts from his betrayal, but he was also betrayed," she said softly, the breeze flirting with the strands around her ears.

Kyra was betrayed.

I didn't want to talk about Kyra with her. At least not right now.

"Can I get in?" I wanted to feel the cool water against my skin.

Xael smiled, a mirror to my own.

With a nod, she was in a one-piece, and I was in my black bikini from the first night Kyra had really touched me.

I swallowed and shut my eyes, remembering his hands and lips against my skin.

Xael stood, dragging me up with her, our hands staying connected, and we waded in.

She pulled me under and beneath the surface, the warm water hugging close to my skin. I opened my eyes underneath, expecting the burn of the water, but it was simply a beautiful abundance of colorful fish and coral.

Xael smiled at me and spoke to me without words.

"I find being underwater calming, so I thought I would paint a picture for you today since this space and time are ours. It can be anything you want."

She let go of my hand and gave a flick of her wrist, and we both had mermaid tails of glittering scales. I laughed out loud and gasped, covering my mouth.

I didn't need to breathe oxygen here.

Of course, I didn't.

It was a dream of Xael's creation.

"I ripped a mermaid's tail once. She deserved it," I confessed.

Xael laughed, loud and bright, sounding just like me.

Today, the water didn't scare me like it had in the trial.

It was as if the pains of my past couldn't wrap their claws around me in this world. I was eternally grateful for the emotional reprieve. So, I let myself enjoy this pretend-world for as long as possible, becoming a creature of the sea like the rest of the world, and my problems didn't seem to exist.

Until things started to go dark, and Xael smiled sadly at me.

"I'll see you soon, Greer. Be brave."

Our rainbow world of water and the beautiful meadow above faded into a darkness that sucked the world dry of color. I was plunged back into reality to deal with whatever would come next.

TWO

KYRA

I was lost in my father's domain. Which was also mine now, apparently. How fucking ironic.

My father had barred me from Greer's room.

Again.

I was told not to speak to her about anything regarding the realm, the gods and goddesses, or any information pertaining to our current situation, which was hilarious because I knew very little. I was also a glorified prisoner because my father said I couldn't be trusted not to do anything reckless for Greer, which is why I had these damn manacles on. My powers were useless since I had no access to them. The manacles acted as a warning system to my father when I did or said anything against his will.

He was right, of course, to restrain me. I was ready to burn down the entire realm to free her, but I didn't know how to leave or go to the mortal realm.

Hell, I didn't even know how Afton had moved through the realms or why my father had only visited once a year. Was there some reason they couldn't all go to the mortal realm at any time? They had been waiting for Greer, but why? Why now? What were all the rules at play here?

I mentally put it on my list of things to figure out because the more I knew, the better I could help Greer with this situation.

I needed to talk to Greer without these damn shackles on. She deserved an explanation. In my defense, I had no idea what his plan was. The curse that my father had put on me at a very young age prevented me from revealing my true identity until now. But she didn't need excuses. I owed her an apology, especially now that my father had lifted the curse. I guess he didn't think others finding out would be a threat anymore. How ironic that in my efforts to protect her, I had to betray her and break her heart.

There were still many details I didn't fully understand about the curse. I knew I was tied to him and the infernal realm. But what exactly was I supposed to do as the Prince of Hell? I wasn't going to join my father. He was delusional, power hungry, and lethal. I had never heard of any other children from the gods and goddesses, either. I couldn't be the only one. The gods and goddesses were immortal, so it's not like they needed someone to take over for them. What exactly was my role in my father's grand scheme?

An ache shot through my chest, and I rubbed at the stone embedded in my sternum. It was now a smattering of red and black. Like the two parts of the stone were fighting for control. Sometimes, I would wake with a searing pain in my breast-bone, and I noticed that my eyes would go black when I was speaking with my father, through our minds. It was a disgustingly invasive thing that was apparently a part of these damn manacles.

So here I was, stewing in my thoughts, wandering idly through the halls of my father's house, trying to find a way out of this with only about a tenth of the necessary information I needed. I had, at least, been granted the ability to go throughout the palace instead of only having doors open to the throne room or the bathroom. I had found that this place was an extension of his power. It bent, transformed, and warped to his desires.

Hence, the decor changes in the throne room, and why, at first, the doors only allowed me into certain spaces. He had slowly permitted me to wander into other spaces and corridors.

I had made it a point to avoid my father and the other guests, though. I didn't want to speak to him or any of them. There were new faces and people every time I stumbled through the hallways of this place. Some days, the floors were shiny indigo tiles; other times, they were cold, hard stone. I wondered if the house changed as quickly as my father's mood.

It was not a comforting thought.

Outside the mansion was the rest of the afterworld. My father had other henchmen monitoring the rest of his domain. I knew very little about what lay in the infernal realm. I knew there were places where people rested and were free of their physical bodies. I also knew some people were damned and tortured for eternity.

There were no windows, at least none that allowed me to look out or explore what was beyond these walls. No door I had encountered led me outside, and there were still a great many doors I could not open.

I felt like I was in a messed-up horror video game where someone else was controlling me. All I could do was go through the motions or be forced through passages that surely would have something terrifying around the corner.

The best way for us to escape was to play nice with my dad, but the thought made me want to light something on fire and watch it burn slowly. I didn't want to do that until I could talk to Greer and tell her what happened. She didn't need to think that I was on my dad's side any more than she already did.

I scrubbed my hands across my face and sighed.

Absentmindedly, I turned to the right, in what felt like the same damn hallway I had been wandering in for gods knows how long, when I heard voices from somewhere up ahead. I froze and slipped back around the corner, pushing myself flat against the wall.

It was my father and someone else.

"Does Verity know he's here?" the voice said.

"Not yet, I'm waiting for him to be less angry. His love for the timewraith is standing in the way of the reunion. He needs to control himself. I can't very well add fuel to the fire. You know she already sent him away when he was young with her magic and only permitted him to come here when he would willingly make the choice. But I didn't anticipate him coming because of love for the wraith. It makes things more difficult. I hoped his coming here would fix the divide between us, and we could rule as a royal family. How it always should have been if she hadn't gotten so furious and sent him away. She might very well lose control as well. Both hot heads they are," my father grumbled in his low voice.

"Love is such a fickle thing. Once it's admitted outwardly, the spells and bindings become tricky to deal with. If I had gotten to your son and the wraith before they said it to one another, I could have driven them apart. Alas, the realms seem to have other ideas. It's a shame we haven't been able to visit Earth because of the others who reside there. This whole thing over Xael, our silly little time goddess. How she complicated so much, for us, for so long. But now we have her wraith, and we can right the realms once again. You know, I could try to speak to Kyra and the wraith. Get them to denounce their feelings. Then, I could spell them to fall madly in love with someone else?" the other voice said, light and twinkling.

"It's too bad Verity always knew my tricks and has warded herself; I could have helped you, Riordan. We may have avoided this whole mess in the first place if I had been able to manipulate her feelings," the voice added and sighed.

Who was Verity? They couldn't go to Earth on a whim, but, apparently, Afton could. What magic prevented them from doing so? Who was Xael? One of the original twelve? I didn't know all of them, but I knew some of them from the visits with my father. He only spoke of maybe four or five. Afton was one of them, and Farren, Phayre, and I couldn't remember the others. I cursed myself for not listening when my father had visited me.

I had been so young and naive.

I had no idea what would happen years later. How important simple bits of information could have been at this very moment.

I assumed the other voice was Farren, the god of love, beauty, and sex. It was said that Farren had beauty beyond comprehension and was androgynous, straddling the line of all sexualities, genders, and identities because love is love. They knew not of those social constructs but only what was true in the heart. Farren was said to be able to manipulate the emotions of others, and love magic was said to be the most complicated and some of the most powerful because matters of the heart always were.

I swallowed, thinking of how Farren spoke of manipulating Greer and my feelings. I did not know the rules of how and when love magic could be used, but I knew there were loopholes and hidden clauses, so it was easy to be tricked and taken advantage of.

I was trying to commit this conversation to memory. There was a lot of information to unpack here. Was my father in love with someone named Verity? Was that my mother?

He had never spoken of her. I had asked when I was younger, and he had avoided the question. Was she the real reason I was sent to Earth? My father had acted like I had needed to learn the ways of mortals, but I still knew so little of him and the curse, so maybe there were more things to uncover here.

"It seems the realms were always destined to come to this point, Farren. I doubt there was much we could have done in between now and when Xael cursed us and the humans. If my son would just cooperate, this wouldn't be so difficult. I will let you know if I need your assistance. Right now, I'm interested in seeing how things play out," my father grumbled.

The voices faded away, and I could no longer hear their conversation.

I had a lot more questions now than answers, but a mental to-do list was forming in my mind.

First and foremost, I needed to talk to Greer.

Then, I needed to talk to my father.

Finally, I would need to talk to this Verity.

I closed my eyes and took a breath. Suddenly, I realized I wasn't alone.

"Son, you cannot eavesdrop on me in my own home. "

My eyes flew open. My dad stood in front of me in the form that most resembled my adoptive father. It disgusted me and made me want to shove my flames at him. But I swallowed my anger and tried to play nice.

For Greer. For our escape.

"It wasn't intentional. Who is Verity?" I asked, pushing myself off the wall and facing him.

He was taller and broader than I was. A deliberate power tactic, I'm sure.

He eyed me with his scarlet eyes, a mirror of my own. I

could see him calculating what this information would cost him. His hair was long and black in this form, and his lips twitched, as if my question amused him.

Bastard.

"If she's my mother, I think I deserve to know," I said, lacing steel in my voice.

"Soon. You need to learn to behave first." He dismissed me and winked out in a black hiss of smoke.

"You can't keep me in the dark forever!" I threw up my hands in frustration.

I let out an exhale. There was no way I was going to be able to talk to Greer about my plan. I would have to play the role of the perfect Prince of Hell to get answers and get us out of here. She would have to hate me for betraying her for a little longer. The thought made my knees weak and my heart ache.

I just hoped my dad would keep Farren away from her so she couldn't denounce her feelings for me.

Fuck.

This whole situation was impossible.

I started walking again, thinking of how long I would need to keep this up.

I didn't exactly know what they planned for Greer, but I knew it couldn't be good. Nothing involving my father ever was.

I would do whatever was necessary to protect her and get her out of here, even if it meant sacrificing myself in the process.

THREE
LUX

I was sitting at our dining room table, looking at nothing. How was it possible to feel so much and yet be able to do so little? It felt like we failed, monumentally so. And that failure was sitting on my chest, slowly suffocating me.

Greer and Kyra had been gone for twenty-four hours.

They had whooshed out of the room, leaving Waverly, Sutton, Nova, and me dazed.

I knew they had taken her from Earth. If she were somewhere in this realm, I would have been able to find her. I was a shifter, for gods' sake, my tracking skills alone could have helped me find her thousands of miles away. She was my best friend; I knew her almost better than I did myself.

And she was gone. It was like a part of my body had been ripped away, but I couldn't tell you where the pain originated; it was lurking everywhere. There was no manual for how to deal with someone stealing your family away.

"Tell us, Wave," Nova said from the kitchen.

She walked over and sat across from me.

I blinked a few times. My body was frozen in place, unable to process what the fuck had just happened.

"The President is announcing that the new winner is taking a secluded, extended vacation to recover from her new immortality with her new boyfriend, Kyra. When they return, they will do the post-victory interviews," Waverly grumbled, looking at her phone and sliding in next to Nova.

"What an annoyingly blatant cover-up," I griped.

The rest of the world had no clue that their winner was in a losing battle with a whole bunch of childish immortals. My blood started to boil, and the urge to smash my hand through something was strong, but instead, I just sat looking at the only people I could trust.

We all looked like we had seen better days.

The last hours had been an absolute shit show, and they were all currently staying at mine and Greer's place while we tried to figure out what the hell we should do next. Waverly's long, dark hair was piled on top of her head, and her pink eyes were red and puffy. She was in an oversized gray hoodie and biker shorts.

Nova was tense, her gaze shifting side to side. She looked like she was ready to jump into battle at any given moment. She kept rolling her neck side to side.

Sutton was currently out, checking in with his contacts about what was happening in the infernal realm. It made sense that they would be taken there, considering who Kyra's father was. They could have been taken to the celestial realm, but for some reason, it seemed Ky's dad was calling the shots of this kidnapping, and that was most likely their base of operations.

What would hell be like for them? Sure, their bodies would survive, but what about who they were? Their hearts? Their minds?

I stuffed those thoughts away. Otherwise, I would head straight into a panic spiral. Gods, I knew I had looked better. I had spent the night that Greer and Kyra had been taken flying the skies in my dragon form, snarling and breathing fire into the sky to release some of the anger and heartache from my body.

It didn't work.

"I think we should pay the President a visit. He's working with Kyra's dad, so he obviously knows something. He can give us some insight on how to get them back and how to stop the gods and goddesses from whatever it is they are doing," I said, staring out the window. At least that was a whole, coherent thought.

"How are we going to get to him? You don't just demand a meeting with him," Waverly said, her pink eyes widening. Her normally glowing golden skin looked dull from the lack of sleep and adrenaline spikes of the last few hours.

"I can get us in," Nova said casually.

I raised an eyebrow at her, and she smiled.

"He won't say no to me," she added, her smile turning sour.

"Okay?" My brain was working at half the speed it normally did, so I wasn't sure if I had missed something or was just too fried to understand her implications.

"He has been trying to get me to either work for him or sleep with him for pretty much over a hundred years." She sighed and rubbed her hands along the muscles of her shoulders.

"Gross," I said, making a face of disgust. The President was nasty and powerful. And a misogynistic asshole. He made my skin crawl.

"You don't need to do this, Nova," Waverly said, grabbing onto Nova's silver star-studded deep brown hand.

"Yes, I do. For Greer and Kyra, and the rest of the world, it's a small sacrifice," she said, her fiery orange eyes hardening.

"And I can handle him, you all have only seen a fraction of what I can do, my power is deadly and destructive. I would happily use it on him, and he'll welcome it. It's what he wants. And he does love getting his way," she said, rolling her eyes.

"What does that mean?" I asked, tilting my head to the side, my brain was still three steps behind.

I knew Nova had extreme power, but she hadn't used a lot of it. In fact, none of us had really shown what we were capable of. There wasn't much need in everyday life to show off your magic. It was more like an identity card to get what you wanted, when you wanted, without having to do anything.

And what did she mean about the President wanting it?

"I guess you'll have to wait and see," she replied, trying to sound playful, but it fell flat.

Despite my curiosity, I wouldn't push her to tell us. I had a feeling we were going to see what Nova could really do at some point or another. In reality, I didn't know how much more torment I could take. If we could at least space out the horrible events happening in the future, that would be fucking great.

"I'll call his office now, I bet I can get him to meet us tomorrow." She stood suddenly, dropping Waverly's hand, and walked towards the balcony. She pulled out her phone and began pacing and talking with her hands.

"If we can get a meeting and Nova can control him, then I can get him to speak. You can hide like you did in the victory ceremony, just in case," Waverly said, thinking out loud. Her eyes crinkled in worry.

Nova came back inside and smiled tightly at us.

"A bargain has been struck. Tomorrow at twelve. He knows that I'm associated with Greer, so he would be an absolute idiot if he didn't suspect something, but I told him I would make it worth his time." She narrowed her eyes.

I didn't exactly know what would make the whole thing worth the President's time, but I wasn't going to ask if she didn't volunteer the information. One thing at a time.

My phone buzzed with a message from Sutton.

**Sutton: Found something. I'll be gone for
a few days looking into it. Don't
worry, I'll be fine. See you soon.**

"Sutton's out for the next few days chasing a lead."

"I know you're worried, Lux, so are we. But Kyra and Greer have one another, and from what we understand, she's an essential part of their plan. And she's immortal now, so she will survive." Nova walked over to sit beside me and gave my hand a squeeze.

"Some things are worse than death. I'm afraid of what will happen *because* she will survive. What will happen to the Greer we know and love?"

My whole body shook. I knew all about what physical and emotional pain could do to someone. I had seen it happen again and again. It wasn't something I wished on anyone.

What would these people do to her to make her comply with their plans?

I wasn't going to wait and find out.

↔

The next day came agonizingly slowly. It seemed like time was moving at a glacial pace since Greer and Kyra had been kidnapped. My sleep quality was absolute shit, and I was more exhausted today than I was yesterday. But we had a job to do, one that would, hopefully, alleviate the pain in my chest and the anxiety in my belly.

Nova, Waverly, and I were ready to meet the President.

I was hidden in Waverly's hair, a small ladybug perched on the cuff of her ear. I hated being this small. It made me incredibly uncomfortable. I would much rather be in my tiger or even my dragon form. Yes, I could hide and be inconspicuous, but I thrived on announcing my presence and using strength and power. Being sneaky, quiet, and agile were not exactly my strengths. But here I was trying to stay hidden behind Waverly's raven colored waves as she and Nova checked in at his office.

From what I could see through the limited visibility of Waverly's hair, we were in a waiting room.

"He is ready for you now," said a feminine voice.

I was itching to jump out and slash the President's face with my tiger claws. But knew that would be incredibly unhelpful to our cause. In fact, it would probably make this situation ten times worse. But gods, did I want to rage at something, and he was my best target.

"Great," Nova replied in a clipped tone.

We started moving, and I lost even more visibility because of Waverly's hair. I skittered across her ear, and she shivered slightly. I didn't dare say sorry. I just made a mental note not to tickle her again.

"Nova Zemen, what a sight you are, and you brought the siren with you. Waverly Banks. What rare, powerful beauties I have in my presence. Please, make yourself comfortable. Drink?" he said in his booming voice. Waverly slowly sat next to me.

"No thanks," Nova said, her voice sounding guarded.

"A shame."

I heard glasses clinking and liquid pouring, followed by a groan and nails scratching against leather.

"What can I do for you today?" he said joyfully, as if he didn't know why we were here.

"Where is Greer Roberts?" Nova was not wasting any time.

"Ah, well, I don't know. See, I don't ask questions, I simply do as I'm told," he said with a smile in his voice.

"*Tell us what you know about her kidnapping,*" Waverly sang in her siren song. She invoked truth in others, something we desperately needed right now.

"Ah, little siren, your power won't work on me."

Waverly tensed beneath me. This was not going as planned. Why wouldn't her song work?

"I learned a long time ago how to arm myself against your kind when the original kingdoms reigned. It's a shame that the ways of magic and power have been lost as the years go on. We have all been reduced to rules, regulations, and laws that inhibit us from being our most powerful beings. We are weakened by it. It's about time that true power was unleashed," he said, chuckling slightly.

Was he actually serious? This pompous asshole was going to give us the runaround, and it took everything in me not to spew fire at his face. What did he mean that it was about time "true power" was unleashed? What were all these random magical loopholes that we were now discovering?

"Why did you agree to this meeting?" Nova asked bluntly.

"You said you would make it worth my time. I have been trying to get a taste of you for a long time, Nova," he said slowly.

There was malice, and something else, in his voice. I imagined the look he was giving her would have made anyone want to vomit. This was bad. Very, very bad. We needed to abort this mission, but there was no way I could communicate that without revealing myself.

"I want to see your power, Nova Zemen," he goaded.

"No," she declared flatly.

"Not even if I threaten your little siren girlfriend? You did say we had a deal," he goaded with an edge in his voice.

"You thought to come in here and use her against me. Why should I not do the same?"

Claws scraped against wood, and fear trickled through my

veins at his implication. We actually had no idea what he was capable of. We were not immortals like he was. The damage he could do to us was infinitely worse than we could do to him.

"I suggest you keep your little shifter caged, as well. There isn't much that Luxton Gilmore can do against me. But you, Nova Zemen. You... are dangerous."

His footsteps sounded, and his power closed in. My body froze. He knew I was there?! How?!

Godsdamnit.

"Come out and play, Mr. Gilmore." His breath was hot on my back as it brushed over Waverly's ear.

I winced, fluttered out from her hair, and transformed into my natural state. There was no more reason to hide, and I could shift better here than tucked away on Waverly's ear.

The President was leering over Waverly. Nova's jaw was set. As I stood in front of him, a snarl ripped out of my throat, and he laughed in my face.

"Fools, you are. You don't stand a chance against them. It's much better to join the winning side. They have already taken your little timewraith and the Prince of Hell. They're both already on the right side. The only one of you powerful enough to go toe to toe with them is you, Nova. But will you? Will you embrace your power? Or will you be like Hyacinth has been all these years? Weak. Unable to make tough decisions and spill blood. Hiding from the world. Why fight what's in your veins? Don't you want to get your hands a little dirty?"

He towered over Nova, who was straining in her chair, grabbing the leather armrests with a vice grip. The President was huge, broad, and covered in gray, steely skin.

He smiled, and his flat, white teeth transformed into jagged edges, sharp and deadly. He was goading her. Trying to make her act. My body was aching to transform, but I held back, waiting for the right moment to strike. I couldn't let my rage get the best of me. The point was to get answers, not inflict violence.

"How dare you speak about the original goddess with such disdain. You have no idea what you are talking about!" Nova spat, sitting rigid and tall in her seat.

"But I do. You forget that I am one of the oldest living immortals. I saw the rise and fall of the kingdoms. I was chosen long ago to usher in a new age. I simply had to wait and play along until the time was right for the true reckoning."

Waverly's face had blanched. I didn't know what to do. I shifted to my tiger in a flash, and the President was on me, wrapping his hands around my neck and squeezing hard. Choking, I tried to shred his skin, but it was no use. This was how I was going to die. Tears spilled from my eyes as the air was forced out of my lungs.

"Show me what you can do, Nova, or I'll crush Luxton's throat. We had a deal!" he roared, his grip on me tightening.

I was losing air quickly, but this could not be my end. No fucking way. I changed into a king cobra slipping through his crushing grip. Before he could react, I sank my fangs into him, and I changed again into a ladybug. I flew to Nova's shoulder.

He bellowed out in pain as the poison from my fangs started to push through his blood, and he cursed. His skin was incredibly hard to penetrate. I wondered if that was part of his power.

I changed, again, to stand behind Nova, my body shaking. Waverly had moved beside me. It seemed as if Nova was the only one who could handle what was happening in this room. I cursed myself for not being, at least, a little more prepared.

Nova stood then, and her energy pulsed and swirled around, the swell of something deep and foreboding settling in the air. She moved her hands and fingers in an intricate pattern, as if she were painting, and the President's dark eyes went wide and then feral.

"I will not let you hurt anyone else. A deal was struck, and I am a woman of my word," she snarled and moved towards him, continuing to twist her hands and wrists until he was on the ground laughing hysterically.

"Do you feel that, President? When the poison hits your veins, it is mine to control. I'm not weak. However, I do choose to wield my power with care," she hissed, and the President's eyes started to roll back into his head as he spasmed on the ground.

"Not quite," she whispered, and raised her hands.

His body went rigid, and then he was hovering in the air like a rag doll while Nova's hands moved idly. What was happening? I had never seen anyone manipulate someone so effortlessly. Was this the extent of what she could do? It was terrifyingly beautiful.

"Everyone always underestimates poison in their veins, the pain, the searing heat embedding itself into your very being. It won't kill you, of course, being an immortal and all, but gods, it will be excruciating," she said wickedly.

His face was contorted in a sneer. His eyes were unhinged with something. He licked his lips slowly.

"Is this the best you can do, Nova?" he hissed.

"Not even a little." She flicked her wrists, her fingers twisting his body in unnatural angles, and he cried out. My own body hurt looking at the bent angles of the President, but I couldn't even begin to feel sorry for him. He deserved this and worse.

She threw a hand up towards the door.

"Call the guards off or I'll stop," she commanded, walking around his floating, unnaturally large and broken body.

"Don't come in here!" he growled.

His eyes looked feral and filled with something like... lust. It made me want to gag.

"More, Nova. Show me more."

He licked his lips, slowly this time, and she closed her fist. Every part of his body twisted more as he howled in pain, and she slammed him to the floor.

"Tell me what you know," Nova demanded.

"They took her to the infernal realm; you won't be able to get her back. Time moves differently there; she has been there for weeks now. You are probably too late," he said, nearly delirious, his eyes glazed over.

Weeks?! No, no, no. My stomach plummeted to the ground, and I staggered back a few steps, grabbing onto the wall to balance. What were they doing to them?

"How can we get there?" she raged.

Blood started to pour from his eyes, ears, and nose. I gagged, leaning my forehead against the wall, and Waverly looked away.

The most powerful immortal in the city was at the hands of the most powerful blood witch I knew. And he liked it. Nova looked indifferent, like she was used to silly men in power doing her bidding.

My head was spinning. It felt like the world as I knew it didn't make a damn bit of sense anymore.

"I don't know, but ask Hyacinth. She can help you. That's all I have."

He was panting, and then Nova brought her hands together, interlacing her fingers, except for her pointer finger and thumb. She pressed down and brought it to her heart, whispering something.

Blood stopped leaking from the President's body, which returned to its normal state. He floated towards his chair until he was lightly set down. His eyes were closed, and he looked as if he could just be sleeping.

Nova cleared all the blood from the office with a. snap of her fingers, so it looked normal again. Hypermasculine and over-the-top power, but that was what it had looked like before.

This was madness.

"Holy shit, Nova," I shuddered, gaping at the President's limp body.

"We need to go." Nova's voice held no negotiations.

"Lux, get small, again," Waverly said quietly.

I didn't say anything. I had no words, so I shrank down and landed on Waverly's ear once again.

We walked out past the assistant, and Waverly painted on a smile, giving her a little wave.

At least we got some of the information we needed, but I had even more questions now. Like, who the hell was Hyacinth? And what the fuck had I just witnessed in that damn office?

FOUR

GREER

I was sitting in what appeared to be some sort of formal dining room in the house of hell—a nickname that I was using inside my head for where I was currently trapped. The room was huge. The table was an unnecessarily long, shiny stone slab with large wingback black chairs hugging the sides. Everything was dark. The walls were a bleak gray, and a huge fire roared on one side of the room. A tremendous iron chandelier hung above us, lit with hundreds of candles. There were servers milling around the outskirts of the room, and they looked to be all different species in the same dull uniform. They all wore the same expression.

Empty.

Were they creatures of hell or beings stolen from Earth? Or maybe something else entirely?

I had been winked into the room, so I didn't get to see any other part of the house. There was a door at one end of the room where the servers flitted in and out, but that was the only viable exit I could see currently.

My manacles were a constant companion of suffering. My wrists were bruised and angry, the pain radiating to my fingertips all the way up to my neck. I refused to show that I was affected. I had been through worse before, so surely, I could deal with the constant agony of these damn cuffs.

Interestingly, I had been dressed up. I was put in a dark maroon floor-length gown that hugged my body, leaving my entire back exposed. However, the rest of me was covered from my throat to my wrists, where it connected to my handcuffs like a godsdamn fashion statement. They were now gold and glittered with diamond studs around my throat, wrists, and ankles, where they ended in strappy gold heels.

My hair had been pulled back from my face and was in an elaborate braid down my back. I had been made over. The exterior of me was polished and shone to hide the jagged pieces of who I was and who I was forced to be.

Earlier in the day, I had been woken up aggressively and then been shoved around in a haze as people poked, prodded, washed, and dressed me. I was shown a three-second view of what I looked like in a mirror, and I was shocked. I looked like Xael, but not. Hollow, but oddly regal. The juxtaposition of how I looked and how I felt on the inside was evident. I had wanted to roar, but I didn't. This was not the time for that fight. I needed to formulate a plan, and I needed to play nice to get what I wanted. If I couldn't play well with the others, then I would make them put me down so I could visit Xael in my dreams.

I would survive this. There really wasn't any other choice. Death wasn't a friend I could turn to anymore, so instead I would become my own harbinger of pain.

Sighing, I looked at those sitting around the table.

They had sat me across from Kyra, who was right next to his father at the head of the table. I couldn't look directly at him. My heart hurt endlessly, and my neck was killing me, like my head weighed a thousand pounds, and every shift of my muscles sent zaps of misery through my body. But I stole glances. I couldn't help it. The physical and emotional pain were all rolled together, and in some ways, it was comforting. It was at least something I knew.

Kyra looked absolutely breathtaking in his dark red tux. He wore a black dress shirt slightly open, showing a small peak of his stone, which was now marred with red and black. His hair was as unkempt as ever on top, but short on the sides. His scarlet eyes raked over me.

I didn't know if his manacles were still on. It was difficult to tell from the way his suit fit. At least he didn't have an actual dog collar like I did. Were they torturing him in the same way, or was that just a special treatment for yours truly?

There were six others at the table, including Kyra's father. He was in an all-black suit. He looked sort of like Kyra, but not exactly. It was like his form was too big and too broad for this human form. He had the same scarlet deep-set eyes, shapely mouth, and strong jawline, but it felt forced on him. His hair was dark and long, going to his shoulders.

Afton was among the guests, and I wanted to flip him off, but refrained. The woman who had touched me and unlocked the cage I had around my power was also here. I didn't recognize the others. They all looked humanish, but I knew that they were controlling themselves around Kyra and me. They all radiated power and energy. Who knew exactly what their natural forms were like?

We had been served wine, and the others chatted idly while I tried to swallow the bile in my throat. Kyra's dad had been ignoring us since I was shoved into my seat. I should have been trying to listen to what they were saying, but I couldn't think with the roaring in my ears and the ache in my arms. I wanted to stop time for just a moment. Just to breathe for one fucking second, but I didn't know how to do that without losing more of my shit.

Xael and I hadn't talked about using my powers at all,

actually. I silently cursed myself for taking too many moments to try and find reprieve when she had shown me the dreamscape she could manipulate in my mind. I should have started training with her right away, but I still felt too raw to try. The escapism she offered was addicting when all I was used to was a barrage of anguish.

I exhaled and tried to count back from one hundred. My mental count got to forty-three when Kyra's father started to clink a fork on his glass filled with blood-red wine. The sharp noise made my brain hurt.

"Thank you all for being here," he boomed.

I tried to keep my face neutral instead of sneering at his pleasantries.

"Appetizers will be served shortly, but I think we all should introduce ourselves."

He smiled with too white teeth and chuckled as if he found this all amusing. He turned his full attention to me. I wanted to shudder under his eyes, which didn't seem scarlet at all but instead looked bloody. I straightened my spine.

"Wraith, you can address me as Riordan, or God of Hell."

"And you can call me Greer," I smiled sweetly.

The air crackled with something, and I stole a glance at Ky. His mouth was set in a hard line, his eyes had gone wide.

"Greer it is, wraith." Riordan tipped the wine to his lips, unbothered by my sass.

"You all know my son, Kyra," he said, turning his full attention to Kyra, who went rigid underneath his gaze.

"How are you finding the infernal realm?" Afton inquired from my right. He was still about six feet away, since the table was massive, but I could feel the iciness of him when he spoke.

I ground my teeth together in an attempt not to snarl at him. I had not known who he was at the time. I had assumed that he might be an ally, but I had obviously been wrong.

"Delightful." Kyra grinned, but it didn't reach his eyes.

"I believe you are already familiar with Afton, Greer? He has been the only one who has been able to visit Earth regularly since he is the god of travelers, mercenaries, tricks, and many other forms and feats of entertainment." Riordan tilted his chin at Afton.

I looked at him then, and he smiled, the motion nearly cracking my psyche wide open. He was wearing a light blue suit that complemented his icy eyes and blonde hair.

"Thank you for the help in the trials." I tried to make it sound sincere and genuine, but my voice was strained.

"Of course. We couldn't have you too damaged before you got to us." Afton winked at me, and I hated him all over again.

What they didn't realize was I was fucked up from the day I was born. They made sure of it when they cursed Xael's magic.

"Cerena, you have also already met. She is the goddess of nature and energy. She released the last of the boundaries from inside of you to fully accept the power of time."

Cerena smiled. Her mahogany hair was pulled into an intricate updo, so her umber shoulders were on full display. She wore a gold, strapless gown that shimmered and glittered in the firelight. Her eyes were purple today. They had been blue when she freed me. I wondered if she changed her eyes depending on what she wore.

"So nice to see you up and walking around looking put together, little pet," she purred, batting her long eyelashes.

I wanted to claw her eyes out when she called me her pet, but I refrained. If I showed violence now, I would never make it out in one piece. They would make sure of it.

Instead, I simply nodded and took a sip of my wine. It tasted expensive, and I idly wondered if I should be drinking it, but I didn't care. I needed something to do with my hands and mouth. The liquid ran down my throat and heated my belly. The more I drank, the more the world dulled, and I was desperate for a reprieve from my own feelings and the heaviness of my limbs.

"Phayre is the goddess of heavens and light. She oversees the celestial realm," Riordan continued.

He nodded to the woman who sat at the head of the table at the opposite end. She was the one who had grabbed my chin before and basically told me I would be their puppet. Her hair was more of a golden blonde tonight, and her washed-out skin appeared slightly rosier tonight. Her white gown flowed in billowy panels down her lithe frame, and gold swirls swirled on her skin. Her eyes were blue and bright. She wore a vivid pink lipstick like a dressed-up ghost Barbie.

"You're looking much more obedient tonight, Greer darling." Her voice dripped sugar.

I took another sip of wine to prevent myself from saying anything that would most definitely get me in trouble before I even knew who the rest of these people were. There were only two left on Kyra's side of the table.

"This is Farren. God of sex, beauty, and love... He helped pick out your attire for this evening," Riordan said, smirking slightly.

Farren was beautiful in a way that I had no words for. It made my mouth water, which felt odd.

"What do I look like to you, dear?" Farren quirked his head to the side and beamed.

Farren looked like straight sex on a stick. He looked like Kyra in a creepy way. I shook my head, and the image became fuzzy, and then it settled into what I assumed was his normal appearance. I swallowed and took another sip. The more I drank, the less I could think.

He now had golden skin and short, dark blue hair, full pink lips, and honey eyes that looked at me like he could devour me whole. Farren wore a bright purple suit that hugged his small frame, and a white button-up, which was slightly open, exposing more smooth skin.

"I would honestly prefer not to answer that," I said, finally realizing that everyone genuinely expected me to answer.

Farren laughed in a light, twinkling sound that made me want to laugh, too.

More wine for me, then.

"And finally, Estoria, the goddess of health and fertility," Riordan pointed to the woman who was the closest to Kyra.

She was a full-figured woman with her sepia skin and long, golden brown braids intertwined with blonde strands that had been perched on her head to resemble a crown. She wore an emerald green gown that went up to her throat and flowed down like a waterfall.

"Hello, Greer," she said, and her eyes matched the color of her gown.

She was the only one who gave a somewhat nice greeting. I smiled at her and then took another sip of wine.

I stared at my glass and realized that it kept refilling itself, and I had no idea how much I'd had to drink.

Not the best move, Greer.

Too bad I couldn't convince myself to care right now. I wondered if I would have a higher tolerance of alcohol as an immortal, but it did give me some liquid courage.

"I thought there were twelve original gods and goddesses." I leveled my gaze at Riordan, who only blinked as a reaction to my question. "I'm assuming you all are part of that original group." I tilted my head to the side.

Farren laughed, and Phayre scoffed.

"They teach you nothing in the mortal realm; no wonder we need to take it back," Cerena huffed.

"Indeed, but the rest of the original twelve are not here. They are on Earth, except for Xael. Her power is within you now." Riordan set his wine glass down and leaned back in his chair.

"What?" I said, practically spitting out my wine.

"Oh, Greer dear, there is so much you do not know." He smiled with pity in his eyes. "Don't worry, you will learn, but now we will eat."

He clapped his hands, and a flurry of staff swarmed us and delivered our feast. There were so many things on the table, and it all smelled delicious. I was ravenous, but my head was reeling.

On Earth?! I had never heard of any gods and goddesses being on Earth. How much of what I had learned in school was true? Was that what was on the other side of the world in the Eastern Hemisphere?

My head was drowning, but my stomach growled. I tried not to laugh, suddenly feeling a little tipsy. I looked at Kyra, who was already staring at me. My body felt light for the first time in days. Weeks? Months? I had no idea. His eyes shifted to his father, who was talking to one of his staff members.

Without breaking eye contact with his father, he started to move one of his fingers on the table, like he was spelling something out. I looked at him wide-eyed and shot glances around the room, but everyone was ignoring us.

He smiled at me as I watched his finger move with just a whisper of smoke gone in the blink of an eye if you weren't looking. His manacles must be gone.

I didn't know exactly what he had said, but I think he spelled it out.

We will not fail.

His gaze came back to mine. Something sparked in his eyes, and the corners of his mouth tipped up. My heart clenched. I didn't understand what he was trying to convey, so I bit my lip and kept drinking, wanting the alcohol to muddle my thoughts to the point where I felt absolutely nothing.

Maybe Kyra wasn't as far away as I thought. I just needed to talk to him, but I didn't know how.

I started writing my own words.

Together?

My fingers ached from the act. My heart was ready to explode out of my chest because, if we were to be noticed, I would be the one to pay. Did it matter? My body could survive anything, even if my mind couldn't. Immortality kept me alive, but it didn't keep me sane. Pain was my friend. So, if that was the price, so be it.

His eyes went wide, and he nodded curtly once, then he whipped his head as his father began to finish up his conversation with his staff.

Maybe we could do this. Together.

I didn't say anything else the rest of the evening, afraid of what else I would do when I barely cared to be alive.

FIVE
LUX

"So, are we going to talk about what just happened?" I paced in front of the large couch, snuggled into the corner of the living room.

Waverly was sitting with her feet up on the glass coffee table, a frown slashed across her lips. She hadn't said anything to Nova since we got back here, and Nova was perched far away from her on the armrest.

"You just kicked the President's ass, and he asked for it. What was all that about?

Hyacinth? Who is that? What the hell did he mean by us returning to true power? What the actual fuck is going on?"

I threw my hands up and fought the urge to stalk around in my tiger form. I released a growl, trying to get my composure under control.

"He has propositioned me on several occasions to handle him with my powers. You know I can use blood control, I've used it on you before, Lux. But it isn't pretty. It takes away free will, and I could use it on thousands if they were in my range. However, as a blood witch, I am subject to some of the most stringent rules and regulations of any specialized power or species, because I'm seen as inherently dangerous. Even though there is beauty, life, and light in it... people only see it as dangerous, evil, and cruel. In the President's case, he wants it for himself. Power always has duality. It is the wielder who decides what to do with it.

"He has said to me before that he thinks that people like us, as in me and him, should be able to run free and use our magic for all sorts of desires. He fetishizes power, including mine. He sees beings as playthings and possessions. It's repugnant. But it was a way to get answers. A way for us to manipulate him, instead.

"Clearly, he has ties to the original goddess of magic, Hyacinth. Blood witches are special beings from her bloodline from years ago. I'm a direct bloodline. I have similar power to what she can wield. She would know how to move between the realms, but she may not help us if she is aligned with Kyra's father. However, it's worth a try," Nova finished, standing tall and crossing her arms.

Waverly had a full-on scowl now, and I looked at Nova hard.

"Men in power fucking suck." Waverly scooted closer to her and grabbed her hand.

"He's a nasty bastard and deserves to actually have his ass fully handed to him. Thank you for doing that even though I know it wasn't easy." I grabbed her other hand. Nova's fire eyes dampened, and a tear slipped out.

"It's exhausting having to be strong, but not strong enough to scare people. And to use my power, but not too much because I might break a rule, but enough to make me useful."

She closed her eyes and exhaled. Her silver stars shuddered across her skin.

"But I think I have a way I can try and reach Hyacinth. I've never spoken with the original goddess, but my grandmother did. I can link us and ask her for her guidance. That way, she won't see us as a threat to her plans if she is aligned with Kyra's dad. I will simply tell her I want to lean into the original immortality history or some bullshit like that."

Nova squeezed both our hands and got up to do her own pacing. I plopped down on the couch and sighed loudly.

"Okay, what do you need us to do?" I asked. "Whatever you need, we've got you."

"Let me go get my book, and I'll see." She walked over to the hallway where she had taken up shop in the guest room.

"How are you holding up, Wave?" I slid closer to Waverly, who was frowning again.

"I want to know how he resisted my song. That's never happened before. I don't have as many rules and regulations as blood witches, but we are close to the next step down—or step up, depending on how you look at it. I don't know of any way for people to do that. There is a lot of siren lore that was lost in history. So, maybe because he is so old, he remembers how to fend us off? I don't know, it doesn't make sense. It bothers me." She tugged at her long, dark hair.

Nova returned with her spell book. It was practically medieval, with a thick, worn, black leather casing with pressed whorls and swirls across the cover. It could easily weigh about twenty pounds. She slammed it on the coffee table and sat before it, crossing her long legs.

She mumbled something with her hand hovering above it, and her stars shone bright and then winked when the book opened and gently fluttered to a page. She scanned the text. I craned my neck to see, but the words were in some language I couldn't read. They were arranged vertically and horizontally across the page, with slashes of numbers and symbols breaking up the pages.

What a mess. I shook my head and decided it didn't matter because I couldn't read it anyway.

I hoped Kyra and Greer were holding up.

Kyra still hadn't had a chance to tell Greer who he was. At this point, I assumed she knew, and it didn't go over well. She had been thrown into the trials, then immortality, and then her powers ripped through her.

And then she got kidnapped.

Super.

It was almost unfathomable what she must be going through, and my heart hurt thinking about whatever was going on down there. It would not be good. I was genuinely worried about who she would be after.

She had demons before, but now she'd have to reconcile with those previous traumas as well as her current ones. Before, it was so dark she had turned to death to alleviate her pain, and I had helped pull her out with my bare hands. That was no longer an option. It had never been a healthy option, obviously, but I wondered if she had found another way to cope that wouldn't come at the cost of her hurting herself more than she already was.

The thought sent a shudder down my spine.

I knew that when you did what you needed to do to survive at the time, it would come back with a vengeance to wreak havoc on your life when you were feeling safe again. I didn't want that for Greer. She had already been through hell and back, and now she was there again.

Literally.

I wanted to pull her in and tell her we would figure this shit out like we always did. We would fight for happiness, love, and light together until the day I died. I hadn't thought much about immortality for myself in a while, but now, with Greer being an immortal, it felt like something I should entertain.

I had always told my parents I didn't want it.

I didn't want it so I could be powerful forever, but rather so that I could have more time with my loved ones. Even Kyra had become like a brother, and he was immortal. But I wasn't sure what his fate would be, being the Prince of Hell and everything. I could only imagine what it must be like to be back with his father, who had been absent and manipulative his whole life.

I wouldn't want to be back with my mom and dad, even though they were my parents. They had always treated me like I was an inconvenience because of what I chose to do with my life, who I chose to love, and what I believed in. They never got or understood who I was, and I was relieved when they died several years ago. Maybe that made me a bad person, but I didn't give a single fuck. I didn't deserve to be treated like an afterthought, which was why Greer had become my family.

Now, it had grown to Kyra, Waverly, Nova, and maybe Sutton...

I wasn't exactly sure what had been going on there. We had been flirty and there had been banter and light touching, but nothing had really happened. I wondered if anything would come to pass, considering we were all at the beginning of what could possibly be the fight for our lives and others.

We had no idea what we were up against. We barely had any information, except that they had been waiting for Greer and had orchestrated her stepping into her power. They needed her power to reclaim the mortal realm. And who the hell knew what that meant?

Were they going to wipe us all out? There had been chaos in the old kingdoms, and there was a ton of bloodshed when the gods and goddesses were involved, according to the old texts. So, what exactly did that mean for modern society?

There were also accounts that claimed they had a serum that could kill any immortal they didn't like... So, they were practically all-powerful.

"Earth to Lux!" Nova snapped her fingers in my face, and her fiery eyes danced.

"Sorry, what's up?" I leaned forward.

"I need a dragon scale from you." She smiled sweetly.

"It says that? Seriously?" I was genuinely surprised.

"Yup, cough it up, please." She held out her hand expectantly.

I changed the skin on my hand to a dragon's and popped off a hard golden scale for her.

"Thank you." She snatched it up.

Nova and Waverly had been running around gathering supplies and things for this spell, and I had been gazing off into space, moping about the whole situation. I stood and straightened my spine.

"I'm sorry, I was distracted. What else can I do?" I rubbed my hands together.

"Nothing, I think we're almost ready," Nova insisted.

We walked over to the dining room table, where Nova had already set up a circle of candles. She lit each one and placed my dragon scale, a piece of hair, some sort of leaves, a white flower, and a few other random things in the middle.

She lit each candle, twelve total. The flames danced as we hovered around her. She brought out the same knife she had used to slice her and Kyra's hands when we had accessed his memory.

She cut her hand and drizzled blood over all the items, whispering in the witch's tongue. Everything started to hiss and sizzle as the flames of the candles jumped.

"More blood... more sacrifice..." Nova grumbled and went to make a second slice.

"Can we use mine?" I offered my arm, and she nodded, making a gash that stung, and held my arm over the items.

"Mine too." Waverly stuck her arm out, and Nova smiled before placing a light kiss on the inside of her wrist. Waverly blushed slightly, and Nova made an incision while Waverly winced.

We all held our arms over the flame of the candles and saw the blood drip down in fat red drops. Suddenly, the hissing grew loud, and the room filled with smoke. An ear shattering crack, like thunder, rumbled through the penthouse, shaking everything from the furniture to the light fixtures.

"What's happening?!" I screamed over the noise.

A wind swirled around us, lifting Waverly's hair and my braids as Nova's eyes widened.

"It was too much," she whispered.

She whipped her head back and forth as the wind began to swirl around us and smoke filled the space. The flames danced higher and higher. I wondered idly if it would destroy my apartment. Another crack rumbled.

"There was too much power with our blood!" Nova screamed and grabbed both of our arms. She shoved us both to the floor as a piercing flash of light cracked through the space and a boom shuddered, sending us all sprawling in different directions.

I couldn't see, and my ears were ringing. I crawled on my arms and legs, coughing, and waited for my vision to clear.

"Nova," I wheezed out. "Waverly!"

I couldn't see anything, but the white cloud of smoke snaked into my nose and my mouth. Then a snap so loud it made my ears ring. The penthouse looked exactly the same as it did moments ago, except a woman was sitting by the candles. She wore jeans and a long-sleeve shirt with sleek black booties. She looked like she could have been Nova's relative. She twisted an aquamarine curl around her finger. Her long, muscular legs were crossed, and she drummed a few pointed, red fingernails on the table.

"I was wondering when you would call, Nova Zemen. I've been waiting," she said, her voice low and silky.

My mouth dropped open, and I could feel her power wrapping around me like a warm blanket.

"The siren and the shifter." She nodded towards me as Waverly was being hauled up by Nova. "Now, let's talk about your friend the timewraith, Greer Roberts, and the Prince of Hell himself, Kyra Valequay." She smirked through her dark purple lips.

I swallowed. It looked like she already knew exactly where this conversation was going. I just hoped it wouldn't end in any—or all of us—dead.

SIX
GREER

"Xael, where are the other gods and goddesses?" I inquired.

It was the same night as the terrible dinner where I was introduced to six of the twelve original gods and goddesses. My body felt positively effervescent in this realm. Light as air and free from the aches that constantly plagued me.

As soon as I had been dismissed, I went straight to my room to go to sleep as quickly as possible in the hopes that I'd get some serious answers from Xael. I had been recovering for long enough. It was time for me to face the reality of my situation.

"Ah, you met the five that sided with Riordan," she replied.

Today, we were in a forest. No pond in sight, just an opening in a circle of dense trees. We were seated in the middle of the small meadow facing one another. Xael was dressed casually again. Sometimes, I had to fight the shiver that snaked down my spine when I gazed at her because it was like I was looking at and talking to myself. It was eerie, to say the least.

"Greer, whenever the gods and goddesses wanted to leave Earth and let their creations kill one another for sport... Well, you remember I told you I fought to give my powers to humans, *correct? And I did. No one really liked the idea. When I released my power out to you all, it was Riordan and Phayre who gathered the others to strip me of my immortality. At the time, they all agreed that it was a just punishment, and they needed their combined powers to release me from my immortality. But it left things out of balance.*

"You, Greer, as the timewraith... You settle the balance. You are a substitute for me in the balance of the original twelve. You also possess the power I had, which was fundamental in creating the world in the image of the original immortals."

I nodded my head and closed my eyes, trying to absorb everything she was saying.

"Let me show you," *Xael said, and I opened my eyes.*

We were no longer in the forest but rather in a throne room almost identical to the one Riordan had held me, except the coloring was more neutral.

Xael was in the middle of the room with what I assumed to be all twelve of the other immortals looming around her. Some I recognized and others I didn't. Power crackled through the air, creating little sparks of energy. A few of the immortals were yelling while Riordan held up a lengthy knife poised above Xael's head as tears ran down her cheeks.

"He wanted to kill me. If my power was to be absorbed by others, they thought it should be them, not the humans," *Xael said, watching the version of herself get absolutely berated by so many powerful beings. My heart ached at the sight.*

Suddenly, three immortals shoved Riordan away, and a few others joined, placing themselves between Xael and those I knew to be followers of Riordan. One of the immortals gathered Xael up in her arms and gently rocked her side to side.

"There were some who were on my side. Some who realized that killing me would alter the fabric of our world. So instead, five of them agreed to take me to Earth and protect my body in an eternal sleep."

The scene changed, and Xael was put into a glass casket by the woman who had given her comfort in the throne room. She waved her hand over Xael's body, and almost immediately, Xael fell asleep, and the scene went fuzzy.

I found myself stumbling back into the forest of our dreamscape. I didn't know what to say. How had this history been so lost to those of us on Earth?

"They gave up their spots in the celestial and infernal realm for a piece of earth as long as those who voted to end my life stayed away. Thus, the mortal realm became divided into two hemispheres. The east, for those who wanted me to live, and the west, for those who wanted me to die, never to interact with one another again."

Blinking my eyes, I realized that's why the Eastern Hemisphere was never spoken about. The gods had decided long ago what our fates would be.

"They would agree to stay divided until the one who could act as my replacement could be found, made immortal through the trials, and accept the power. Now the original twelve have been somewhat restored, because of you, but it means the realms are vulnerable to the power of the original twelve again. Before, those who spoke out against me didn't have enough power to tip the scales and take over, and the five who went to Earth didn't have enough power to stand up to the others. But with you, Greer...

"You seem like an easy pawn to control, Greer. You do not know of our ways, our magics, or powers. If you side with those six, they can take back the mortal realm and do whatever they want to the earth, just like the chaos before. If you side with the other five, then there is an equal chance for both sides to fight for what they want. They were waiting for you because they can't make a move without you." Xael looked exhausted, bags suddenly apparent under her eyes.

My mouth was wide open. So much of what we had been

told had been lies and deceit about our history, about everything. There were so many more nuances and intricacies in the politics at play than we had ever been told.

"But if there must be balance, how can there ever be peace? Clearly, you are all divided to the point of no return. I mean, it's been thousands of years," I said, not understanding what this meant. "How are we supposed to fight this? I don't even know how to leave the infernal realm. How can I even get back to earth?"

How could anyone be victorious in this? It felt like we were set up for failure. Immortals forever battling for the most power. An impossible cycle.

"There are ways to keep balance and keep the mortal realm safe. There are old and ancient ways only the goddess of magic would know. She will know how to find the answers and then how to put them into action." Xael smiled fondly as if remembering something sweet.

With a wave of her hands, Xael produced an image in front of us of the woman who comforted her. It took a moment to realize that this woman had an uncanny resemblance to Nova.

"Hyacinth. She is the one who currently guards and holds on to my body."

"Okay, what about the others? On earth? They will help us, right?" I asked. I was sure we would need their help to keep the others from destroying the mortal realm.

"Some of them, perhaps. Hyacinth will. Briar, the god of war, will. If his sister, Raelyn, will. And Armello, the god of the sea, no one knows exactly where in the world he is. He roams the waters, and I don't think he has been seen since the big split thousands of years ago. Damari, the goddess of raw physical strength and power, will fight for you if you prove you are worthy. She doesn't respect those who hold weakness." Xael was frowning slightly.

"So, the only yes we have is Hyacinth?" My eyes went wide,

and a sinking sensation settled in my stomach. "There isn't a way to protect the mortal realm without them, is there?" I whispered, even though I already knew the answer.

"No. There isn't, and they might be persuaded to the other six, because they have been on Earth for so long. The reason they fled to the realm in the first place was because they disagreed with the others, and they were my friends. But I have been in my eternal sleep for so long, I no longer know who is friend or foe. I made a terrible mess of things. In trying to do what I thought was the right thing, I created even more chaos for those around me."

My head was pounding from all this new information.

"What happens to the Immortality Trials? Now that they have what they were looking for? The power of time isn't in humans anymore, is it? It's just in me?" I had been thinking about this for several days. Everything I knew to be true felt muddled and messy.

My whole life had been a fucking game that I was destined to lose, but I didn't. I won the trials, but by doing so, I actively fell deeper into this ridiculous power scheme. Was there no escaping these frivolous gods? Was I forever destined to be played with like a broken doll, desperate to be left alone?

The trials were a goddamn curse, and I had willingly welcomed it. My entire life had been one big disaster after another. Sure, I had power now, but what did that mean if everyone around me just wanted to use me again and again?

My immortality was a deadly reminder that no matter what, I would suffer for eternity, in all the realms. There was no end. Just eternal damnation. I thought I had dealt with the worst of my demons. My body was desperate for a peace that was slipping further through my fingers the more Xael and I talked.

"I don't know, Greer. They liked the trials for entertainment as well. They think it's amusing that their creatures still fight to the death for immortality. The power of time is no

longer in humans; only you. I am, again, so sorry for the loss, hopelessness, and trauma it caused you. It was supposed to be a cure for humanity, not a disease. I'm so sorry your mother was taken from you because of what I and the others did. And that it haunted you for years in the same way." Xael grabbed my hands and gave them a squeeze. Tears were falling from her eyes, identical to my own. I squeezed back my own tears threatening to spill.

I knew this wasn't entirely her fault. She was doing what she felt was right, and it got all kinds of fucked up.

"You said that I should have wanted to enter the trial, but I didn't. I now know that I was most likely forced into the trials by the six here, but why wouldn't their curse and your magic drive me to it? Why did they have to hire someone to be me and enter me? How did they know it was me?" I chewed my lip. These were other things that I didn't have answers for. There were so many blanks that needed to be filled in. My old friend hopelessness kept trying to creep in, and I did my best to keep snarling at it and telling it to go the fuck away.

"I don't know, Greer. It's something I have asked myself. Afton oversaw keeping tabs on all mortals who showed the "time sickness." The fact that you looked exactly like me was a pretty clear indicator that they should have been wary of you. But I don't know why you weren't drawn to it. It is something I have thought of as well, maybe when my magic and their curse collided, there were clauses and loopholes created that we didn't even know of...." She seemed unconcerned.

"What about my dad? Do you... Do you know anything about him? Did he have anything to do with it?" I said quietly. I didn't know my dad, and I had never wanted to know him, but I felt like if he had had a hand in this, I should be aware.

"From what I have understood, your father abandoned you and your mother because he was not a good human, not because

of anything else," Xael said mournfully, like the thought pained her.

So, my dad was simply a piece of shit?

Great. Add it to my list of other traumas.

"Okay, so how do I leave this realm? I know I need to get away from them, but I'm always chained, and I need to know what's happening with Kyra. I don't want to leave him, even though he practically destroyed my heart." I winced, the pain in my chest a constant amongst all the other things I was dealing with.

"But I don't know how long they will wait before they start to use us against one another and before they make a move against the mortal realm. I'll do my best to stop them, but I can't take them all on by myself. I'll need help." I tried to focus on what exactly my next step needed to be. One foot in front of the other.

"I don't know how you will be able to leave the infernal realm. Unless Riordan grants it, or Afton takes you. I will search my own mind for the answers, but I don't know. In the meantime, I will train you in the power of time and help you fight, so when the time comes, you can escape. I'm sorry, Greer. I wish I knew how to get you out of the realm." Xael's cheeks were wet once again.

Darkness started to slip into our sunny little grass patch.

"You are being woken up." Xael scowled.

"Thank you, Xael, this is making a little more sense now. I'll see you soon." I gripped her hand hard.

"Be brave, Greer." She cupped a hand on my cheek.

The darkness swirled around, and I was surrounded. In a breath, everything was gone, and I was being thrust into my physical body once again.

SEVEN

KYRA

Greer and I were being forced into training.

We were told our bodies were weak from being in the mortal realm for too long, and real immortals were trained in the art of magic, old school weaponry, and the ways of the gods and goddesses. I tried not to roll my eyes when my father lectured me about it. It was low on my priority list to know the ways of his realm, not that I told him that.

For the most part, I was still being ignored and punished by him. My plan of trying to get on his good side was going absolutely nowhere. I hadn't seen Greer since the odd dinner the other night, when she had asked if we were doing this together.

Well, I assumed that was what she was asking.

She had looked so overwhelmed and anxious. I wanted to rip off the manacles and hold her and kiss away the worry. My body ached for her, and my heart hurt knowing she was in pain. I was doing a fucking terrible job of protecting her and being any sort of knight in shining armor.

Not that she needed me to save her, but this mess was my responsibility.

So here we were in *training*.

But it was a test. They wanted to see how far we would go for each other.

Both of us were in decent fighting condition due to how much we trained together for the trials. I wasn't that good at using weapons, but I was damn good at using my magic. However, Greer didn't have any training with her powers, but she was a menace with a dagger.

We were in a huge room, covered in black mats, with miscellaneous gym equipment and weapons nestled into different corners. The ceilings were high, and there was a viewing deck where some of the original twelve were likely sitting, along with other immortals, civilians of Hell, and random people. All loitering around, watching the spectacle.

Greer was on the far side, away from me. She had been led in by Phayre. She was dressed in leather leggings, boots, and a short-sleeve T-shirt. If I weren't so worried about her safety, I would be salivating at the way she looked right now. Something in her posture, though, made it clear she wasn't as scared today as she had been a few nights ago. Her long red hair was braided, falling nearly to her low back. The urge to run my hands against her skin was strong, but there was no way that would be allowed.

I was sitting with my father in tactical pants, boots, and a black shirt as well. My father clearly favored the form that looked most like me, with his own personal add-ons. He was always taller, broader, and just *more* than I was. He radiated power. It felt like his magic was always on me, breathing down my godsdamn neck.

"Now, if you show me a real fight. Then, I will keep these off and trust you to meet your mother." My father waved his hands, and my metal manacles clanked to the floor. I rubbed my wrists and narrowed my eyes.

"A real fight? What exactly are your expectations here?" I demanded. I needed to know exactly what I needed to do in order to have some semblance of freedom.

"Show no mercy." He smiled, flashing all his teeth, making my stomach knot. His blood-red eyes flashed black.

I blinked as the only recognition.

"Welcome, friends and honored guests! Today, we will have three rounds of combat before each of our new immortals begins to learn the ways of old. The first round will be brute force. The second round will be weapons. The third and final will be a weapon of choice and, of course, their powers," my father boomed, facing the glass box that housed the cheering section. They roared, and my father grinned at them and then at me.

"Don't embarrass me, Kyra." He winked at me, but it felt anything but playful.

I looked over to where Greer was, and Phayre yanked on the collar around her throat and pulled her close. The fire in my veins roared as Greer grimaced and ground her teeth. Phayre whispered something in her ear. She grabbed Greer's chin in her hands and got inches from her nose.

Greer went rigid, and then Phayre pushed her away with a smile and a wave of her hand. Her manacles crashed to the ground from her wrists, ankles, and finally the collar.

Greer swallowed, and a flash of something lit her eyes.

She wanted to run.

She wouldn't get very far.

I wanted to grab her and tell her we could make it. We could find a way out, but I knew that was a lie. I had no idea how to get out of here without Afton or my father's help. Neither one of them was lining up to do a damn thing to help Greer and me besides hold us hostage.

She squared her shoulders and rolled her neck. Rubbed her wrists and rolled her ankles. She walked towards the center of the room, which held a large rectangular mat. I walked with her, holding my breath. This was the closest I had been to her without the manacles, and I still hadn't explained to her what had happened. We hadn't talked.

We were so close.

But so far away. A chasm separated our hearts even though our bodies were an arm's length away.

We stepped up to the mats, and the air between us felt heavy and thick.

The manacles had left angry bruises on her neck and wrists. I assumed she had matching ones on her ankles. I clenched my jaw and exhaled loudly. Greer's green eyes flashed, and I couldn't place it. I wanted to fall at her feet and tell her how much I loved her and how sorry I was for everything that happened. That I didn't want this.

"Ky," she said quietly.

"Greer," I choked out, tears welling in my eyes.

"BEGIN!" My father roared, and I whipped my head to where he was smirking.

Greer was on me in an instant, swinging with a right hook aimed at my jaw. I side-stepped her, which she was expecting. Her left knee slammed into my side. I let out a groan as I grabbed her leg. I used her momentum against her and pulled her to the floor as I wrapped my legs around her.

She landed with an "oof," and I lost my grip on her. She pounced on top of me, straddling me, and she slammed her arm against my throat. Her body felt so good against mine, even though my airway was cut off. I wanted her to stay there with a little more friction; her strong thighs pressed around me made me feral. I was trying to decide what I should do to make this seem legitimate, even though I just wanted her pelvis to grind against me.

I looked up at her, and her eyes were unfocused. I gasped for air and went to buck her off with my hips, which made her eyes go wide as she pushed harder into my body.

"She told me if I didn't give this my all, she would hurt you." Her voice was barely audible.

Fuck.

I knew we were being baited against one another, but this was just cruel.

I grabbed her thighs and pulled up as she yelped and lost her balance on my throat with the upward momentum. I wrapped my arms around her waist and then flipped her over on her back.

"I think I can find a way out, but I need to win, too," I whispered as Greer's eyes narrowed into slits.

She pulled her legs up, wrapped them around my chest, and slammed me down. I landed with a groan as she sprang up. She was ready to pounce, but I had already vaulted up.

There were cheers from the watching deck.

I pushed my too-long hair out of my face. My breath came out in pants, from fighting and from being so close to Greer for the first time in weeks, without the look of betrayal in her eyes, but instead, something else shone—like hope.

I charged her and slid down at the last second, sliding through her legs and taking them out. She smacked the ground, face-first, with a crack. I scrambled to see if she was alright, and I heard my father's booming voice.

"Don't help your opponent, if she can get up, keep going," he boomed with a chuckle.

Greer rolled over, and blood leaked from her mouth and nose. She pushed herself up, and I looked at her in horror. I had just knocked the love of my life down, on fucking purpose. Godsdamnit.

She spat on the floor; her eyes were determined. She nodded at me like she understood.

We both had to put on a show.

I pushed forward once again, and Greer slipped by me and slammed her foot into my back. I arched and twisted, grabbing her foot, and pulled her down with me. We landed in a grunt, and I was on top of her in a second, slamming her hands down and putting my mouth inches from hers, my hair long enough to shield us from the onlookers.

"Win, Kyra, get us out of here, please. Don't hold back," she whispered, her breath warm against my mouth, and she arched underneath me. I had less than an inch of distance to press my lips to hers, but I knew it wouldn't be a good idea. It was a terrible one, actually.

"First round to Kyra!" My father yelled.

I leaned back and looked up, masking my features. Painfully, I removed myself from Greer's body and offered my hand to pull her up.

Her hand met mine, and I sent warmth through the connection; her body shivered, which brought me a deep sense of satisfaction. A smirk spread on my lips, and was met with a downturn of hers, which sent a deep cut straight to my heart. I tried not to show that I was hurt. We were still so far apart despite everything.

"This doesn't mean I trust you, Ky," she grunted through clenched teeth, staring at our hands.

She went to pull away, but I held on tight.

"I know, I'll fix this," I murmured, and something softened in her before her gaze flashed to the viewing deck.

She let go, her hand falling limply away from mine, and wiped her mouth again, spitting on the ground where more blood splattered on the mat.

"Pick your weapons, round two begins in five minutes," my father commanded.

Greer reached for a long dagger, and I grabbed for a short sword.

Wiping a towel across my face, I closed my eyes to catch my breath. How were we going to last the next two rounds without causing more irreparable harm to our relationship or each other's bodies? I sighed and scrubbed my face with my hands.

Greer looked at me and seemed to be trying to tell me something, but all I could think of was how much I missed the feeling of her and how much I wanted things to be different for us.

"ROUND TWO, BEGIN!"

And so, we did.

EIGHT

GREER

My face hurt like a bitch, and my tongue ached from biting it when Kyra had swept my legs out from underneath me. But if Kyra thought he could get us out of here, then I would let him figure it out.

Xael and I had been trying to puzzle out how to leave the infernal realm for a while now in my dreams, but she didn't know how. Traveling through the realms was a messy business with the rift between the original twelve. I wasn't exactly sure how Riordan had been able to do it once a year with Kyra. Xael said that they might not have been able to detect him on Earth if he were there for less than a certain number of hours and didn't use his power. His power would be like a beacon for the rest of the gods and goddesses who resided on earth, so maybe he had been careful.

I just added it to the ever-growing list of things I didn't understand and needed to find answers to. There were so many fucking rules and loopholes, it made me want to scream.

Right now, I needed to make this fight as close as possible so Phayre would keep her grabby hands to herself. She said she would hurt Kyra, that she would make him her own *personal* pet if I didn't play well. I didn't need to know any more details to know that the idea of it made me want to vomit. She practically salivated when she talked about him, and it gave me the biggest ick. I was mad at Ky, but I still loved him, and *no one* deserved to be treated like that. And no one touched what was mine.

I swallowed hard and told myself to get my focus together, because I was planning on winning this next round. I wanted to show these assholes that I wasn't helpless. That, when I wanted to, I would strike. They underestimated me, and it would be their downfall.

Ky let out an exhale as we circled one another, and it was his tell. He ran at me, his short sword drawn, and he swiped at my belly. I smiled wickedly and ducked, shooting my leg out at the same time, so he tumbled and rolled over his own sword. I spun my dagger around in my hands and turned, waiting for him to get up.

If they wanted a show, I would give them a damn show.

Kyra looked a bit confused, and I smirked.

He lunged again and arced up with his blade. It sang against my dagger as I brought it up to parry. I pushed him off with a snarl and attacked. I swiped and jabbed ferociously, making him step back.

He was breathing heavily, sweat trailed down his brow, his long hair clung to his forehead, and all I wanted was to run my fingers through it. Scarlet eyes followed me, bright and intense, never once leaving my skin. He blocked my blows, doing everything he could to keep up. I knew Kyra didn't train with a short sword; he had never needed to rely on anything except his powers. I knew so much about him that it made my heart drop to my belly in the pit of grief, which I tried to keep locked down.

He wasn't nearly as quick and agile as I was, and I nicked his bicep, his chest, and his cheek in what looked like untrained swings but were controlled points of attack. Suddenly, he dropped his sword from his wide arch coming from my chest to his bottom hand, catching it before it hit the ground, and thrusting up.

Snatching his bottom wrist with the sword, I squeezed and twisted. Hard. He yelped and dropped his weapon. I used his own momentum to twist it even harder and then pull through his arm, so he spun around, and his arm was behind him. Kyra roared in pain as I pushed harder, slamming his back into me and bringing my other hand with the dagger up to his throat.

My body hummed as it was pressed into his back. It was like my skin remembered the way Kyra's hands felt trailing down my body and how he felt when his mouth was on me. I fought the urge to shiver as a wet heat started to pool between my thighs. I bit the inside of my cheek to check myself, because now was not the time to be horny for Kyra—he still had a lot of explaining to do.

My eyes were barely level with his upper back. He was taller and broader than me. He tried to squirm against me, but I pressed the tip of the dagger to his throat and gently trailed it down his throat to his chest, feeling the give of his skin slightly as he leaned into it.

I gasped, not meaning to cut him, but he whipped his head to the side and gave a quick shake of his head.

"SECOND ROUND, TIMEWRAITH!" Riordan announced.

"Greer," Kyra pleaded.

I pushed him away gently, but didn't let go of his wrist. I eased up on the grip, and he turned to look at me. Heat and arousal were apparent in his gaze, and I swallowed again.

It was as if I were telling my mind to stop, but my body was intent on not listening. The nicks on his olive skin and the tear that had followed my dagger's path from his throat to his chest haunted me. It exposed the smooth, hard planes of his chest, revealing the top of his abdominal muscles. I stared and licked my lips involuntarily.

Kyra grunted, and my eyes whipped up to his.

The corners of his mouth tipped up, and I rolled my eyes.

"Round three starts in five minutes," Riordan concluded from his position on the sidelines.

I sheathed my dagger and grabbed a water bottle, downing the whole thing.

No one had seen my power since that day in the throne room when I had exhausted all my energy and passed out. But Xael and I had been practicing together. I wanted to flex my time muscles.

But I needed to let Kyra win.

I wouldn't show everything I had learned, but I would show a taste, because I wanted them to be afraid. They needed to feel the darkness that now coated my skin and lived inside my veins.

I wanted them to see that I was a monster of my own making to the people who would choose to stand against me and hurt those I loved.

Kyra had discarded his shirt entirely, putting his stone on full display in his chest. It looked... wrong. It was cracked, with black and red etched across his skin, like the colors were at war with each other, and the veins leaking from it were a patchwork of dark scarlet and inky black.

All his abdominals were on display, and the V on his hips made my mouth water. He turned to grab a dagger this time. His black and gray flame tattoo that enveloped his back tensed and bunched over the muscles as he rolled his shoulders back and flexed his hands, exposing veins and corded muscle.

The wet heat started to work its way into all parts of me, clouding my eyes and judgment for a moment as I pictured throwing myself on top of him and licking the sweat off his hip bones and sucking at the pulse point on his throat.

I closed my hands and breathed deeply.

I would not blow this because I was horny for the man who had lied to me. But I wouldn't let anyone else get to have him, either. Phayre would lose a hand if she attempted even a taste.

"One weapon and your powers, don't hold back. The last one standing wins. BEGIN!" Riordan demanded, and we both stepped up to the mat.

I kept my dagger sheathed at my thigh as Kyra and I just stared.

His hands began to lick with flames.

I shivered because I had never seen Kyra go all out with his powers before. I got little snippets, but there weren't many instances where a full display of power was necessary on Earth. He had a regular job, which he got because he had power, not because he needed to use it, or it meant anything for his skills.

The flames licked up to his forearms, and he pushed his palm forward, a fireball shot at me, and I pressed my energy out, slowing it down the second before it connected. Kyra's eyes went wide while I easily side-stepped it.

He sent a wave of fire pushing towards me, and I pushed my energy out, not needing to use my hands as a conduit. I stopped it right in front of my nose. Xael said that when I was in control of the time realm, I could move in the realm. But the more I moved, the less control I would have over the time around me, so I needed to make calculated movements that didn't expend too much energy; otherwise, I would lose focus and let time snap back to normal.

So, I took five quick steps to the side, where Kyra was frozen, his eyes still fixed on the wall of flame extending from him by about ten feet. I pulled the energy back to me, and the flames hissed, then dissipated, and Kyra's eyes flashed to me as I stood to the side of him, twirling my dagger.

He flexed his fingers, and my dagger heated before exploding in my hand. I shielded my face and pushed my power out in a quick burst, falling to the ground to avoid the shrapnel.

I had never seen Kyra's explosive power. It was the most dangerous thing about him. There was so much I still didn't know about the man I had said "I love you" to.

Not letting my mind wander too far, I rolled and pushed up and let go of time again. Kyra slammed his hands together, and my dagger's explosion pulled in and fizzled to ashes. I gaped openly at him. I didn't know he could do that, either.

I guess I wasn't using that anymore.

"You've been practicing," Kyra noted. It was not exactly a question, but I could see in his eyes that he didn't understand how I had been doing it and how I was proficient at it.

Xael said to think of it like a "push and pull." Pushing the power out meant slowing down time to almost a complete stop, and pulling meant I could speed it up around me, which could be very useful in combat, but was much harder than pushing.

I had learned to use it in close combat training with her, pushing and pulling to find openings in an opponent. It was easiest to push it out and halt time entirely when I did little movement of my own, because my control slipped as I started to move my physical body. It was a delicate balance.

I needed to use my agility to put my power to the best use.

Roaring, I sprinted toward Kyra, pulling at time to close the distance between us quickly. He pressed a heated ball of flame out, and I pushed out time to slow it, ducking and landing a kick to his abdomen, sending him sprawling and sputtering for breath. I snapped my powers back, launching myself at him, and he let out a plume of flames headed towards me. Twisting midair, I barely avoided the heat.

He leapt up, and we circled each other once again. He was an offensive fighter. He shot out another wall of flame, and I paused the world around me, ran behind him, and snapped up his dagger.

I lost my control on time, and his flames pulsed forward. It was as if he sensed me behind him. Kyra whipped around, roaring, and I pressed the dagger to his chest. He hollered and leaned into it. In horror, I paused time and pulled it out, but not before it sank an inch deep.

I screamed, and his eyes went wide and narrowed.

"It's okay," he whispered as his body's momentum crashed into mine and he rolled to the floor. I scrambled away, holding the dagger in my hand.

I looked up at our audience. Riordan and Phayre were frowning, their heads bent together. If Kyra could let me hurt him, I could let him hurt me.

I screeched, a sound that was all the pain and sadness I had been keeping at bay since I had arrived here. It shook the arena, and I pushed time out in a burst, then snapped it back as I ran towards Kyra. He shot a flame column at me.

He expected me to deflect it. I feigned an ankle roll and plunged myself into the heat of the flames, screaming as the flames burned my arm and my leg. It was white hot, sharp, and searing. I yelled again and fell, smelling charred flesh. The flames around me had dissipated.

I whimpered and blinked my eyes, black dots floating in my vision.

Kyra bellowed in anguish, and the world spun and faded in and out of focus.

"Greer." Kyra's scarlet eyes were bright and blurry, not from my pain, but because tears swam in them and fell on my shirt, soaking through to my skin, the pain in my arm and leg shrieking.

"I thought you would deflect like you had been doing," he confessed, looking in horror at what I imagined was charred flesh.

I was struggling to stay conscious as my pain receptors fired off, telling me to stand down.

"Find a way out," I choked out, and I caught a glimpse of the muscle exposed and the skin peeling off. My stomach rolled.

Kyra looked at me in panic and gritted his teeth.

"I'm so sorry, Greer. I never wanted to hurt you," he admitted as I slipped out of consciousness and heard his dad howl.

"KYRA IS THE WINNER!"

I let the blackness fade and turned to welcome Xael in my dream.

The pain was still searing even in here; in this place where so much else couldn't seem to touch me.

Greer, my child. You have sacrificed so much.

I have news. Hyacinth is talking to Nova.

They are finding a way to get you out.

My body felt heavy and wrong.

Nova... Lux... Waverly... Even Sutton.

My friends.

I couldn't focus on any one thing.

I slipped from the dream state too quickly; my body was being handled by someone, and a new warmth slipped over me. There were flashes of Xael holding my hand. Of someone else holding it... somewhere else.

I didn't know what to think between the pain, Xael, and everything.

So I retreated to my own darkness until the chaos around me settled down.

NINE

LUX

"Hyacinth?" Nova asked, sounding guarded.

"In the flesh, darling. Surprised to see me so well informed?" She uncrossed her long jean-clad legs and stretched her arms out before she got up and walked a circle around the room.

"You all can have a seat on the couch, if you'd like. I'm not here to smite you or anything." She laughed lightly, as if that wasn't something she might actually do.

I glanced at Waverly, who was pulling Nova to her feet, and I got up, blinking.

"But you could... Couldn't you?" I asked, moving to sit on the couch far away from where Hyacinth had settled into the corner. She tilted her head and tossed her long aquamarine hair back.

"Luxton Gilmore. What interesting familial power you have. The dragon isn't something I have often seen in shifters since the original wars." She narrowed her eyes and flashed her teeth. "Most were killed or destroyed at the greedy hands of all the others' creatures with the intent to be the best, despite what it meant to climb to the top. They had little regard for peace, harmony, or longevity." She clicked her tongue.

"Uh, I didn't realize." I didn't know what to say. I had hardly ever asked about my family's origin. My parents and I weren't exactly the conversing type.

"They always try to snuff out what's unique and different if they can't control it." She pursed her lips.

"Hyacinth, you clearly know why we summoned you. What do you know?" Nova questioned from where she was standing, with her arms crossed and her legs wide, like she was gearing up for battle.

"Aw, Nova, my dear, one of the greatest blood witches from my line. How straightforward you are. Your friends are trapped in the infernal realm. There is no way for them to leave unless Afton takes them out or Riordan allows them free passage," Hyacinth responded casually.

We all collectively groaned. Hyacinth smirked and held up a finger.

"Except, with my help and the help of one other, you can create a short portal window that will link us together." She folded her hands together and exhaled loudly.

"Okay." I motioned for her to continue, knowing she wouldn't have suggested something so confidently if she didn't already have a plan.

"Greer or Kyra will need to establish the connection with the other person. We will need to do it soon because Riordan is preparing to make his move, since Greer is in his grasp. He can overthrow the contract that has kept us separate for thousands of years. With Greer's power—and most likely his son's —he will be able to move freely to the mortal realm and destroy it. Most likely, he will come for Xael and try to recruit the others before he puts the rest of his plan in motion." Her expression turned serious, her eyes hardening and her voice deepening.

"I imagine Riordan has kept Verity hidden away, but she has started to grow restless with her son near," Hyacinth continued.

I felt like we were starting a book in the middle, and I had missed the first hundred pages.

"Who is Verity?" Nova asked, the only one currently capable of asking coherent questions.

"Kyra's mother, of course, and Riordan's prisoner," she spat, settling onto the couch.

"Kyra's mother is a prisoner?" I already knew Riordan was bad news because of Greer, but why did he hate women in general?

"Yes. Verity is one of my daughters."

Waverly's mouth dropped open.

"Not literally, little siren, but a descendant of my power. I created several from my own magic to spread the witch bloodline. Verity was one of the originals I created. Riordan and she met at our solstice celebration, where I was too preoccupied to notice him move past my wards." She looked upset and disappointed in herself, as if she were the one to blame.

"Sounds like he's been an ass his entire life," I mumbled under my breath.

Hyacinth laughed loudly then, her eyes sparking to life.

"Yes, Luxton Gilmore, he has been an absolute thorn in my side for the entirety of my immortal life," she proclaimed.

"He and Verity quickly became enamored with one another. He failed to mention, of course, that he was king of the infernal realm. She would have never given him the time of day if she had known. We are honest and transparent with our people in the Eastern Hemisphere. She would have known to stay away if I had equipped her better," she bit out.

"You can't possibly blame yourself," Waverly insisted.

Hyacinth looked at Waverly with brows raised.

"I don't. Riordan is the one who needs to take responsibility for his actions. However, I can't help but feel like I did her a disservice. She has been gone for a long time. My feelings and the sorrows of the past are not why I came here. When Verity became pregnant with their child, Kyra, that is when Riordan decided to reveal who he was to her. She exploded with rage, and for the rest of her pregnancy, she planned her escape. As soon as Kyra was born, she used her magic to send him to the only place she knew to be home." She tapped her fingernails on the table. Clearly, this story did not sit well with her.

"She created a spell so powerful that Riordan had to stay away from Kyra, and the only way Kyra could come to hell was if he willingly agreed, which he did, because of Greer. Verity knew the only way he could escape was with her help. She has mourned her child for years."

Waverly swiped at her eyes, and Nova reached for her hand.

"She sacrificed her life for Kyra's, and Riordan has never let her go because of it." She stood abruptly and clenched her jaw.

"So, how will she aid Greer and Kyra to bring them back?" I asked in a small voice, not wanting any of the lethal-quiet rage pulsing off Hyacinth aimed at me.

"I don't know, exactly. Verity's magic has always been completely her own. She may open a portal. She may give them the power to travel. But she will need more than what she has. Spending time in the infernal realm will have weakened her significantly. She will have to borrow from her sisters or me. I will give it to her, of course. The war that is brewing has been coming to a boiling point for centuries."

A war? It was one thing to know that a fight was brewing, but a war was nearly inconceivable. What would that mean for Earth? For us? For these immortal beings?

Waverly sucked in a breath, and Nova narrowed her eyes.

"Greer has the ability to balance the world or destroy it with Xael's power. She will need to make wise decisions on how to proceed. But know that you have my support. I would suggest trying to find Armello as well." She looked at Waverly.

"Who is Armello?" Waverly questioned.

"The God your kind descends from. He hasn't been heard from in, well, since the divide and the great wars. But your songs could help you in finding him," she mused.

"I don't know what that means," Waverly whispered, looking unsure of herself.

"Go to the seas and sing, my dear, or travel the waters. The ocean will take your message for you, and it will be Armello who surely answers your call. You might even be lucky enough to catch Briar as well," she mused.

"Who is Briar?" I asked.

"Armello's best friend. He was in love with Xael at the time of her fall, and those boys have always stuck by one another's side. So, I would imagine if you found one, you have a good chance of perhaps finding the other," Hyacinth replied.

"Great, another fucking god," I grumbled.

Hyacinth looked at me with pity. "Oh, dear Luxton, you will need the help of those of us who reside on Earth to challenge the others who do not."

"I don't understand what you mean. There have been godly beings on earth this whole time?" I questioned.

Nova's eyes zeroed in on Hyacinth.

"That's why the Eastern Hemisphere is off limits to us, isn't it? You all have that side, and the others have ours. I assume over the fallout of Xael herself." Nova concluded, piecing together the puzzle much faster than me.

"Yes, my child. How perceptive you are. There are more details and nuances than that, but that is the basis. I will tell you more details when you retrieve the timewraith. But know that, at some point, you will have no choice but to find

Armello, Briar, Damaria, and Raelyn. Xael's body is with me and mine. She has been preserved since her fall from power. Her body is still fit as a magical vessel." She pursed her lips.

"Who the fuck is Damaria and Raelyn, then?" My head was spinning.

"Another tale for another time. I have not seen or been contacted by any of my godly kin in years. People with power have a funny way of pushing others away who can challenge them. But in order to restore balance and stop the war that is to come, you will need all the help you can get. At minimum, you will have to have six on your side, including the timewraith, to feed the balance of the universe.

The Eastern Hemisphere has been ours since the fall of the kingdoms. We have warded it accordingly for the safety of our people, and the people of the west would rather accept that we are barbarians that don't want anything to do with you all than ask smarter questions." She blinked rapidly, like it made sense that most of the people in the West were just assholes who believed whatever they were told.

"But the original twelve hold many grudges, and most of us just want to be left alone without the squabbles of the original hierarchy. You will need to be clever and demonstrate to those on Earth why their aid is requested. They once saw Xael's reasoning, but time has a funny way of turning the tide."

"Will she want her powers back?" I asked suddenly. This was much bigger than we had anticipated. The trials looked like a joke compared to what was actually happening. The whole thing was a ruse. We thought our greatest obstacle was getting Greer out of the death match for immortality. But it turns out that was her saving grace, and the real danger has just begun.

"I don't pretend to know what Xael's agenda is regarding the timewraith. She has been in a hypnotic sleep for years. But know that you all will need to decide how you will aid in this fight. Greer is the key, but there is a reason you all came together. Fate has a funny way of setting the course and letting you decide your own destiny." Hyacinth spoke in vague riddles, and it only added to the overwhelm of this situation.

"So, what now? Will you contact us when Verity reaches out for one of your kind's powers?" Nova asked skeptically.

"I will. I suggest you bolster your own magic and skills to prepare for what is next. Once Greer comes back, you will need to put your magic to good use. And it seems as if the West has let these things slumber and discouraged ethical practice most of your life." She looked at a watch that had magically appeared on her wrist.

"But that story can be told another time. Be prepared to receive your friends. Kyra and Greer will not be the same as you once knew them to be." She nodded to us.

"Nova, come here, my daughter." Hyacinth beckoned with her hand, and Nova stepped up slowly.

"I bestow you with the gift and love and power of your kind. The protection of the original witch and all after her." Her hand glowed, and her fingertips dusted Nova's forehead.

"You will be able to contact me whenever you need. Our link has now been established. Use it wisely, child, as I am a very busy woman." She winked, and then she was gone.

Nova touched her forehead where Hyacinth had made their connection. A few stars popped up around where she had touched her, glittering and sparkling like diamonds flirting with the edge of her light purple hair, dusting the crown of her head. They shone more brightly than the others, capturing your gaze with a bewitching light.

The elevator door dinged, and we all whipped around. I changed into a tiger and roared a warning as Waverly tied her hair back. Nova had her hands poised to puppeteer.

Shadows swept in from the opening doors, dousing the

room in a smoky haze, before Sutton glided in, a small smile on his lips as we all stood silent and still.

"Relax, it's only me." His lips turned up.

"Godsdamnit, Sutton." Nova rolled her shoulders.

"It's nice to see you," Waverly said, going in for a hug.

I hung back. I didn't know what Sutton and I were to each other. My nerves always felt raw around him. He felt untouchable until I could feel his shadows slide against my side and practically purr in my ear.

"It's nice to see you," I said, clearing my throat.

"You too," he uttered, his smile growing a millimeter before he settled himself at the table.

"I have some news." He folded his elegant fingers together.

"Good or bad?" Nova asked, sliding in across from him.

"A bit of both."

"Fucking great," she sighed.

"Alright, let's hear it." I pulled out the chair next to him.

"I want the bad first, then the good." Waverly sat next to Nova.

"Okay, the bad first, then."

"Oh, before we get started, Hyacinth was just here," Nova said, leaning back in her chair.

Sutton's eyebrows lifted a fraction in surprise. His expressions were so damn hard to read. I was an open book about my feelings. They were practically written in bright red letters across my forehead, but Sutton was cool and collected most of the time. Barely a hair out of place.

His bright red lips curled up slightly, "I'm sorry I missed her."

"We can fill you in on what she said later." Waverly dismissed the visit like we hadn't just been in the presence of the original witch of all time.

Sutton nodded, and his small grin disappeared. "So, the bad news," he started, drumming his long fingertips against the table like he was debating on how to most delicately break this terrible news to us.

"The darkness of hell is stirring, and the creatures there are excited. They said that Riordan does, indeed, have Greer and Kyra. There are very few ways for them to leave. So, as of now, they are stuck in the infernal realm."

"Hyacinth has a way for them to come back. Verity, Kyra's mother, is a witch and is trapped down there, too, apparently. They will exchange messages in the way only they can," Nova recounted.

"So, part one of our plan is basically being done for us," I chimed in, feeling relieved that we, at least, had one thing figured out.

"Right."

Sutton tilted his head towards me and eyed me up and down. I swallowed and forced myself to look at his dark eyes. They pulled you in and made me want to rake my teeth across his skin.

A small curl of those damn red lips happened again, and I swore he could practically hear my thoughts.

"Once they are retrieved, however, Kyra will struggle with the power of hell. I imagine, at this point, his crystal is turning back to the original magic that beckoned him home. He will be at war with using the cursed fire inside him."

"What does that mean exactly?" Waverly frowned.

"He will be a beacon for the creatures of the infernal realm. There are ways to use this to our advantage, but it means, most likely, we will be pursued by much of what lies in the depths of despair in hell itself." Sutton shrugged like it wasn't that big of a deal.

It sounded like a pretty fucking big deal.

"But, you also are cursed?" Nova asked.

"Yes," he replied.

"And what can you tell us about that?" Waverly asked in a soothing voice.

"It's a generational curse. Passed from my father to me. A punishment by Raelyn herself at the request of my mother. Something that I am now forced to bear," Sutton said, weighing his words carefully. There was hidden meaning in this curse, and clearly Sutton was not ready to disclose this secret.

"So, that means you at least know Raelyn? Your mother asked for aid; perhaps you can appeal to her the way your mother did?" I said, feeling a little more hopeful about our situation since Raelyn had helped his family before, even if it ended up screwing Sutton over in the long run. Sutton grimaced.

"It's a bit more complicated than that. I..." Sutton cleared his throat and closed his eyes. His mask slipped on again as he continued, "We can at least try to reason with her, I suppose."

Nova quirked her brow. "Well, you'll need to reveal that sooner or later, but right now, we will let it rest. In the meantime, we need to get you to the sea." She turned to Waverly, who looked terrified.

"I haven't been to the sea in a very long time," she whispered.

"Why not?" I asked. With the way Hyacinth had spoken about the sea and sirens, I had gathered that it calls them.

"I almost died," she confessed.

"I need a drink," I mumbled, standing up.

"Yeah, me too," Waverly snickered.

"Strap in, motherfuckers, because it's going to be a long night," Nova announced, passing around a bottle of tequila.

"Bottoms up," I said, and let the clear liquid burn its way down to the sinking feeling in my gut.

TEN
KYRA

I had been locked in a damn cage.

Images of Greer's skin peeling off and exposing her muscles haunted me. The smell of seared flesh felt permanently ingrained in my nostrils. I had nearly gone berserk when my father tried to shove me off her. I clung to her hand as long as I possibly could before he took her away.

He had told me not to worry, that her immortality would prevent her from dying or incurring any long-term injury. Riordan had the audacity to laugh and say that she was already becoming accustomed to extreme pain with her manacles. The flippancy with which he spoke about her well-being sent me into a tailspin. I hadn't realized that hers were a constant source of agony.

Without much thought, I had flung myself at my father, and then everything went black as his power flooded into me and sent my body flying and my consciousness breaking. I had been shoved into my room until I had calmed down enough to have a conversation with him.

Now, I paced my room like a feral animal. All the furniture had already burned to a crisp. I wasn't proud of my rage, but I had fucking hurt Greer.

Again.

And my father was doing it constantly, without care or thought of how her body might recover, but what about the rest of her?

I wanted to cut off my own hands and strip myself of magic. The thought of contributing to her pain was unbearable. I wasn't any better than my father if I did this to her. How could I be so fucking careless?! Hours—or maybe it was only minutes—passed by. I couldn't be sure how long I paced.

Finally, my father appeared at the door.

"I see you redecorated," he commented, smirking.

"Have you ever really loved someone?" I demanded.

His eyes flashed, and his brows furrowed. I'd caught him off guard. That was not the response he was expecting.

"What are you getting at, Kyra?" He bristled.

"I would burn down the world. This one, the mortal one, all of them for her. Don't you understand that?"

He scoffed.

"I would give up my magic, my immortality, and my own body for her. And if that doesn't scare you, it should. The lengths I will go to for her are immeasurable, and the longer you play this game where you try to divide us, the more dangerous it gets for you. Every way you inflict pain on her skin, I will pay it back tenfold," I spat.

"You should be careful what you say, boy." His power expanded to fill all the empty spaces in the room. It zapped and heated my skin, as if waiting for the opportunity to consume and destroy.

"Don't say I didn't warn you," I said, not bothering to get up from where I sat on the floor with my back against the wall.

"They say love magic is the most powerful," Farren retorted, materializing behind my father, smirking while my father scowled. He whispered something in my father's ear, and his face softened.

"Threats for love are so fun, aren't they?" Farren joked, giggling, and then he disappeared.

"Did you love my mother, then? Are you capable of love?" I wondered if it was possible for my father to have any sort of empathy and compassion, or if his narcissism and selfishness consumed every part of his life.

His scarlet eyes widened, and he suddenly looked thousands of years old.

"I did love your mother. I still do." Sorrow crept into the timbre of his voice. I wasn't falling for it, though. This man had no capacity for love.

"Do I get to meet her? I played your game. I betrayed Greer again—nearly fatally injured her, despite her immortality. Which should make you gloriously happy, so will you keep your end of the bargain or not?" I stood abruptly.

I was tired of feeling like I didn't have control over anything.

"You will get to meet her. The fire that flows through your veins also flows through hers." A ghost of a smile appeared on his face.

I wasn't sure if he meant it literally or figuratively, but I wasn't going to let the opportunity pass me by.

"Great, let's go." I stalked towards him, and he held out a hand.

Why was he letting me win this fight so easily? What was his angle? I couldn't fathom why it would benefit me to see my mother.

"First, I want to show you the true identity of the realm, as I have now given you access to move around my castle. You can now leave the estate and travel to the outer lands if you wish, but I wouldn't suggest it. I doubt you will be interested in exploring them much after our tour." He clapped his hands together.

"Is this your idea of building a relationship? Giving me a tour of your hellscape?" I almost laughed out loud at the ridiculousness of it.

"If you are to rule alongside me, then you must see the realm for what it is in its entirety." He moved out of the doorway and ushered me through.

I kept my mouth shut and decided that a rebuttal would do me little to no good at this point. Pain shot through my crystal. I gasped, clutching my chest and nearly falling to the ground.

"Kyra?" Riordan almost sounded concerned.

Almost.

"It's nothing," I gritted out and rubbed at my chest.

"Your crystal is making demands of you, is it not? The original gem's magic is being fed here." He smiled, as if this brought him all the joy in the world.

"Well, it's very fucking painful. It feels like the magics inside me are battling against one another." I scowled.

"They probably are. I told you not to taint my original gift."

"Curse," I corrected.

"Semantics." Riordan waved his hands. "The powers granted to you from the Immortality Trials and the powers granted to you from me are fighting for space in the crystal. Eventually, one will win out and annihilate the other," Riordan stated as he walked in front of me down the hallway.

"Fucking fantastic."

I knew I would need to find a way to either force both powers to coexist or deal with this stabbing pain for the rest of my life.

"You could just surrender to the infernal realm power," Riordan commented, as if the choice were obvious.

"No, thank you." I ground my teeth as the pain in my chest retreated to a dull ache.

Just add it to the list of things I needed to fucking figure out. Right now, I needed to pay attention to my selfish father and his tour so I could get my bearings and then meet my mother. Maybe she would be an ally. Maybe she would be able to get us out of this hellhole.

"Are you ready to see our kingdom?" Riordan said.

"Let's get this over with," I sighed.

"There's the spirit. Alright, Son, welcome to the realm of the Infernal."

He snapped his fingers and transported us in the blink of an eye with a swirl of smoke and a zap of power. I coughed and waved my hands around, the smoke clouding my eyes.

"That was fucking dramatic."

"We are now outside of the estate." Riordan set off, and I had no choice but to follow. I looked back at the sprawling castle. It looked like a fortress of death and decay.

"The infernal realm is not all that complicated," Riordan said. "My estate is the central location, and everything else branches off."

Letting my gaze travel wide, the sprawling hills of sand greeted me. The temperature was so hot that the heat waves floated off the soil in dancing curls. Whips of spiny tails and snapping jaws occasionally sprouted through the sand, as if the beasts here were swimming beneath the grains, waiting for something or someone to fall into their maw.

A pack of small, furry creatures sprinted across the endless sand dunes, and in a flurry of screams, teeth the length of my arm sprang from the golden-brown sand and chomped on the pack of animals. Blood burst from its mouth as the ones who survived scrambled away, shrieking, into the distance.

"Delightful." I swallowed and tried to keep my face neutral.

"The climates of my realm are intense. As are the living beings who inhabit it. They deserve it, and I take great pleasure in watching them suffer. Those I have deemed worthy stay with me in my estate."

His eyes looked gleefully at the bloody mess left behind from the murder we just witnessed. My stomach rolled.

"So, your pets stay with you?" I asked.

"These are all my pets, Kyra. You would do well to remember that, considering they will be yours, too." Riordan smiled. "Our first lesson can begin now. You watched those creatures die, and it brought you discomfort. You will have to get over that. In fact, here comes another horde of sand bunnies, kill them."

"No." The response was immediate. I didn't want to kill innocent animals.

"Then you won't get to see your mother," he smirked, and I closed my eyes, breathing deeply.

"How do I know you will keep your word since you keep moving the targets?"

"You don't really have a choice, do you? Do it. Now." Riordan's voice boomed around us, and nausea rolled through me. I watched the small creatures sniff and bounce about.

"I'm so sorry..." I whispered.

I tried to make it fast. My fire flew so hot and so fast that it should have killed them on impact. But these small animals were accustomed to the heat of this damned desert, and they shrieked and ran. I sent another flame after them, hoping this would do the trick, and after several moments of torture, they fell to the ground in a heap of charred flesh. Vomit rose in my throat, but I swallowed it down.

"See, wasn't that fun?" My father chuckled. I said nothing.

We continued to walk through the desert, but I couldn't bring myself to look at any creatures that crossed our path.

The desert ended abruptly as if slamming into a wall of winter was the most normal thing to happen after walking through a literal oven. A tundra swept around us, an invisible barrier separating the two areas. The temperature change was immediate, my teeth chattered, and cold seeped into my bones. Snow and ice covered everything while a small blizzard blew around us.

"Why must the climates be so extreme?" I asked.

Riordan had led us to a frozen lake where a large, shadowy animal thrashed underneath.

"Death is extreme," he replied, and I scoffed at that. "I want you to bring me the head of that creature." Riordan pointed down towards the creature skimming the lake's surface.

"No!" I yelled.

"Kill it or I tighten your beloved cuffs so much her hands fall off." His eyes were deadened, and his voice was cold.

"You wouldn't dare," I growled.

"Try me."

Riordan's power surged forward, then shoved me back a step. What choice did I have with him? I was his puppet, and I didn't have any way out of this without hurting the ones that I loved.

Without any more words, I walked toward the lake. Heat flew from my hands, skating across the frozen water, melting the thick sheet that covered the surface. Soon, there was a hole big enough for something the size of that creature to come through.

"We don't have all day," Riordan chided, and my jaw clenched.

How the hell was I supposed to get this animal's head? My flames would not work underwater. I could heat my body enough to jump in, but what good would that do when I would need some type of weapon? My explosive power should still be able to create force in water, just not flames. Gods-damnit, I would need to go in.

Looking back at my father's smirking face once more, I took a breath and dove into the lake.

ELEVEN
KYRA

The water was a shock to my system. My body seized up, and for one terrifying moment, I was frozen. My eyes were open, trying to track this underwater beast, and I could not move. The animal's reaction to my entrance into its domain was immediate.

It was at the opposite end of the lake when I had taken the plunge, and now it was moving impossibly fast. It was a massive creature, similar to a whale and shark combined, if both of those had grown exponentially and looked like it exploded from the depths of hell itself. It was gargantuan, nearly the size of Lux's dragon, with a mouth full of daggers. Fins like long swords sprouted from its back and sides, its dark eyes homed in, determined to never leave mine.

It was closing in, and I was still screaming at my body to move. I didn't know how immortality would work if I got ripped to shreds and swallowed whole by something, but I was not interested in finding out.

Sending all the heat I could muster through my blood, I got my limbs moving and dove deeper into the dark water. My goal was to get the creature above me and blast it with my explosive power, sending it flying and sprawling to the surface. From there, I would have more fire options, but I needed to get it out of the water first.

As I pumped my arms and legs further into the murky depths of the water, the creature prowled closer and closer. My heart was thundering in my chest, and soon I would need to breach the surface for air.

Fuck. Fuck. Fuck. I just needed to get it underneath the hole I had created in the surface.

The closer the creature came, the faster it went, and I was running out of time, my lungs screaming and thrashing in my chest.

I just needed it to get a little closer. It was now so close I could make out the markings on its slippery skin. Dark grey stripes and dots covered its body. It was terrifyingly beautiful.

Even though this beast was coming for me, it wasn't really its fault. I was in its territory, and it was forced to deal with the conditions it was given. This was all my father's fault; his way of keeping me in line and using Greer against me. He didn't give a shit about who he hurt or what he did. He reveled in the suffering he caused and wanted me to do the same.

Finally, the creature ventured right where I needed it. In a surge of power, I sent explosive energy out and up, hitting the poor animal right in the gut and sending it careening towards the surface, where it slammed against the corner of the ice and flopped over onto the surface.

Blood ripped from its stomach, and I pushed power out below me, sending me after it. My head was going fuzzy, and my stomach clenched as I broke the surface and inhaled deep lungfuls of air.

Immediately, the cold ripped at my soaked skin. My fire erupted around me, sizzling the liquid and drying me in an instant. The creature heaved next to me, its intestines exposed and its insides spilling out in a red, gloppy mess across the ice. Its chest heaved in and out, trying to breathe out of the water.

"Be quick about it, the blood will send other animals coming. Unless you want to bring me their heads too," Riordan called, and the urge to flip him off was immense. Instead, I walked up to the creature and called a blade of fire into my hand so I could cleanly cleave the animal's head.

"I'm sorry," I whispered, the creature's large eyes tracked me. I walked around and lifted my fire sword high. In a last-ditch effort of survival, the creature thrashed its mouth, catching my hand with the fiery weapon. Its teeth sliced through my forearm skin and crunched the bones in my hand while I bellowed.

Blood gushed out of my arm as I called another sword in my other hand, swinging erratically, trying to get the creature's jaws off me as the feeling disappeared in my chewed-up fingers and lightning strikes of agony ricocheted through my body.

My sword made contact, and the beast let go in a scream right in my ears, nearly exploding my eardrums. Its head flopped away from its body, and I ripped the rest of my flesh from its maw.

My legs collapsed underneath me as I fell to the ground, my sword going out. My arm was a mangled mess of torn tissue, broken bones, and exposed muscle. I couldn't control the vomit that spewed out of me next to the creature.

"Well, wasn't that fun?" Riordan asked. He was suddenly right next to me, looking at the creature and then back at me. "I wasn't sure how you were going to accomplish it, but this will do. Come, there is more to see."

"I need to go see a doctor or a healer of some sort," I ground out, swaying even with my knees on the ground.

My mangled arm was pulled close to my body and, before

my eyes, the tissue tried to knit itself together. I could feel every pull on my nerves and body. My vision went hazy as the pain continued to pound through my entire being.

"Not until we are done. Now stand," Riordan growled, and I stumbled to my feet.

"What are you going to do with the head?" I asked, looking at this poor, mangled creature who did not deserve this fate.

"Nothing, I just wanted you to do as you were told." He lifted his brows and continued to move.

There was no room for me to say or do anything except focus on setting my feet one in front of the other to follow my dangerously careless father as he took me through the rest of his realm.

The day felt impossibly long. My body agonizingly continued to knit itself back together. I wasn't asked to do any more horrendous tasks, but I knew this was only the beginning. We walked through several other terrains, all of which I couldn't exactly remember because my mind kept going foggy from the immortality working its magic on my broken flesh. Every time I faltered, Riordan was there telling me that if I didn't keep going, Greer would pay the price. So, even though it was excruciating, I kept going. Finally, we made it back to his estate, and I collapsed into a chair. My eyes closed, but I knew my father still lingered.

"Do the other gods have children?" I asked finally. The question had been a constantly nagging thought nearly the entirety of my time here. The idea of Riordan as a father was laughable, and the more I thought about it, the more I realized no one else had children.

"No."

"Why not?" I opened my eyes and realized we were not in the foyer of the castle anymore, but a room filled with bookshelves, a desk, and a fire. I didn't know how we got here, but I was still sitting in a chair, and at the moment, that was all I cared about.

"The others do not have children because we were never supposed to be able to conceive children," Riordan replied.

"Why?" My head was a mess from trying to navigate this day, but this was important. If nothing else, I could get some information out of him, since he seemed delighted to watch me suffer.

"Can you imagine what chaos we would have reigned if we all could reproduce at any given time?" He chuckled.

A drink appeared in his hand, and then another. he offered it to me, and I took it gingerly. I watched him sip his drink before I tasted mine. I didn't know what his motive would be in drugging me now, so to hell with it. My body was craving a reprieve from having my arm chomped off by a giant whale shark, and this was the best thing I was going to get right now.

"You mean more chaos than you have already caused?" My voice was a little stronger now that the liquor warmed my belly. I looked down at my arm, and things were moving along a little faster, now that I wasn't constantly fighting to stay upright and walk through the dangers of this realm.

Riordan rolled his eyes. "The way we created beings around us was either from our magic or our blood, but never from our own seeds. Verity was a very special case, and so were you."

His eyes seem to soften at her name. But what did that even mean? He hurt those he claimed to care about. It seemed like the more he thought he loved you, the more he wanted to crush you underneath his fingertips.

I wanted to fling my drink at him for even acting like he gave a single shit about me or my mother. He was avoiding my question with his bullshit non-answers.

"We met at a solstice festival and fell in love. She is a very talented witch from Hyacinth's original bloodlines." He took another sip, and I filed away that information to dissect later.

"She did not know who I was at the time, and Hyacinth herself was preoccupied; otherwise, I'm sure she would have dissuaded her from getting involved with me. I confessed to Verity that I was infertile but had always wanted a child." He looked thoughtfully into the fire, and I sat up straighter.

"But you forgot to mention that you were infertile because you were the God of Hell?" I clenched my teeth and gripped my glass hard, wanting to shatter it in my palm.

"Our love was strong and powerful. I thought we could overcome that small hiccup." He took another long sip of his drink. "She began working on a spell that would allow us to conceive a child. By all means, it should have failed, but she was skilled in ways that many were not, and we borrowed love magic from Farren himself. The combination of the two and the power of your crystal..."

"My crystal?" I rubbed my chest as it ached dully.

"Yes, it began as a small crystal that both of us ground up and ingested. It was infused with her magic and the magic of love. We tried many different formulas to be able to conceive, and one day it worked." His eyes glazed over, like he couldn't believe it himself.

"And the other gods and goddesses were just okay with you having a son and finding a secret way to conceive a child?" I wondered how any of the gods and goddesses ever agreed on anything, considering they all only had their best interests at heart.

"Some were displeased, but Verity was protected. She is still the only one, to this day, who knows the way to conceive a demigod child. Demigods can be created in other ways, but it is difficult and often takes away from the power of the true god. Conceiving our way didn't take anything from me at all. But after she found out who I really was, things were never the same. As her way of punishing me for doing this in the first place, Verity sent you away with her own spell. You were never allowed to come back here unless you came willingly." He smirked, like we shared some inside joke.

"Greer," I whispered, rubbing my brow.

"How convenient all of this fell into place." Riordan looked smug as hell.

"How could you visit me on earth, then?" I wanted to get as many answers as I could since his tongue was getting looser by the minute.

"Oh, Afton had a way of making me undetectable to magic and for several hours of travel. It was tricky work to control and conjure, which is why I could only use it once a year. Magic for us, and from strong beings, has loopholes that can be exploited, but the consequences, especially for those without immortality, can be deadly." His glass refilled in his hand, and so did mine.

I nodded, trying to keep all this information organized to help set Greer and me free.

"And what happened after Verity sent me away?" I wasn't sure if I would be able to handle the answer.

"She became quite inconsolable," he said quietly.

"What does that mean, exactly?"

"She hated me. She still does, I believe. Her rage has fueled her for your entire life. She is sequestered to her own quarters and is on what you would call 'house arrest.' She knows you are here. Her protection spells alerted her the minute you set foot into this realm. She has been raging even more to meet you. Demanding little thing." He chuckled like she was a simple amusement and not a real-life person whom he betrayed, tricked, and used for his own fucking agenda.

"When can I meet her?" I asked, my heart ached in a new

way for a mother I never knew and for another woman mistreated by another disgusting male.

"Tomorrow. She is becoming even more difficult to manage the longer you are here without having met her. You both need to be taught a lesson from your ongoing tantrums," Riordan said, and I didn't have it in me to fight back on it. Whatever he dealt out, I could handle, and I would do my best to protect my mother and Greer, if given the chance.

"And when can I see, Greer?" I needed to see how her injuries fared.

"You are released from our time together and may go see her now, if you wish." The corners of his lips turned up.

"What's the trick?"

"No trick, son."

I didn't believe that for one godsdamn second, but I sure as hell wouldn't waste another opportunity to see her again. There was zero energy left in my body to uncover his motives at this moment. If I had to pay for these visits later, I would.

"Well, this was not exactly what I anticipated happening." I stood on wobbly legs and set the glass down on a table nearby. My fingers were now able to wiggle around with minimal pain, but I kept my arm hugged close as the healing power of immortality continued to do its work.

"Another time we will take the long road around and I'll show you all the secrets this place has to offer." His eyes flashed black.

I swallowed and nodded, not knowing what that meant. More tasks for me to complete. More ways for him to control me with agony and fear.

"How do I get to Greer?" I still didn't understand the layout of the house, considering it was ever-changing and based on his own movements.

"The estate will respond to you if you simply ask to be taken to where you wish."

I grimaced and walked out the nearest door and into a hallway. I breathed deeply for the first time in hours. My father was a constant enigma. I wasn't even supposed to be allowed to be here, yet here I was, another fucking anomaly. My poor mother, having to deal with his sorry ass for years.

I set aside those feelings and stood idly in the hall.

"Take me to, Greer." I didn't know what else to do.

A dancing light appeared on the floor in front of me, and I took that as a sign to follow it. My steps were hurried through hallways and foyers until I arrived at a door that I assumed was her bedroom. The door unlocked in front of me, and I grabbed the knob, breathing hard.

Who knew what state she would be in right now? I didn't know how her healing would go, considering her arm had literally been fizzled right off by my flames. It made me want to punch a hole in the fucking wall and burn this place down. My rage had no place here, though, so I opened the door to see her fast asleep with bandages wrapped around her. Red hair was flying everywhere, and her pale skin was on display through the tangle of black sheets. I sat next to her bed, lay my head down on the sheets, and let the rage and sorrow fill me.

Tears flooded my vision as I wept quietly next to her, clutching the fabric beneath me. All the emotions of the day poured out of me, and I mourned the mistakes I had so foolishly made.

I don't know how long I let my silent tears pool beneath me, but I stilled when fingertips brushed my scalp. I looked up to see Greer's eyes still closed, but her fingertips were right next to me. I gently kissed each one, and a small sigh escaped her lips.

"I'll fix this. I'll fix everything, I swear," I whispered, and even though it pained me, I left. Gently, I closed the door behind me and ran my hand through my hair.

I needed to prepare for what was to come. My mother, a

talented witch who broke immortal rules, would know how to get the fuck out of here. I just knew it. But would it be enough to get Greer back?

I didn't know, but I would do everything in my godsdamn power to get us out of hell.

TWELVE
LUX

"Who wants to go first?" I took another pull from the bottle, looking between Waverly and Sutton. It seemed we all needed a bit of liquid courage before we spilled our secrets.

Waverly bit her lip and looked down. Nova squinted her eyes at Sutton, who pretended to be preoccupied with something on his pant leg.

"Do you all need some warming up, then?" Nova asked loudly.

"Please," Sutton grabbed the bottle from my hand. Our fingertips brushed, and I tried not to shudder. Sutton seemed unbothered, to say the least.

"Okay," Nova rolled her shoulders. "Okay." She reached out and grabbed Waverly's fingertips. Waverly scrunched her brow and held on tight.

"I have lived a long time, as you know..." She started, and silence filled the space as we waited for her next words.

"I have played many roles and parts in this world. And it has not always been kind to me, and I have not always been kind to it." She exhaled loudly.

"Nova..." Waverly whispered, slowly rubbing her hand with her thumb.

"I have been a mercenary and an assassin. And I was good at it. Sometimes, I liked it. But often I did it because I felt like I had to, because there was no other choice. But that is not all of who I am and what I can do. And it's not something I often engage in anymore. In fact, it has been many years since I have thought of that time in my life." Nova had a ghost of a smile around the corners of her mouth.

No one said anything as she continued.

"The President knows my past and likes the violence. You could say men like him are disappointed that more of us aren't like that anymore. As society has evolved, we have evolved to not have to take pieces of ourselves and sacrifice them for those who would not do the same for us." Nova scowled. Sutton shifted beside me, his mouth in a flat line.

"He has been harassing me and borderline stalking me for quite some time to push me to a breaking point of letting my own demons overtake me," she hissed, crossing her legs.

"So, when the time comes where we face off with him again, because there will be another..." she said darkly, her stars shining bright for a moment. "I will kill him." Her fiery eyes danced.

There was tension in the air at Nova's confession.

"That is my warm-up. I am telling you that when the time comes, when I have access to that damn formula, I will end his life. Without regret, without a second goddamn thought. That motherfucker is mine, and he will die at my hands for the power he so greedily takes and wields over others. That bastard is mine, and his death is a prize that I will take deep joy in winning. My blood lust is not to be trifled with or to be interfered with, do you all understand?" Her stars grew brighter with each word.

"Deal." Waverly squeezed her hand. "As long as I get to

watch." She placed a peck on Nova's cheek, and Sutton gave a small smirk and a nod.

My brows shot up as an idea started to form in my head.

"I need to find a way to access that formula then. Not only for you, Nova, but to level the playing field. The gods think this gives them the upper hand, but we can use it as well. We need that serum."

I shot up and paced back and forth. "Nova, your blood lust is fucking genius!" This would be a way we could add power to our team. A way to increase our chances as we were faced with the impossible.

"I have another idea that I don't think you all will like." Sutton sighed and ran his hands through his strawberry blonde hair.

"What?" Waverly asked, chewing her lip.

"We also need more Immortality," he said darkly. "I know you all have your own feelings about it, but we cannot deny that the gift of Immortality also brings a power surge. And now, it's reversible. So, we can take on the power and then get rid of it if we so choose, but we need it. Choice is a luxury we do not have anymore, in this regard."

"But we have no idea how that actually affects the body and our powers?" I said darkly. "Yes, we knew taking away immortality makes you killable again, but we know that immortality is a painful process for most. Would your body be able to go back and forth through the cellular transformation without losing something? Your humanity, your magic, or something else?"

"We don't. But we need more than what we can offer now. The formula to reverse immortality and having immortality ourselves is the best way we can arm ourselves for whatever is to come. Selfishly, it might be able to help me break this fucking curse on myself," he added quietly.

"It's a good idea, Sutton." Nova slid her arm around Waverly.

"How do we get immortality?" Waverly wondered.

"Xael is the goddess of time. Her power was used for all the Immortality Trials winners. Xael has essentially been reincarnated through Greer; thus, Greer, in theory, has the power to do the same thing. Her power should be able to give immortality." Sutton thrummed his fingers together.

"Is there a manual for that?" I crossed my arms across my chest and sighed.

"Not that I know of, but now that Hyacinth is on our side, and Greer has the power, we should be able to figure out a way to gift it. But it means that Greer's powers are vulnerable. People will want to take advantage of that, and just like the formula to take away immortality, the power to give will also be priceless." Sutton's black eyes swarmed with shadows as if lost in thought of what this would all mean.

"But first, we must get her and Kyra out of the infernal realm. Then, we get immortality, the formula, and get the rest of the gods on board on earth to help us overthrow the fuckery happening in the infernal realm." Waverly easily slid into her commander mode.

"Immortality and the serum would be powerful bargaining chips to get these gods and goddesses on our side," Nova commented.

"We would practically be gods ourselves," I whispered. I didn't want immortality. It was one of the last stands I had taken against my parents, and I wanted to hold to it desperately. It was my rebellion against what they had wanted for me and what I had wanted for myself, but I couldn't deny that this could be a tipping point in gaining aid from those original twelve who were on earth. It could make all the difference.

"Okay, so now we need to get to the sea." Waverly's eyes filled with tears.

"Your turn?" Nova grabbed the last of the tequila and handed it to Waverly.

"My turn." She gulped down the bottle and set it down with a loud crack. "I ran away when I was young. I couldn't have been more than twelve at the time. What's unfathomable is I can't remember what my sister and I had been fighting about. I grew up on an island off the coast, and the water was a constant companion. The ocean was our backyard. But I was upset one day, and I fled to the mainland. We had a few relatives who lived on the coast, and I thought I was old and grown enough to be here because my emotions were high from whatever fight we had." She swallowed and dropped her gaze.

"I tried to return after what I had done. We weren't supposed to travel across the ocean by ourselves. I came back to try to reunite with my sister and my parents. But something had happened. My parents did not answer my call, and instead, I was met with a hurricane that nearly killed me, sent by my sister. I was banished at such a young age," she whispered as a tear slipped down her cheek.

"Wave." I reached out and grabbed her hand.

"I still don't know what happened, to this day. I never went back to the ocean, and I never went back to our island. I stayed with my aunt on the mainland, who changed once I returned. I asked her if she knew anything, and she told me one day I would be told, but now was not the day."

The air in the room thickened.

"So, I denounced them as family and never went back. I've avoided the ocean ever since. I don't know what happened, and I am scared to know now. It was so long ago, but my heart broke as a child. How could they do that to me? How could they send me away?" she sobbed out.

"I've avoided looking for answers because nothing will be good enough. I don't want to invite that pain back again. But I knew one day I would not have a choice. I have isolated myself from the family I once knew. I have no idea if they are alive or dead. Either way, the ocean has not been my friend for a hundred years," she said solemnly.

"We all seem to be paying a great cost for this godly skirmish," I whispered.

"It seems to be no coincidence that we have all been brought together and must pay dearly for what is to come. The gods have been letting the world be their playground for too long." Nova's voice was made of steel.

"How long do you suppose we will wait until we hear back from Hyacinth?" Sutton asked.

"As long as it takes. She said Verity will reach out to her. In the meantime, I think we should rest and plan for tomorrow." I stood as Waverly wiped tears from her face.

"The sea. We should go tomorrow. Let's rip off the band-aid," Waverly murmured, a mask of stone sliding over her features.

"Are you sure, Wave?" I crouched in front of her and Nova.

"I'm sure."

"Let's regroup in the morning." Nova pulled Waverly up and tucked her into her side.

"There's been a lot going on tonight," Sutton commented as he, too, stood tall, and the shadows danced around him.

Waverly said nothing as she and Nova walked back to the guest room, so it was just Sutton and me standing in the living room.

His features softened, he opened his mouth to say something, and then closed it abruptly.

"Uh, how are you?" Feeling foolish almost immediately. I couldn't get a read on Sutton. Sometimes we shared a moment, and then in the blink of an eye it would disappear.

"I'm okay," He smiled through his ruby red lips. "How are you feeling about the formula?"

I got lost looking at his mouth before I realized he was hinting at the fact that my parents had made the serum and died for it.

"It's complicated," I mumbled. My relationship with them had always been strained, but I never wanted them to be manipulated by the gods. It all felt wrong and despicable. It seemed like years ago, Greer and I had been sitting in my office uncovering one mystery after the other.

Sutton nodded like he understood. "And Greer?"

My heart crumpled, and my face fell. It was easy, amongst the planning and doing, to forget the gaping hole in my heart where my best friend used to reside.

"I feel like I failed her. She's already been through so much. She's strong, but I wish she didn't always have to be." My heart ached for her and Ky.

"We did the best we could with what we had. The gods and goddesses almost always find a way to get what they want." The dark smoke that swirled around Sutton's eye thickened with every word.

"What happened to you? And your family? You don't have to tell me, but you know my family trauma, so I'm here if you want to share." I shrugged my shoulders, trying to be nonchalant. But in reality, I was desperate to know Sutton more. Something about him made me want to learn the inner workings of his head and trace the lines of his body.

"That is probably another story for another time," Sutton replied darkly.

I nodded, crossing my arms across my chest.

"Lux..." Sutton started and then stopped abruptly.

"Yes?" I tried not to sound hopeful.

"I do like you," Sutton mumbled under his breath.

"And I like you." I wondered where this conversation was going.

"I like males," he blurted out awkwardly.

I had never seen him look shy or pensive, but with every word that came out of his mouth, his face scrunched up more.

"So, you think I'm attractive?" I smiled and walked towards him.

"Obviously, yes." He stepped closer to me as well.

"So, what are you going to do about it?" I whispered it like a dare.

"Fuck," he mumbled as we both took another step forward.

My heart rate started to quicken at the thought of Sutton's lips against mine, and his hair intertwined in my fingertips. He smelled like smoke and spice. I wanted to inhale deeply and imprint it on my brain.

"I'm not good at this. I'm basically cursed at this," he muttered, his lips merely centimeters from mine.

"I don't know what that means exactly, but I assume a kiss won't hurt anybody, right?" My tongue slid across my lips. I just wanted to taste him, to see what Sutton would feel like.

"A kiss would be harmless," he said, sounding unconvinced.

I slid my hands into his hair and grabbed, gently exposing the column of his throat.

"Are you sure?" I whispered across his skin, hovering my lips against his throat.

"Fuck," he muttered again.

"Can I kiss you?" I said, sliding my hands down his narrow shoulders and letting them land on his waist.

He swallowed loudly.

"I don't know if it's a good idea." He practically whimpered, his eyes squeezed shut.

"Why?" I ran my nose along his jawline.

"I don't know if I will be able to stop, once we start."

His muscles tensed as I ran my hands up and down his back, roaming lower and lower. He was holding himself back as if he were in pain. I didn't know what this curse was and why it had such a hold on him, but I didn't want to push it.

"Okay, maybe another time." I wrapped my arms around him, instead, and pulled him against me.

"What are you doing?" He seemed almost panicked.

"It's a hug, we can stop if you want." His muscles quaked with tension until finally he started to relax and melt into me. His head rested on the crook of my neck, and his arms clung to the front of my shirt as if he wanted to bury himself inside me.

"Just talk to me. When you're ready," I whispered in his ear.

Sutton didn't say anything, but tears pooled against my skin. I didn't know how long we stayed wrapped in one another's arms, but eventually he broke it off. His face was composed and controlled once more.

"I should go." He turned to head out the door. I grabbed his hand, and he paused for a moment.

"Stay, there's plenty of room for you here." I didn't want him to be far away.

He hesitated for a moment. Sutton, always so confident and mysterious, appeared flustered by whatever this was between us.

"Sure," he said finally, and I dragged him to one of our guest bedrooms, showing him where towels, extra clothes, a toothbrush, and other random things he might need were. My body was desperate to go to him. To wrap him up and hold all the pieces of Sutton together, even if he wasn't sure where he belonged right now. He could belong with me. But I didn't do any of that. Instead, I walked out and shut the door behind me, aching for a man I wasn't sure wanted the same things I did.

I didn't know what to make of Sutton. Whatever plagued his family and cursed his heart prevented him from so much. It must be a heavy burden to bear if the thought of being intimate with someone sent panic through his body.

We all had our own demons, mine just happened to have kidnapped my best friend. I went to bed with more questions than answers, but at least we had a plan for tomorrow.

I wouldn't leave Greer behind. Not today. Not tomorrow. Not ever. With those thoughts resetting my resolve, I fell into a dreamless sleep, hoping that tomorrow would bring better news.

THIRTEEN
GREER

"How are you feeling today?" Xael asked.

The burns on my body had faded from puffy red gashes to white lines along my skin, but I couldn't see them here in the dreamscape. Soon they would be nothing but scars; however, the searing pain of Kyra's fire had lasted longer than I was ready for.

In some ways, the pain was welcome. It was a constant companion. It reminded me that I was still alive and human, despite being an immortal. I was still me, who experienced agony and sorrow, but I knew it had cost me time to heal. It had been a long time since I had seen Kyra. I knew that it had cost him, too.

"Good, the burns are healing nicely. They will leave marks and scars, but I believe the worst of the pain is over."

I sat across from Xael. A mirror image of myself, her brows drawn together.

"Shall we take a walk together?" Xael offered her hand, and I grabbed it, pulling myself up as we moved through the magical forest.

The greenery around us bloomed into a kaleidoscope of colors *as creatures moved around us and the sun created a twinkling rainbow, dusting the ground. It was something only dreams could be made of.*

"Magic is often a two-sided coin," Xael cautioned after we walked for a while.

"There are dark and light parts of it?" I guessed.

"Yes, Kyra's fire can provide warmth, light, and love. But on the other hand, it holds destruction, fear, and pain," she said, reaching out to stroke a light pink petal of a rose. I leaned down and gave it a sniff. I hadn't seen a tree or a flower in a while outside of this space together.

The outside world slowed, fading away the longer I was trapped here. My hurt towards Kyra was fading. The scar on my heart, the match to the ones on my body, was healing with time.

"My anger towards him is less," I confessed. "I think I understand more now about why he couldn't tell me. It doesn't make it go away, but I know that it was for my own safety. He simply didn't have much of a choice when it came to his father."

Xael nodded as we continued to walk, coming to a small opening in the treescape. I turned my face up to the sky, relishing in the heat.

Gods, how I missed the sun. The city. Lux.

Our home.

"Curses of old are fickle, as you know. Time can allow us clarity we didn't know we needed," Xael said, looping her arm through mine and pulling me along.

Her words were meant as a comfort, but I could feel the stakes getting higher and higher. I had the power of time, yet things were slipping past me too quickly. I had just learned to control mere moments, to push and pull the speed of it, yet I couldn't grasp my hands on how long I had been down here or how much time had passed in the mortal realm.

"The curses of gods and goddesses seem to fuck up a lot of shit," I grumbled, and Xael laughed.

"I don't disagree. We are terrible even when we have the best of intentions." She sighed and ran her hand along the long braid of wine-colored hair hanging down her chest.

"You're getting stronger, though. You are comfortable with pushing and pulling time while in battle and in moments. We will keep training your stamina to hold longer moments in between. To jump from one moment to the next is like bringing the ends of a piece of paper together as opposed to running the whole length of the page."

I nodded, understanding that the concept of time was difficult to unpack. What moments did I need to slow down, and what moments needed to be sped up?

"You must also understand that this power has the ability to destroy physical bodies and things," she warned.

I turned to look at her. "What do you mean?"

"I'll show you," she responded, pulling herself away from me and standing in front of a sturdy-looking tree.

Xael's eyes scanned the ground, and she picked up a few small rocks. Throwing one at the tree, it simply bounced off back to the ground.

"If you throw something, like this rock, at something as strong and impenetrable as a tree, nothing may happen. But if you increase the speed, the impact is greater. Try throwing this at the tree while speeding up time just around the rock." She handed me the stone, fitting it comfortably in my hand.

I hefted it up and whipped my arm back before letting it fly, focusing all my time energy on that stone. With a crack, the rock embedded itself into the tree and created a crater with slices splintering from the center.

Damn, that was more powerful than I thought.

"The velocity and force of it change when I manipulate time." I was surprised that I hadn't realized it sooner.

TIMEWRAITH   113

When Kyra and I fought, I had moved my body in a defensive way. I was avoiding and using the snaps of time to find openings. I wasn't operating in the time-space as an offensive move.

Xael waved her hand over the tree, and it went back to its beautiful, untouched state, before the rock had done any damage.

"Yes, you must be careful how your touch affects people in the manipulation at all. You could cause irrevocable damage. Immortals won't die, but as you know, it doesn't mean they can't be gravely injured or disadvantaged. Bodies and minds are not invincible. You are meant to live forever, but it doesn't mean the vessel you are in is meant for repeated abuse or strain."

"Okay, so basic physics. Be careful when I interact with actual objects and beings outside of myself while I'm moving through time. And immortals may not be able to die, but we can break." This thought had been haunting me ever since I arrived. My manacles were a constant source of pain and a reminder that, at this moment in time, immortality felt like a curse. What was the point in living forever if every day was filled with sorrow? It felt like there wasn't one.

"Exactly. In theory, you could push someone, and they would crash into the wall when time returned to normal." Xael smiled devilishly.

"Even a god or goddess could be incapacitated by a small movement while I manipulated time." I returned her grin.

"Yes, but I would caution you on using it until you are ready. I was not a fighter in the same way you were, Greer. I didn't often use my abilities for offensive fighting or training. You are much more equipped to fight this than I ever was. But they will use their own powers against you and their thousands of years of skills to best you. You may be able to surprise them now, but be warned that they will learn how to fight you quickly and

without mercy," Xael spoke softly, like the memories of her own fight haunted her.

"I will be wise when I strike. Especially because the first chance of escape may be our only one."

I let my fingertips trail the flowers and trees around us. Craving the connection to something living that wasn't in Riordan's fortress.

I wondered how the others were faring in the mortal realm. What were they doing and sacrificing for Kyra and me? I knew Lux would burn it all down to get back to me because I would do the same for him. What version of ourselves would be present when we reunited? It felt like I didn't know who I was anymore. I was trapped. Turned inside out by heartache and manipulation.

"There's something else you should know," Xael said hesitantly.

I snapped my eyes up to her. She took a deep breath and loudly exhaled.

"Oh gods, what?" I asked, even though I was afraid to know the answer.

"Your blood now has the power to give immortality," she confessed.

My mouth dropped open.

"Seriously?"

"Yes."

"How much of my blood?" I was almost sure I wouldn't like the answer.

"I don't know the exact measurement, but a decent amount," she said lightly, like she didn't just drop a bomb of powerful information. "However, it must be given consensually. People cannot simply gut you open and feast on your insides in an attempt to obtain immortality. You must allow it to happen."

"What a lovely visual," I muttered. "Does that mean they

took blood from you?" I wondered if that's how they had managed to give the power so freely to the winners of the trials.

"They stripped my power, so they had no need. My blood does nothing without the power of time in it," she said mournfully.

"This feels heavier than the other parts of this," I whispered.

I could give immortality to my friends if I wanted. Would they want it? They had never wanted it in the first place, but we could no longer deny that having immortality bolstered your powers and your bodies in ways that were quite advantageous. However, I was now intimately familiar with the downsides of it. The grief that came with always healing and being alive, even when you didn't want to.

But to drink my blood? The thought sent a shiver down my spine. A new responsibility I was not yet ready for.

"It is. It's a heavy burden to bear, as it is your choice alone on who gets to live forever." Her eyes closed for a moment, and she breathed out.

"I'll do my best not to fuck it up." I tried to tease, but it fell flat.

"I know you'll do what you can, Greer." She said it like she believed in all I could do fully and without any shred of doubt.

"Can we practice now? I want to see how much force and impact I can have in the time snap." I wanted to know and understand my own strength. How much could I push, and how much could I really accomplish? Xael nodded and led us a little further into the forest until a large clearing opened up, and she set the scene. Dummies were set up around, and weapons materialized in front of me. I grabbed a dagger and took a few moments to breathe.

I could do this.

Time trickled through my fingertips, and I moved, pushing and pulling the current around me. Slashing through the dummies and going at them with a vengeance that seeped from *my bones. Rage fueled me, and I let it fly. I pretended these dummies were Riordan and Phayre. I tried to picture Kyra, thinking it might help, but it made me want to vomit.*

My anger at him had fizzled out, and a dull ache was left. I wanted him to be the balm. The salve that I couldn't seem to get to. The only tincture for this wound.

My breath released in puffs, and I looked around at the carnage around me. I had slashed and cut, making what would feel like shallow cuts in real time, but left the dummies in shreds in the time current.

"So, you see that the force and energy are different when you move here, my child?" Xael said from behind me.

The sweat from my brow threatened to slide into my eyes, and I wiped it away.

"I will have to use more or less care depending on the enemy," I responded, realizing that this part of the time magic thrilled me as equally as it terrified me.

"Yes, but we will practice so you can be precise and conserve your energy appropriately."

Stamina and endurance would be necessary for the battle ahead.

"Again." I let the frustration run through me, and I slashed through it. Each strike pushed me further until I couldn't feel or think; I could only do.

Our dream worlds were suspended in time. I didn't know how much I trained. My energy flowed effortlessly and without limits. I was in the middle of manipulating the time around me when I was yanked out, and I cried out.

In here, time was on my side, but in the infernal realm, it was my greatest enemy.

"What were you dreaming about?"

Gasping, I sat straight up, and immediately my arm tingled with the fresh skin and scars from the burn. I looked over to see Phayre sitting next to me in a chair which almost looked like a throne. A glass of wine in her palms, and her eyes glittering like a cat.

"Killing you," I said with a tight smile. I imagined hissing at her and smacking the wine glass out of her holier-than-thou hand.

She laughed loudly and threw her head back, nearly taking her wine with her.

"Aren't you feisty today? Is that any way to treat your keeper?" She stroked her hair.

"You're a captor and a manipulator. This is what you wanted, right? Kyra and I are at odds. One of us is paying the price of fighting each other. I am sure you preferred me getting burnt to a crisp. So, you're welcome," I grumbled and swung my legs over the side of the bed and breathed deeply.

The transition from the dream state to my reality was aggressive today. My head pounded, and my heart was still racing.

"Greer, my pet, you are serving a very specific purpose for us here. And you're immortal now. No need to be so dramatic. We unlocked your power." She acted as if it were the greatest gift I could have received.

"I didn't ask for this. And you unlocked it because you wanted it for you, not for me," I sneered.

"Tsk, tsk. Semantics. Anyways, I came to deliver some news that is rather fun!" She sprang up and placed her long fingertips on my shoulder. I resisted the urge to push her off and simply stared into her eyes. Her wine glass sat abandoned on the bedside table, and I desperately wished she would forget about me, too.

"What's the news?" I couldn't imagine it would be anything I would be excited about.

"We're hosting a party! A ball, if you will, and you will be our guest of honor!" She clapped her hands together.

My eyes went wide, and I ground my teeth together. "What's the celebration?"

"The beginning of our reign, pet. Now that we have you, we can start to make the mortal realm ours. It was simply a waiting game, and you see, we have all the time in the world." She dug her fingernails into my skin.

Gripping her arm, I manipulated time around me, and an audible crack filled the room. Her wrist limply fell away from me.

"Don't touch me again," I snarled, standing up and backing away.

Phayre's mouth opened in an o, and she looked down at her hanging wrist like a minor inconvenience.

"So, the timewraith knows how to play with time to hurt others, does she?" She blew on her wrist and, with another crack, shoved it back in place in one gruesome motion. "Be mindful of how you use your tricks, wraith. I have my own, too," she snapped, showing all her teeth, and her gaze went unfocused.

In the blink of an eye, the cuffs on my wrists were on fire. Shrinking. Digging into my skin and burning the flesh that had just healed. I cried out, but as soon as it had happened, it was over. The heat settled down, and the metal expanded. But the indents were there, and the smell of my skin still hung in the air.

"Thanks for the heads up," I gritted out.

"How did you learn to do this? Xael hardly ever used violence in her days." Phayre seemed curious, like she wanted to understand the malice behind my eyes. Like she wanted to see what I could release on her if I snapped.

"Physics. I'm not just a pretty face."

"Well, someone will be here to dress you for the ball shortly. Be on your best behavior, and maybe you'll get a little reward. A little uninterrupted time with our Prince of Hell, if you will?" Phayre lifted her brows and snapped her fingers, and she was gone.

I breathed a sigh of relief. I couldn't decide if it made any real difference pissing her off. She wanted to control me either way. I would be careful not to show my hand too much, though. Snapping her wrist had been a momentary lapse of control.

The thought of seeing Kyra made my heart swell. I wanted us to be right again. We would need each other if we were going to get out of this place, and I only hoped he had been keeping up his end of the bargain.

The door opened, and a flurry of people swarmed in, ready to push me and batter me into a horrendous gown, I'm sure.

I sighed and hoped tonight would be the beginning of Kyra and me, too. We needed to get out of here. And fast. The clock was ticking, and it was a countdown that I couldn't control.

Fourteen
Kyra

"This ball is fucking archaic," I grumbled, looking at myself in the mirror.

A dark red suit and scarlet eyes stared back at me. They were getting Greer ready as well. She was the guest of honor. I couldn't tell what angle, exactly, they were playing at with Greer and me.

One moment, they wanted us to tear off each other's skin, and the next, they acted like our love was exactly what they wanted. My head was still spinning from my day traversing hell with my father. My arm was now fully healed, but the memories of that creature's teeth tearing at my skin made me itch. The image of torn flesh and exposed bone was enough to make me vomit again.

Maybe there was a way to play this game and win, without both of us sacrificing our bodies constantly. A way to spin our story so that it would appear in their best interest to celebrate our love. One of us would need to play the devoted servant to their cause, and neither one of us was very good at doing that.

Damnit. I couldn't defy my father when Greer was on the line. It was a lose-lose situation.

But tonight, I would at least be able to hold her during a dance, and hopefully, she would give me a better chance to explain, now that I was given a longer leash.

Gods, I hoped tonight would be the night that I met my mother. My dad had been dangling that in front of my face for some time. If I played along tonight, he said he would take me to her. I didn't have much faith in his promises. Not after he made me kill those creatures with such thoughtlessness.

A knock on the door jarred me from my thoughts, and it swung open a second later to allow in my father, dressed in an all-black tux. A crown of dark metal and glittering rubies sat on his head.

"Kyra, you look almost as handsome as me!" My father chuckled. I tried not to wince at the almost-compliment.

"Thank you." I rolled my shoulders back and swiped my hair out of my eyes.

"Are you ready for the ball?" He beamed at me like everything in his life was falling into place in the exact way he had hoped. "Your arm looks perfect."

"Yes, I suppose it's fine now." It most definitely wasn't. "And I will dance with Greer tonight. Don't try to stop me." I squared off with him. Better to just get it out there and see if he really was going to try and make me pay for it now. Or worse, make Greer bear the cost.

"Wouldn't dream of it. Just keep your temper in check, and then we will visit your mother." He smiled wolfishly. There was malice behind those eyes, but I couldn't do anything to stop it.

"It could be to your advantage, you know, if you let Greer and me spend time together." I was testing the waters, trying to find a way that didn't require my body to be mangled in order to get what I wanted.

"Hm, and how's that?"

"We will be better as allies together than enemies who are

scorned and separated." Steel laced into every word. That, at least, was true.

"I'll take that into consideration," he said noncommittally. I wanted to punch him right in the face.

"Love is a powerful magic," I said, not ready to let it go.

"Is that a threat?" Amusement danced across his face.

"A promise. That love can be more powerful than fire or time. Not that any of you know what it could do, considering the only person who truly understands is Farren. None of you seem to be capable of that emotion or that power anyway." I shouldered past him and out into the hallway.

He grabbed my shoulder and wrenched me back, delivering a hard blow across my face. It happened so fast, I didn't have time to react. I only felt the sting of his slap after, and tasted blood from where my lip had split open. I reared back and stumbled into the wall, flexing my hands for the next attack.

Riordan smiled broad and wide at me then. My face turned to stone, and my heart pounded. Was he this violent with Greer? How would I even know? We couldn't speak to one another, and he certainly wouldn't tell me the truth.

"Maybe we are so powerful that we don't need it, son. What good has it done me this far?" My father asked smoothly, as if he didn't just backhand the shit out of me. "You may want to clean up that bloody lip before we enter the party." He shoved his way forward, and I followed him silently, not having anything else to say to him as I wiped at my mouth.

Laughter began to filter in the hallway as we got closer and closer to what I assumed would be a transformed throne room.

I breathed deeply as we pushed through the large, dark, metal doors, and the space was flooded with gentle candlelight. The room was filled to the brim with beings, including all the powerful six and many other subjects.

I scanned the room for the only face that mattered and came up empty. The hall glowed and dazzled with energy, and I couldn't fucking care less. The only thing that was keeping me sane was the thought of seeing Greer and holding her. I needed to know if she was okay. Or as okay as she could be in this situation.

"Enjoy the party, Kyra." My dad disappeared and left me to fend for myself. Not that I minded being alone, but it was rather the principle of leaving someone at a party where they knew maybe two percent of the population, after physically assaulting them, like he couldn't be bothered to bludgeon me anymore because he had important guests to tend to.

Phayre came out of nowhere and grabbed my arm.

"Kyra, darling! You look splendid," she slurred slightly with a glass of champagne in her hands. I steadied her as she dipped to the side.

"Thank you," I said curtly, snatching my hands away, not wanting to linger on her very long.

"Your wraith is lucky to have you. And, I will say, I would love to piss your father off," she said flippantly.

I half listened to her and nodded.

"You know, if we slept together, it would positively rile Riordan up in the most delightful way," she said seductively.

My eyes snapped to her.

"No, thank you." I put some distance between us, not knowing what she was capable of either. She had been cruel to Greer before, who knew how far she was willing to go to make everyone's lives miserable.

"And here I thought you would find fun in fucking over your father." She laughed giddily.

"Aren't you both on the same side here?" I scrunched my brow. My head was throbbing from the movement, but I ignored it and kept my eyes alert, searching for my girl.

"Yes, dear, but that doesn't mean I don't like to watch him suffer a bit." She threw back her glass and waved her palm.

"No matter, I see you are a lost cause to the wraith. Her entrance is scheduled soon, so you can wipe that lost puppy dog look off your face. It isn't the most becoming." She went to touch my cheek, and I winced from the fresh pain.

"Hmm, daddy not playing nice?" Phayre gripped my face harder, and I batted her hand away.

"Thank you for the information. Have a good evening, Phayre," I replied curtly and walked away from her giggling.

Grabbing a drink, I slunk around the moving bodies to the sway of the music and nearly ran into Farren.

"Just the person I wanted to see," Farren said. He was decked out in a tuxedo jacket on top and a full black ball gown on the bottom.

I stilled, not sure what to do. Farren was an unknown card. One I didn't know what to do with. Distance was the safest bet. A room full of immortals and hell's guests was not the moment for me to lose my shit. But damn, did I want to.

"Don't look so frazzled, Kyra. I have something to give you." Farren handed me a small black envelope and a tiny vial.

"Give this to your mother when you see her and tell her I never stopped fighting for her." I thought I caught a glimpse of sorrow flicker over his features before he disappeared into the crowd.

Confused, I looked down at the envelope and potion of black liquid swirling in the small glass. I pocketed it and told myself I could ask my mother about it when I saw her. Hopefully, she would be in good spirits to help, even though I had no memory of her or any idea what state she was in.

She could be an absolute asshole like my father. I had no idea.

I had thought Farren was on my dad's side, but maybe

things weren't exactly as they appeared. It made me wonder where everyone's allegiances truly lie and at what price? Could they be persuaded, or paid, in some way to release their coveting eyes from the mortal realm? To simply exist here and not crave what they couldn't have?

Phayre's proposition seemed out of spite, but not out of desire to truly relinquish the power of the mortal realm. I would need more information about each original immortal to see where their true motives lie.

A hush fell over the crowd as the thoughts of espionage floated around in my head. I looked around to see what had stunned everyone into silence. Then I saw her. My heart nearly broke open looking at her. She almost floated in, down a set of stairs I had hardly noticed when I had entered.

Greer looked divine in a waterfall of black silk. It circled one arm and shoulder, showing off her powerful arms, hugged down her chest, and spilled onto the earth. When she walked, her legs poked through thigh-high slits. A corset with glittering diamonds hugged underneath her breasts and circled her waist.

The lights danced off her wine-colored hair that was pulled back and braided in elaborate plaits. Rubies dripped from her ears, and a stunning red choker was at her throat, and ruby wristlets. Their way to control her, I was sure.

I swallowed, thinking of all the things I wanted to do to her in that dress. The first thing was fixing the mess I made with my curse. The second being how I could apologize again and again with my body, if she would forgive me.

Just because there was a good reason for me lying didn't mean that it wasn't any less painful. She was allowed to feel angry and hurt, even though I did it to protect her. I had no choice. But I understood what made us *us* was not holding on to secrets, and this one... it was a bomb I detonated.

Greer smiled politely through red-stained lips and made her way through the crowd, where people looked at her like she was a zoo animal.

"The timewraith," was whispered across the room in murmurs. It was the first time she was publicly acknowledged by all the people in the infernal realm and my dad's court. There had been whispers and sightings of her, but nothing like this announcement.

Her attention scanned the crowd. I hoped it was to find me. Gently, I moved through the throngs of people, making my way to her as her gaze danced across faces. Her green eyes simmered when they found me, and her lips curled up in a bright smile. It nearly stopped me in my tracks.

Godsdamnit, I loved this woman.

The world around us slowed as we moved toward one another, almost as if time had turned to syrup. I realized, as she moved towards me, that she was manipulating the time current around us, on purpose or by accident, I wasn't sure.

I held out my hand to her, people floating out of our way, and when our fingertips connected, it was like a lightning strike. My nerves fizzled, and I sent warmth into her palm while I drank her in.

"Greer, you're breathtaking," I said quietly, trying to resist the urge to throw her over my shoulder and drag her away from this mess.

"So are you, Ky." Her voice was soft.

"Care to dance?" I needed to be closer to her and feel her body against mine, like I needed air to breathe.

She smiled and nodded as I wrapped my hand around her waist and pulled her close, breathing her in. My whole body was on fire. She melted against me.

"Hi," I whispered in her ear.

"Hi."

"Greer, I'm so sorry," I murmured against her skin. "The

curse could have killed you if I spoke of it; it was a chance I wasn't willing to take. But your feelings are valid, I know it was a betrayal, and the 'why' isn't an excuse."

She sighed and pressed herself against me. I gripped onto her hand and waist a little tighter. The feeling of her here made every blow against me worth it. I would take on an army if it brought me back to her arms.

"I know, Ky. A lot has happened since the trials. Too many things weigh heavily on me. I want to let this one go. I'm tired of holding onto the anger," she said.

Eyes followed us as other couples joined in the dance. I hadn't thought I would also be a spectacle, but I was. The Prince of Hell, a child that should have never been born, with a timewraith that wasn't expected. Suddenly, I had the urge to run away. But there was nowhere to go. I had to stay if I wanted to meet my mom.

"Does that mean we can work on being okay?" I asked, twirling her gently, my skin desperate to feel hers on mine without the greedy eyes of everyone in this room.

"Yes, I still love you, Kyra. I just need some time to build our trust again," she answered, as I pulled her against me.

"Anything you need, just ask. I love you with my whole heart, Greer." The ice between us slowly melted. "Are you okay? Are they... hurting you?" This was the question I needed an answer to, even though I knew what the answer would be. The real question was if she was alright enough to make it out of here. But I was more afraid of that answer. I was the one who got us into this disaster with my father, and I was determined to be the one to get us out.

"Can we talk freely?" she whispered against my cheek.

There was a commotion at the center of the room. A clattering of metal and a groaning, almost like a large latch or door was swinging open. Suddenly, huge metal cages lowered from the ceiling. The whole crowd held their breath as these monstrous contraptions hung over our heads.

"Our entertainment for the evening!" Riordan roared, and the crowd erupted in cheers.

"Oh my gods." Greer clung tighter to me as we both took in the sight. Beings from Earth were trapped in these cages. All sorts of people, beaten, bruised, and bloodied. Witches, animalia, shifters, other magic users.

"No," I whispered as Phayre clapped her hands, emitting power, and all those trapped in the iron bars were forced to dance along with the music. But they moved wrongly. Jerking side to side as if being controlled by someone else. They moaned and cried out in pain, but everyone in the room looked delighted as they kept up their own revelries.

"Someone, surely, was being punished. But between the two of you, who could it be? Hmm? Or perhaps it was just a little taste to let you all know that this is the order of things. A preview of what fun we could have with Earth," Phayre said, sliding right past us and laughing maniacally as she stroked her hand across both of us.

Greer and I locked gazes. Her eyes shone with tears, and I knew mine burned with pent-up rage. When would this madness stop? Every action had a consequence, and I couldn't keep track of whose transgression, however small, led to this atrocity.

"Kyra," Greer breathed. She brushed tears away from her cheeks. It was then that I noticed her wrists. They were puffy and raw.

"You never answered my question," I replied, pulling her wrist to my mouth and giving a light kiss. Her eyes closed, and she swallowed.

"I don't know how much time we have, but your mother supposedly can help us. You need to find her, talk to her. It might be the only way," she whispered.

"How do you know?" I tried to barely move my mouth. I purposefully turned away from my father's obnoxious stare.

"Xael."

"What?"

"When I sleep, she visits me in my dreams."

My mouth hung open. I had no idea that was even possible.

"Oh, Ky, there's so much to tell you, but it's dangerous here. Find a way to talk to your mom and get us the hell out of here. Then we can share what we've found." She smiled softly at me.

I closed my eyes and breathed deeply. Did this mean my mother could be trusted? If so, why would my father ever allow us to meet?

"Ky." Greer had stopped moving and placed her hands on either side of my face. My eyes squeezed shut, not wanting to shy away from her touch. Anyone else's I could not stand, but hers I craved.

"Look at me," she commanded.

I opened my eyes and focused on her fingertips against my skin and the fire burning in her eyes. It was a welcome sight to see the fight in her irises once again. I wanted to stoke that fire and let it roar. Bring it to life and let this whole godsdamned world burn down by her hands.

"Together." She trailed a fingertip across my lips.

The urge to kiss her and wrap her body around mine was so strong I nearly gave in. But I didn't want to mess up anything else. We hung in a precarious balance here. Our relationship and the space we occupied in the infernal realm were very delicate.

We both looked up at the torture chambers above us, a horrible reminder of what our fate could be if we didn't stop them. Was it too late for these people? Could we help them, or were their fates already too far out of our reach?

"Together." I splayed my hands wide on her back.

"Gods, I want to touch you more. I want to forget about all of this. The pain," she choked on her words. "The terrible things that are already happening and whatever horrible future these monsters have in store. It's selfish, but I just... I need to hate this world and who I've become just a little less," she confessed, and I knew there was so much more on her heart, but we couldn't get into it here.

"Me too, you're what I dream about, Greer." I moved us slowly into the dance again.

"Anything fun happen in those dreams?" she teased, trying to lighten the mood.

"Oh, you have no idea." I bent down and murmured in her ear.

She chuckled at that and then stiffened. "Your dad is walking over to us."

Godsdamnit.

"Kyra." He paused. "Wraith." His voice raked against my skin.

"Greer," she corrected, her smile turning feral.

"Right." He laughed like she had told a joke.

"I need to borrow my son. You don't mind, do you?" There was a challenge in his voice. He didn't give her an opportunity to answer before adding, "Do you like the entertainment?"

Greer frowned and said nothing.

"Ah, don't worry too much over them. They were tortured for quite a long time. It was brilliant, honestly. My necromancers set up a spell for them to dance every time one of us immortals claps. Isn't that delightful?"

Bile rose in my throat, and Greer's gaze turned murderous.

"That isn't exactly what I could call it," Greer's words

came out icy as her eyes fluttered back up to the dancing corpses.

"You will learn, Wraith. Anyway, my son is now mine."

She took one last look at me, and that gaze felt like she was trying to tell me everything she couldn't say and everything our bodies couldn't do.

"Goodnight, Greer." I grabbed her fingertips once more and gave a squeeze. She looked down at our palms, and her eyes softened.

"Goodnight, Kyra." Then she was gone. Shuffled into the crowd, pulled into a conversation with Phayre, and shoved at a new dance partner, where she stiffly accepted and moved robotically through the motions.

"How much longer do I need to play this game for you to let me meet her?" I pulled myself away from the woman I loved to face the man I despised.

"Oh, the night is so young, let's meet some of my favorite people, shall we?" His face was lit up with joy.

I grimaced as I was carted around and introduced to dozens of people. Countless people asked for a display of my fire magic and were absolutely delighted when I created a fire orb.

They seemed fascinated by me. That Riordan had used his own powerful magic to create an heir had them in awe. It was Riordan's way of flexing his strength. Showing the people and the court here that even the rules of the gods and goddesses had nothing on him.

I was a campaign token as he spoke openly about how the mortal realm would soon be his to rule. One person asked him who would reign over the infernal court, and he said, "My son, of course." I nearly spit out my champagne.

"You can't be serious?" I said when we moved to the next person.

"I am very serious. Why do you think I worked so hard to have you?"

"Why not let one of your henchmen rule, like Phayre?" I grumbled.

"Because they don't deserve a whole realm," he replied, like the answer was obvious. What he didn't say was that he felt like he could control me more easily because he could threaten me at any time, and I would fold. Just like I had been. My manacles may have been gone, but his power over me was not.

I said nothing while we moved throughout the room. My eyes wandered to where Greer was also being paraded around. We were the most interesting playthings in the whole room, orbiting one another but never getting an opportunity to get closer than we were before.

Time seemed irrelevant as, again, I was presented like a trophy my dad had won. Until finally a clock struck loudly somewhere, and most of the crowd was too intoxicated to continue to move responsibly.

"Your duty is done, tonight. Tomorrow morning, your mother awaits." Riordan disappeared, leaving me standing in the middle of the godsforsaken ballroom to find my own way back.

Greer had disappeared with Phayre, who was her constant keeper.

I shuffled through the dark halls, the vial and envelope still stashed in my jacket pocket. My mind wandered again to what court dynamics and politics were at play.

For some reason, I had the feeling my mother would help me make sense of it. I knew she had some answers for me. I wasn't sure I was ready to hear them. Sighing, I finally found my way back to my room.

Greer kept floating into my head in that gods damned black silk.

She would be the end of me, not this hell or my father, but Greer. I closed my eyes and welcomed the dreams of me worshiping her body and making her come again and again until I could make it a reality.

She and I would be reunited again, and then I would rain fire down on all those who scorned us.

Fifteen

Lux

The sun had just crested over the horizon, bathing the sky in reds and oranges. It was a beautiful sunset. One that danced with crimson and gold. Waverly stood between Nova and me in the sand. She had shucked off her shoes and sunk her toes in. Her shoulders were tight, and her mouth was in a hard line.

Sutton stood on the other side of me, and I was all too aware of him. I wanted to tear down this wall between us, but I didn't know how. I didn't want to fuck up the group dynamic, but there was something between us that was powerful and strong like the ocean. Pushing and pulling us together with forces larger than us.

"I need to sing to it," Waverly said finally.

Silence had hung in the air as we drove here to experience it at first light. Waverly had insisted we wait for the sun to be rising for her to sing. It was the same beach Greer had washed up on during the trials. The image of her bloody and screaming flashed through my head. Gods, how that seemed like years ago, and it was only a month or two.

Nova scanned the beach and basically read my thoughts.

"This is where the trial was. Odd that now it's harmless. Just a beach that has seen and experienced so many horrible things." She slung an arm around Waverly and kissed the top of her head.

"Places seem so unassuming when you don't know the history of what has happened. It's important to know where you've been and where you will go." Sutton's voice was low, and his face was turned away.

I looked at him out of the corner of my eye. He would often say things like this. Like he had seen a thousand lives lived and lost. It made me worry about him, just as I did with Greer.

They both had been through too much. I suppose the same could have been said for some of my experiences, but I was never without care or basic needs or even luxury. I was just without empathy.

"Okay, I can do this." Waverly walked her way towards the slow lull of the tide. Her dark hair whipped around her as the breeze picked up.

"What do you think will happen?" I blurted.

"Nothing at first, I assume." She set her shoulders down and clenched her fists.

"The water will most likely carry the message to where it needs to go. Water is a living, breathing entity that carries memories and emotions," Nova commented.

"I will send my song, and we will see who answers. Hopefully, Armello will, or at least someone who can help us find him, and we can get some answers on where to go from here," she supposed.

"I wonder how much those on Earth actually know about what's going on in the infernal realm or with the trial or even that Greer exists. Hyacinth seemed to know, but I can't help but wonder if the others washed their hands of this years ago," Nova said thoughtfully.

"What a fucking mess," I added.

Tensions were rising here, and I could only assume the same could be said in the infernal realm. Who knew how much time had passed there? It was days for us, but it could have been weeks or months for them.

Gods, I hoped Greer and Kyra had at least found a way to reconcile so they wouldn't be so alone. Greer was hurt, and for good reason, but Kyra had also been betrayed, and his options were limited. Nova using her spells for him was a slip in the magical curse. It would have been impossible to find and understand it otherwise.

"Okay, here goes nothing."

Waverly waded into the water, letting it come up to her knees, and took a loud breath. The water hugged around her as she began.

Those who are lost.
Need to be found.

Aid is needed.
And urgency is headed.

I ask for the presence.
Of those who can pay penance

I beg thee for a message.
A way to connect.

For I am a siren of the sea
I ask that the water travel for me.

Let this song ring true and clear.
The end of the mortal realm seems near.

Let the past and future collide.
And the sea shall soon provide.

Waverly sings this last song.
In hopes that we can once more get along

Her words slithered around us and hung on our skin. A gentle coaxing. Guidance to do as she said. Her voice rang high and musical. I had heard no other sound so sweet.

She stood with the words dancing around us for a few more moments before running a hand through the water and turning back to us.

"It's done." She looked sadly at the ocean before us.

"How will he return the message?" I wondered if we would need to set up camp permanently near the ocean to get answers.

"I assume he will track my siren stamp. When I interact with water, it's almost like a gentle ping or text message. If you will it to others, they know how to tune into the siren signal and track it. I imagine that Armello or even my sister might be the ones answering this call. They will find me, I'm sure. One way or another." Her pink eyes became watery, and she blinked rapidly, her dark lashes fluttering.

"Wave?" I looked at her, crossing my arms.

"I haven't sung a siren song since Greer and Nova, and I were all together." She looked heartbroken.

"I know, answers will come soon, though. We're all worried." I grabbed her hand and squeezed lightly.

We made our way back to my car, toweled the sand off our feet, and headed back to the city. The drive was mostly silent, everyone preoccupied with their own thoughts.

"I need to get the serum," I blurted out.

Sutton sat in the passenger seat and looked at me quizzically. "Yes, you do. Do you have someone you can put on it? Someone who will stay quiet and loyal to you?"

I did. For the most part, I was well-liked by my employees. I tried to be a better and different boss than my parents. They had ruled with intimidation and manipulation, not just over me, but everyone else. If you didn't like what they had to say, you had better luck quitting and finding another job than convincing them out of their own ideas.

"Merritt was the one who discovered it in the first place. I'll have her and someone from my biomedical team on it and the chemistry division."

"You'll need the bio composition from the victim's blood," Waverly said from the backseat.

"Anything else?"

"Yeah, I'll grab what I can from the case of the murders. Nova, is there a way for you to run a blood analysis on them?" Waverly kept her eyes at the window as she spoke, her cheeks still wet.

Nova scrunched her nose, and her stars danced. "I've never been asked to do that before. Let me look to see what information I have about detecting isolated compositions in someone's blood. I could maybe tell you what poison is used by the taste, smell, compound, but it's not a guarantee. Mostly, I could just tell you it's been tampered with, but not what exact chemical caused it and how much of it was used." She furrowed her brow, tapping her finger to her lips.

"But you think you could look into it?" Waverly turned and faced her, finally. Her lashes stuck together.

Nova gently brushed her fingertips across her rosy cheeks.

"Yeah, it will be a fun challenge. I haven't discovered something new about my powers in quite some time. The possibilities are endless." She winked.

"Great, so now we just wait," Sutton said, a ghost of a smile playing on his lips.

"Now, we wait." I did not feel satisfied with that answer at all.

"I have an idea." Nova smiled wolfishly from the back seat.

"What's your idea, Nova darling?" Sutton drawled.

"I was invited to a party," she said.

"We're seriously going to go out when all of this is happening?" Waverly said in disbelief.

"Well, it's not any party, love. It's a swanky one with past immortality winners and, unfortunately, the President. However, I think for research I need samples of those beings who have immortality in their blood right now, and seeing as we don't have any of those with us right now..."

"So, I can go stab some of the immortals trolling the city?" Sutton asked wickedly.

"Exactly. We will each oversee tagging some people, and then we will compare it to our own blood without immortality. It's something to do, and we can get dressed up and look hot. Plus, it's good recon on what the upper crust of the city knows about the mortal realm takeover," she explained.

"Gods, why does this feel like such a terrible idea?" I murmured.

"Because it probably is." Sutton teased. "Which is why I love it."

"Great, it's settled." Nova clapped her hands excitedly.

"When's the party?" I said as we drove back into the city of Odessa, the glass and metal looming overhead.

"Tonight."

"Of course, it fucking is," I grumbled.

"Lux, you were definitely already on the guest list, and so was I. We get plus ones. Easy. Don't you pay attention to the goings on in the city?" Nova commented, almost scolding me.

"I barely go to any of the parties anyway. Before, I would only go if Ky texted me saying he was going to be there and that it would be important." My heart clenched again at the thought of him at the hands of his father.

Nova nodded.

"I'd love to be your plus one tonight," Sutton purred next to me, and my stomach did some funny things.

He reached over and placed a hand on my thigh and looked up with his dark eyes that swirled with smoke. I swallowed.

"Hey, eyes on the road, Lux." Waverly teased.

I gritted my teeth while Sutton started to rub down the length of my leg.

"Yes, behave, Luxton," Sutton scolded.

Godsdamn, this was going to be a long day.

↔

"You look great," Sutton complimented. He leaned against my door frame, his ruby red lips glittering, and his dark eyes sparkling. He wore an all-black suit. No tie. It hugged his slender frame perfectly. His long fingertips were gently folded in front of him, and his long, strawberry blonde hair was slicked back.

"Thank you, so do you." My mouth suddenly felt very dry.

Sutton was all cool lines and dark smoky images. I was loud and brash. My deep violet suit cut close, and I had a white button-down open across my chest to show off my tattoos. I would love to make these elites a little uncomfortable.

Sutton walked over and placed himself behind me in the mirror. We locked eyes, and something electric passed between us. We were about the same height. I was broader and more muscular. Thick arms and legs to his delicate lines and limbs.

"Hello," he whispered, smirking and locking eyes with me.

"Hey," I said, smiling back at him.

"Are you ready?" He stepped away. My body pulled to him like a magnet, but I stayed rooted where I was and simply turned around to face him.

"I suppose so. Does Nova have what we need to take our samples?" I cleared my throat. Heat was making its way across my cheeks, and I wanted to tear off both of our clothes with my leopard claws.

"Lux, Sutton, get out here!" Waverly called, and the tension between us snapped.

Sutton winked and left my room, and I trailed after him.

Nova and Waverly both looked stunning. Waverly, in a fuchsia dress that slid down her body and accentuated her generous curves, and Nova in a short silver playsuit.

"Okay, here's what we're working with." Nova put several things on the table.

"What are we looking at?" I asked quizzically. There were four small packs of what looked like little needles encased in small buttons.

"You will take one of these." She held up the small needle with the flat, round back on it in between her fingertips, and it almost disappeared, minus the tip.

"And just give a gentle poke," she pricked her own finger-tip, and a gel-like substance covered the needle after the blood dripped down.

"The gel-like liquid encases the blood on the needle so I can study it," she announced.

"Got it." Sutton snagged a pack, sliding it into his jacket pocket without a second thought.

"So, everyone feels totally fine and natural, stabbing random immortals at this party without them noticing?" Waverly asked, with a frown.

"I mean no. But hey, we've done stranger shit, you know?" I grabbed a pack and slid it into my jacket, wondering how I would discreetly place the needle between my fingers without stabbing my own fucking hand.

"True." She sighed, grabbed the pack, and looked at it. "I don't know where to put this."

"Here," Nova grabbed it and slid it in between Waverly's breasts.

I snickered, and Waverly batted her hand away.

"How am I going to get it out so no one else notices?!" She laughed.

"I don't know, get creative." Nova winked and slid her pack into a clutch she had placed on the counter.

"Ready?" Sutton asked, the corners of his mouth twitching.

"Let's go stab some people," I said, and we were off.

The party was on some fancy rooftop. The place reeked of booze, luxury, and stuck-up elegance. There were many people there who used to be associated with my family and who made a point to come over to me and offer their hellos. They inquired about what I was doing with my time these days and how I was so kind to rent out my building to those less fortunate.

I did my best to smile and not snarl at them. Some gave sneaky appreciative glances at my bare chest, and others looked on in distaste. We all quickly got separated through the throng of bodies as we moved and weaved through the crowd. I was by far the most sought-after and spoken to. I was able to nick a few people successfully, who I knew had immortality, after I offered to fill up their cups. They didn't even notice.

Nova forced people to give her a wide berth, and men tended to flock to Waverly like puppy dogs who had lost their owner. Sutton moved through the crowd like smoke, undetected, unless he wanted to be seen.

I had finally filled my pack of samples when the President

stalked over to Nova with delight in his eyes. Bile rose in my throat, and I started after them.

"Don't, Lux." Waverly grabbed my arm and looked after them, her eyes strained.

"Wave." I looked between her pained expression and Nova's stone one, as the President was getting deeper into her space.

"She told me not to interfere, and I have to assume that means you, too. She can handle herself. Come get a drink with me." She walked over to the bar and ordered two glasses of champagne. We made our way to a quiet spot near the balcony edge, and Waverly threw the drink back quickly.

"I'd ask if you're okay, but I know you aren't." I did the same and motioned a waiter over to bring us two more glasses.

"I hate him, and I hate him more for being impervious to my siren song. Like, could he be an even bigger asshat?" She groused and snatched the second glass up.

"Probably, but let's not find out what that means exactly." I chuckled and scanned the crowd for Sutton.

"What's the deal with the two of you?" She knew who I was looking for.

"I don't know. He has some secrets, I think, and some baggage I don't understand. Maybe it's like Kyra and his curse. It can be deadly to others. I really like him, though. I'm pulled to him in a way that I haven't had with other people. So, I'm just letting it breathe, even though all I want to do is tackle him to the ground," I confessed, realizing that, in theory, I didn't know much about Sutton. I just knew how I felt when we were around one another.

"I get it, Nova was the same way. We barely knew each other, but I knew that there was something there, and I wanted to hold it in my hands and nurture it. Let it grow into something really special." She gazed out at the city skyline.

"What's even more unthinkable is that we are here at this

party and Greer and Kyra are doing gods knows what in the infernal realm."

"I know you're worried, Lux. You and Greer have been through so much, but she's our friend, too. We're doing what we can with what we've got. When they come back to us—and I do mean when—we will get answers. We will figure this shit out. This—us and them, it's important," Waverly said, her tone low and authoritative.

"I know it is." I looked over to where Nova had slipped away from the President and had looped her arm into Sutton's. They were making their way over to us when a scream ripped through the air.

A pop and woosh sounded as a pipe burst through the floor, and water sprayed everywhere. More screams followed as several more pipes popped. Water, marble, and debris littered the ground as people began to panic and run.

Things moved in slow motion. The water suspended itself in midair and then began to move as if it were sentient. People looked around, trying to find a water warlock or witch manipulating the liquid, but no one seemed to be the culprit.

The droplets formed and twisted, as if controlled by something else entirely, until it spelled out the word "Evanya" and then burst. It dissipated nearly as quickly as it had formed.

The partygoers held their breath until the water stopped. It was as if it had only caused a moment of inconvenience, and then everyone was back to their own devices again.

"What the fuck was that?" Nova walked over to us.

Waverly's face had gone a few shades lighter.

"What?" I said, looking at her.

"What does Evanya mean, Waverly?" Sutton asked, searching her pink eyes.

"That's my sister's name. Her full name. We only ever called her Eva." She chewed on her bottom lip.

"So, what does that mean?" I asked.

"It means she got my message, and that it's serious. I only ever called her Evanya when it was serious," she whispered.

"We need to go to your family's island, Waverly." Nova rubbed her hands down Waverly's arms.

"Tomorrow?" I said.

"Tomorrow," Waverly agreed.

This was what we finally needed to get some more fucking answers.

SIXTEEN
KYRA

"You ready?" Riordan inquired, looking almost annoyed. It was hard for me to tell, as he always slipped on a mask of confidence. But something about my mother obviously put him on edge. I thought it tipped in my favor, considering I was actively working against my piece-of-shit dad. My mom could be the key we needed to figure out how to get out of here.

"Yes," I replied curtly. He had woken me up early and led me through a maze of corridors and down countless flights of stairs and elevators. It felt like we were truly going to a dungeon where he was the only one who knew the pathway. My senses were on high alert as I tried to track our journey down into the depths of his estate. Why would he need to keep her so far away? Was there a reason he couldn't just evaporate there? It was his kingdom after all.

We arrived in front of a sleek metal door. He stood in front of it, frowning. I shivered and tried to bring heat to my hands, but nothing happened.

"Magic doesn't work down here," I observed, understanding why we had to take the long way through the entire fucking castle.

"Your magic does not, no." He frowned at the metal door again.

"And what exactly did you do to this metal to take away people's powers?" I asked, trying to understand how that was even possible.

"An old trick of the gods. Your mother actually designed it. We have limited resources for it, and she refuses to make more. She was the only witch smart enough to figure it out, and here we are using it against her," he smiled smugly.

My mouth dropped open. "You really despise her so much that you would use her own magic against her?" Hot anger raced through my veins, and if I had the ability to use my fire-power, I certainly would have taken it out on him right then and there.

"Don't be a fool, Kyra!" he hissed, his eyes darkening. "I love your mother more than anything else, but she will not cooperate. We were a goddamn miracle team, your mother and me. But she attacks me every time I enter her chambers. She is inconsolable and has lost her damn mind. Screaming and hurling things at me. Refusing to share magic and spells that others cannot recreate. This is the first time in decades she has said coherent words to me. I allowed this visit to happen because she has agreed to cooperate once she has met you. She will make more of this magic and provide other spells that we had developed together, or you will pay the price. Or maybe Greer. Or perhaps both." He slammed his fist on the door, and it bent slightly. He huffed and straightened his shirt.

So, this visit was a deal made not by me, but by my mother. What was she sacrificing to make this happen?

"How could she have made such a thing?" I asked, wondering how this metal could even exist. My mother appeared to have discovered many things in the crevices and cracks of magic.

"Your mother is the smartest godsdamn witch in the whole world. Even more so than Hyacinth sometimes. She was able to fabricate things that should not even exist through pure tenacity and perseverance. Like you, for example," he said, admiration in his eyes.

"It's a wonder she didn't see through your lies," I commented, leaning back against the wall.

He was stalling, and I was done playing nice. He wanted to play dirty with Greer; I would do it with my mom.

"Love is a powerful magic; you don't get to choose who you fall for, and she proclaims it was her greatest weakness. Even though it cost *me* everything," he whispered harshly. There was more to that story, from my mother's side, I was sure.

"You wanted to control her; loving her and owning her are not the same thing." I knew I had struck a chord. He was someone who conquered and took what he wanted with little regard for others. My mother may have loved him, but that didn't mean she consented to being his possession.

"You think you understand, Kyra. But you don't. I have lived endlessly, and you have lived so little." His eyes narrowed, and he exhaled loudly. "Let us go in."

He placed a hand on the door, and it swung open to a glass corridor. We stepped through, and something filtered over us, like we were being scanned. Then another door opened at the far end of the hall. I had no idea what it was scanning for, but my magic was useless, and I didn't have any weapons on me. I hadn't been allowed any.

"Verity!" my father boomed next to me as we made our way through the door.

The space opened to what felt like a modern-day apartment. A living room sprawled out in front of us with relatively updated furnishings; a small kitchen was tucked in the corner alongside a dining area. A hallway branched off to the right into what I assumed were several other living accommodations, like a bed and a bathroom.

"Don't make me ask again," Riordan threatened, looking around.

Silence followed, and then shuffling. Slowly, she emerged from the hallway in black joggers, a tank top, and slippers covering her feet. It was like looking into my own face. She was my height. Her dark hair was braided loosely, and she looked like she was no more than thirty-five.

She had lacerations on her skin. Fresh, from what I could see. Raised, angry, red marks and cuffs that looked a lot like Greer's. Purple and blue surrounded her forearms and hands from where the metal dug into her skin.

"Here," she grabbed a file off the counter and handed it to Riordan. I stood frozen in place. Her face was unreadable, and his was practically gleeful.

"Thirty minutes, Riordan. That's what you agreed to. Alone. These damn things are on, you have the spells, and I am speaking to you nicely," she gritted her teeth and shook her wrists at him.

"If these do not work, I will feed our son to the dessert monsters and make you watch. Is that understood?" Riordan said the words so casually, and my eyes went wide.

"Yes."

"And if you don't come back out in thirty minutes, I will do the same to her and Greer. The clock is ticking." Without waiting for my answer, he turned on his heel and left. We had hardly any time.

"You're immortal," I said, looking at her and not knowing why that was such a surprise. Obviously, my father wouldn't have it any other way. Which meant she was literally trapped in here for eternity.

"So are you," she whispered and walked closer to me, our eyes nearly level. "Kyra?" She said, letting her fingertips hover above my face like she wanted to touch me but didn't know how. "You know who I am?" She questioned, letting her hand fall. Her muscular frame took up space in the room, her energy filling every inch around us.

"You're my mother," I whispered, trying to memorize the lines of her face. The thick brows, the angry marks across her body, and now the smattering of tattoos snaking up around her arm and then her neck.

"And you're my son." Her eyes filled with tears, and gently they started to fall. Her hand flew to her mouth, and I had the urge to wrap my arms around her and hold her, so I knew that she was real. That she actually existed and wasn't something made up by my father.

Tears fell down my own cheeks, and I knew I needed to get answers because time was so precious, but nothing came out.

"You are so handsome and powerful from what I can gather." She tilted her head to one side, and her hair fell into her face slightly.

"You're quite the powerhouse yourself from what I gathered," I said, and she walked us over to sit.

She scoffed. "Yes, well, not powerful enough to not be duped by your father. But I suppose being manipulated by the gods is nothing new, especially those who reign here. Why are you here, Kyra? You consented to come to the infernal realm, and in the process, I see that Riordan broke your curse, but other things are causing your immense pain." She scanned my body as if reading words on a page.

"What are you able to see?"

"My power is complicated, Kyra. But, right now, I'm trying to understand your magical reading. Your spoken curse is gone. But the crystal in your chest seems as torn and broken as you are right now," she commented wearily.

I nodded. "The pain is getting worse. It was clear and red after I won the Immortality Trials and was granted new powers. But since everything began here, obsidian has crept back in. And Riordan has plagued me with many special treatments for disobedience."

"Start at the beginning, my child. Tell me everything that transpired for you to end up in front of me in the shortest manner possible. I'm so sorry I sent you away when I did. I hope that your adoptive family was loving and kind. Hyacinth said she would make sure it was so, and I would give my life for her and her word."

I could see the guilt and hurt in her eyes and her heart. It was palpable in the way her shoulders went rigid and her fingertips twisted and turned in her palms.

"I know you had no choice; I know what it means to be controlled." I laid my hands on hers and gave them a squeeze. She looked down at our palms and smiled.

"Your story, Kyra. Quickly, we don't have much time. You being here is a blessing and a curse. One that I have now paid greatly for, but I am selfish. Even if those spells damn the world, I had to see you."

"I thought I was the one who pushed to see you. It did feel too easy... But you've paid with more than your magic. He's hurting you, as he does me. As he does anything he deems in need of breaking and bending to his will."

"My body will heal even if the memories never leave me. Do not worry about me. Protect yourself in whatever way you can and make sure that when you endure his wrath, it is worth it. So, tell me, how did you come to be in front of me, my beautiful boy?" She held onto my palm.

So, I told her. My father, Greer, the trials, Lux, Nova, Waverly, Sutton, the predicament we were in now, as fast and shortened as I could. I left out so much, but I could feel the minutes slipping by.

"Greer is Xael's chosen one?" she whispered in awe.

"Yes, she said she comes to her in her dreams and that you might have the means to help us escape this hell, literally."

She smiled, sitting back and crossing her legs. Her fingertips slipped from mine, and I sank into the couch.

"Oh, my dear, Kyra, I have been preparing for this day since I sent you away," she said, looking smug.

"Are you able to help us?" I asked, feeling hopeful.

"Yes, Riordan knows many of my secrets, but not all of them. I have been waiting for you for so long. Not only will I help you escape my dear boy, but I will go with you." She breathed deeply, and I looked around, wondering if my father would be privy to the plans that were spoken aloud.

"Don't worry, I have magic-proofed my apartments from your father; it drove him wild for years, until he learned how to accept it. I took parts of his DNA and used it to fortify my walls against him. And he wouldn't dare let anyone else help him when it comes to containing me," she said.

"Oh, I almost forgot, Farren gave these to me for you." I pulled out the vial and envelope. Her eyes softened as she looked at the small tokens.

"My dear, Farren." She held the vial in her hand and ripped it open. "He will help. He had tried to get to me for quite some time, but Riordan never allowed it. This is the first contact I have had with anyone but him in... I can't remember how long."

The memory of Farren talking to my father about trying to trick Verity came back to me, and I wondered if it was his way to try to contact my mother in some way to help.

"What's the vial for?"

"A missing piece for a potion to be able to connect with Hyacinth. We will need her help in creating a portal to your friends. I assume they are anxiously awaiting your return, even if it has only been a few days for them. Time is a fickle thing here." She stood and paced around, tapping her finger to her lips.

"I have been siphoning magic using my spelled metal for years. Anytime Riordan or any of the others use it, it gives back to me, even though I told Riordan it stops me from practicing magic as well."

"You've been pretending for years to be weak and feeble?" I was astounded by her dedication.

"I don't think Riordan fully bought it, but he did think that my heartbreak over losing you, and sending you away, ripped out a part of me that my magic fueled. I have been crafting a plan for years, my dear boy. When you play with the gods and goddesses, you must think twelve steps ahead, because they have the power, but I have the cleverness," she said, and I realized then Riordan had never been a match for my mother. That bastard had gotten lucky. She fell for him; otherwise, this would have never happened. She had been playing the long game for revenge ever since.

"Your metal sucked some power from me." I chuckled at how brilliant she was.

"How fun." She winked and smiled apologetically. "You will need to be ready at a moment's notice to leave. There will not be another chance. Our time is nearly up. And I don't desire to see anyone eaten alive and then reformed, so I suggest you go. You will know when the portal has opened up. Greer will feel it especially like time itself is ripped in two." She stood then, ushering me towards the door, a look of worry on her face.

"Thank you for being on my side," I said, wanting to move in for a hug. "Can I hug you?" I asked, unsure how to end this reunion.

Her grin was contagious, and we embraced each other. The weight of her arms around me felt like coming home. My shoulders could finally relax, and the ball of tension sitting in my stomach eased.

"Kyra, you must be ready. I do not know where the portal will open, only that I will do my best to make it so. Good luck."

I nodded and turned to leave.

"Thank you, Mom. Words cannot describe how much this means to me and Greer. I'm excited for you to meet her. She is a force to be reckoned with, just like you."

She winked at me and chuckled. "Can't wait to meet her and all your other friends."

"Okay, goodbye."

I went to the door, took a deep breath, and entered the glass chamber once more. The walk back to the metal door felt like it stretched on forever, until my father flung it open with a sinister smirk on his face.

"Oh, you were almost out of time. How I would have loved to see some extra entertainment today. Regrowing your whole body is nasty business as an immortal, especially after being eaten alive." Riordan sighed, as if the disappointment was almost too much for him.

No words left my mouth as we made our way back to the main part of the mansion.

"I will call on you if I need you. If you go visit your little wraith, I am sure she will show off her newest scars," he said and disappeared.

My mind fractured into a million different ways that he had hurt her, and I went running. My heart pounded in my chest as I weaved my way through the halls. My stomach plummeted at the thought of seeing her broken and bloodied just like I had done to her in that damn fight.

Finally, I arrived at her door and pounded my fist against it, hoping she was whole. She flung open the door, and the sight that greeted me was devastating.

"Hi, Kyra," she said. "Did you want to come in?"

Her eye was nearly swollen shut, a deep bruise settling into the ring around her socket. All along her hands and neck were raised marks. Almost every inch of her exposed skin was black and blue, and her hands were covered in little lacerations. I couldn't tell if they were defensive or some sort of sick pattern carved there by my father.

What had been done to her after the ball? We needed to get out of here before it was too fucking late. It was time to plan our escape, because I didn't know how much longer either of us would last.

I swallowed hard and nodded. I slipped past her body, my arm brushing up against her. The urge to slam the door behind me, wrap her around me, and press myself into her was strong, but we had more important matters to attend to.

SEVENTEEN
GREER

Kyra looked disheveled. His hair was so long now and always in desperate need of getting brushed out of his eyes.

His scarlet eyes roamed over me. I knew what he saw. Phayre had just left. Another session with her using my body like a punching bag.

She had forced me to use my time magic offensively, but I paid for each blow. Phayre commanded me to break her arm. She would giggle with glee, snap it back into place, and then deliver a blow to my face, my stomach, my ribs; no place was off limits.

The pattern continued, and the darkness I thought I knew before had nothing on what I clung to now. Every time she came in, my wrists and throat screamed, and I retreated back to that place of hopelessness. A place where my mind and body were not one.

Where thoughts of my death were possible and welcomed, a place where no one could touch me or see me, I simply ceased to exist. A place where I could finally find peace before the rest of the world came slamming in.

"Greer, who did this to you?" Kyra choked out.

I didn't know how long we had been standing there, my eyes vacant and my brain begging to be anywhere but here. I grabbed his fingertips and held them to my heart.

"Ky, I don't want to talk about it." I couldn't delve into my wounds right now. They were locked up tight for me to be able to survive. When I could finally release them, I didn't know what would happen, but right now I didn't want to feel Phayre's rage or Riordan's orders. I just wanted to feel him. To erase everyone else's touch.

My collar had been removed, but not before it branded my skin, my cuffs were still old friends, and I had no idea why Kyra was allowed to be here, but I didn't care. If this were my last chance to feel something with him. I would take it.

He placed his hand against the door and leaned into me, so our bodies were connected everywhere at once and not nearly enough. His fingers tightened around mine, and his chest rose and fell, his hair tumbling forward.

"Please, just tell me if I'm hurting you," he breathed out.

"There's no pain I don't already know. Do your worst," I begged.

If they wanted to tear us apart, they were already succeeding, and at least this would be ours. A delicious memory to carry us through to whatever the end might be.

I dropped his hand and cupped his face, searching his eyes for something to make me feel like a person again. He looked practically feral as he stood eerily still. I tucked his long black hair behind his ears and tilted my head to the side.

"Kiss me, Ky," I said, and the words crashed over him. "Use my body for something else besides agony."

He pushed into me, my back pressing steadily against the door as his mouth was on mine. My bones ached, but I wouldn't tell him to stop. At least this pain I could control. This was done by my own fucking hand and not theirs.

Kyra tasted like fire. His lips burned me with an addictive flavor. I wrapped my hands around his neck, a leg around his waist, inviting him to touch more of me.

He grabbed my ass and lifted me up as his lips continued to travel down. I thrust my body into him. There was too much heat and too many clothes blocking our bodies. I had been in a drought, and I was dying for him to quench this relentless ache and thirst in my body. It had been so long since I knew pleasure. Knew a touch that wasn't threatening.

He grunted and moved us toward the bed, never once breaking contact. He laid me down, and I panted, looking up at him. It was a different kind of torture, how much I had missed him. How much my pain ached for his touch and the sensation of his searing lips and palms.

"Gods, I missed you." He let his eyes soak in every detail of my battered form.

The scars that seemed insistent on staying, and the welts and blood blisters that took forever to heal. He gently moved to take off my shoes and socks. He took his time caressing every inch of newly exposed skin. Tears pricked my eyes at his thoughtfulness. It was almost too much. My body no longer knew what gentle was. It didn't know love, not from others, and certainly not from myself. I didn't know how to fight anymore. All I knew was how to survive.

"Just make me forget, for one moment, that we are in this place, make me yours again, Ky. Please, for the love of gods."

I wanted to pretend I was back in my own room with my friends just down the hall and that nothing existed outside of us and our love, and that the world wasn't falling apart. That after this, there were so many things expected of me. And that if I failed, people would die. I was already dying, but the end was always out of sight. Never coming to take me away in a merciful bliss. Instead, I was forced into a purgatory filled with people who were always chipping away at my soul, ready to put me back in exactly the way they wanted.

Ky answered by kissing the inside of my ankle, running his hands up my thighs, and peeling down my leggings. I hadn't put any panties on today, and when Kyra stripped my legs bare, he breathed deeply.

"Fuck, Greer, I could look at you all day." His eyes were watery, and I wondered if he really could. Could he look at this version of me and still love me the same way he did before?

He took even longer to trail his way up my legs, gently nipping the insides of my thighs and running his warm hands against my bare skin. I groaned and arched up, wanting him to taste or touch me where I needed him most. Heat built in my lower belly, and I knew I was leaking onto the bed. My body still remembered, even if my mind spiraled and fractured into a million different feelings.

"Can you touch yourself, beautiful?" Kyra said against my hip bone, and I reached down to find my clit. I started to gently circle my center, and Kyra sat back on his heels and just watched as I used my fingers to draw pleasure. This, I could do.

Gods, if he could just tell me what to do, then the rest of my noisy brain could focus on that and nothing else.

"Can you put a finger in, baby?"

He licked his lips, and I nodded, sliding one finger in as the other built momentum on my clit. Still, he watched with fascination and reverence as if nothing could bring him more joy than to watch me pleasure myself. And it felt good. Like, I was slipping into a reality where this was truly possible.

"Ky," I moaned. I pressed myself further and further towards a climax. Maybe he could erase everything that had been etched on my skin. He made it seem so easy to forget what had transpired before.

"Don't come yet, Greer," he whispered and took my hands away from my wet pussy and licked them clean. My inner thighs quivered as I watched him devour my essence.

"Gods, you're exactly what I need," I said, and he smiled, placing a light kiss right above my clit. I squirmed, wanting him to do more for me.

"And you're delicious," he said, and pulled me up to remove my top and bra. He ran his hands over my breasts and cupped them gently, sliding his nose against the sensitive skin there. He took one nipple in his mouth and sucked as I wrapped my leg around him and clung to him. Pleasure built in me as he took his time giving attention to each bud.

All that mattered was his lips and his hands. The bruises and scratches faded away, and there was only him.

"Why are you taking such a long time?" I whined while he continued to nip, suck, and pleasure every part of me.

"I'm savoring you; I haven't had you in weeks, Greer."

He came back to my mouth, sliding his tongue to dance with mine while gently kneading his hands on my hips, careful to avoid the purple flesh there. But I wanted him to press himself into my skin, to press so hard that those marks were now his.

"Less clothes for you." I clawed at his pants and shirt. He chuckled and shucked them off effortlessly so I could see all the lines of muscles and scars. And that shining crystal that looked like it was a battle all on its own.

In my own pain, I forgot about his. What war was he waging alone? I didn't think I could shoulder my own pain and his, so I didn't ask. Not now, not when we could escape into one another.

I touched the stone gingerly, and he shuddered, the red blinking bright. The shadowy onyx almost shrank away.

His cock was hard and ready. I salivated thinking about it in my mouth and inside me.

He pulled me up before I had a chance to admire him fully.

"Greer," he whispered against me, and our bodies finally got to touch fully, our hands exploring. My inner thighs and pussy were slick with arousal. I grabbed for him, and he felt so fucking good in my hands. I wanted to push him inside me now. The ache for him hummed through my blood and made my mouth water.

"Ky." I turned towards the bed, and he pulled me down on top of him, so my breasts pressed between us.

"Let me taste you, hands on the headboard, princess, and that pussy... I want to drown in it," he growled.

I smiled, the feeling foreign on my face. I climbed on top of him and made my way to the top of the headboard that had once held my shackles. Now, it would be my throne for Ky's face.

I positioned myself right over him, and he blew on me. I shivered while his hands wrapped around my thighs.

He reached up and licked me cleanly, lapping me from front to back. I shook as he slammed me down on top of him, and I cried out. His tongue danced around my clit as his hands moved to my ass and massaged the soft flesh there. I cried out as I rode his face and moved against him. I could think of nothing else as Ky pushed me into a realm of pleasure.

"That's it, Greer, take what you need," he said in between mouthfuls of my pussy.

Ecstasy curled at my spine and spread everywhere as his tongue worked wonders. I moved, throwing my head back and grinding into him. Gods, he felt good as he slipped a finger inside me, and the combination of my hips moving, his mouth, and his finger sent me flying off the edge. I screamed. My orgasm ripped through me, and I pulsed around him, moving against him until every last drop of my orgasm had been extracted. I breathed heavily as he lifted my hips and slid out from under me.

He kissed up my spine and positioned himself behind me.

"Please, Ky."

I needed him inside me. This moment was too precious to waste a single second. He eased himself in, and my body sighed like it had been waiting for him all along. He felt so incredibly right. He pulled me up, so I was against him, and he kissed along my neck, not thrusting as he rubbed my nipples with my own wetness.

"Gods, I could drown in you," he whispered in my ear, then he let me go, and I placed my hands on the headboard.

"Hard, Kyra, I want to feel every inch of you. Don't worry about the bruises, just, please, fuck me like before," I begged.

There was a pause, and I was afraid he would say no. So afraid he would turn me away, when all I wanted was this one last time. Like nothing had changed, even though everything was different. But he didn't reject me, he obliged.

He pressed all the way into me and then pulled all the way out. He started slow and built to an unrelenting rhythm set to ruin me. He felt so good pounding into me. His hand came around to rub my swollen and aching clit again. I screamed as he moved fast, and my pleasure shot through me at a jolting speed. Right as I was on the edge, he slipped out, and I moaned.

"Greer, look at me," he said, and I turned around. "I want to see you the next time you come." He pressed his lips against mine, and I tasted myself on him.

"I want you to see all of me when I come for you, Ky." I positioned myself over his beautiful cock. I sheathed myself on him, and he fluttered his eyes closed.

"Gods, you feel fucking perfect."

He opened his eyes and placed one hand at my clit and the other on my ass while I rode him. Our eyes never left one another, even as I bit my lip and sweat dripped down my chest.

I mentally captured this image in my head. A time when I was powerful and capable of more than being a vessel for other people. A time when I could take what I wanted and be given the same in return.

I groaned as we both toppled over the edge, and I collapsed on top of him, wrapping myself around him and breathing heavily, taking in his scent and the smell of our lovemaking.

"I love you, Greer Roberts," he said into my hair, stroking my spine and holding me close as I curled around him. I sighed into him and felt at home for the first time since we had been in this hellhole. But I knew it couldn't last. There was always a price to pay, and who knew when the next round of torment would begin.

"I love you too, Ky," I said against his chest.

Barely above a whisper, he pressed his mouth to my ear, "We're leaving. My mother, she knows a way out. Be ready, and I'll come get you."

I didn't dare make a sound or any indication I heard him. Who knew what ears could extend to us? They would have gotten an earful of our sex, but I didn't care. I wanted to wrap myself around Kyra and get into his skin. What would they do anyway? This wasn't even a plan. It wasn't even the outline of a plan. It was a fleeting idea that may or may not have merit.

"I'm going to get up now."

I slid myself off him, and I leaked down my thighs. I walked to my bathroom, and Kyra followed behind me.

"May I?" He nodded to the shower. I smiled and let him turn it on and invite me underneath the warm spray. He gently lathered his fingertips and explored every inch of my body, letting his lips wander to my breasts, his teeth leaving little traces on my ass.

His eyes and fingertips kept lingering on the marks Phayre

had made, but I wouldn't speak of it now. I wouldn't sacrifice anything else to her. Especially not this moment.

I returned the favor and traveled down his strong arms and the planes of his chest and abdominals. Heat started to build again, and Kyra was hard against me.

"You really did miss me..." I wrapped my hands around him, sank down to my knees, and placed his cock in my mouth. I ran my tongue around the length of him and sucked on the head, loving the feel of him on my lips.

"Greer," he murmured as I grabbed his ass with one hand and placed my other at the base of him. I wanted all of him again. My ache for him couldn't be solved with just one time. But if this is all we had, I would take as much as I could.

"Again." I stood and guided his hand down as I hiked my leg around him. He bit my shoulder as he finger fucked me, and I groaned, grabbing my breasts and pulling hard at my nipples.

"More, Ky," I whined, and he lifted me up and positioned himself under me. I slid on easily as the water sprayed around us.

"Fuck fuck fuck." He pumped into me, and my head lolled to the side. My fingernails dug into his chest as our mouths crashed together. This was messy and desperate, not sweet and thorough like before.

I was starved, and he was my salvation.

"Come for me, Greer," he purred against me, and I rubbed my clit as he pumped into me and I fell apart on him. While my orgasm ripped through me, Ky roared my name and flooded into me, both of us pressed into each other against the wall.

"If that was our last night, I'll take it," I whispered against his cheek. His eyes searched mine as if trying to decipher those words.

"I would die a happy man," he whispered, "but no one is dying tonight. Soon things will be different."

The spray of the shower created steam and hissed around us.

I wanted to believe him. Gods, I really did. Kyra Valequay was the only one in this place I could really trust, even if he had hurt me, too. But maybe this time... this time would be different.

EIGHTEEN
GREER

"You should go," I said quietly.

Kyra's brows furrowed, and it was hard not to be distracted by his beautiful naked body. We lay there silently for what felt like too long. Maybe I should have used my power to prolong this moment, or speed it up, but I couldn't bring myself to do either.

"Greer, I want to stay."

His fingertips brushed mine. I sat up in bed and left his side. My body was aching, but not as badly as it had been before. I dressed quickly, needing to be anywhere but here right now. This intimacy was too much. And I wasn't sure what it would cost.

My body was resilient, but my spirit was faltering. He talked of escape, but there was no real plan. The likelihood that this would work was abysmal, at best. I was slowly coming to the realization that this could be my life for the rest of eternity. The possibility wasn't a distant fear anymore, but a real-life nightmare. I wasn't sure how I would survive it.

"I can't do this with you tonight... I need some time to

think. This was amazing, and I just need a moment alone." I couldn't look at him lying there with hurt in his eyes.

"Okay, I'll see you soon, then."

I kept my gaze trained on anything but him as he shuffled around. When the door finally closed, my lungs released the air I had been holding onto, and I slumped against the wall, sliding to the ground. My exhaustion weighed heavily on my bones, but beneath it, there was a restlessness in me that I couldn't shake.

How was it possible to be so tired, yet so keyed up at the same time?

"Can I go to the training facility?" I asked the empty air. I knew I was always being monitored in some capacity. There was no answer, but a knock sounded quickly at the door.

"Farren," I said, surprised as I opened the door.

"I'm to be your escort to the training facilities, to bar you from using anything too pointy," he said, smirking.

I nodded, not sure what to say. With no words, he led me through the halls towards the place Kyra and I had fought. Where my skin had burned, and I had lost some pieces of myself.

"Have at it, but don't touch any of the weapons. Those cuffs will shock you anytime you get too close to something that you shouldn't," Farren stated. "I am surprised you want to train considering your... condition." He waved a hand over my body, and I knew that he was talking about Phayre beating the absolute shit out of me as well as my sex-crazed hair.

"I'm fine," I responded under his scrutiny and turned to jog away from him, so I could start running laps around the training space. Time almost ceased to exist as I pushed myself to the brink of collapse. But that was the thing, my body was ready to rest, but my mind wasn't. If I could just break myself enough to actually silence all the screaming sensations in my brain, then maybe I could legitimately find a moment of peace.

I loved Xael and our dream realm; it was a comfort I didn't take for granted, but right now, I needed to be without anyone else in my head. Even just myself in there was driving me mad.

At some point, Farren left, and Phayre had taken his place. I hadn't noticed her come in, but I knew the moment she replaced him. The first shock sent me flying as my whole body convulsed, and I screamed in pain as her electricity shot through me. My legs flew out from underneath me, but I still had momentum from jogging. The ground greeted me painfully, and I slammed down hard, gasping as all the air left my lungs.

"I am your new keeper now. Keep training, wraith, but be warned, there might be some surprises along the way," Phayre giggled happily, and slowly I shoved myself up, saying nothing.

The fight in me tonight was gone, and all I wanted to do was prove to myself that I was still strong. I still had some control, and I still was Greer Roberts. Even though my body begged and pleaded for me to rest. I didn't, I just kept going. What other choice did I have? Numbness flowed over me like a cool breeze, and I embraced it for as long as I could.

Hours passed as I lifted weights and ran through fighting drills by myself. The shocks would come in rapid succession sometimes, and then wait long periods, where I would foolishly think I got a reprieve. Every time, Phayre squealed with delight and then yelled at me to get up and keep going. And every time I did.

My mind would try to reach back towards Kyra and our short time together. But it made me feel too vulnerable, too raw. He was supposed to be the one who made everything better and loved me no matter what. But what if I was unlovable after all of this? What if the person he knew before was well and fully dead, and this new version of me was someone he couldn't stomach?

Maybe that wasn't fair. We had both done things we regretted, but right now, I was going down a dark hole that left me dizzy and delirious. Who was I outside the confines of this place? What would be left of me if we did escape?

Those thoughts kept me going. I tried to outrun the answers, but I never could. They kept haunting me through every kick, squat, and punch I threw. Finally, my muscles screamed at me to stop, and I listened. With a heavy thud, my knees hit the training floor, and I sprawled out, closing my eyes. Now, I could welcome rest. I was sure of it.

"Had enough, little wraith?" Phayre purred.

I cracked open my eyes, and she was right above me.

"Get up." She sent electricity through my veins again, and I moaned, rolling over and breathing heavy.

"Get up, wraith. Otherwise, I will—" she didn't get to finish her words.

There was a loud crack and boom as the air around us shifted, and a buzzing filled the space. Phayre's attention swept around looking for the source.

The doors to the training facility blew open, and a woman I didn't recognize stepped through. There was something about her, though, that seemed familiar. Her eyes were alight with fury, and she looked from Phayre to me and back again.

"Greer?" she asked, and I nodded, my tongue not working so well after the many volts of electricity given to my veins. My immortality kept me healing constantly, but it couldn't keep up when I kept running headfirst into pain and didn't rest or eat enough.

"Verity?! How did you get out of your cage?" Phayre seethed, walking towards her.

Verity laughed maniacally.

"Oh, Phayre, I have looked forward to hurting you for a very long time." Verity's hands flew open in the blink of an eye and towards Phayre. The manacles that adorned Verity's wrist flew off and attached themselves to Phayre's skin as she screamed, falling to her knees. Phayre tried to throw her power around, but the manacles worked the same way Kyra's had. Her body convulsed, and her eyes fluttered rapidly while her power was thrown back into her own skin.

"How... how is this even possible?" Phayre gritted her teeth, and I stumbled to a standing position.

"You all forget that I am the daughter of Hyacinth in one of her truest forms. If I didn't want to be captured all this time, do you think I would have been? The spells that Riordan stole from me are laced with my own fail-safes, ones that cannot be discovered except by me. There is no magic that I cannot dissect, unfold, and reform to do my bidding, given enough time," Verity snarled, stalking over to where Phayre was spitting insults at her on the ground.

"You are coming to take the wraith? And do what with her? You have no hope of overcoming us, even with your fancy little tricks. I wasn't ready for you, Verity, but I will be, and you will wish death were an option once I am done with you!" Phayre screamed.

Verity backhanded her across the face. Phayre's lip split, and I gasped.

"Oh, I can't wait to get my hands on you!" Phayre yelled, teeth red and mouth swollen.

"Enough!" Verity placed her fingertips on Phayre's head, and she collapsed.

"You... you can overpower a goddess?" I said, words forming finally. There was no way this was real.

Verity's smile was small. "Yes, in some ways. This was a bit of planning and luck. Greer, we must go to the throne room now. The portal to your friends and out of this place's time is limited. Can you walk? Use your powers?" She offered her arm for me to grab onto, and I clung to it.

"I... I am so tired..." I whispered. Verity scanned my face.

"I know. You only have to make it a little further. These cuffs... are they power reversing or control?" Her fingertips swept over the metal, and I fluttered my eyes closed.

"Control. And pain."

"Greer, I don't have time to get them off gently. We will need to leave them behind, but I would need time to break the metal's magical binding. However, there is another way, one with more pain. Hopefully, after that, you will never see them again." Verity wrapped her hands around mine, and I looked into her eyes. They looked like Kyra's. Ones that could bring comfort and support, if I would just let her.

"Okay," I whispered, not sure what else to say.

"I am so sorry, my dear," Verity said, gripping my hands in hers. She continued to speak, but I couldn't understand her anymore. Was she speaking a different language, or had I finally lost my mind? A sound erupted around me. Like a vase shattering into a million pieces, and then the flashing heat of pain as each bone in my hand, wrist, and lower arm ruptured underneath Verity's palms.

It hit me like a freight train, moving in waves of agony rippling across my skin. With what was probably quick and efficient, but felt like years of torture, Verity slipped the metal cuffs off me, and they hit the floor with a clang.

Immediately, my body felt lighter as I stared at the things that had been my worst nightmare for so long.

"I am so sorry," Verity whispered again. She quickly grabbed some weapons and pushed me towards the exit. "Take this, at least."

She tucked a dagger into my back pocket, and I nodded numbly, still unable to move my fingertips properly. It was like I was seeing it all happen from above, not really in my body, but rather watching myself being forced to go through the motions. There were cracks and pops as my bones tried to fuse themselves together, and endless screaming. My vision dipped in and out of focus as Verity hustled us to the throne room as quickly as she could. The feeling of power continued to grow around us like a bubble ready to burst until Verity flung open the doors.

Riordan stood by the entrance with Farren by his side and Kyra restrained in front of him. Right behind them, a crack in the air was forming. It was glowing bright and beautiful; fissures of light were fracturing from the center, and I could feel the pull of the portal.

"Riordan," Verity growled.

"I knew you would try to pull something with your tricks, Verity. You are not as clever as you think." Riordan laughed. "And I have a few tricks of my own." The portal continued to groan and grow. "I promised you a monster, didn't I? One that would swallow you whole."

My mind couldn't comprehend what he was saying as several giant creatures filled the room. An oversized four-legged creature with the mane of a lion and rough leather of an elephant tromped in with tusks the length of my entire body and teeth to match. Another bug-like creature with snapping pinchers and a scaly body ending in a tail spiked and dripping with what could only be poison. The liquid dropped to the ground in a pile of steam and hissing. The last one was a hoofed creature with tall, spiraling horns poking out from its head. Leathery wings sprouted from its back, and claws meant for shredding adorned the tips. All of them were coming right for us.

There was nothing I could do. My power and body were

too tapped out to do anything. I had so foolishly run from my feelings and straight into this sad state, only to be given the opportunity to escape when I was at my weakest.

"Now, Farren!" Verity screamed, and the whole throne erupted into chaos.

NINETEEN

LUX

"Lux, get the fuck up!" Nova hissed, and I sprang up disoriented, my eyes heavy with sleep.

"What's going on?"

We had crashed after the party with plans to head to Waverly's birth island to get some damn answers. I swear to gods, my eyes were only closed for .3 seconds before Nova shook me awake.

"Hyacinth is here." Her eyes were wide, and her stars glittered. The room was still dark, and all I wanted to do was get a godsdamn night of sleep.

"Fuck her," I said grumpily and rolled over, stuffing my face into my pillow.

"Luxton Gilmore, get your ass out of this bed right now before I drag it out my fucking self."

I knew she would use her magic on me to make me get up, so I threw the covers off and stalked after her. I didn't bother to put a shirt on. Why, out of all the nights, did Hyacinth have to come in the middle of this one?

"Luxton, you look rather deliciously disheveled," Hyacinth commented as I walked into the living room, where

Waverly was already perched on the couch, and Sutton scowled. Everyone else was more decent than me, but I didn't give a fuck at this point.

"Hyacinth, what an interesting surprise to see you here in the middle of the night," I retorted, sitting next to Waverly as Nova paced the living room.

"Well, it wouldn't be my first choice to spend the middle of the night here, but alas, here we are." She smiled. It looked as if we had torn her away from a party as well. She was clad in a dark emerald pantsuit, and gold glittered along her throat and hands.

"You were interrupted?" Nova crossed her arms over her chest and tilted her head to the side as if trying to imagine what party she could have possibly been at.

"Yes, Nova. I'm an eternal goddess. As such, I do have a life to live. No matter, Verity contacted me."

Everyone's eyes whipped to her.

"She found a way to you?" I whispered.

Greer was now closer to coming home, and the realization punched me in the gut. I missed her terribly. Kyra would be with her, which sent another hit to my abdomen.

"Yes; however, we have very little time to prepare," she said, leaning into our couch.

"How little time?" I questioned.

"A few hours perhaps?" she replied, unbothered.

"A few hours?!" Sutton's ruby red mouth dropped open.

"Yes, we will need to move swiftly. In the infernal realm, it will be a full day or two for Verity, Kyra, and Greer. It also sounds as if Farren may be joining them." Her voice softened on his name, and I wanted to ask more, but there was no time.

"So, we don't have an exact time range, then?" Waverly looked ready to spring into action.

"Not exactly, but my guess is we have three to five hours," Hyacinth informed us, still in no particular hurry.

"Well, what do we need to do?" Nova said harshly.

"Tsk tsk, I want to know what you all have been up to since we last saw each other, as I am now invested in the likes of you all." She set her chin on her hand and smiled beautifully.

"Well, I received a message from the sea. From my sister, I think, but I have a feeling she will know something about Armello. We were planning on going to the island where I was born tomorrow, but considering the change of events, we may be delaying that particular trip." Waverly clenched her fists like she couldn't decide what to do with her hands.

"Ah, Evanya, is your sister correct?" Hyacinth questioned.

"Yes, do you know her?" Waverly asked, turning to her eagerly and leaning closer. Hyacinth's expressions flashed from pity to sadness to steel.

"Yes, my siren. The tragedy that happened years ago was told across our nation." She patted Waverly's hand. Waverly looked at her and opened her mouth, then closed it again like she wasn't sure what to ask next.

She finally settled on, "I don't know what happened to her."

"I believe it is her story to tell," Hyacinth replied.

Waverly nodded and hid her face, but not before a tear slid down. Families were so fucking complicated.

"We're working on a plan to get immortality for ourselves and get the serum to take it away. It seems to be the most logical decision for the battle ahead." Nova narrowed her eyes.

"A serum to take away immortality? Why am I just now hearing of this? Who invented such a thing? It cannot be possible," Hyacinth hissed, her nails digging into the chair. She looked genuinely fearful despite her obvious anger.

"My parents, the other gods hired them and killed them for it. It's dangerous, and we're trying to understand it more. We've been doing our own research into what that means for the body and the magic inside of us. But the formula disappeared, so we are working on confiscating it." I barely contained my snarl.

"Well, at least your immortality will be easy to gain," she said flippantly.

Sutton raised his brow and then narrowed his eyes. "What do you mean?"

"Greer can give it to you," she said, as if it was common fucking knowledge.

"What?" I choked out.

"Her blood grants it with consent. She can grant it to all of you. It's part of the power of time." Her body relaxed back in her chair, but her eyes were calculating.

"Well, I guess that makes this easier..." I mumbled, not really loving the idea of drinking Greer's blood but grateful that a somewhat easy solution fell into our laps.

"And that's what we have, so can we get moving on preparations for this spell or portal retrieval or whatever the hell we're calling this?" Nova's impatience formed a line on her forehead.

"Yes, yes, I have heard enough. Let's begin." Hyacinth started listing out all the ingredients we would need to create, contain, and sustain a portal and then close it. Nova raced off to her own home, where she tended to keep her special ingredients, and Waverly had a few items she had snatched from the Federation of Extraordinary Cases.

Sutton headed to Kyra's place to go get some of his things to act as a better grounding beacon, and it was my job to rifle through Greer's things to find something that we could tether her to as well.

"What about Verity and Farren?" I asked, not knowing how we would get something for either of them.

"Don't worry, shifter, I have them covered. Verity was with

me for quite some time, and Farren has always been by our sides. Go get your timewraith's things."

I nodded and went to search for something meaningful. I pulled out a photo of us from college and found that old ratty t-shirt we both got on orientation day, but only wore when we wanted to make fun of our university. It made my heart ache to think of how much we went through and how many more things were sure to come.

"I got some of Kyra's things, but I didn't know what would have been the most valuable for the portal." Sutton stood in the doorway looking down at me.

"I'm sure whatever you grabbed is fine," I replied, standing and turning to face him. His eyes traveled down my chest to my low-hanging sweatpants, and it sent heat to my groin.

"You still haven't put on a shirt?" he commented, his mouth twitching at the side.

"No, but I'll grab one, since everyone is so concerned about it." I winked as I slid past him, brushing my bare skin against him.

He followed me to my room and watched with hunger in his eyes as I pulled a fresh shirt over my head.

"Better?" I asked playfully.

"Not exactly, but it will do."

For a long moment, we just stood, staring at one another. It pebbled my skin and made the room feel thick with all the words unspoken.

"When I get immortality, Lux..." Sutton started, then stopped, closed his eyes, and licked his lips. I wanted to bite his cherry red mouth.

"Yes?" I stepped closer, into his space, and ran a hand down the smooth skin of his arms.

"This course, this burden, should be less. And then I want to tell you and show you everything I haven't been able to say."

He opened his eyes, and the dark irises were full of promises and secrets yet to be shared.

"Okay," I whispered across his skin.

I slid my hand to the back of his neck, then moved it into his hair, and tilted his head to the side. A little moan slipped from him that made my dick go hard. I licked up the column of his throat and inhaled his scent, wanting to wrap myself in it.

Sutton's hand moved down and cupped me, and my groan matched his.

"Soon." He stroked me on the outside of my sweats. I pressed into him and bit his collarbone.

"Soon," I growled in response, wanting to devour him. He broke away and looked down.

"You might want to wait a few moments for that to go away. It's obvious, if not impressive," he purred and slid out of the room.

I breathed deeply and rolled my shoulders and neck side to side. I tried to let the thoughts of Sutton naked and underneath me fade away, reminding myself of the task at hand.

Everyone was gathered in the living room by the time I had gotten myself under control. Nova and Hyacinth were setting up the space. The furniture had been moved, and candles and other items were scattered in a circle around the floor.

Nova chanted over a bowl while Hyacinth mixed something else.

"What can we do?" I asked Waverly, who had placed herself off to the side, where she could watch.

"Nothing. We were instructed to wait. You might want to get dressed for a battle. I don't think this will be pretty."

I noticed then that Waverly had changed into one of her tactical uniforms and had some weaponry strapped to her. Sutton and I nodded at one another and went to get changed.

We came back in our own gear, and I grabbed a first aid kit just in case.

Nova and Hyacinth were in constant motion, either mixing, placing things, or flipping through books. They stayed that way for about an hour as the rest of us paced and loitered around unhelpfully.

"You are so similar to her, such a talented witch." Hyacinth surveyed Nova's work.

Nova smiled and wiped sweat off her forehead. "I hope that's all we need," she said and looked at the rest of us.

"Now, we wait." Hyacinth plopped down at the dining room table since all the living room furniture had found a home elsewhere.

Four hours passed.

"If you all want to take turns catching naps, I'll take the first watch," Nova offered and gulped down some water.

It was still the middle of the night, and we were not in top physical condition for fighting.

"Fuck it. At this point, I think it will make it worse. I say we all just wait," I replied, and Nova nodded.

And we did. For another two hours, then the sun started to peak through the windows.

"Are you sure it will happen today?" Nova said, looking at Hyacinth, who had been a statue for the last several hours.

"Six hours have passed, which is a bit longer than I was anticipating... I hope nothing went wrong," she mused and looked worried for the first time.

Suddenly, the room shifted. The air turned thick and syrupy, and the temperature dropped rapidly, spiked, then dropped again.

Hyacinth's smile widened.

"Fashionably late."

The portal had started to form.

TWENTY
KYRA

"Sleep, Riordan." Farren shoved my father's heavy body away, and he hit the ground hard.

"Off." Farren flitted his fingers, and my bindings flew away from me. "We cannot kill him, Kyra, and we have limited time. We need to handle these beasts and leave. Our battle with Riordan is another day."

I flexed my fingers and stood looking at my father's body crumpled on the floor. A man who wielded his words and power like a blade every chance he got looked positively mortal without the constant sneer on his lips. He didn't look like someone who would take joy in hurting people for eternity. He looked almost like any other man. Too bad the truth was even worse than what most people could imagine.

"A little help here!" Verity screamed as Greer swayed on her feet.

She looked unwell. Her face was pale, and sweat clung to her body. It had been hours since I had last seen her. After she had asked me to leave, even though it felt like we had reconnected, she couldn't even look me in the eyes when I exited the room. Her body had been abused before, and she had shunned my concern. But now, even though she appeared to be healing better without the cuffs, her steps were wobbly and her gaze unfocused.

The feral bloodthirsty beasts were closing in on them. The portal yawned open a little wider.

"Don't let them go through!" Verity yelled as she slashed out against the winged creature. She landed a slice of magic against its abdomen, and it reared up, charging towards where Greer was blinking unsteadily. It's gaze an endless pool of black zeroed in on her.

"Greer!" I shouted.

Her eyes widened, and she shook her head. At the last second, Farren winked right next to her and pulled her out of its path. The other two creatures surrounded my mother. I desperately wanted to pull Greer into my arms, but they needed my help.

I crafted fireballs and sent them careening towards the animals. They exploded on contact, but nothing happened. The flames danced across their forms as if absorbed.

"Your fire won't work against them! It stems from Riordan, so they are immune." Farren yelled from where he was facing off against the claws and hooves of the winged beast. It lowered its horns and charged, ready to impale Farren if he hadn't leaped out of the way.

The tusked animal lumbered towards me, shaking its head and stomping its foot as if it would love nothing more than to crush me under its hulking weight. My mother was cornered by the one with pinchers; it not only had venom coming out of its tail, but it would spew streams of the bright green fluid out in bursts if anything got too close.

"Fuck!" I bellowed. I called upon my explosive power, pulling it from the depths of my chest and shoved it out to detonate a small, controlled charge underneath its feet, sending it flying towards the wall.

"Kyra!" My mother tossed me a sword, and I caught it, squaring up against this creature. How was it that a sword could cause damage, but my fire wouldn't?

"The soft underbelly is where you need to stab it. Otherwise, it won't die," Farren called out from the other side.

Greer was clinging to the wall limply, looking as if her heart might stop beating at any moment.

"What's wrong with Greer?" I asked my mother as we slowly turned back-to-back, keeping the creatures in front of us.

"Her heart has taken so much damage. She was training to exhaustion. Now that the cuffs are gone, her body can heal faster, but that doesn't mean her soul will. That's something her magic can't touch." Verity's eyes glistened as she looked at the shell of a person that was left of Greer. My once vibrant, headstrong girl was now carved and cut up into pieces because of this wretched place. I wouldn't allow any more of her to be strewn about these desolate halls. This ended now. These beasts could tear me to shreds if only Greer could have another chance to find herself again.

When we made love, she was coming back to who she was. Her fire was coming alive again. But it had only been a moment. One we had both indulged in and one that I hadn't realized cost her more than she had let on.

"Focus, Kyra. We have to get out of here, quickly. Others will surely come!" Verity leaped towards her monster and slashed out with her sword. We were all managing well enough with our monsters, except for Greer. She had slumped to the floor behind Farren. At least she was out of the way.

The massive creature before me huffed and stood ready to charge me again. I stood my ground, ready for it. With a roar, it stomped towards me, its huge feet slamming against the ground, and I waited as long as I could, until I could smell its rancid breath, and then I slid underneath it and stabbed upwards. Thick, dark red liquid rained down on me, and the creature bellowed. It staggered forward several steps before it crashed down to the ground, my sword still embedded in its thick underbelly.

Wiping my face free of the creature's blood, I ran towards Greer, where she huddled in the corner.

"Can I touch you? I need to get you out of here," I said gently as her gaze hung on the fallen creature.

"Okay."

I scooped her up in my arms. The portal was nearly the size of five grown adults, now crackling and sparking with energy.

"Mom! Farren!" I shouted as they continued to battle the creatures before them. Farren had suffered several slices to his arms, but he was holding his own. I turned to look at my mom and nearly caught the huge scorpion's stinger in my chest. I fell back with Greer still cradled in my arms, and she moaned out in pain.

"Did it get you?!" I scanned her looking for blood, and she shook her head.

"Run to the portal! I'm right behind you." Verity yelled, launching herself onto the creature's back and stabbing into its skull. It screamed and flailed about, trying to throw her off and catch her with its pinchers.

"That's my girl!" Farren cheered as he pulled his knife from his beast's lifeless body.

"Go! The portal is shrinking," Verity's eyes widened in horror. I followed her gaze, and my heart sank. The portal was now pulsing and closing.

Verity's beast finally fell, and she wasted no time leaping off its back as the throne room doors flew up. Phayre's angry screams ricocheted off the hall.

"Don't let them get away!" she screeched, and we ran for it.

Bursts of magic and life crackled around us, and Greer's body clung to mine like it was the only thing keeping her from floating away. The portal was on the other side of the massive throne room, and there was debris everywhere.

Farren and Verity were at the back, warding off attacks as I cleared a path forward, hoping to gods we'd make it, because there would be no mercy after this. I took one last look at my dad's form. He was starting to rouse, his eyes squeezing, and his fingertips moving.

"Hurry!" Verity panted as we sprinted across the room.

I threw Greer through. She disappeared in a wink, and I reached back and grabbed my mother's hand, flinging her forward and then shoving Farren ahead of me.

"You won't come back from this," Phayre hissed, too far away to do anything about it as I jumped through the portal behind Farren.

We had finally escaped. But at what cost?

TWENTY-ONE
GREER

"Fuck." Everything hurt, and I felt useless. The monsters in the throne room nearly took us out, and all I could do was fall apart in the corner.

I counted to ten and opened my eyes, letting my heart swell and feel full for the first time in months. Lux, Nova, Waverly, and Sutton stood staring at our little band, as well as a woman who looked larger than life.

I almost stopped believing this was possible. I was starting to lose hope, but my friends proved me wrong. Finally, a little ray of sunshine in what had been the most hellacious time of my life.

"Lux," I whispered, looking at him, tears welling in my eyes. That was all the permission he needed. He scooped me up in his arms and hugged the living crap out of me.

"Godsdamnit, it's good to see you." Lux squeezed me hard, and I was too tired to care that it hurt, but the good kind. The kind that felt like love in the best way. He then held me at arm's length. "Are you okay?"

"Um..." There was no way to answer that right now.

"Stupid question. I know you've been through hell. Literally. But I'm glad to see you in one piece and of some sound mind." He snickered, and I couldn't help but laugh, too. Was I of sound mind? I didn't know anymore. But gods, it felt good to see my beautiful best friend again.

"Move out of the way, Lux." Nova shoved him off and grabbed me. Waverly slathered herself up against us in a three-woman hug.

"I love you all so much," I said in a muffled voice against Nova's skin.

"We do, too, and we have so much to tell you," Waverly said, her pink eyes watery.

"She needs some healing, even though she may not say so," Verity said, eyeing my hands suspiciously. The bones had reset themselves, but the soft tissues were screaming, even if they looked semi-normal right now.

"Let me grab you something," Nova replied, running off to grab one of her concoctions to speed the process up and dilute the pain.

I looked over to where Kyra and Lux were embracing. Sutton was smiling off to the side. He was not the touchy-feely type, but I could sense his relief in the way his shoulder drifted down with every passing moment.

"Hyacinth," Verity whispered and embraced the woman I didn't know. It was easy to put together that we were in the presence of the goddess of magic herself. Farren brushed off his pants and looked around at all of us. His slashes from the beast already fading to pink scars.

"Now this is an interesting lot indeed." He stood, locking eyes with Hyacinth.

Tension crackled in the air that I couldn't quite place, and they walked slowly to one another. Farren touched Hyacinth's cheek, and she leaned into his touch.

"Hi, my love," Farren whispered, pain in his voice.

"Hello," she said, and I felt like I was intruding. We all

looked at one another, clearly sharing the feeling of missing a key piece of information.

"I didn't know if you would still care for me," Hyacinth said quietly.

"I never stopped. I played the game to protect our girl, but I never stopped thinking about you." The two of them embraced in a way that only long-lost lovers can.

"Why don't we all take a moment to collect ourselves. We'll clean out the space and resemble the living room while you all get cleaned up or grab some food. Your favorites are in the fridge, G," Lux said, and I nodded, tears spilling down my cheeks once more.

It was like I had never left. Maybe that meant the last few months could be a horrible, distant memory.

"Take this, and let me know if there's something else you need, okay?" Nova came up to me with a glass of bright orange liquid, and I slung it back in one go.

"Thank you," I whispered, avoiding her watchful gaze. There would be a day to share everything, but today wasn't it. Everything was too fresh. Moments ago, I thought I would be damned to hell for my entire existence. I needed some time to reconcile my reality with what it could be now.

"Greer." Kyra held out his hand, and I took it tentatively as he led me to my bathroom. "I'll go grab some clothes for you."

He shut the door behind him. We needed to talk as well, but every part of me was weary. The kind that made you feel like your limbs were full of metal and your heart was a heavy stone.

I sighed and looked into the mirror. There was something different on my skin, in my eyes, behind the bruising and battle wounds of what hell did to me. I didn't know how I felt about it. This *difference*. So much had changed so rapidly, I hardly recognized what I had become. Who the fuck was I?

The badass who completed the trials felt like someone else. The woman in front of me looked even more broken than I had been before.

Nova's potion was already working wonders, dulling the aches and abrasions, and my hands were starting to feel normal again. On the outside, technically, I was a whole person. But what about the mess inside of me? I didn't want to think about it.

We needed to keep our focus ahead. But how could I do that with so much of my past weighing me down?

Kyra returned and handed me a pair of leggings and an oversized sweatshirt with some fuzzy socks. My heart clenched.

"Thanks."

He smiled softly and left. And I just let him go, unable to sort through the mess in my head to find the right words to ask him to stay. To ask him to hold me together.

I needed a minute to breathe. There were so many pieces at play. So many I didn't even know existed until such a short while ago. Now, I needed to be the woman who had her shit together to face off against the evils of the world, even though I was cowering in a throne room less than an hour ago.

"Okay, Greer, you can do this." I painted on a face of bravery and strutted back to the living room. Two original immortals were draped across my couch while my best friends bustled around and Kyra's mom paced about. Gods, what a sight this was.

"The timewraith I have heard so much about." Hyacinth was the first to recognize my presence.

"Yes." I sat between Lux and Kyra.

"Well, what should we start with this evening? My time is limited, and Farren and I have somewhere else to be," she said, gripping his hand and pulling him into her lap. They giggled, and Verity beamed at them. It was sickeningly adorable.

"Shall we start with the immortality spell?" Verity suggested.

"What?" Kyra said.

"Greer will give immortality to all those here; it will only help you all along against the fight to come," she said, as if it were obvious. "You all are not immortal, yes? I believe Hyacinth said we would need to be prepared to help you all and Greer."

My face went blank as I thought about my friends becoming immortal.

"Right now?" I asked, my voice quivering as I cleared my throat. Everything inside me was exhausted. Could I dredge up the energy to do this now? It didn't seem like I had much of a choice.

"Yes, the sooner the better," she said.

Kyra scowled next to me. "What does this spell need?"

"My blood." Xael had told me it needed to be freely given. I just didn't know how much was needed and what the toll would be on me, or everyone else, for that matter. But in this, I could be useful. This I could do without having to bare too much of my shattered self.

"Gods, seriously?" Kyra exclaimed.

"We don't have to do this now," Lux said.

"I think we do, unfortunately. Are you up for this, Greer?" Nova questioned, and I nodded. What was a little blood between friends?

"Who wants to go first?" I asked, sitting up taller.

"I'll do it. In case something goes wrong, I don't mind being the guinea pig," Sutton said, and Lux looked like he wanted to argue, but kept his mouth shut.

"Well, let's begin," Hyacinth said as Farren hopped off her lap.

Hyacinth and Verity came together and reached out their hands to Nova.

"Hi, Nova, I'm Verity. Kyra's mother."

"A powerful witch, too, if I am not mistaken?" Nova responded by taking both of their hands.

"She is the best of us," Hyacinth said with motherly adoration shining in her eyes.

"I will share knowledge between the three of us so we may help prepare Greer."

Nova nodded, and they all closed their eyes as they linked together. I desperately wished Xael were here to hold my hand. To help me the way that Hyacinth helped her magical children.

"Okay, so the preparation is more for those who receive, since Greer will be donating the blood?" Nova pursed her lips.

"That is correct," Hyacinth responded.

"Well, Sutton, we're going to give you a healing, strength, and vitality potion before you take Greer's blood to help facilitate the transition," Nova said.

"If you'd like to say Xael's sacred oath, then you can, Greer, or you can make your own." Verity laid a hand on my arm.

"Let's do Xael's." I didn't know what I would say as I gave the power of time to someone. This felt like the job of the original time goddess, not her wraith. And definitely not the Greer Roberts who was here today.

"I'll write it down and you can read it." She squeezed my arm, and Lux ran off to grab some paper.

"Are you feeling okay about this?" Kyra whispered behind me, his hand landing gently on my low back. His touch was warm and comforting. I didn't deserve it after kicking him out of my room with no explanation, but he leaned in close, and I closed my eyes and took a moment to just breathe him in.

"What could go wrong?" I said jokingly, but it fell flat. Everything could go wrong; we all knew that to be a possibility.

"The chances of magical beings not surviving the transition are very low. You were the real gamble as a mortal, but Xael's power was already cemented in you and just needed the right key," Farren winked at me. His gaze tracked Hyacinth's every move.

"Right." I nodded.

"Okay, I made four batches of this beefed-up healing potion." Nova stood in front of me with a small tray of what looked like shot glasses. The liquid in them was a darker orange than what she had given me earlier.

"Bottoms up, everyone." She toasted and slammed hers down. Sutton, Waverly, and Lux did the same, wincing at the taste a little.

"The oath." Verity presented me with a piece of paper.

"I consent to give the gift of immortality to those brave enough to weather the obstacles of time and strong enough to use it for good. If you agree to renounce the selfishness that can plague us as years pass by, I…"

The script said "the goddess of time," and I could suddenly feel the weight of this promise looming over me. I didn't know what tomorrow would hold, but I supposed I could do this now. Give this protection to those I love. Perhaps I didn't need to take on everything at once. This could be enough for today, and when the time came, I could decide what type of goddess I was meant to be. It wouldn't be the same as Xael, but it would be something. It's all I had right now, and damnit, it would have to be enough.

"I, the timewraith, bestow this gift and curse unto you. Be wise and gentle through your many years."

I nodded and swallowed, the words heavy in the air and on my shoulders.

"How much blood will be needed?" Kyra said.

"About two ounces," Hyacinth informed us, snapping her

fingers. An odd-looking machine appeared in front of us. It was clearly designed for extracting blood.

"This looks very medical." I eyed the contraption and tried not to wince as she grabbed my arm and tied a rubber band around it.

"Well, did you think I would just slice you open and let you drain while they lapped it up from you?" Hyacinth said incredulously while getting a bag and needle ready.

"Honestly, yes. Yes, I did." I answered, marveling at how this all was so odd. Yesterday, a goddess was beating me senseless, and now another was gently relieving me of my blood.

"We're a bit more civilized than that now. Xael did have a special dagger she used when she wanted to share her blood, but we will keep this clean and tidy."

A small prick hit the inside of my arm, and I sat still while the bag filled. I looked away, unable to watch it settle in the plastic. No one said anything as the gift of my blood kept giving until Hyacinth pulled the needle out.

"Okay, she's ready." She steadily poured the blood into four small cups while Verity bandaged my arm. I knew it would heal quickly, just a small prick among the many other things my body was working to fix.

"Sutton?" Lux looked at him longingly. Sutton had steel in his eyes, and shadows danced around him.

"Let's do this." He took the small cup and threw the liquid back, wiping his already red mouth off as I chanted the sacred oath.

His shadows pulsed around him, and the air hissed. Shadows tornadoed around the room and blurred everyone out of focus, as if they were at war with one another. Sutton roared, hunching over the ground. Lux stood still in horror as Sutton growled and grimaced through the swirling gray mass around him.

"It will be over soon," Hyacinth whispered, watching carefully.

The swirling slowed, and Sutton's panting breaths could be heard over the hissing; then, all at once, it was still as if his powers and body had settled. No one said anything for a few moments, all eyes on Sutton as the shadows shrank away and the room returned to normal. His eyes were fluttered shut, the rise and fall of his chest seemingly steady.

"How are you feeling?" Verity walked to him, and his eyes flashed open, peeking at Lux before they landed on Verity. She scanned his face, her brows furrowed.

"Different," was all he said before he sat, avoiding everyone's eye contact. It wasn't the answer or reaction I was expecting. My attention volleyed around the room trying to gauge what everyone else was feeling, but no one else said a word. The tension in the room was thick until Verity broke the spell.

"You feel immortal," she explained. "So, one down, three to go."

"I'll go next." Nova took the liquid down in one pull. Her stars started to shine and spin as my mouth moved through the words a second time. Her hands balled into fists, and blood leaked out of her eyes, mouth, and ears. My stomach dipped at the sight, but Verity's gentle voice in my ear assured me it would be fine. Nova's stars swirled and swirled across her skin until a flash disoriented us all. Nova roared.

The light settled as quickly. It had not taken nearly as long as Sutton's episode, but it had been equally as terrifying.

Verity strolled over quietly and wiped the blood off her skin.

"Happened to me, too; a bloody mess," she mumbled.

Waverly stepped up next. "Let's fucking do this."

She grabbed her cup and slung it back as I chanted for the third time. The sound of the ocean's roar filled the room as her hair flew around her. She opened her mouth to a guttural scream that pierced our ears and made our eyes water. The transformation levitated her, suspending her above us while a pink glow emanated from her. Then the whooshing, screaming, and roaring stopped. She collapsed on the ground.

"Waverly!" Nova rushed forward, but she sat up quickly.

"Gods, that hurt like a bitch," she said, and everyone chuckled. It was like a bubble of tension had burst in the room, and we could all finally have a moment of relief.

I was so tired of all the pain and wished I could spare everyone I loved from even an ounce of it.

"It really does." Nova smiled at her and helped her up.

"Everyone's blood feels immortal except you, Luxton." Hyacinth looked at Lux expectantly.

This one was harder. Lux didn't really *want* to have immortality, but it was the best way we could protect ourselves from what was to come.

"On the bright side, we also have a way to undo it. Kind of..." I knew it wasn't comforting at all. It would basically kill us, but to be honest, that wasn't an unwelcome thought. In fact, it was rather comforting.

"Well, I can't have all you assholes live forever without me, so here goes nothing." He drank it down, his eyes never leaving mine. The words of the chant rolled off my lips, and when the concoction was gone, his gaze flickered to Sutton. So fast that if I wasn't paying attention, I would have missed it.

Lux's skin started to ripple and peel and pull open. Talons punched through, his teeth grew, as he morphed into every animal on the planet at once, painfully, and aggressively. He yelled, squirmed, and thrashed as the magic and immortality coursed through his body.

"Godsdamnit." He breathed heavily while his body settled into his normal form and collapsed on the couch. I rushed over and looked into those golden eyes I knew so well.

"You, okay?" I said, and he nodded.

"Well," Hyacinth said in the aftermath of this final transformation. "If you don't mind, we're leaving for a while." She tucked Farren in close.

"You know how to reach us." Verity nodded to Kyra and Nova and, in an instant, they were gone, probably off to the Eastern Hemisphere. I stood in awe of what had all just happened here. How could any of this even be real?

"I think we need a drink," Kyra said.

"I second that." Lux stood.

"Pizza, too?" I asked hopefully.

"And chocolate," Nova added.

"Don't look at me, I don't have any requests." Waverly held up her hands.

"Sutton?" Kyra said, looking at the necromancer.

The corners of his mouth tipped up. "All that sounds great."

"At some point, we should share our stories, but I need some rest first... And so do all of you." I blinked at the sunlight filtering in through the window, surprised it was morning. "You all were up all night, weren't you?"

"Yup, so pizza, drinks, and chocolate are great for breakfast, and then we can all sleep for hours. Then we'll talk. I just drank your blood and would love to get that taste out of my mouth as soon as possible." Lux hugged me as he walked by into our kitchen, and gods, it felt good to be here with my best friend again.

"What did it taste like?" Suddenly, I was a bit curious.

"Like blood," Sutton teased, humor evident in his tone over his answer.

I burst out laughing, and my giggles turned a little delirious as the weight of fatigue, hunger, and everything we'd endured began to seep out. There was so much to do, and where did we even start?

"Come on, food and drinks now, then sleep, then we figure out what the hell is going on in the world." Kyra sighed, eyeing me from head to toe.

"I would just like to say that this is truly the most abnormal day I have ever had, and I've lived longer than all of you," Nova mused.

"No more unusual things today. Save something for tomorrow," Waverly added.

Who knew what tomorrow would bring? It sure as hell couldn't be anything good. But right now, at least I could rest knowing that hell wouldn't greet me when I woke.

TWENTY-TWO
KYRA

I watched Greer's form sleeping next to me. She looked peaceful. This was the first night we had gotten to sleep together in what felt like months. I was still unsure of how long the afterworld had held us hostages. It felt like all the time in the world and yet no time at all. She had almost immediately collapsed after we had all eaten, drank, and joked.

But she was putting on a front. Her smile didn't reach her eyes, and she would absently rub her skin or flinch when someone moved a certain way. We hadn't talked about our last few moments in that wretched place, and we certainly hadn't talked about everything else.

It was as if, for the moment, we were playing pretend. A game where we could be happy without the heaviness of what hell had done.

Greer's form beside me helped ground me. I was still trying to wrap my head around all the politics of what was going on and what the original twelve would do to win. Farren had surprised me, but his intentions aligned with ours. Clearly, his love for Hyacinth was there. I was sure they had run off to bang each other for days after so much time apart.

My mother had promised she would come back and speak with us more after she had seen what used to be her home. We had all been displaced for what felt like eternity.

Greer mumbled in her sleep and scowled, pursing her lips. I gently brushed my fingertips across the wrinkles of her forehead and her plush lips.

It felt good to simply be with her again. Things felt like they could go back to whatever version of normal we had before. I was grateful to see everyone here unharmed, but I was worried about what all of us had been through to get here. Perhaps we all just needed a little time before we could share what we had found out.

Something had happened to Greer right before she came to the throne room. I just didn't know what. It haunted her in those last few moments, and she was held captive by it.

My skin felt too tight, my muscles restless. I planted a light kiss on Greer's temple and slipped out of her room to go sit on the terrace and watch the sun for a while.

"Couldn't sleep?" Lux said as I settled down next to him.

"Nah. I haven't seen the sun, or outside, in... Well, I don't know how long, but it feels like months." I let the sun warm my skin and breathed deeper than I had in a long time.

"Hyacinth mentioned time moved differently down there," Lux commented.

"How long has it been up here?" I wanted to know what the difference was.

"About two weeks."

I nodded. It was likely close to two months down there, then.

"I was worried about what state you and Greer would be in. Together, and separately, but it seems you all were able to mostly figure it out. I know she must have been hurt." Lux's gold eyes shone. He knew she would have been devastated when she found out my truth, and that felt like only one of so many sins I had committed against her.

"She was, she had every right to be, and my asshole father lifted the curse pretty much as soon as I got there, which made it even more suspicious, you know. So, it took a while. Things happened that I don't even know about; she endured so much. But we made it," I admitted.

"I'm glad we're at least back together." Lux smiled.

"How are you feeling about the immortality?"

"I don't feel much different, but it hasn't really hit me yet. My parents always wanted this; it was an act of rebellion to not want it. And here I am," he replied. "I'm still figuring out the alternative formula for it that won't lead to imminent death, but I'm hopeful I will crack the code soon."

I laughed, because only Lux would call it that.

"We have a lot to figure out," I commented.

"Yeah. We do," he replied.

We sat in silence for a while, so much unspoken between us for the time that had passed. It wasn't uncomfortable, but rather a breath before all hell would break loose. Farren's allegiance shift had been a surprise, and it might just be what we needed to stand against the others in the afterworld. But I wasn't so sure.

We had no idea how the others on earth would swing. They had chosen the mortal realm years ago, but it didn't mean that they would choose it again. Hyacinth had created her own community here, but I didn't know about the others. They could have isolated themselves for all those years, for all we knew.

"Ky," Lux said, and I jerked awake. I must have dozed off at some point. I looked inside and everyone was in the living room, just like before. It was an unnerving sight. So much had passed since we had all been together last. My heart clenched, thinking of how much Greer had been through in the after-world, and how much was still ahead.

"Fuck... well, here we go." I pulled myself out of the chair and left the sunshine behind to follow Lux.

"So where shall we start?" Greer was already snuggled into the couch. I sat beside her and felt unsure of what to do. I didn't want to act like everything was totally back to normal when I knew it wasn't. She took the guessing game out of it and wrapped her fingers around mine. I sent heat through her palm, and she gave me a small smile in return.

"Tell us what happened when you disappeared. Start there," Waverly instructed, and Greer obliged.

She recounted how her power was released. Her dreams with Xael. She skimmed over what I knew to be painful parts and left out what I was sure was much of her own time with Phayre. It was her story to tell, not mine, so I didn't comment. But I did add little tidbits about my dad, my mom, the outside of the afterworld, the court, and any other blanks I could fill in for our team. I left out details of my own pain, too.

It was something we would both need to confront eventually, but right now, it could wait.

They sat silently, waiting for us to finish. Greer's grip on me turned tight when she talked of the physical and emotional pain of the power transformation. There were a few tears shed around the room, but mostly just silence.

"Well, Phayre sounds like a cunt," Nova said when we were finished.

"She really is." Greer leaned heavily into me now. They barely even knew the half of it.

"Now it's your turn," she said, and they began.

It had only been two weeks for them, and in the outside world, everything was fine. We supposedly were taking time away from the trial shenanigans. They told us of how Waverly had been contacted, Hyacinth's arrival, as well as a vague statement from Sutton about the things he had discovered. Lux added that he was working on finding the anti-immortality formula.

"Well, this is a lot," I mumbled.

"Yeah, you could say so," Lux commented, furrowing his brow.

"So, it sounds like the next step is to figure out your family, Waverly, and see if we can actually get into contact with Armello?" Greer bit her lip.

"Yeah, we can go tomorrow and see what Evanya has to say," Waverly said, her eyes clouding.

"We should make a public appearance, too, as a sign of resistance to my father and the President. It should be calculated and planned, though," I said, thinking of what would be most advantageous to our group.

"Then we will need to find the others on Earth. We'll have to go to the Eastern Hemisphere and, realistically, probably split up again. Briar, Raelyn, and Damari still need to be contacted. And I would like to see Xael's body." Greer added the last sentence quietly.

"I can get us into contact with Raelyn, but she probably won't be happy to see me." Sutton cringed, and I looked at him quizzically. He was still the most mysterious. I didn't quite know what his burden was, what his curse had done to him and his family, but Raelyn appeared to be at the heart of it.

"Raelyn can connect us with Briar, then, since they are siblings, which just leaves Damari." Lux's gaze lingered on Sutton, almost pleading for him to spare him a look, but he blatantly refused.

"Maybe Farren and Hyacinth will have some ideas. I only know what Xael told me. That we would have to prove ourselves for her help. The best chance we have is to stack our odds against them. Right now, they are down an original immortal, but I bet it means that they will be out there hunting to recruit. We know, at least, that Hyacinth and Farren won't take their side. And I'm obviously not on their side either, but the others are still out there, so we should act quickly." Greer squinted her eyes like she was figuring out a puzzle piece in her head.

"We'll definitely need to split up then to cover the most ground," Waverly said.

"What if I go with you tomorrow, Waverly, and see if I can help you with your sister. And, if Armello is there, maybe he will be more understanding since he and Xael were close?" Greer said hopefully.

"Sutton and I can work on Raelyn," Lux said, and I raised an eyebrow at that.

"That leaves Nova and me to work on Hyacinth and Farren. But my mother will be there as well, and maybe she will have some insight into Damari." For some reason, I had the utmost faith that my mother could do anything. She had defied so many odds already and, like Greer, she still stood her ground.

"Okay, so it seems like we kind of have a plan?" Greer continued to gnaw on her lip.

"This is so fucking messy because of my damn father," I growled, feeling hot rage course through my veins.

"Yeah, well, parents suck," Lux commented.

"Today, let's take a breather, and tomorrow we'll go on our day adventure and report back?" Greer said. Her eyes looked like they were pleading for a moment to forget everything around us.

"Deal," Nova said. "I need to collect some supplies, and I think we all need to sit with this immortality a little longer."

"I need to get out of here for a little bit, Lux. Want to take a walk with me?" Greer looked at him, and Lux smiled.

"Yeah, G, let's take a walk."

Greer got up and left with Lux.

"You're lucky she forgave you," Nova hummed beside me.

"I know." Did she, though? Because things were not the same between us, and it was mostly my fault.

"Don't do it again, you asshole." Waverly threw a light punch at my shoulder as she walked by.

My mouth dropped open, "It wasn't like I had a choice. Sutton, you know how curses work to hold you hostage, don't you? Back me up on this."

Sutton's gaze was deadpan. "No, I think I'll let you drown in this one." His dark eyes glittered and swirled.

I laughed hard for the first time in months.

"Fuck you guys." But godsdamn, it was good to be back and out of hell.

Twenty-Three

Lux

"What's the deal with Sutton?" Greer asked when we were barely two steps away from our building.

"Gods, what happened to 'how are you?'" I laughed, and it felt good to just be in the same space as my best friend again.

"Fine, how are you?" she started again, her green eyes sparkling, but she was hiding things from me. I could always tell. Her shoulders were stiff and her smile a little forced.

"Better, now that you and Ky are both earthbound."

I squeezed her arm a little harder where we were looped together as we strolled the city streets of Odessa. The hum of the metropolitan and gasoline in the air felt very normal considering all that was happening unbeknownst to those around us.

"Okay, and?" she questioned as we continued our walk through the tall buildings toward our favorite park.

"And, I don't know. It's complicated. He has some baggage, obviously, and a curse himself. He did say he was hoping that turning immortal might release some of the chains on him that this curse had, but it's generational. And deals with Raelyn, so I'm thinking that whenever we deal with her, it won't be good." I didn't exactly know what plagued Sutton, but it was something about being untouchable and isolated; whether it was a literal meaning or just a metaphor was still unknown to me. The more knowledge I acquired about magic, the less I actually knew. It was like its own living and breathing entity. The wielder could only control so much.

"So, nothing has happened?" She winked at me, her dark red hair whipping around as a breeze picked up.

"No, I mean, we've had some moments of intimacy. A heat-laden kiss, some touches, smoldering glances, but nothing too juicy, you know." It sounded like I was in a PG-13 film, not an adult relationship. Gods, I wished it were more, but I would settle for anything I could get with Sutton.

She hummed at that, clearly displeased with that answer. "Well, we all know how curses can affect your relationship," she grumbled, her frown very dramatic. Ah, now we could actually get somewhere.

"Okay, but Ky didn't have a choice. Not that it invalidates your feelings, but it seems like you two are less volatile than I expected. We all have fucked up families, you know."

She shrugged as we sat on a bench and watched as people walked by. "I know, and we did sort of make-up, at least with our bodies." Her mouth twitched up in a smirk. "But it still hurts, nonetheless. We need to have a lengthier conversation, but I don't have it in me right now. I want to enjoy being here for one second without clouding this time with all the bull-shit." She bit her lip and curled in on herself. "Phayre was a nightmare come to life."

I wrapped my arm around her and placed a kiss on her temple.

"I'm sorry for everything that happened to you, Greer. I'm here for whatever you need."

"I just feel like we're at the beginning of this chaos and trying to stop it before it erupts, but nobody fucking knows what's going to happen. They want to destroy and pillage what has been built here. They were playing with corpses for god's sake for entertainment down there." She swiped a tear from her eye, and I didn't know what else to do but hold her close.

"They're power hungry and fucking ruthless. It makes me want to vomit and crawl into a hole and then forget this all happened. The fighter in me is so lost," her voice broke, and she choked back tears. "I don't even know what version of me was able to get through the trials, because right now, I am just so done." Her eyes closed briefly, and she let out a sigh.

"Greer, you don't have to do this alone. I know, it's strange that everything out here is normal while the world is on the precipice of something truly unfathomable. You took the brunt of that for months, let yourself have a moment to heal, to simply exist," I whispered. Her time there was unfair and cruel, and gods, I wished I could take the pain away.

Greer said nothing for quite some time and then changed the subject. "I wonder what the Eastern Hemisphere is like."

"Well, I imagine if Hyacinth is running things over there, then it must be okay. Probably similar to what we have going on here, but less gross?" I suggested hopefully.

"We'll all be taking a field trip there soon, I assume, but what we will find there is yet to be seen. Even Kyra had limited exposure to what it had to offer since his adoptive parents lived in such a rural area. They wanted to shy away from the spotlight, and here he goes shoving himself right into it," Greer said, picking at her fingernails.

"They've been talking about the next set of trials." I didn't know how the subject change would land, but I thought she would want to know.

"I figured they would. We need a way to stop it before it

happens. Those blood contracts cannot be signed. I need a plan for that, too. The gods just want them for fun now. A giant contraption of entertainment, as if people's lives weren't more than a few minutes of fame." Her lips curled up in disgust, and her fists balled up. There was a little bit of that fight that she was missing.

"Just add it to our ever-expanding, impossible to-do list."

"Yeah."

I sighed and tried to think of a bright side, besides the fact that we would all be together and then splitting up again soon. I didn't know what any of us would face when we met with these original twelve. So far, it was fifty-fifty of being great and being an absolute disaster.

"I don't know what I'm doing, Lux. How the hell do we stop the big bad six... well, five now, I guess. When we barely knew they existed until a few months ago? I was being picked apart daily, and I can't... I can't do that again. How are we supposed to do this?" She asked, and I didn't have an answer.

"I don't know, Greer. We'll figure it out. I wish it didn't fall on our shoulders, but here we are nonetheless." I wrapped an arm around her and pulled her in tight.

"It feels like it landed on my shoulders, and you all got sucked into the hellish vortex that is my life." Her voice trembled, and more tears started to fall down her cheeks.

"Either way, we're all committed to this and committed to you. Hell, we drank your blood. We might as well fight the whole godsdamn world for the people we love." I tightened my hold on her as she wiped her tears with her hand.

"On the bright side, I do have cool powers," she giggled.

"Yeah, like really cool ones, you'll have to show me all of that soon, G. I know it's got to be absolutely badass."

I grinned widely, just picturing Greer raining hell on all of them like she did in the trials. She would find her way back to herself. It might seem impossible now, but Greer was a fighter.

Even if she didn't believe in herself right now, we would remind her who she was.

"We should go back." She stood and held out her hands to me.

"If you say so." I wrapped my fingers around hers and pulled her in for another tight squeeze.

"Either way, we'll do this together. Our little two-pack has expanded threefold, and now, we're practically a full volleyball team," I teased. She chuckled, and we walked arm in arm back to our place.

The city pulsed around us, and we took our time going back to the apartment where more planning and plotting would take place. The mortal realm was undisturbed as of now, but it wouldn't stay that way for long, considering Greer's powers were fully awakened and the players were now getting ready after years of waiting.

The world was a powder keg, and we were going to do our best to nix the fuse before it was lit.

When we arrived back at the apartment, everyone worked on their own things. Greer went and joined Kyra as he poured over his computer and phone. He had brought over things to set up camp here as our headquarters. Nova was combing through her spell books, and Waverly was on the phone.

I spotted Sutton on the terrace and headed towards him. He was so beautiful it almost hurt. His pale skin was in such contrast to his dark eyes, ruby-red lips, and strawberry-blonde hair. The shadows around him would ebb and flow, like smoke staying close to a burning fire.

His lithe body floated as he moved with the grace of a dancer. I desperately wanted to clash my sharp edges with his and see what would happen. My stomach always fluttered with him, wondering what secrets he held on to and what was the special key to get them out in the open.

"Hey." I walked over and stared out at the city with him, my fingertips brushing his.

"Hi." His dark eyes swept to mine, and his lips curled slightly. The only hint that he was excited to see me.

"How are you feeling?" I turned to face him completely and stroked my thumb along his hand.

"Different." His gaze was glued to where my thumb made small circles on his skin. An image of all his skin on display flashed through my mind, and I shut it down quickly with a swallow.

"Different how?"

"Like the curse inside me won't shatter my bones the way it once could. I mean, it still could, but it won't kill me, so there's that," he said casually, like he wasn't just talking about his own mortality.

"Do you want to talk about it?" I stopped moving my thumb and fully placed my hand on his, gently prying his fingertips away from the rail and interlocking them with mine.

"I do, but not yet. I need to see Raelyn first." His eyes softened, and there was sadness in his voice, but also something that sounded a little like hope. "And you?"

"Me what?"

"How do you feel?"

"I think I'm at peace that this decision was mine and not my parents. It just so happens our interests aligned in the end, but it wasn't for them. It was for me, for you all, for the mortal realm, really." I wondered how much more we would have to sacrifice for this fight we never asked for. Greer and Kyra had already been faced with so much, and this was just the beginning.

"A fight so large the rest of the world may never know it even existed in the first place." He pursed his red lips and scowled.

"I don't even know what we're up against, exactly. What

does a war with the original immortals even look like now? Years ago, it was a bloodbath, but what does a modern-day world explosion look like? I can't even fucking fathom it." I ground my teeth together and gripped Sutton's hand tighter.

"Well, we're about to find out, I suppose." He lifted his lips to my knuckles and kissed lightly, sending little shock waves through my body. I wanted to shiver and purr from his soft mouth, but I refrained.

"Sutton." My voice came out breathy.

"Lux." He stepped into me and slid his hands around my neck. He smelled like cinnamon and something sinful.

I wrapped my arms around his waist and pressed our bodies together. His dark eyes simmered, and I tightened my hold on him, running my fingernails up and down his spine to see him quake.

"You know they can see us," he whispered into my ear and nipped at my skin.

"I don't give a fuck," I growled into his ears, and heat went straight to my groin. I grabbed his chin and slammed my lips into him, not caring that everyone could see. My feelings for Sutton were not a secret to anyone.

His lips met mine with the same fervor as we battled for dominance with teeth and tongues and clawed at one another's chests. I bit his lip a little too hard and drew blood, the metallic taste of him filling my mouth. I sucked on his lip to soothe it, and he groaned into me, pressing his hip bones into mine.

He reached his hands down and grabbed my ass, hard. I laughed into his mouth. He smiled against me.

"You have a wonderful ass, Lux, truly a work of goddamn art. And all these tattoos, I want to trace every single one of them with my tongue," he said it like a promise.

"Why wait, then?" I searched his eyes for the answer as to

why we couldn't do more than this. What difference did it make? What did this curse do to him?

"It's not just about the physicality of this, Lux, it's about all the other stuff. It's complicated." Sutton sighed into me, and our moment of heat was broken. Instead, I wrapped my arms around him and held him tight, not wanting to let go of him.

"Soon."

"You don't owe me anything, Sutton."

"But I would like to."

I didn't know what else to say. So, instead, I just held him close and breathed in deeply all that was Sutton. I don't know how long we stayed like that, but eventually it was time to go inside and plan for our trips. The next few days would be long, and we would need to be prepared. I just hoped I was prepared for whatever truths Sutton had to share.

I hoped my heart could take it.

↤↦

"Okay, we're all clear on the plan?" Greer addressed us the next morning. We were all geared up to go our separate ways. She looked better, less haunted this morning, and I was grateful for it.

"Yes, you all have the magical item I gave you, correct?" Nova paced back and forth in a violet purple playsuit.

"Yeah, right here." I held up the small coin necklaces each of us was wearing.

"Think of them like magical walkie-talkies, okay? There's no guarantee our cell phones will work, especially depending on where everyone is going." She rubbed her forehead.

"Everyone reports back tonight, either through their coin or meeting back here, if you can." Kyra looked around at all of us as if this might be the last time he could.

"Everyone, be careful." Waverly used what felt like her siren voice because I had a strong urge to be extremely cautious.

"Wave." Sutton raised a brow at her.

"I know, I can't command you all to be careful. It's too vague, but I really want all of us to come back here in one piece." Her lip trembled.

"Immortality will protect you all," Greer insisted.

"But it doesn't mean your pieces will be the same once they are broken. Immortality isn't invincibility. And we are dealing with gods and goddesses who could be very angry and vengeful." Kyra narrowed his gaze, his scarlet eyes on fire, looking right at Greer.

"Got it, don't get too fucked up because it will be a bitch to stitch ourselves back together." I tried to lighten the mood.

"Okay," Greer said quietly.

"You ready?" Waverly grabbed for Greer's hand and gave it a squeeze.

"Okay, we're leaving." Greer stood there for a moment.

"See you on the other side." I gave her shoulder a little nudge toward the door.

It was like we were all stuck in this moment. Nobody wanted to take the next move to leave one another, but we had to. There weren't any other options forward.

"Right. Okay. Go team." Greer smiled shakily and left with Waverly, who had slid a mask of steel into place. She had been through some shit with her job, so I knew they could handle whatever came at them together, but the thing was, we didn't even know what was possible anymore. And Waverly had wounds that needed to be healed by first ripping through the scar tissue.

"You ready, Prince of Hell?" Nova smiled wickedly at Kyra. He rolled his eyes and chuckled. Only she could get away with calling him that.

"Hyacinth, Farren, and your mother are expecting us. Let's open this fucking portal." She made quick work of opening a portal with some chanting and salt before it swirled and popped open.

"See you on the other side," I repeated, and Ky and Nova hugged me quickly. Sutton was forced into Nova's embrace, but Ky just gave him an awkward shoulder pat.

They stepped through the swirling vortex, and it popped shut in a flash as soon as they left.

"We travel by shadows, Lux. Are you ready to face my past with me?" Sutton tried to make it seem lighthearted, but I knew this would be heavy.

"I'm here for you. Let's go."

I grabbed his hands, and Sutton closed his eyes. The shadows swirled and swarmed, and I shut my eyes, too. The air around us turned ice cold, and my hair whipped around while the shadows picked up speed, creating a tornado-like wind around us.

"Here we go!" Sutton shouted, pulling me close and wrapping his arms around me. My eyes flashed open to see him smiling. "Now."

Everything went black as we fell and fell and fell, clinging to each other like our lives could be preserved between our bodies. Until we crash-landed, and we were a tangle of limbs and groans.

"Is this it?" I whispered, not able to see anything in front of me.

"Yes, I guess I never asked," Sutton whispered close to me, but I still couldn't see him.

"Asked what?" I grabbed around on what felt like a dusty concrete floor.

"If you're afraid of the dark."

I hadn't been before, but something in his voice told me that maybe I should be.

TWENTY-FOUR
GREER

L ux had arranged for a private helicopter to deliver us to Waverly's home island. We all agreed that it might be safer than going by water, as Waverly wasn't sure what to expect from her sister or the island she grew up on. Waverly looked out at the ocean and thrummed her fingertips against her thigh.

I grabbed her fingertips and squeezed them tight. We rode in silence over the roaring rotors. The pilot would come back when we called for him, but he wouldn't be staying. We were both prepared for a fight or something else. I had my daggers. Waverly had started to favor a staff that she could add spikes to with the press of a button. It was pretty badass, if not absolutely fucking terrifying.

But I was grateful to be here with her. To have something to do, something to occupy my hands and my head while I sorted out the mess of who I was.

A lush island came closer and closer. The helicopter landed on a soft, white sand beach. The foliage and greenery went on forever across mountains and glistening blue lakes.

"Don't trust it," Waverly said. We thanked the pilot and hopped off onto the beach.

"Don't trust what?"

"The beauty." She scowled and looked around us as if waiting for something to jump out.

The helicopter roared to life and took off, leaving us behind, and I swallowed, reminding myself that Waverly swam this as a child. I was a strong swimmer, too, so it wasn't like we were trapped in a territory where we didn't have a feasible escape route. At the moment, there was nothing to be terrified of, except for the fact that I did not trust myself to perform the way I did in the trials.

But Waverly did have connections here. Her sister's name had obviously popped up for some reason.

We watched the helicopter fly away until it was just a speck in the sky, both of us staying put as the ocean lapped against the beach and the sand hugged our boots. Waverly walked over to the waves and sang gently to them.

"They will be here shortly. It's best if we wait for them." She sighed and plopped down into the sand.

I sat next to her and looked up at the cloudless sky, the sun shining warm and bright above us.

"How bad will it be?" I asked. Surely it couldn't be as bad as hell. I shoved the memories of Phayre's torture aside and the monsters that lurked there and dug my hands into the sand.

"There's no telling, really. This island is nicknamed 'the Island of Death.'" Her eyes narrowed, and her lips pushed into a flat line.

"Is that meant to scare people away?"

"Most definitely. Sirens often ended up as people's pets back in the day, and my sister never wanted history to repeat itself, you know? So many things were put in place to protect us from the outside world."

"No, I didn't." A voice came behind us, and we both

whipped our heads around. A woman, who looked very similar to Waverly, stood there with her arms crossed. Her hair was dark like Wave's, but cropped close, and long scars dotted one side of her face. She was full-figured, like Waverly, but taller and not as soft. A little rougher and tougher looking. Her eyes were the same shape, but they were a deep purple instead of Waverly's cheery pink. Her skin was a bit darker, like she spent all her time outside in the sun.

"Evanya," Waverly whispered, standing up and facing her. Tension fizzled and cracked in the air. The forest behind her started to shimmer and glitter and shake, then it fell apart, piece by piece, like a fractured mirror. It sloughed off to show a gate and a wall made of metal, like a glimpse into another world.

"I wasn't sure you would come." Her voice softened.

"You answered my call," Waverly whispered.

"And who is this?" She threw her head in my direction.

"Greer, a friend," I replied, not sure how much we could trust Evanya because I didn't know how much Waverly really trusted her. She seemed cautious, rather than dangerous, at least towards us.

"Your magical lineage?" she inquired.

"Uh... complicated?"

She chuckled loudly at that, like it absolutely delighted her.

"I'm interested to hear more, but come, little sister, I will not force you out like I did before. And I will answer all the questions I'm sure you have." She turned, and the door opened to a metal passageway. We looked at each other and decided we had no other choice but to follow.

We went through silently, and the doors slammed shut behind us. I jumped at the sound, sweat breaking over my brow. We were not being captured; this was a conversation.

Not a kidnapping. The treetops grew over us, accompanied by a wire netting, while we traversed the hallway.

"We follow intense security protocols. We don't want people nosing around in our business. We take the security of our people very seriously," Evanya said, walking in front of us, the dirt crunching underneath her boots. We ended up at a doorway, and she placed her palm on it, and it beeped. A groan and click sounded as the door in front of us opened, and we all stepped through into a cityscape. A mix of rural and modern technology.

"Whoa," I breathed. This place felt like another world. There was a bustling city market with food stalls and goods off to one side and skyscrapers on the other, while sleek ships flew overhead.

Evanya cut left and entered a building that looked to be made of stone and clay, but when you stepped inside, it was all modern lines and fresh tech. She gestured for us to sit around a table where someone bustled in and set water and a tray of snacks down.

"Where would you like to begin?" Evanya said as the man left, and we were alone once again.

"Why did you almost kill me when I was just a child?" Waverly said, her molars practically cracked with how harsh the words came out of her mouth.

"Okay, let's start there. You know that most of our people have some siren blood. Not as many as strong as ours, but some nonetheless. Power of persuasion and truth were used as a weapon long ago, and it was almost taken from us once more. When you left, Waverly, I thought someone had kidnapped you. I sent out an SOS to Armello himself. But instead of getting help, someone else answered my call. A disgusting man and his cronies ransacked our security system and stole from us. Not our high-end technology, but ancient secrets of our people, including the way to ward yourself against sirens," Evanya hissed. She stood and paced the room.

"Why does this sound like President Adonia?" I looked at Waverly.

"I was thinking the same thing, and I bet that it was another one of his missions on behalf of the gods to get more weapons in their arsenal against those who were left here on earth." She fisted her hands and scowled.

"You will have to explain more of this to me. But long story short, we were invaded when you left because I was careless. I needed you to stay away, Waverly." Evanya ran a hand over her face and closed her eyes briefly.

"That man killed our people without a second thought. And I couldn't have him getting his hands on you. He seemed intent on trying to steal a young, powerful siren for himself. Instead, he stole a secret. I would make that same decision today. I would rather have him know our ancient teachings than take and torture one of our own." Evanya slammed her hands down on the table in front of us as tears rolled down her cheeks.

My heart beat fast, looking between the two of them. So much was taken from them when they had only been trying to love and protect each other.

Waverly's face was impossible to read, but her body shook.

"Wave." I squeezed her thigh.

"You could have reached out to me!" she cried out, standing swiftly and throwing her hands down by her side.

"I was ashamed!" Evanya returned to her pacing. "I let our people down. I couldn't watch your face as I confessed to you that I'd done the same to you. I was a coward. And the longer I let it go on, the more my anxiety built around it until I decided it was best to wait for you to come home. It only took a hundred or so years, but I would have waited forever, Wave. I love you so much. I was willing to do what it took to keep you safe." Her words tumbled out, and she stood right in front of Waverly, gripping her shoulders and shaking her slightly.

"I appreciate the apology, but more than words will be needed to fix this wound, Eva." Waverly brushed her sister's hands off and leaned up against the wall like everything was too heavy to handle. I understood that feeling in my bones.

Evanya looked helplessly at her sister, and tears fell freely down her face. They both had suffered so much and were forced to be separated from one another.

"I just want to have my sister back," Evanya whispered, collapsing into her seat once again.

"I know, me too." Waverly's eyes were still closed. I didn't know what to do, so I just sat, twisting my fingertips in my lap. Sadness and heartbreak filled the room.

"Did Armello ever come?" Waverly finally asked.

Evanya's eyes darkened, and she wiped the tears off her face. "Yes, but it was too late, and things got messy..."

"What does 'messy' mean?" I already knew where this was going, but I hoped, maybe, I was wrong.

"We were involved," She snapped.

"Eva..." Waverly warned, pushing against the wall and standing tall next to me, as if she were ready to fight her sister on my behalf.

"I'm not angry at you for asking, Greer. Armello was not helpful while we were under attack, and then he was marginally helpful after. And then he became an extreme nuisance after that," she spat.

"So, you two fucked?" Waverly asked with a smile creeping into her voice. She folded herself back into her chair, arms across her chest.

"Yes, and then he claimed the sea called back to him, and he needed to roam the waters once more. Blah, blah, blah. He got what he wanted and then left. At least he was a good lover at the time. But he couldn't do much to help recover what we lost. He simply came and went," she explained flippantly.

"We need him to come back," Waverly said evenly, watching her sister's reaction. She winced only slightly.

"Is that absolutely necessary?"

"Yes, we're on a bit of a mission." I hoped that our chances of getting Armello on our side didn't solely depend on the relationship that did or did not exist between him and Evanya. Why was everything so godsdamn complicated?

"What is this mission?" Her brows shot up as her interest piqued.

"Well, the short version is the original gods and goddesses are up to some fuckery. Some of them want to take over the mortal realm." I wondered if that would be enough information to get this party started.

"Why? This realm was terrible when they all resided here. It was war and chaos. It was best that some of them got the fuck out of here." She leaned on her elbows and looked at me quizzically.

"Yeah, well, apparently, they're bored now and ready to fight for it. There's also the small issue that I'm the timewraith." I dropped that bomb, wondering what it would mean to someone who grew up with more truthful tales of the gods and goddesses of the realms than I ever did. We were purposefully left in the dark, like I was always playing catch-up with the snippets of information others knew.

"Seriously?" She simply blinked.

"Seriously. And now that I have been awakened, so to speak, they might have what it takes to tip the balance of power back in their favor. They kidnapped me and the Prince of Hell once and held us for over two months. So, I'm sure they will try to take me again or at least recruit more of those living on earth to their nefarious quest." As in, killing people indiscriminately and using their dead bodies for whatever they wanted, I thought to myself.

"I didn't know there was a Prince of Hell. Children are forbidden for the original rulers," she said, narrowing her gaze.

"Well, apparently Riordan broke some serious laws with a powerful witch to conceive him, so I don't know what to tell you." I didn't feel like I needed to bring up my relationship with Kyra into this. Not now, when I didn't even know what was going on with us.

I craved his comfort, but kept him at arm's length. It wasn't fair, but I was doing what I could to become myself again after our time in hell. Our relationship needed some serious work, and us sleeping together before we talked about anything was probably not the most appropriate way to cope.

"Well, shit. Okay. I'll call Armello. He won't want to leave his precious sea and island hopping to get disturbed by the other gods and goddesses, so I am sure he will be on your side with the others who still reside on the mortal side. But it will cost you." She smiled like she had a secret.

"After everything you put me through, you're going to ask for a price. We're asking for your help because we have no other way to get in touch with him. The message I sent out was for him, and you intercepted it!" Waverly threw an accusatory finger at her sister.

"I intercepted it and squashed it so no one else would come the way someone else came the last time! And what I am asking for won't be unreasonable!" she hissed.

Both sisters were up on their feet, leering at each other. It was the perfect image of sibling rivalry at its finest.

"Then what is it?" Waverly shoved her sister, and Evanya scowled, pushing her back. I wondered idly what it was like when two sirens sang at each other. I couldn't imagine it would go well.

"I want immortality!" she snarled, getting in Waverly's face and cornering her against the wall.

"That's it, huh? You just want to live for fucking ever and fuck up some more shit?!" Waverly shoved past her and looked like she was ready to smash her fist into something. I had never seen Waverly this angry before. I could practically see steam coming out of her ears.

"Waverly, it's fine, I'll do it!" I would give it to her sister with no questions asked if that is what it took to keep people safe. It was an easy thing for me to do.

"But why does she get to ask for it? Why do you think you deserve it after everything?" Waverly paced around the room and waved her hands around randomly.

"Because I want to spend the rest of my life making up for the years lost, you idiot! I fucked up, and I want to take time to mend it and get my baby sister back!" Tears ran down her face again, and it was like the air in the room got sucked up.

"Well fuck, that's a good reason." Waverly plopped down next to me, looking utterly exhausted.

"We need to make some preparations first, but then I can grant you immortality," I assured her. "How did you know it was possible?"

"The siren's island is old, and many traditions, legends, and history are passed down through here. We know more than you probably think. If only I had the opportunity to share it, Wave. I'm sorry." Evanya hung her head in shame.

"I'll make a few phone calls, and we can get to work on your immortality. Then, you can get Armello to come here," I said.

Waverly nodded, knowing that Nova would need to be consulted again for the exact steps of the ritual.

I just hoped that I wouldn't need to give out immortality at every bargaining opportunity. But we needed Evanya on our side, and she was our best bet at finding Armello and the first step in recruiting more gods and goddesses to our cause.

TWENTY-FIVE
KYRA

"Aw, we meet again so soon, friends," Hyacinth greeted us at the door to her giant house. It was a mansion of witchcraft and magic. It was all black on the outside, while the inside sparkled with dazzling splashes of color, mid-century modern furnishings, and random knick-knacks that seemed more for magic-wielding than anything else.

"Why am I not surprised that this is where you live?" Nova looked pointedly at the black walls and elaborate wallpaper, which featured pink alligators.

"I'm a colorful woman." She guided us to a sitting area where Farren and my mother were already lounging, waiting for us.

"Kyra!" My mother hugged me, and it felt good to see her again, so vibrant and free. I wanted to soak up all our time together and relish in her knowledge, learning what it means to have a mother.

"Hello, darlings," Farren said from his corner of the couch. Hyacinth slid next to him and dusted her lips across his brow.

"It's good to see you again, Farren." Nova squeezed his shoulder as we sat across from the three of them.

"Tell me your updates, then." Hyacinth waved her hand, and coffee and tea appeared in front of us, while a steaming cup plopped into her hand.

"Well, Waverly and Greer are going after Armello. Lux and Sutton are pursuing Raelyn, who will hopefully also provide a lead on where Briar is. And we're here, talking to you about Damari." My mother beamed at me, like she was so proud of what I had accomplished in such a short amount of time. It was odd to be on the receiving end of someone's adoration, especially a parent.

"And how is immortality settling in, Nova?" Hyacinth pointed her gaze at her.

"I feel mostly the same, I believe, nothing new to report here." She unfolded her legs and reached for a cup of coffee.

"Well, Damari is going to be a bitch to get a hold of and deal with, so that's the bad news." Farren clicked his tongue like it was a simple inconvenience, and not a monumental issue.

"What does that mean exactly?" I asked, thrumming my fingers on the oversized chair I occupied.

"She is vicious. She will most likely not answer my call, but perhaps she might answer Greer's? She had a soft spot for Xael, and I think it was mainly due to the intensity and outrageous limitlessness of the power of time. She wanted Xael to use it more aggressively, but that wasn't Xael's style. However, in some ways, Damari respected that. However, she did not like that I often outwardly disagreed with her. She just really was not a nice lady. But that goes to show the power that Xael had over people. She could melt the toughest hearts. So, I will try my best to reach out, but I will also give you the information to try and reach her on your own."

I nodded, taking it all in. There were so many fucking

power dynamics at play that it made my head spin. Was Greer in a position to be able to handle another power-hungry immortal? What else would she need to sacrifice until there was hardly anything left?

There was so much going on in that beautiful head of hers, things she was keeping to herself. It made me worry about how she was really doing. Her brave face wasn't fooling me.

"What about you, Farren? Has anyone tried to come for you?" I tilted my head to the side and studied him. If Hyacinth trusted him, then so did I. But I couldn't shake the memory that in hell he had appeared close to my father. A confidant that Riordan trusted deeply.

"No, and I doubt they will. I think Riordan always knew I was playing a game way out of his league. So, as long as I kept him happy, he didn't seem to mind," Farren confessed. Apparently, double-crossing people was completely fine and normal in the infernal realm.

"Okay, and the others with Riordan? Do you think they will stick with him?" I asked, leaning forward.

"Well, we all know Phayre won't switch sides. Afton won't stand up for anything, and he wants to be able to travel more freely. The red tape of all of this aggravates him, but he's not malicious like the other two." Farren hummed and tapped his finger to his chin.

"So, maybe we can work on Afton and get this shit stopped before it actually starts." I looked at my mother, whose beaming smile turned into a frown.

"Unfortunately, I don't think that will happen, Ky. Your father has been planning this for years. There will be a combustion point. They've made it too far to go back now, and we will simply have to be ready for whatever that battle looks like." I nodded, not fully understanding what this would all come down to.

"So, we try to limit the ripple. We keep people out of it who don't need to be a part of it and try to cut the serpent's head off. What about the others we are missing?" Nova said, sipping her coffee slowly, her stars seeming a bit dull.

"That leaves Cerena and Estoria. They are lifelong soulmates and will do what needs to be done to protect one another. Similarly, to Briar and Raelyn, who always stick together because they are siblings, Cerena and Estoria are great lovers and will never deviate from one another. It will be hard to convince one without the other, and they do not like change." Hyacinth set her coffee down and sighed.

"This is all a bunch of frivolous politics that cost people their lives." I buried my head in my hands.

"Yes, it is," my mother responded.

"Okay, so depending on what the others come up with, and how Damari responds, is how we move forward." Nova drew everyone back in, trying to keep us on task.

"Exactly. But in the meantime, I would like to show you some of the Eastern Hemisphere while you are here. You portaled directly to my door and have seen nothing of how we choose to enjoy our lives and our magic." Hyacinth stood and reached out a hand to Nova and me.

"We will show you what the Western Hemisphere has hidden away, and what your adoptive family was too scared to get close to." She looked at me, and I looked away.

I knew my adoptive family stayed away from the big cities and only went from rural town to rural town to keep me under the radar. I couldn't help but wonder if Hyacinth could have found me or maybe some of my mother's people if I had been on a longer leash.

It didn't matter now. The past was the past. But there were lots of unanswered questions that I would probably never get to the bottom of.

"Before you all go, I'm going to talk to Ky for a minute." Verity grabbed me and looped her arm in mine.

We walked out the glass back door, and it felt like we stepped into a fairytale with a beautiful garden adorned with lantern lights and cozy seating.

We walked through the maze of flowers and arches, encountering small ponds here and there.

"Does it feel nice to be back?" I asked as we continued to walk arm in arm. It felt strange, but in a good way.

"Well, it certainly looks different, but Hyacinth always loved interior design and trends. I haven't gone back to see the people I once knew. I'm afraid. Can you imagine that? I left them willingly at first, and then obviously, I didn't stay away willingly. Hyacinth knows how manipulative love can be, but not everyone else does."

I nodded, wanting her to continue.

"They don't know about you or exactly what happened. Hyacinth kept it a secret. Said it's my story to share, but I guess I don't know how to share it. This doesn't exactly feel like home anymore, but it certainly feels better than when I was stuck in hell with your father. So, you could say I'm feeling a little displaced. And soon I will have the courage to face those I once knew, but right now, I simply don't." A few tears slipped down her youthful cheeks.

"I think you should be allowed to take as much time as you need. We all need different things while we heal and reac-climatize to things around us. You went through hell for years. I think staying here with Hyacinth in her home while you figure it out is a perfect way to do that."

"I would like to get to know you, Ky. I was hoping you might let me see your memories of when you were a child sometime... You don't have to answer now, but I would love to get to know who you were and how your adoptive parents treated you, and how I can be here for you now."

My heart clenched, and I knew that this woman would always be my mother.

"They were wonderful, a bit traditional at times, but kind, nonetheless. I always felt a bit disconnected, but we all did our best, you know?"

"I understand. And Kyra?"

"Yes?"

"You need to take care with Greer. She needs time to heal and may never be the woman you once knew. Hell has a way of changing people. Phayre did unspeakable things and... I had to harm her to get her cuffs off." Verity's eyes swelled with more tears.

I swallowed, "What did you have to do?"

"I didn't have time to get them off magically. So, I had to shatter nearly all the bones in her hands and wrists to slip them off." Verity scrunched her eyes closed and shuddered violently. "I didn't know another way."

Bile rose in my throat, but I swallowed it down. "You didn't have a choice, but thank you for telling me. I imagine there are many more things that Greer faced that I have no idea about."

"She will come to you in time. You just need to give her some space and let her navigate her own healing."

There was nothing else for me to say. She was right, and every new detail I gathered about Greer's time in hell made me want to rip the entire realm apart. We walked in silence for a while. Verity and I are in need of our own healing as well, though not to the same extent as Greer. We had been worlds apart, and now trying to fit it all back together again would be hard.

"I'd like to visit you some more, if you're okay with that," I finally said as we made our way back to the house.

"And I, you, Kyra. We've got all the time in the world to figure this out now."

Gods, I hoped she was right.

We needed to make sure there was still a world to live in before that happened, but either way, this felt like the beginning of something powerful and new.

↤

Nova and my tour with Hyacinth started with a map.

"This is the Eastern Hemisphere, as you have been taught by the Western ways." Hyacinth unrolled a large, lamented piece of paper which showed the world how the Western ways were taught.

"This is not true?" Nova questioned, squinting at the map. It had the large Western Hemisphere as a huge mass with juts out on either side. Tiny islands littered around the continent, and then there was the Eastern Hemisphere. It was small, in comparison, maybe a fourth of the size, with broken land pieces. It looked fragmented. Random pieces of land were thrown about. It looked small and feeble beside the West.

"I didn't realize that this was how it was taught in the Western schools." I squinted at the map and realized that it was easy to think that the East was rural and unimportant just by the way the map was laid out.

"But here is what our continent actually looks like." She unrolled another piece of paper and floated it above the current one.

The Western Hemisphere's size shrank by about 30% and then the Eastern Hemisphere matched the land mass with larger connections and islands clustered together, like a unified body as opposed to broken pieces of glass.

"Gods, this is alarming but not surprising. Easy way to keep order in the realm by acting like the Eastern Hemisphere wasn't unified or dignified. A way to control us without us even fucking knowing it from a very young age." Nova seethed her stars glittering darkly.

"Greer had mentioned that little information was given on the Eastern side, and I definitely felt like a zoo animal half the time and avoided questions about it so as not to draw further attention to myself." I didn't know if that had been the right move when I had been crowned a winner. But the sides of the world had been divided for so long, and I didn't realize how much until right now. I had selfishly been trying to protect myself in the best way I knew how.

"What is taught about the Western Hemisphere here?" Nova questioned her eyes, never leaving the map like she was memorizing the lands on the page.

"The truth, in my domain, the other places I have less control over, and thus their education isn't under my supervision. But I do not lie to my people here. They know the truth, and they have elected leaders and officials. I simply am here as an advisor to help share knowledge." She pointed to one of the large bits of land called Elyria.

"We are here, in the middle." Her fingertips traveled across the map to the center of Elyria to a city called Archer.

"I grew up here." My fingertips went far away to a small island in the north. "Bieri." I could cover the whole thing with my thumb so easily on this map.

"Your adoptive parents are still there?" Nova looked at me with understanding in her eyes.

"No, they are in the west now. Just south of us. Small beach town," I pointed to where the West was and let my fingertips brush the southern edge. Nevara.

"How is immortality handled here?"

"Ah, well, it's not really," Hyacinth said, thrumming her fingers.

"My people vote on it every year, on whether they would like access to it, and most of the population does not want it.

They will live many years, as most are magic users of some kind, and those who are not sometimes ask for it. It is not sensationalized, like it is in the West. You must take a year-long course on the pros and cons of immortality and pass the exam before you can be eligible. Education and access are free to everyone who turns twenty-five," she explained.

"That's very civilized..." I thought of the bloodbath that was the immorality trials.

"And how do you grant it?" Nova tapped her finger on the table below us.

"Xael's body is here, and can still grant the power. Her gift of time is gone, and her body is in a permanent comatose state, but her wish was that the gift would be free. When Riordan stripped her of her power and sentenced her to death, he could not take what she was born with in her blood, and that was this gift. Magic is a fickle thing when threatened. I believe it was the last fight she fought for herself, even if she doesn't know it." Hyacinth's eyes watered, and tears dripped onto the map.

"Xael's body is here?" I looked around like I expected it to just be lying around.

"Underneath us. I have a lab and state-of-the-art homeostasis installed to keep her body alive, as I believe there is a way for her spirit to return, and Greer could possibly be the answer."

"What?" I nearly fell to the floor.

"You think Greer can revive Xael?" Nova looked at her incredulously.

"Xael visits her in her dreams, does she not? She is a corporeal being when they speak. You cannot kill a goddess as easily as Riordan thinks. You can make it hard for her to come back and be earthbound, but to eradicate her completely from these realms? Impossible, to my knowledge. She is a part of this world itself." Hyacinth spat like she was giving the finger to Riordan himself.

"Well, this is an interesting turn of events," Nova grumbled.

I needed a minute to wrap my head around this.

"Does Greer know?" I held on to the table, gripping so hard I might snap it in half.

"I don't know. I doubt Xael has brought it up. She probably feels it is selfish. You would have to ask Greer. When she comes here, I will speak with her and show her Xael's form. She deserves to know," Hyacinth said.

"Knowledge is power, and Riordan seems to be great at fucking taking what he wants and giving scraps to the rest of us," I said, glaring at the map. How he had manipulated an entire country to believe a falsehood was truly impressive and disgusting. But if you controlled the narration, then you controlled the truth, and the people who believed it.

"Well, now that that shit is out of the way, would you like to go see what my world actually looks like?" Hyacinth rolled up the maps and carefully put them away.

"Sure, let's go see what other lies we discover today," Nova chuckled, but there was fire in her eyes.

"The team is going to get a kick out of this."

I could just see Lux's face when we told them what we'd learned. Gods damn immortals and their childish fucking games.

Twenty-Six

Lux

"This is a graveyard." I looked around and had absolutely no idea what time it was. I hadn't heard anything from the others, but we had shadow-traveled here. At least, that is how Sutton had explained it to me, but as my eyes adjusted to the midnight sky, the only thing that twinkled was the stars and moon above.

We had exited the main part of a mausoleum, which had been our starting destination.

"Yes," Sutton looked through the graves at a leisurely pace, seemingly unbothered.

"Why?" I tried not to shiver.

Sutton was comfortable around death. It was his magic, but death was not comfortable to me, and even when Sutton had interrogated our dead victims last year for the serum, it had scared the living shit out of me.

"I'm looking for someone specific," Sutton said, humming slightly as he strolled through the stones.

"Who would that be?" I was almost afraid of the answer.

"My father." He frowned as he happened upon a rather unassuming marker.

"Do we have to dig him out?" I tried to hide the horrified look I was sure was on my face.

"Unfortunately, we do. I need the body, even if it is severely decomposed."

I almost vomited on the spot.

"Exactly how are we going to get the body?" I asked, holding my hand up to my mouth and willed the nausea to go away.

"Lux, you're a shifter. I need you to shift and help dig this up."

I laughed hysterically at that. "There is no fucking way I'm grave digging a dead ass body out of this ground!!" My voice sounded shrill and so unlike me, but I did not want to touch Sutton's dead father.

"Please, I'll reward you greatly." Sutton's red lips broke out into a seductive smile. My mind went to all kinds of terrible ways that his mouth could be used. Damnit.

"Are you really dangling sex in front of me so I will dig up your dead father? Is that really what our relationship has come to?" I licked my lips, and suddenly the nausea was gone.

"Yes, Luxton," Sutton whispered to me, and his shadows swirled, caressing my body, and touching me everywhere and nowhere at once.

"Well fuck." My voice was hoarse as he stepped away from me. "Fine," I grumbled as I shifted to a bear and scowled at Sutton.

"Look at you. Your grumpy face is even cuter when you're a bear."

I rolled my eyes at that and started to paw through the dirt.

"Good boy." Sutton patted my fur, and I shivered at his praise.

The work was quick, and in no time, a pile of dirt was sitting next to Sutton, and my claws were scraping a wooden coffin. It was plain and lacked any personalization. I looked up at Sutton and turned my large, furry head to the side.

"Just make a bigger hole to the side there, so I can stand. Then we can rip off the lid."

I nodded and kept digging until there was plenty of room for both of us to stand. I shook off my fur and paws and shifted back to myself.

"Hi, my little honey bear," Sutton said, placing a peck on my cheek. My body reacted without thinking. I slid my arm around him and pulled him close.

"I don't think there was anything little about me," I growled and ran my nose up and down the column of his throat.

"Hm, no, I'm sure there isn't much that's little about you, except perhaps your patience." He chuckled and nipped at my ear.

"As hot as this is, we are standing over your dead father," I whispered in his ear, wanting to be literally anywhere but here so we could continue. Why was nothing easy with Sutton?

"Sadly, he was always ruining something of mine, so it makes sense that he would take this from me as well." Sutton sighed and moved close to me so we could pop the lid off. I extended claws from my fingertips and pulled the top off with Sutton's help.

Sutton muttered a few words over what was mostly a decaying skeleton, and I tried not to gag. The smell itself would have caused me to run, let alone the open bones and skin hanging off it. Another round of nausea threatened to overtake me. Sutton seemed unbothered, but I suppose he had built up a tolerance to such things.

"Hello, Father." Sutton crossed his arms and leaned back on his heels as the skeleton that was his father sat up rigidly.

"Godsdamnit." I nearly fell back at how quickly he moved.

One eyeball was still intact, while the other was completely gone, along with all the skin on that side. This was truly the stuff of nightmares.

"Haunting me in my grave even, Sutton?" The skeleton practically spat on us.

"You're being an asshole still? Even now that you're dead? How typical," Sutton hissed back.

"Why have I been raised? Tell me what you want." His jaw was clicking, and I didn't even understand how this was possible, considering he had no jugular or vocal chords. But a voice leaked out of him, nonetheless.

"Where is Raelyn?" Sutton got straight to the point.

"I don't know, after she cursed me, and then I cursed you. I never saw her again," his father replied.

"Liar. I know she kept tabs on you and told you that if you were ever ready to break the curse you brought upon your family, that you could find her to pay the price."

Sutton walked around and got right into the skeleton's face despite the decaying flesh looking nothing like a human being, let alone his father.

The one eyeball twitched, and then a huff of air came out of somewhere that I think was supposed to be an exasperated sigh.

"Fine, yes. The letters Raelyn sent with the address were kept in our family P.O. box. You know where to find it, and you know the code."

"Have fun in hell, Dad." Sutton snapped his fingers, not even giving him another opportunity to respond, as the bones collapsed again.

"Let's cover it up. Then we can talk."

I nodded, not wanting to push him, but really wanting to get the hell out of here.

"I got it," I softly grazed his arm, and he looked at me longingly before hopping out of the hole. I returned to my bear form, shoved the lid back into place, and started to work on all the dirt once more until we had a semi-undisturbed grave again. Sutton was the prince of secrets, and the more I learned, the less I understood.

"Ready to shadow travel again?"

I really wasn't.

"Sure."

But I did want to get the hell out of here.

He held out his hand and wrapped his long fingers around mine. The swirling happened again. Our asses landed back in my apartment as we crashed onto the couch. For what felt like the hundredth time in the last hour, I held back vomit.

"Fucking hell." My stomach would never recover.

"It's a bit jarring, isn't it?" Sutton laughed. It sounded beautiful. I wanted to hear that sound repeatedly until I could hear nothing else. There was still a decent amount of light outside as the sun hadn't even begun to set.

"I'm going to shower the dead off of me, and then I can have this conversation." I stood and headed to my room.

"Do you want some company?" Sutton said silkily.

I froze in place, my tongue heavy in my mouth.

"If you want to," I said, not sure what it said about us that we were ready to get down low and dirty after we had just dug a grave and exhumed his father.

Sutton didn't say anything as he sauntered toward my room. Heat shot through my veins, and I carefully stalked after him. My mouth watered at the sight of his graceful movements.

He gently sat on my bed and eyed me up and down.

"You first," he said, looking hungrily at me. I didn't need any other encouragement, so I whipped off my shirt, displaying all my tattoos and umber skin.

"And you?" I was practically panting.

He gently removed his shirt, and I gaped at his beautiful

chest. Slowly, I closed the distance between us and reached for his exposed skin. My lips dipped and moved across the planes of his torso, circling his pink nipples. He groaned and leaned into me, grabbing onto my neck. I nibbled my way up his throat until his lips were captured in mine.

A ringing sounded through the room, and we broke apart, confused.

"The coins!" Sutton scrambled out from under me and ran out of the room to where he had stashed the coin in his jacket. Someone was calling.

"Lux? Sutton?" Waverly's voice ran through the small coins that had been tossed onto the kitchen counter.

"We're here," I replied, catching up to him. I looked between the two of our shirtless bodies and smiled.

"What's up?" Sutton said smoothly.

"Greer and I have to stay for a while. We're working on getting in contact with Armello. Just wanted to update that we won't be coming back. We'll keep your pilot on standby, but it could be a few days." Waverly sounded tired.

"How are things there?" Greer's voice pushed through.

"Uh, good. We're working on where to find Raelyn. The first piece of the puzzle was found, and we're working on the rest. Sutton made me go grave digging," I added casually.

There was a long pause where no one said anything, then Greer and Waverly's laughter sang through the coin.

"That made my day. Hope it went well. We already talked to Nova and Kyra, and it seems like they're going to need some more time, too. Until we are reunited! Love you!" I could practically feel Greer's hug from the other side of the coin.

"Love you, too." Then the coins went dead.

"Where were we?" I turned on Sutton, licking my lips.

More ringing filled the space.

"Mother fucker!" Sutton threw up his hands, and there was nothing to do but laugh. "Literally what?"

"Jeez, Sutton, you could act a little happier to hear that we aren't dying in a ditch somewhere," Nova purred on the other end of the phone, and I could feel her amusement.

"You won't be back tonight?" Sutton guessed for her, his red lips pouting.

"I'm sorry, did we interrupt something? Is Lux tied up somewhere fun?" Kyra's voice pushed through the coin.

"Unfortunately, no, I'm right here," I laughed, covering my face with my hands.

"Great, well, we'll be a few more days. We'll come back when we can. Any word on your end?" Nova asked.

"Not yet, we've barely scratched the surface," Sutton sighed.

"Well, play nice! Bye." Nova let the line go dead before we even responded.

"Is the mood ruined?" I reached up and ran my hands down Sutton's spine. He shivered at my touch.

"I'm just waiting for someone else to interrupt." Sutton scowled at the coins.

"Okay, well, why don't you order us some food? I'll shower, and then we can talk and revisit this." I gestured between the two of us.

He agreed and retrieved his phone from his pocket.

I made quick work of scrubbing the dead off my skin and tried not to linger too much on the memories of Sutton. The sight of him, the feel of him.

I came back to the living room feeling fresh and revitalized. Sutton had changed as well and cradled some sushi on the couch.

"Hey." I sat next to him and grabbed some food.

"You smell nice." He sniffed my way, and I grinned. The walls of Sutton were slowly crumbling down in the form of cute compliments.

"So, want to tell me about your father-situation and Raelyn?" I gently placed my hand on his thigh.

"This doesn't need to be a sob story, but it will sound like one. I made my piece with it. My father cheated on my mother almost the entire time they were married, including when she was pregnant with me." He popped another roll in his mouth and chewed thoughtfully.

"Sounds like a piece of shit," I added, and Sutton's mouth formed a thin line.

"He was. He had other character flaws, as well, but that was the most glaringly obvious. So, my mother asked for help from Raelyn. For knowledge on how to get away from him. She didn't have a lot of resources, and Raelyn had been her grandmother's preferred goddess. Raelyn saw a kindred spirit in my mom and helped her, cursed my dad in the process."

I nodded, wondering how often gods and goddesses really went around enacting curses.

"Part of the problem was that my dad went to attack Raelyn, and she didn't take kindly to that. She cursed him to be unlovable and alone. Unfortunately, because of the way the curse was worded in the passion of the moment, it extended to all his kin. Raelyn was embarrassed that her curse had not excluded me. My mother no longer thought of her as a kind goddess, but instead was horrified at what had been done to me."

"So, she fucked up, was too embarrassed to say it? And you have now had to live with the consequence ever since?"

"In so many words, yes." Sutton scowled.

"For quite some time, Raelyn would allow the curse to be lifted from both of us if my dad swore a vow of celibacy, isolation, and devotion to her. As in: no contact with anyone, ever, to release us. But of course, he declined. She would only allow *him* to lift it from both of us, and I have suffered the consequence of being isolated or involved with people ever since. I was told that I was incapable of love and being loved. There would always be a point in relationships of any kind where that person would get a vacant look in their eyes and run from me. There was no telling when it would happen. It was like they were sand slipping through my fingers. There one minute, and gone the next," Sutton whispered.

"Sometimes it would happen in a few days, and sometimes it would be months, but it was always painful. It happened without fail."

My heart nearly broke in two. No wonder he had said so little up until now and kept everyone at a distance; it was either that or watch them flee.

"But immortality has changed that?" I questioned, trying to understand all that was being said.

"In some ways, I think it has. It has strengthened me and weakened the curse. I often think immortality has been a way to reverse curses over time, as curses were not meant to last forever without constant love and care. So, I'm not sure what exactly is happening inside me, but you, Luxton, are the first person I have cared for in a very long time that has returned the sentiment." Sutton suddenly looked shy and insecure.

"I've been with many men, but only physically. You are the first person that I have had genuine feelings for in what feels like a lifetime. And I'm afraid that if we sleep together, you will wake up and run like everyone else had been forced to."

I didn't know what to say.

"I don't have an answer for that right now. All I can say is that I like you, and I want to explore being with you. I don't foresee waking up and all that changing. Isn't love supposed to conquer all?" I said, thinking of the stories we were told when we were younger.

"You love me?" Sutton's eyes went wide.

"I know that I care about you, but I'm not sure I know that I'm in love with you," I said. Sutton's eyes darkened.

"Love often takes time," Sutton said, and I didn't know if he was saying that for my sake or for his. "All this to say, we will need to bargain with Raelyn to lift the curse. It still lingers in my body. We'll see if she will help. And then we see if Briar will join as well."

"Where do you find the answer for where she is located?"

"My family has a storage place where they keep their after-effects. I can access it. I just didn't want anything to do with it after my mother passed."

"So, we work together," I placed a gentle kiss on Sutton's temple, and he sighed.

"Together."

We sat in silence the rest of the night, letting Sutton's story fill the room.

TWENTY-SEVEN
GREER

The potion was prepared for Evanya, and I had already drained some blood.

"You ready, Evanya? It will be painful for a few moments." I handed her the first vial for healing, like Nova had instructed, and then gave her the cup with my blood.

"Let's fucking do it." She drank the first vial easily and hesitated at my blood.

"Okay, let's do this." I chanted the spell and waited for a breath. Eva tossed back the blood like a shot. She grinned with bloody teeth. Waverly and I looked at each other with eyes wide.

"Eva?" Waverly reached out to her not a second before she screamed and crumbled to the ground. Shaking and writhing in pain. We both looked at each other, horrified, until she stopped suddenly, gasping and rising.

"Motherfucker, that hurt like a bitch." She rubbed her hands down her body.

"You good?" Waverly looked at her suspiciously.

"Yeah, I'm good." She nodded at me. "Thanks, Greer."

"Sure, now we can talk to Armello, right?"

"Straight to the point, I see. I like it. Well, he's coming for dinner tonight, so you'll have to wait until this evening to meet him, and I'll warn you he can be a lot."

Waverly and I looked at each other wearily.

"What does that mean, exactly?" I scrunched my nose up. "A lot," as in horribly cruel and gruesome? Or "a lot," as in a big personality?

"It means he's a bit unhinged and a shameless flirt, but we will see how he behaves tonight." Evanya pursed her lips. "In the meantime, I'd love to show you our island." She beamed like nothing would please her more.

"Do you feel up to it, Greer?" Waverly asked, and I nodded, curiosity getting the best of me, considering a lot of what I knew about the world came from the very westernized version of what I was told. Which, apparently, was all false. And I sure as fuck didn't want to sit alone with my own thoughts right now. I flexed my wrists and reminded myself that I was free. There wasn't anyone lurking around waiting to cause me unspeakable agony.

"Let's do it."

↤

Evanya started in what she called the plaza square. Everything was a beautiful blend of new-age technology and rich, cultural traditions. It was like looking at a world come to life in a way I had never seen before. We walked through numerous buildings, stalls, statues, and museums, where the history of the sirens was told and celebrated.

This is truly amazing." I whispered while we strolled through one building after the other.

"How about a little training, timewraith?" Evanya inquired smugly after our beautiful town tour.

"Magic or physical or both?" The last time I trained, I

made choices, which led to me falling apart when I should have been strong. I didn't want that to happen again. I was fucking better than that.

"All of the above." She winked at me.

"Alright, let's see what you're made of, Evanya." I nodded at Waverly, and she grinned. This could be a redemption moment. One where I was free to wield my power and prove to myself that I could not be contained by anyone.

"Greer gets the first round, and I get the second."

I thought it would be good for them to release their tension, and I had really never seen Waverly's full power, and she hadn't seen mine.

Evanya led us through the colorful city once more until we arrived at an arena full of magical training simulations, physical fighting, and equipment for movement and magical practice.

"It's like a gym with all the added extras of having magic to work out." Evanya looked proud of the space, and it was truly spectacular. We didn't have a lot of spaces in the Republic, which celebrated or encouraged the use of magic like this. There were so many rules and regulations around the use of magic that many only used it in small ways. Even so, if you had it, it made you better, and if you didn't, it made you weak.

"Do we, like, suit up or something, or how do we do this?" I asked, unsure of how this would play out since the last time I had battled someone was in the arena in the infernal realm with Kyra, and that hadn't gone too well.

"Yup, we'll put on some protection suits." She gestured to one of the staff members. She showed us where we would get magically geared up, and where to pick our own weapon of choice if we wanted anything. Waverly and I slipped on tactical gear. I always traveled with two daggers strapped to my person. To my surprise, Waverly picked up a couple of chains and wrapped them expertly around her body, intertwining them between her breasts and around her waist like a corset.

"Since when do you use chains?" I smiled, looking her over. "You look hot."

Waverly laughed, and it twinkled around like wind chimes. "It's my preferred weapon. I don't use them often, as they are seen as rudimentary, and the FEC likes us to use electric guns. But they are an ancient practice of my people, a way to reclaim our power when we were hunted during the wars. It makes me feel closer to my lineage. And it is hot." She winked at me, and the corners of my mouth tipped up.

"Things feel different here. Freer than the republic. Fewer rules, but more respect for boundaries. More truth in how people live and breathe." I didn't realize how constricting the Republic was because I did what I could to fly under the radar when I was human.

"We have a diversity of people here and a deep sense of community. There are those with and without magic of varying degrees. There's power in the community, which is why it was so hurtful when I wasn't welcomed back. I know now that my sister did what she thought was best, but it still stings. I've missed so much and had to deal with so much other shit as a siren in Odessa. Most sirens stay close to the sea, coasts, and islands because the water feels like home, and I've been afraid of it for so long. So much time wasted." She turned her gaze to the ground.

"But now you and Evanya have all of the time." I grabbed her hands and gave them a squeeze, drawing her pink eyes to my own.

"Thank you for doing that." She squeezed back, and her gaze softened.

"Thank you for being my friend, before and after all this mess. I don't know what I would have done without meeting you, Wave. I have been so naive to so much around me, and you helped open my heart and my mind to more. Thank you. It's a privilege to be here with your sister and for you to share your home." I wish I could put into words how much her friendship had meant to me all those months ago. The olive branch she extended to me long ago meant more than she knew when I was so angry at the world and in need of more love and support.

"We don't abandon our friends, G." Her gaze was full of steel, and I wrapped my arms around her short frame. One day, I would tell my friends all that happened in my time away. I knew they would still love me and cherish me, but I wasn't strong enough right now to admit it to them or myself.

"No, we fucking don't. Let's go beat your sister's ass," I teased, and Waverly looked gleeful.

"Oh, this will be interesting for sure."

We moved back to where Evanya had told us to meet, and we went over to a corner of the arena where a few people were milling around. Evanya waved as a small crowd started to gather.

"Welcome the timewraith, Greer Roberts," she boomed through her siren voice. It sprinkled my body, magic wrapping itself around my ears. "And my sister, Waverly Banks, has returned. The first round goes to Greer." She pointed towards me with a javelin and smiled broadly.

"You will lose." Her voice sang, and the power sank into my bones and limbs, and for several moments, I wanted to lose. I wanted to quit right then and there. I pulled at time around me like taffy and breathed through the command. I willed it away, clenching my fists and huffing out air.

"That's a shitty way to start the fight," Waverly commented as I snapped time back to normal.

"We're pulling out all the stops, no?" Evanya smiled wickedly at me.

"Let's go."

We stepped up to the center of the space, and someone gave a whistle.

"Begin in 3, 2, 1..." I manipulated time as the one came out of the mouth of our announcer, and moved through the space to end up right behind Evanya while the one came to an end. I kicked into her back and sent time back to normal. She went flying across the stage.

"Fuck," she spewed, landing fully on her belly.

"We're pulling out all the stops, no?" I responded as she got up and spat.

"Time's a tricky bitch, huh. Stay still," she commanded, and this one was laced with more intention, with everything she had, and my body refused to move. It was a sweet caress, and I paused time around me to breathe through. Evanya moved in slow motion towards me as I tried to fight the command. Siren's truths had to have a time limit. So, I stretched it until I could wiggle my fingertips and toes. I finally found movement. She was nearly on top of me and went rolling to the side as her javelin arced wide.

I got up and faced her.

"So, the commands don't work as well with the manipulation of time." Evanya stared at me, delight crossing her features.

I charged her without a second thought and swiped in with my dagger. She blocked with her javelin. There was barely any time for magic as we traded blows and strikes, punches, and kicks. It was a blur of time itself, and I barely had the space to slow down or speed things up. There were short bursts where I could land something, only for her to come swinging with the next. She had years of training with her weapon and her power. I had months.

"Aren't you tired, Greer?" she sneered. We breathlessly circled one another. I wiped at my brow and kept my distance.

I was tired; my thoughts and actions were getting sluggish. I could barely keep up with her.

"I'm scrappy, what can I say?" I smiled at her and felt alive in a way I hadn't felt for quite some time.

"Doesn't sleep sound wonderful?" she practically whispered, and my eyes felt heavy. I couldn't fight this one off as easily. The suggestions of sleep slipped into my body and bones easily.

"Shit." I stumbled forward as the command got stronger.

"You've worked so hard. You deserve some rest," she soothed me, and stood straight. Slowly, she made her way towards me, her javelin pointed down.

"Rest, timewratih. You've fought hard enough."

My mind and power had zero safety walls left in place. I collapsed to the ground, fighting the call of sleep while it curled around me like a blanket.

"We can work on this, Greer. I can help train you, but now you will sleep, and I will have won."

I slipped into darkness without a second thought.

⟻

"You fell prey to the siren song."

I woke up sprawled in front of Xael.

"Shit, I did. She's good." I sat up and looked around to see the very familiar meadow.

"She is. One of the best, I believe, since her people trust her to lead," Xael agreed. "But you did good, Greer. You tried to fight with your powers and your body. You are learning that there isn't always an easy way to keep up with both, and you need to make quick decisions to save time and energy to continue to survive." Xael beamed at me like she couldn't be more thrilled that I had lost.

"Well, I'm glad you're excited about this." I laughed.

"I see you are making progress on gathering your allies. Farren is a bit of a surprise to me. I had believed him and Hyacinth to have had a rough breakup when they first separated, but it seems like their love story is timeless. And Verity has proven a helpful ally."

"We're working on it. Hopefully, Armello will help us. I don't know how it's going with the others, but maybe we can swing the vote our way and avoid this whole gigantic conflict in the first place." I wanted to stop this shit before it started. If we could get control of things before we had a big blowout on Earth, that would be ideal. But I didn't know if that was a realistic hope. We could only prepare so much for what was to come because we didn't know what the fuck was really out there.

"My hope is that the casualties will be minimal, and you can come to an agreement, but it didn't work when I was stripped of my power, and I am not sure it will work now. I am rooting for you all, but I am skeptical." Xael thrummed her fingers on her thigh.

"We'll keep training. I know we haven't for a while, but I just wanted to enjoy my time in the mortal realm with my friends." I felt selfish for pushing Xael out of my dreams the past few nights, but I needed time to just be me, without the whole fucking power of time on my shoulders. I also didn't want her to see those last few moments in the infernal realm. I didn't want to talk about it; I was barely holding myself together as it was.

"You don't need to apologize, Greer. It is a large burden that has fallen on your shoulders, child. You will soon have even more to navigate. Evanya will wake you shortly; so, until next time." Xael waved, and before I could respond, someone was shaking me.

WAKE UP.

"Wake up!" Evanya stood over me with Waverly at her side, looking pissed.

"I'm up." I shot up. "Honestly, that was a sneaky bitch

thing to do. Nicely played." I held out my hand to match her own while she hauled me up.

"It's a great siren trick. There isn't always time and energy to use your powers, but when your opponent is exhausted, they're at their weakest and much easier prey for whatever spell you try and cast. I can teach you how to fortify your mind as sirens aren't the only ones with the power of persuasion, and it wouldn't hurt for you to strengthen your mental walls." Evanya smiled at me, and something blossomed between us, like an appreciation for a worthy adversary.

"I feel like that was a shit last move, but whatever. You ready, Eva?" Waverly looked ready to go, her pink eyes shining bright.

"I'm not even tired." Evanya winked at me. She was a badass, and she knew it. I couldn't even be mad about it.

They walked to the center of the arena. Waverly let her chains wrap around her hands and slide around to her wrists. Eva twirled her javelin.

"Oh, this will be good." Someone sidled up next to me. He had some animalia characteristics, with ocean-like eyes and an almost fish-like quality to him. He was tall and broad, with silk strands of blue hair trailing down his back, and green highlights, almost like fins, running down the lengths of his arms where tattoos and muscle corded.

"Who's your money on?" I asked.

"Evanya, for sure. No way she would lose." The stranger responded, as he spoke, I noticed some of his teeth were sharp between his dusty purple lips.

"I'm rooting for Waverly." I looked at the sisters walking around one another.

The announcer counted down, and the two women launched themselves at one another. Chains went flying as Eva's javelin swung wide to beat them off, but they attacked like two people who had years of pain and trauma to work through. Their voices and songs battled, bouncing off one another like echoes. The magic glowed and rippled around them. They hurled siren songs at one another with little to no movement from either's magic, so it turned to physical brutality. I had never seen Waverly like this. She was confident and strong. Quick and sure as she twirled and threw with her chains like an extension of herself.

"Do siren songs not work on other sirens?" I asked, not knowing whether the stranger would know the answer.

"It really depends on how strong the offensive and defensive powers of the opponents at play are. They both have strength in these attacks. It's not often that people outside of sirens can completely brush off siren songs, without the help of the secrets of our people, but you were able to form some resistance until you couldn't. It's usually a game of stamina and endurance. And the more exhausted you are, the more susceptible you are, but the more tired the siren is, the weaker the song. It's all about flexing the correct muscles, you know?" the stranger explained.

"So, you're a siren as well?" I looked at him, feeling like something about him was almost familiar.

"I am many things," he replied cryptically, and I didn't know what that meant, considering people usually only manifest one power. But in truth, I didn't know that much about all things magic, because I never wanted to listen. The reality I knew to be true was being broken down with every passing day.

The rules of the republic were a carefully constructed house of cards built from strategic manipulation by the original six who currently resided in hell. A giant game of chess.

A scream ripped through the air as Eva caught Waverly's side with her javelin and tore into her skin. Waverly went down. I moved to run towards her, and the stranger's hand clamped around my wrist.

"Don't interfere," he commanded softly, and I froze by his side.

Waverly whipped out her chains to Evanya's ghostly face and pulled her legs from underneath her in an instant. Then she jumped on top of her, wrapping the chains gently around her throat.

"A truce," Waverly commanded, and the color came back to Evanya's face as she broke out into a smile. Between the bloodshed and the blows traded, the tension between them fizzled and faded.

"A truce, sister."

Waverly climbed off her and held down her hand to help her up while cradling the side of her abdomen with her other palm.

"You didn't have to slice me so hard, you moron." She winced as she walked back over to where the stranger and I were standing.

"I guess neither of them win, then," I said to the stranger.

"It was a fight, I wasn't going to seriously harm you, just a little nick. Can you help with this?" Evanya nodded to the stranger next to me, and he beamed.

"Of course, Eva." He strode over to Waverly, put his turquoise fingers up to Waverly's side, and created a webbing over the wound that soothed Waverly's pain. She sighed with relief. Her healing appearing to accelerate with this salve.

"Thank you... I'm sorry, I don't know your name," Waverly said.

"Armello." He looked lovingly at Evanya.

"You're Armello?!" My mouth dropped open.

"I told you he'd be here for dinner," Evanya replied, rolling her eyes.

"Shit, I didn't realize I was talking to you," I mumbled, not that it mattered, I guess. So far, he had been pleasant, which was more than I could say for some of the others.

"Yes, Waverly Banks and Greer Roberts, it's a pleasure to meet you." He grinned, and his sharp teeth showed through.

"You know who I am?" I took a step back, unsure of how to feel about our whole interaction.

"Of course. It's not often that a timewriath pops up and starts to shake things up. Then Evanya invited me to dinner, and I knew things were suspicious, considering Eva usually only calls when she wants something." He smiled seductively at her, and I suddenly felt like I was intruding on something very intimate.

"Oh gods, okay, well, nice to meet you," I said, unsure of what to do.

"You as well." He bowed his head.

"Well, I'm starved. Shall we get cleaned up for our dinner?" Evanya clapped her hands and avoided eye contact with Armello. "Someone will get you squared away with new clothes and a room at my house," she continued, turning to Waverly. Someone materialized out of nowhere to guide us away.

"Shall we, Armello?" She extended the crook of her elbow to him, and he gladly grabbed it and snuggled close to her.

"I've missed you, Eva," he purred.

"I'm sure you have," she retorted as they walked away.

"What the hell is going on there?" I laughed. They bickered on their way out like an old married couple.

"Truly have no idea but oddly excited to find out," Waverly said.

Well, at least we were off to a good start with Armello. It could have been a lot fucking worse, that's for sure.

"Okay, well, let's get this party started then." We walked arm in arm out of the arena, and I sighed in relief. Hopefully, this would go our way and we would be one step closer to figuring out this mess.

TWENTY-EIGHT
KYRA

Hyacinth's home was unlike anything I had ever seen before. There were sleek modern buildings mixed with all the wonders of nature. Greenery everywhere, which reflected off all the mirrored surfaces on the buildings. It was like a giant greenhouse or conservatory.

"This is beautiful," Nova whispered while we walked the streets where people used their magic effortlessly around them, unrestricted, but respectful. No one blinked an eye at the scent of magic which filled the air. The people strolled in all shapes and sizes, a beautiful kaleidoscope of magical diversity.

"It is. We try to work as a collective. Magic and non-magic wielders alike. We have those who have and have not, but it is just like any other skill to be honed. Not all of us can be beautiful speakers, but you can practice with what gifts you have and use them in ways that make sense for you." She and Farren walked hand in hand. People would stop and speak to her or smile at her. She would kindly greet them all and introduce Farren to each one.

They all seemed genuinely happy that she was here. It was

a beautiful sight to see that the people met her with respect and reverence, rather than fear and avoidance.

"You have cultivated a society that seems very kind." I looked around at the consciousness of the collective.

"We have our own battles, but for the most part, we try to be conscientious of the mortal realm and others. Your side of the earth seems to thrive off being powerful and wealthy. My people here want contentment, to be cared for and provided for. It is a different way to live life." She eyed me like she wasn't sure where this compliment came from.

"Do you not trust me, Hyacinth?" I wasn't here to play games, and if I needed to show her my loyalty to my friends and Greer, I would.

"I am a bit suspicious of you, Prince of Hell. You battle with more than you care to discuss." She looked pointedly at my chest.

I thought I was doing a damn good job of hiding the pain there. I didn't want to add to the ever-growing list of shit we need to take care of. I certainly didn't want to concern Greer with this. My pain was minuscule compared to hers. She didn't need to take this on, too.

"I would love for this rock in my chest to not have any connections to hell, and instead be the power I earned in the trials. The powers have been warring with one another for quite some time, and it only got worse the closer and more involved my father was in my life. But I'm handling it fine." That was a lie. I was not handling it all, actually, but rather ignoring it.

"Is there a way to remove that part of the crystal?" Nova questioned.

"Perhaps. Come, let's go somewhere and have a look at it." Hyacinth led her way through the crowds and around the city effortlessly with Farren contentedly at her side.

"This is a beautiful place, darling. I'm excited to finally see it and be here with you." Farren stroked her arm and lay his head against her shoulder.

"Thank you, love." She spoke softly, as if she was afraid to break their contact.

We came to a building shaped like a giant rosebush with a glass door for an entrance. Inside, Hyacinth greeted the person working the front before we disappeared down a hallway. We descended some stairs until we arrived at what appeared to be a medical facility.

"Alright, Kyra. Let's see what we are working with here." Hyacinth motioned for me to get on the metal table in the middle of the room.

"You're going to examine me?" I sat on the table and eyed her suspiciously.

"Don't tell me you're shy, Ky," Nova teased, trying to lighten the mood. She gave me a wink, and I nodded, pulling off my shirt.

"Gods be damned," Farren said, and Hyacinth hissed.

My crystal had only gotten worse, as if the war inside it was leaking like an open wound. Lines covered my chest, fracturing off from the stone. They looked like fresh gashes. Red and black clashed and pulsed with every breath. I had just gotten used to the pain at some point. I had to ignore the aching and sharpness that was nearly constant.

"That looks really fucking bad." Nova's eyes were wide while she studied me.

"It's tender most of the time. But it's fine. We have more important things to deal with," I said, trying to keep my tone light.

"I am not buying it. Lay down, now, before I make you." Nova raised her eyebrows at me, and I obeyed, not willing to cross her.

"May I?" Nova loomed over me with her hands.

"Go for it." I closed my eyes and tried to breathe evenly. I could feel it almost rebel against the scrutiny as it pulsed and throbbed.

"It's like a battle in your blood, around your stone. It seems to be spreading across your body. Were you going to tell anyone about this?" Nova scolded me, her hands scanning my torso.

The branches from the stone went clear down to my hip. Greer had given me curious looks when we slept together, but I played it off as if it were nothing. She hadn't wanted to talk about her scars, so I didn't overshare mine.

"I was going to talk to my mother, but Hyacinth over there seems to just sense the infernal realm's influence that refuses to leave my body, so now it looks like she has saved me the words," I replied curtly. Hyacinth chuckled.

"Oh, Kyra. It didn't start off as evil, but it definitely is in the same vein of magic your father uses, which usually tends to manipulate and control... and is power hungry. It wants all the stones' power back in its court, instead of in the one that was bestowed on you.

"I can perform a ritual that will chase it away, but it will be painful. Your mother should probably be here, too. We will need her power, along with yours, Nova. We can eradicate the virus, as you say, from your body once and for all. But it will force you to rest. It will take time after the spell is cast for it to filter out of you. You may be bedridden for a few weeks."

"You might want to tell your love about this," Farren chimed in.

There was no way I was adding this to her mental load. I would take care of it, and she didn't need to worry about it until it was already done.

"Greer needs to finish her job with Waverly. We do this as soon as possible. My father cannot have any more claim to me than he already does. I think it's how he tracked me as a child, and how he probably still knows where I am now. I do not want to put those I love in danger because my father still has a magical hold on me. Let's get this done." I grimaced as another stabbing pain hit my sternum.

"We will do it at my house, then. Put your clothes back on, Prince of Hell. Let's perform the ritual. The tour is over." Hyacinth swept out of the room, and Nova waited for me to put my shirt back on.

"Are you sure you don't want the others to be here for this? It sounds pretty torturous." Nova eyed me skeptically.

"I don't want to slow any of them down. We'll tell them once they contact us to tell us their jobs are done. Greer will need to come here anyway to meet Xael and, most likely, to figure out what the hell to do with Damari. Let's just tackle one thing at a time." I hopped off the table and walked towards the exit.

"You don't need to die a hero, Ky. We all know that Riordan is a dick and did some terrible shit to you. Lean on the people who care about you. Don't carry this all on your own, okay?" Nova pursed her lips at me.

"I know, but you're here. My mother is here. It'll be okay. The sooner we do this, the sooner we can get started on the healing process, right?" I tried to sound confident, but I didn't feel it.

I knew this would hurt, and most likely, I would be able to feel my father's wrath as his hold on me disappeared. He would retaliate in some way. I just didn't know what that would be yet. And, in some ways, I would grieve the connection. Even though I wanted it gone, there was something to be said about mourning a relationship that could never be. It was more complicated than just wanting to cut ties completely.

"Whatever you say, Prince." Nova winked at me, and I rolled my eyes. The sooner I was just Kyra and less the Prince of Hell, the better.

↩

"Why did you say nothing?" My mother raised her voice at me as I lay on the operating table at Hyacinth's house. She looked at my naked chest, and tears rolled down her cheeks.

"I was going to. I just hadn't found the right time yet." It wasn't a total lie. I had no idea how to bring this up to her, and before, we were just trying to escape. This could wait, but leaving hell couldn't.

"Gods, it's bad. I didn't realize it would be this bad. Unfortunately, for this spell, you need to be awake. I wish we could have known this sooner. It's like an infection on steroids," she muttered.

Nova was gathering supplies, while Hyacinth mixed some things and set up some symbols.

"Recovery will be hard. To completely eradicate this, we will have to do several rounds, after we see how the first one takes. Are you ready to get started?" My mother looked at me nervously, clearly worried for my well-being.

"Yes. I'm immortal, so it's not like I can die." But that was a curse in itself. To never have a final moment where you could feel nothing at all. Sometimes, death could be a welcome sight.

"But you can sure as hell be in a lot of fucking pain, and sometimes that stays with you. Sometimes it haunts you with no end in sight. Doesn't matter now, though. We have to get this out. There is no other option." Nova brought over several bowls and candles, setting them around me. She put some liquid on the crystal, and it hissed and steamed.

I winced as hot pain sliced across my chest, but the heat wasn't new. I could deal with this.

"It will only get worse." Hyacinth had no pity in her voice.

"Looking forward to it," I gritted out as she poured

another round of liquid on my chest. My mother lit the candles and looked over at Hyacinth.

"Okay, here we go." My mother looked at me one more time and pressed a kiss to my temple.

The three of them joined hands and began to chant something in a language that was all their own. The air around us swirled, and the liquid on my skin grew to searing. I dug my nails into my palms and breathed out loudly through my nose. The flames of the candles flashed, their flames rising and dancing.

Suddenly, the air stilled, and then it was as if an arrow shot right into my heart, and searing heat pushed through me. I screamed while it fizzled through my veins and pounded into my skull. It was what I imagined it would feel like to be engulfed by my own fire. And maybe it was a rebirth in a way. A way to be reborn through the ashes.

Wave after wave after wave of heat shot through me, and I thrashed on the table.

"Kyra, I'm going to hold you still," Nova said, but I barely heard her over the roaring of heat in my veins.

The blood control pinned me to the table, and the pain overtook me. It was too much, and I passed in and out of consciousness.

I could feel my father's presence in my mind. He yelled and thrashed, too. He cursed Hyacinth's name, and then his eyes burned into my soul.

"KYRA!" he bellowed, folding over in agony. It was as if I was seeing him through his own eyes, like I was flashing between his body and my own. The power of the spell fizzled and fried my insides.

"Kyra?" My mother's voice pierced through the darkness, and I tried to reach for it, but it slipped through my fingers like wisps of smoke.

"You can do this, Ky. The first round is almost through,"

Nova encouraged me, but I didn't know how I would be able to survive round after round of this pain.

It surely seared off my skin. I thought of Greer's arm with the muscle exposed and the skin stripping off in chunks. What her hands looked like after my mother had to shatter them. If Greer could be this strong, then so could I. I came back to consciousness, free of the blood magic, leaned over, and threw up everywhere, ejecting everything from my body.

"Gods be damned." Hyacinth jumped out of the way at the last possible second.

"It's almost finished its course. The worst of this is almost over," my mother cooed in my ear. Fire roared in my throat and ears. The heat started to die down to a simmer, and sweat coated my skin.

"Sleep now, my child. You have ridden out the worst of it, and now you can rest." My mother's hand floated above my eyes in a fever-like dream, and I slipped into unconsciousness, not knowing how I would live to see another day.

↔

I dreamed of Greer. Her sexy confidence and her beautiful figure. She soothed me in my sleep. Gently tracing her lips across my body, cooling the fire on my skin. I wanted to reach out and tell her I loved her, but she seemed intent on her pathway across my skin. My voice wouldn't come to my call. She caressed me with her lips, and her wine-red hair tickled my skin.

I wanted her to consume me. I wanted to die by her mouth and in between her thighs rather than this heinous fire in my skin. One that I could not control. One that wasn't meant for me to wield, but it was meant to destroy, to push out everything that didn't belong. To burn it all up and have me rise from the ashes. It was so potent and strong, the only thing that could stop the shaking in my bones was Greer's cool tongue as she licked the sweat off my body and sent ice through her fingertips.

I wanted to tell her I was sorry for betraying her and that I didn't want the heat of my fire to consume her, like it was consuming me. It wasn't a death I wanted to inflict on anyone, but one I would have to use nonetheless in the conflict to come. I ached to feel her and talk to her. I wanted this whole mess behind us and our future to be bright and happy, like the people in Hyacinth's world, not in our damn republic.

I shuddered as she gazed into my eyes, and then she started to fade away. I tried to cry out and reach for her, but my body was useless. I lay limp and helpless as I watched her disappear, her smile sad, like this was the final goodbye. I urged my tongue to move, but my mouth felt dry. Words were not mine to command anymore.

This was all for her. For our life together. For one free of my father and the manipulation of the gods, but I didn't get to say any of that. Instead, I watched in horror as she faded away until only her beautiful eyes, ringed in blue, remained, and then I was alone. Helpless. Painfully simmering in my own magic. Until I, too, lost the connection to my physicality.

↔

"We need to do a second round, quickly. Before the hell crystal can gather strength again, we must hit it at least two more times." I heard Hyacinth's voice hiss.

I wasn't sure if I was awake or not. I still felt disconnected from my body.

"Kyra?" Nova's voice floated around me and then fell across my skin.

"Yes." I think it came out of my mouth. I was definitely thinking it. My eyelids and tongue felt like they weighed a thousand pounds.

"It's been twelve hours. It's not enough time," my mother's voice came through.

"I can make it." My voice didn't sound like my own, but I wanted to do the damn thing. Get it over with. The pain would subside. I wouldn't die.

"You sure?" Nova's eyes hovered before me, their fiery orange hue floating towards me.

"Yes. I won't die, just pain. I can do it." My words were slurred and garbled. It felt like the crystal had a hold on my brain and my words. My whole body hummed in a very bad way. Fuck.

"Again," Hyacinth said, and the ritual began once more.

This time, I could see the flames dance on my skin. I didn't know if it was a hallucination or a dream, as I watched my skin peel off in chunks. I could see my own muscles and skeleton before me. My eyes sizzled to nothing.

"Restrain him!" Hyacinth commanded, and I could feel Nova's magic, a whisper in my body. I had been thrashing and didn't realize.

"Second round is almost over," my mother whispered, and I prayed that I would die. At least this would be over. Death would be a mercy to having my skin fried off again and again.

"Rest."

This wasn't gentle; it was forced. My mother put me down again, right before an explosion happened in my chest.

↤

This time I dreamed of my father. His face was filled with rage, and he roared at me.

"How dare you push out the power with Hyacinth's help! This is a betrayal of the ultimate kind."

I didn't know what to do or say. But I couldn't move. It was like he had unlimited access to berate and throw insults at me. His words hit me, each slashing me through.

The power inside me truly was an extension of him. I was sawing off our connection one slice at a time. I craved the release that it would bring. My smile was potent as I realized I would finally be free of him.

His eyes showed black while he pushed flames out of his hands and incinerated the world around him. He lit everything on fire, inviting mass destruction around him. I willed my body to look away. This dream needed to end. I wanted as much space as possible between my father and me.

"Fuck you!" I wasn't sure my mouth made the sounds, but I sent it with my whole being. The air around me rippled and shook until there was nothing left of either of us, and darkness swooped in again.

↔

"Hopefully, this is the last round." Hyacinth sounded softer this time.

"How are you doing, Ky?" Nova's hands grabbed my arms, urging me to answer.

"Fine," I croaked. My voice sounded broken and feeble.

"Fuck." My mother swore. "Last time, my son."

I welcomed the pain this time. It would be the last and final time to hopefully rid my body of what my father had done. My bones ached, and my eyes were impossible to open, but I could do it. My chest felt like it had been ripped open, but I was ready.

"Last time," I whispered.

The pain this time was almost sweet, like a generous lover. It took me fast and quick. And then I was free.

"The end." My mother gently used her hands again, and I fell into a deep, dreamless sleep.

TWENTY-NINE
LUX

It's like I could feel the demons of Sutton's past in this place. We were in some random small town where Sutton's family had apparently stashed their belongings or family heirlooms. It was dark and dingy, barely lit, while we walked through rows and rows of storage containers.

"This is eerie." I shoved my hands in my jacket pockets. There was a chill in the midnight air I couldn't quite shake.

"It's not uncommon for people to store keepsakes of deceased family members here. This place is steeped in death, and items can hold powerful magic after one passes." Sutton strode ahead.

I still didn't know much about his death magic. It seemed like his curse and death magic were separate, not one.

I mean, hell, my magic and Kyra's magic could be quite deadly if we used it that way. There were rules, of course, but death magic was simply another way to wield power. It didn't hurt anyone to speak to their ancestors after they had passed, and shadows and light were just two sides of the same coin.

"How do you feel about being here?" I asked as we settled in front of a non-assuming unit. It looked the same as the others, minus the numbers looming overhead. Each unit had an electronic padlock used to gain entry.

"It's not my favorite." Sutton punched in numbers and sighed loudly.

I nodded as the door pulled up and darkness seeped out. Sutton felt around on the inside and clicked the light on.

It was relatively organized, if not a little bit dusty.

There were normal things you would find in any storage unit: furniture, boxes, filing cabinets, and many other random household items. There were also a few odd things in floating liquid, potions, large spell books, and other assorted magical items.

"I think it will probably be in a small chest. My father would always put the notes in and hide them in a secret compartment with a tumbler lock combination."

"Why so much security and secrecy over a location?"

"It was a part of the curse. Raelyn is fucking brilliant, which is why the mistake of cursing me as well as my father damaged her ego. It was a slip in her judgment and intelligence. Part of the curse was that my father couldn't share her location with anyone, and I believe it constantly changed. I'm not sure. But now that he's dead, the lines of the curse have gotten hazy. Curses can't normally extend to the dead, but Raelyn is more powerful than most people and most of the other gods and goddesses. So, we will see what happens when I open that chest and read the information."

"Gods, this is unnecessarily complicated. Why do the original immortals make everything so fucking complex!" I crinkled my nose as a horde of spiders scattered by.

Sutton looked at me teasingly. "Don't tell me you're afraid of spiders, Luxton?"

"I just don't like the small creepy crawlies."

"You can literally transform into any animal or creature, including the elusive dragon, and you are afraid of spiders?!"

Sutton's eyes went wide, and he could hardly control his laughter as he doubled over, his orange-hued hair flopping into his face. He roared as tears flooded out of his eyes.

I couldn't help it. I joined in on the wheezy giggles, letting the joy of Sutton wrap around me and hold me close.

"I'm allowed not to like certain creatures, okay?!" I gasped for breath and clutched my stomach. Finally, Sutton stood and pushed the tears off.

"That made my entire life. Thank you, Lux." A warm smile spread on his face. I think it was the first one I ever saw. It made my heart nearly explode out of my chest. Gods, I wanted to see that more.

We resumed searching in a comfortable silence, and the urge to touch and breathe Sutton in was so strong I could hardly stand it. Like a spell had been cast, and I was falling into the sticky mess of it.

"I think I found it," Sutton said from further back, and I waded my way through the mess until I found him standing over what looked like a desk with a small black chest on top of it.

"This is it?" I reached my hand out and traced the small carvings of detail on it. It was no bigger than a shoebox.

"Okay, let's try this." Sutton spun the tumbler lock, and there was a moment of silence before a click echoed through the room.

"That was easier than I thou—" A plume of black smoke emitted from the lid. It popped open, and a howl pierced the air.

"Lux, get back!" Sutton screamed, but it was no use. The smoke turned into a snapping beast and was already on top of me. It was the size of a bear with white eyes and yellowing teeth, the length of my forearm. It looked like a wolf made to rival a small car. Its giant paws shoved me down.

Fear ripped through my body while the beast lunged for

my face, and my mind went blank on what the hell to shift into. Saliva from the creature dripped onto my face, and I shoved with all my might against its heavy paws. Sutton yelled and shoved his shadows out, toppling the beast and sending it flying into a stack of boxes.

"Lux," Sutton grabbed me and hoisted me up. The animal shook off the blow and snarled at us once again. The space was too small amongst the chaos of the Sutton's family things for the three of us.

The creature stamped its feet and lowered its head, preparing to charge. I looked over at Sutton, who still clung to the little demon box, and I pulled him towards the entrance.

"Run!" I screamed. The beast charged, slamming into the side of the unit where we had been seconds ago.

We sprinted through the maze of corridors. The howling grew frantic, and the creature burst through the crowded space behind us.

"I need more room to shift. If we can get outside, I can shift to my dragon, and then I think I can take it." There was no other animal I could think of that would rival that thing. It was monstrous, and something in its milky eyes told me that one bite from that thing and we would be done for.

The beast skidded and slid on the floor behind us, its feet pounding against the ground as we ran for the exit. The box was still clutched in Sutton's hands while we burst through the doors into the night air.

With a roar, I transformed. My body creaked and groaned. Scales lined my skin, and wings sprouted from my back. The hellhound exploded through the doors, shattering the glass. Sutton lunged to the side to avoid the spray of jagged shards.

The hound fixed its eyes on me while I roared, my talons scraping against the pavement and my body shaking with rage. The beast snapped its teeth and shook its fur. And the unthinkable happened. The beast grew.

Its legs elongated and its torso rippled with new muscles. His head expanded to rival my jaw, and it stood nearly eye to eye with my dragon form.

"Are you fucking kidding me?" Sutton called from the ground.

The beast of a dog whipped his head around to look at him, and that was all it took. A small moment of distraction before I charged the creature, trying to latch myself on its neck, but it reared back at the last second, and I missed. Instead, I crashed into its chest and we went tumbling.

Swipes of claws and snaps of teeth were exchanged as I tried to get control of the creature. Its claws dug into my flank, and I roared. Black dots sprinkled through my vision while I lurched to the side, my clawed paw coming away bloody. The hellhound licked its lips, and I swear to gods, it smiled at me.

I was too afraid to spew any fire for fear of hurting Sutton. My control in this form was much less than in others, and now, with my wound seeping huge amounts of blood, I was dizzy on my feet.

"Hey, asshole!" Sutton screamed.

The hound turned to where Sutton was surrounded by a tornado of shadows. With a scream, Sutton thrust his hands forward, and his shadows attacked. They swarmed the hound, pushing into its mouth and ears. The creature clawed at its own face, marring its fur and tumbling to the ground.

"Now, Lux," Sutton commanded as he walked, his hands outstretched and his eyes glowing.

The shadows were relentless. I took a deep breath and lunged for the beast, this time finding its neck with ease. Sutton's shadows parted for me, and as I sank my teeth into its jugular, the beast turned to ash on my tongue. Spitting the remains out of my mouth, I transformed slowly. My side was screaming at me, where my own flesh and bones greeted me.

"Fuck me," I grumbled, curling into myself and breathing

heavily. The gash on my own skin took up nearly my entire side.

"No, no, no, no..." Sutton crouched by my side and placed his hand on my wound to staunch the bleeding.

"I won't die, at least," I joked.

Sutton scowled at me. "Yes, but that doesn't mean I like to see you bloodied."

"Get the box and open it."

Sutton's eyes widened. "Right now? Are you serious, Luxton?"

"I need a distraction, please." I pouted, and Sutton rolled his eyes.

The pain was getting more manageable the longer I lay here. If I didn't move for the next few minutes, surely it would get better, right?

"Fine, but there could be another trap."

Sutton walked over to where the box lay close to the building and brought it back.

"Can't be as bad as whatever that was," I said.

"You say that, and yet we are just scratching the surface of what these immortals are willing to do to protect their secrets."

Sutton opened the small hatch that was released when the hound appeared and looked inside.

There was a photo and some random pieces of jewelry. Sutton's face gave nothing away. He traced his fingertips along the small items. He grabbed underneath the jewelry casing and popped it out, revealing a tumbler lock.

"This should be it." Sutton's fingertips hovered over the lock.

"Are you okay?" I asked after several moments of stillness.

Sutton swallowed and closed his eyes. "I have had this curse for so long, and stopped hoping for a resolution many years ago, that this feels like a horrible and excellent idea all at once," he whispered. "I had accepted my fate. I was collateral damage to carelessness and negligent gods. And here I am, opening up this can of worms once again, hoping it doesn't ruin me further."

"It won't, I promise." I didn't know if my words were actually true. But what I did know was that Sutton was no ruined being. He was brilliant and beautiful because of who he was and despite what was thrust upon him at a young age.

Sutton's fingers moved, and he spun the lock. A click sounded, and a small compartment opened. A tiny, rolled piece of paper was inside. We both just looked at it. The bleeding had stopped from the hound's wound, and I was able to sit up, albeit slowly and not without pain.

"That's it?" I breathed slowly. Sutton's hand gently pried it out of the small casing. The paper glittered, and as his hand made contact, it shuddered.

"Well, at least we know the curse won't kill us with immortality and all that, right?" I tried to make my voice light. But the thing was, I didn't know what Raelyn's curse entailed, so who knew what the fuck would happen.

"You have got to stop using immorality as a cure-all," Sutton grumbled, shaking his head. He gently unrolled the piece of paper, scanned it quickly, and it turned to ash in his hand.

"Did you read it?!" I watched the small particles of paper flutter down and scatter, then fade to almost nothing. He was so good at hiding his emotions when he wanted to.

"Yes." Sutton's eyes became watery, and tears slipped down his face.

"Sutton?" I wanted to reach for him, but my body protested, so I simply leaned in close.

"I think I know where she is." Sutton shut the box and looked up to the starry sky. "Perhaps I can finally allow myself to dream of what life looks like without this looming over me.

Perhaps I can allow myself to finally grieve the life I could have had if it were not for the cruelty and vanity of these wretched immortals."

His shoulders shook as more tears came, and he leaned into me, our bodies pressed close. Sutton finally welcomed the feelings that had been budding for years inside him.

"I'm proud of you, you've been so very brave," I whispered into his hair. We stayed like that for what felt like hours, but was merely minutes.

"Can you walk now?" Sutton swiped at his eyes and assessed my ribs.

"I think so, I might need some help," I confessed.

Sutton gently brought me to my feet and slid himself under my arm.

"Let's go home," Sutton said as we walked toward the car.

The word "home" echoed in my brain. Did this mean Sutton was finally letting himself settle into *us*? The life we could have together?

I didn't want to ask any more questions for fear of what the answers might be. So, as Sutton helped me into the car and we drove away from this cursed place, we sat in silence. I stole a glance at Sutton, his lips curving up slightly, and I couldn't help but do the same.

↤

Sutton bustled around my apartment in an anxious hurry, gathering things he needed. I just did my best not to bother him. He barely spoke while we loaded our backpacks.

"Ready?" he asked, grabbing my hand.

I nodded, not knowing what to say, because I still had no idea what the fuck was going on.

We traveled, and it made me want to hurl as we landed right in front of a large black mansion. There were fields all around, like the house had been plopped in the middle of nowhere.

"What is this place?"

It was too quiet here, like we had just walked into a trap, and at any moment, there would be someone who popped up and said "GOTCHA." Oddly, being immortal didn't negate feeling. Immortality didn't mean no pain or suffering, and I couldn't imagine what bad things could happen to an immortal, since they couldn't die.

"Raelyn's house. She picks it up and moves it every so often so as not to garner too much attention," Sutton said. As if magically moving your house wasn't a huge undertaking.

"So, do we just go up and knock or what?" I looked around at the endless stillness of the place. It felt like the whole property was holding its breath. It made my skin crawl.

Sutton shook his head.

"Raelyn, are we permitted to enter?" Sutton's voice carried across the empty land, and it shook the foundation we stood on. Suddenly, everything moved at once. It cracked and fractured like glass. The house in front of us transformed. It grew and grew and grew until we stood in front of what could only be described as a fucking fortress.

A raven fluttered down and looked at us expectantly.

"Hello." I waved at it, and its eyes narrowed into a human-like expression. I wondered idly if that's how I looked when I transformed.

It seemed it wanted us to follow, so we did. Up the long, cascading cobblestone driveway, across a moat, and up to a massive iron door. I felt like I was in a medieval movie.

The door creaked open, and we stepped into what was a very modern mansion. The doors snapped shut behind us, and the bird hopped along, guiding us through the large foyer with two spiral staircases. Everything was carved in dark marble.

We were escorted to a seating area that was black and white, devoid of any color.

"So, this is unusual, right?" I looked around and again felt the oppressive silence.

"It's her traveling fortress. She doesn't like to be called on or bothered, except when it suits her." Sutton looked nervous. His knee bounced up and down, and his already pale skin grew paler.

"My, my, what a surprise."

I could only assume this was Raelyn. She floated in on what looked like wings. I wondered if she had the powers of a shifter. Her tawny skin seemed dusted with gold, and her black wings expanded behind her, but shimmered away as she stepped into the space.

She wore an all-white pant suit, and her hair fell in feathery waves. Her eyes looked like cat eyes, narrow, bright green irises.

"And you brought another shifter?" She smiled at me and inhaled deeply. "A powerful one at that. One with the dragon line. Interesting indeed." Her stare was calculating and cold.

"This is Luxton," Sutton said with a tight-lipped smile.

"Nice to meet you. I'm Raelyn."

I didn't know if I should bow or not. With Hyacinth, it had been informal, but Raelyn gave off a regal vibe. It was unnerving to say the least.

"Sutton, your father is dead in the ground, as far as I can tell. He never did lift the curse from himself and you," she said as if she had no responsibility in it.

Red clouded my vision. She had the power to lift it, and she didn't. Her pride was too much.

"I was wondering if, now that he is dead, you would lift it from me. We also have news of the timewraith." Sutton's voice had no inflection, as if he were trying to seem as uninterested in either outcome.

Raelyn looked at him with narrowed eyes. "You barely have remnants of the curse anymore, Sutton."

"But I would like none of it," he responded, his dark eyes swirling. The shadows around him stirred and shook, homing in on his rage.

"You must do something for me first," she said, and I knew that whatever was going to come out of her mouth was absolutely not going to be good.

"I didn't come here to bargain," Sutton practically spat, and the rage rolling off him was palpable.

"And yet here you are in my home, bargaining. You forget your place, necromancer," she hissed at him, and he practically bared his teeth at her.

"Fine, let's make a fucking deal then." Sutton's eyes narrowed.

I was afraid to know what a deal with Raelyn would be like, but we didn't have a choice.

"Well, this will be interesting," I muttered, and I hoped to gods it wouldn't cost more than we were willing to give.

THIRTY
GREER

"Mom?" I said, shocked.

"This is quite the spread." Waverly and I walked in on a grand banquet set for the four of us. Armello and Evanya were already sitting huddled close together, giggling like teenagers amongst the wide array of food.

"This is a lot," Waverly commented. We made our way over through the sprawling dining room to find our seats.

"Well, a certain God demanded we make it big and bold." Evanya rolled her eyes, her words lacking any real venom.

"It's not often Eva calls on me, so I like to make a splash if you will." Armello gazed dotingly at her.

"Are you both ready to feast?" Evanya opened her arms wide, and we took our seats. Armello raised his glass.

"To the beautiful, Evanya. The siren of my heart." He raised his glass and beamed.

"Okay, you sneaky fuck, let's eat."

I nearly spit out my wine at Evanya's retort. Armello sighed like he expected it, and it didn't bother him at all. We ate in silence for a few minutes before I couldn't contain myself any longer.

"Armello, we also invited you here for me to ask you a question." I didn't want to waste any more time.

Armello's eyes raised his eyebrows.

"Ask your question, Timewraith." He smiled at me in between sips of wine and bites of food.

"As you know, tensions are a bit high since Xael's power became mine. I was kidnapped by Riordan and Phayre, as well as a few others, in a plot to take over the mortal realm. I want to make sure that doesn't happen. So, I need some help from the original immortals to make sure they're not capable of doing that. If it comes to a fight, I would like to fight for the mortal realm. One that is not left to Riordan's control."

"Of course, I will fight for you. Whatever Eva wants, that's what I will do." He nodded.

I didn't realize how tightly he was wrapped around her finger. Would it really be that simple with him?

"Well, that was a bit easier than I anticipated it to be." A weight lifted off my shoulders, and I took a sip of wine.

"However, you might need to be a bit realistic about the others whom I assume you will ask to join your cause. Damari, Raelyn, and Briar. I assume Hyacinth is already on your side, as she was always behind Xael's cause. From the whispers of the water, I have heard Farren has returned to earth."

"Do you have some advice on approaching the others?" I took another sip of wine, curious to see if his words would add any value to the others' recruitment efforts.

"Damari will be a hard sell. Most likely, you will need to do something for her. Raelyn and Briar will follow each other, so get one and get the other. I used to be in contact with Briar, but not anymore. Who could say what state any of them will be?"

I nodded as this echoed what I had been told before.

"I hope that we can keep the mortal realm as is. I do like the way things are here and would hate to see Riordan ruin it with an overarching need to control everything. He is such a power-hungry character. If only he could be satisfied with what he has." Armello looked longingly at Evanya again.

"You say that, yet you were mad when I slept with other people, even though you know I don't do monogamy. I told you that." Evanya pointed her fork accusingly at him.

"So, I had a tantrum! I am not used to being in a relationship with someone who has multiple partners." Armello pouted by sticking his bottom lip out.

"We discussed what it meant for me to be polyamorous." Evanya looked at him, narrowing her eyes.

"Are you sure this isn't a conversation you want to have in private?" Waverly raised her eyebrows.

"Yes, a later discussion, I suppose." Armello waved his hands around.

"I thought this would be harder," I whispered to Waverly. I had trust issues with these immortals. It was hard to know what you could take at face value and what was a ploy for something else.

"Same. I didn't realize he was hopelessly in love with my sister."

"Who knew that it would be so much in our favor to have him obsessed with her?"

"I wonder how the others are doing." Waverly looked nervous. There was no way it would be this easy for the others. We had an in with Armello due to Evanya. Raelyn's connection with Sutton was still unclear. Would it be a good or bad thing for him to approach her?

Damari and Briar were the big unknowns.

"If you'll excuse me, I'm going to go check in with the others."

Armello and Evanya hardly noticed while they flirted and bickered with one another.

"Go. I'll be here with the lovesick teenagers." Waverly waved me off and filled her glass up.

I walked through the enormous dining area to an outdoor patio. I pulled at the coin necklace I hadn't taken off my neck and rubbed it in my fingertips.

"Nova?" I called out with the coin against my lips. It vibrated and hummed as if I were on hold.

"Greer?" Nova sounded breathless. Tired.

"Everything okay?" My heart started to pound, and I had nervous flutters in my belly. A sinking sense of dread hit me. Silence filled the other end of our call.

"Uh, yes. Kyra is healing from a bug," she said cryptically.

"What does that mean? Can I talk to him?"

Another long pause.

"He's recovering. Sleeping," she said slowly.

"Okay. Do I need to come to you? Is he okay?" Anxiety clawed at my throat and chest. A bug wasn't a big deal, but I couldn't help but feel like something else was going on. Did Kyra not want me to know what he was dealing with?

"We should get you and Waverly here as soon as your business is done, and we have enough energy for a portal, but right now, we all need to rest. Hyacinth, Verity, and I have been helping him." She sounded exhausted.

"Okay, does he not want me to know or something?" I whispered, not knowing what else to say.

"He doesn't want you to worry. This feels like something the two of you should talk about, and he insisted you not cut your trip short because he is feeling... out of sorts," Nova replied.

I cleared my throat. "Right, okay, well, I guess let me know if anything changes."

"I will..." Nova's words trailed off, and I had the feeling that she didn't like being in the middle of this.

I desperately wanted to bother her about it, but if Kyra didn't want me to know, there must be a reason, right? Gods, I was tired of us holding each other at arm's length, but I hadn't been exactly the most open with him either since escaping hell. Would we ever be able to get back to just being us? It seemed like such a vast bridge to cross.

"So, we got Armello. He is hopelessly in love with Waverly's sister, so that's an easy win for us. I don't think the others will come along this nicely," I said, changing the subject to something safer.

"No, they won't. Celebrate the win tonight, and we will talk tomorrow."

I let the coin go dead. I should check in with Lux and Sutton. I should also go back to that dinner, but I couldn't. Knowing Kyra was avoiding me made my stomach churn, but what could I do if he wasn't ready to talk to me? If he needed space, then I guess I would give it.

I headed back the way I came and went to my room, willing the hours to go by. I wished I could speed up the time of the whole world, not just my world, so I could see Kyra. Instead, I lay down and willed myself to sleep. To find Xael to talk to her. To have her comfort me, train me, or do something besides sit here and fucking wait.

I closed my eyes, letting myself dream.

↔

"Xael." I breathed.

"I'm here, my child." She sat in our meadow, her eyes filled with understanding.

"I'm worried about Kyra. And this felt too easy with Armello. I know the others will be harder, and I'm not sure I

can do this. I don't want people to suffer. I want to just live my life and not have to worry about some assholes coming in to destroy the mortal realm." I threw my hands up in the air and started to pace in the dream.

"I know, child. This was always a heavy burden to bear. Can I distract you with something else?"

"Sure," I said, needing to literally do anything else but panic about Kyra, right now.

"When you go and see Kyra, you will have the chance to see my body and connect with my physical form," she said slowly, like she was afraid it might scare me off.

"Okay, is that a bad thing?" I sat in front of her, my eyes wide.

"No, I think that I may have an idea. What if we performed the immortality ritual on my physical body with your blood?"

"Would you be able to go back to your body? Would your soul be able to reconnect?" I wondered why I hadn't thought of this before.

"I truly don't know. I operate in a very strange place in the mortal and celestial realm. Physically, my body has been preserved, just stripped of life. My time power still flows in my blood, but I cannot access it like I did before. It exists there, but cannot be wielded by me anymore. But perhaps with the exchange of your blood, I may be able to reconnect physically again. I won't have my powers as they now rest in you, but I may be able to rise and live again as an immortal."

"So, we aren't sure what will happen?" I asked, worried that my blood might destroy her physical form.

"We aren't, but it's worth a try, right? Perhaps I could be of more assistance to all of you on this journey if I were able to phys-ically be in the mortal realm." She looked far off, as if she were unsure of the plan herself. What does immortality look like in someone who no longer could wield their magic? She was an orig-

inal twelve, so perhaps the laws and rules of what we knew to be true operated differently here.

"If you would like to try it, then I'll do it. This in-between space has no rules until we make them, right?" I grabbed onto her hands.

"Greer!"

"Someone calls to you from the mortal realm, child. You would do your best to answer them. Let your body sleep after this. I will not visit your dreams until tomorrow."

"Greer!" Waverly shook me as I woke up, startled. "Are you okay? I got worried when you didn't come back, that something had happened." She chewed her lip and eyed me warily.

"Yes, I'm sorry. I checked in with Nova, and she said whenever we're done here, we should meet up with them. I guess Kyra has a bug? Nova was very vague, and it feels like I wouldn't have known if I hadn't called." I scrubbed my hands down my face and tried not to let this feel like another betrayal.

"I'm sorry, Greer. That sounds oddly ominous. I was just worried, and then I saw you sleeping here and thought maybe you passed out or something. And truly, I did not want to witness any more of what Armello and my sister were up to." Waverly babbled on nervously.

"Wave, it's okay. I was just trying to distract myself from panicking about Kyra and our unnerving physical and emotional distance. Tomorrow feels like a long way away." I sighed, feeling like this night would last forever.

"Do you want to talk about it?"

Yes.

"Not really, but I'm up for a distraction if you have one." I wanted to be vulnerable and pour my heart out, but what if I started and I couldn't stop? What if reliving the past few months tore me into a million pieces all over again? I didn't think I could survive it right now.

"What about if we go for a little swim? Help clear your head and tire you out so we can wake up tomorrow morning and get moving?"

A swim would be nice. I nodded my head and put on my suit. We headed out towards the ocean water.

"I'm trying to conquer my fear," Waverly said as the water hit her ankles. I wrapped my arms around her and thought of the horrifying events of the trial I had to go through.

"Me too," I whispered as we waded in deeper. Stars danced in the sky, and it reminded me of Nova. I wished we were all together again. I needed to touch base with Lux and Sutton, but I assumed if something were wrong, they would have reached out already. What a messy fucked up situation we all were in.

Tonight, we faced our fears in the water, and tomorrow I would see Ky. Gods, I hoped we could figure this out. Pain was the curse of immortality, and both of us had endured a lifetime.

THIRTY-ONE
KYRA

"Kyra," a voice whispered over me. It almost sounded like Greer's voice, but it couldn't be. She was with Waverly, and they were trying to win over Armello. It must be another painful dream. My dreams had a funny way of twisting the knife of physical pain with emotional edges.

"Ky." The voice broke, and sobs erupted. I willed my eyes to open, but all of my body felt too heavy and too vulnerable. Like all my skin was raw and exposed. As if the insides of my heart were strewn about the room in piles of ash.

"When will he wake up?" The sweet imposter of Greer's voice said. Gods, I wished it were her. She made everything better.

"I don't know. He woke up between the first and second treatments, and then again between the second and third, but he hasn't woken up from the third treatment yet. He will be in pain for the next week. His body is new. Free of his father's poison that tainted his blood and heart for too long." It sounded like my mother's soft-spoken words, but I couldn't be sure.

"Why didn't any of you tell me it was this bad?" Greer's voice asked.

"He didn't want to worry you..." my mother responded.

"Well, I'm fucking worried," Greer grumbled.

Everything in my brain felt muddled together and squashed in all the wrong places. I was unsure what was reality and what was just a dream. I willed my hand to lift to let them know that I was awake. I could hear them. If I could only open my damn mouth or my fucking eyes.

A hand settled on my own, and I knew that this was either a very unfairly realistic dream or Greer was here. She squeezed my hand, and I tried to send warmth to her like I always did when we held hands, but the connection to my power felt different. Like there was something blocking it, like a string had been snipped.

"Ky, it's Greer. I know you aren't going to die, but damnit, that doesn't make me feel that much better when I know you're in pain. Why didn't you want me to know?" Her lips kissed my palm, and I willed my body to do anything except lie here.

"The funny thing about immortality is, it doesn't make things like this any better. Pain is pain, anyway it's handed to you. And scars are hard to heal from." Wet drops landed on my hand while she cried silently.

"G, he will wake up soon. He just needs time. His body is learning how to operate without Riordan's touch." Nova's voice was low and silky, meant to soothe.

"I can only imagine the burden it must have been to have Riordan's talons in him for so long. With the curse holding his tongue to this..." Hyacinth almost sounded like she cared. Maybe she was warming up to me after all. I smiled at that.

"Did he just smile?" Greer's hand tightened around mine. "Kyra Valequay, please wake up!" She urged me like she could will it so.

I moved my lips, but no sound came out, just a gentle opening and closing. I pressed my lips together and tried again.

"Don't rush it, Kyra." My mother's voice floated around me. "Some water."

Something came to my lips, and it was like I was swallowing for the first time. I took small sips and started to find the connection to my eyelids. I barely squinted them open. Everyone was blurry, the lights too bright for my irises.

"Maybe we should dim the lights?" Greer asked, her hand cemented in mine.

I tried again, and this time, the soft glow of the overhead lights didn't send my eyelids crashing back down. I blinked a few times until everything came into focus.

"Hi." Greer hovered above me. Her hair fell in a waterfall to the side, and I wanted to run my fingers through it.

"Hi," I croaked out in a voice that sounded like I had inhaled about a hundred tons of smoke. I went to try to sit up, but the most I could muster was lifting my head and neck.

"Don't sit up." My mother's hands pushed my shoulders back down, and her touch felt like irons on my skin. Hot and painful. I winced.

"My skin." I tried to form the words that would make sense of all of this.

"Is probably very sensitive right now, like a raw sunburn," Nova said. She let her hands float over me, and a cooling sensation happened.

"I'm sorry, Ky. I'll let go of your hand," Greer went to snatch her hand away, and I found some strength in my fingertips.

"No, it's okay," I whispered. My palm in hers felt right, and it was worth any discomfort I was feeling.

Greer smiled at me, her eyes watery. "I'm still mad at you. You have some explaining to do. But your crystal is almost fully crimson, and the lines are receding from the rest of your body." She hovered her gaze over my chest and abs.

"That's good, right?" I whispered, words were coming more quickly.

"Yes, very good. You should be fine in about a week. I assume Riordan visited you in your dreams. It tends to be the easiest place the original twelve can access if they try hard enough." Hyacinth looked at me with more warmth in her eyes than she had since we met.

"Yeah, he was really pissed off. It felt like whatever your spell was doing to me was also doing something to him. He was unimpressed, to say the least."

"Well, serves him right for exercising his magical control over you for years, for his gain. The selfish, self-righteous bastard! Just controlling and manipulating everyone he can. He can't even do one thing right anymore by the people he loves..." My mother wiped away a tear and closed her eyes.

"We've all made bad choices in relationships. You're allowed at least one free pass for falling in love with a man who lied to you for a long time about who he was. Gods know we've all been there." Nova squeezed her shoulder.

"What did you find out about Armello?" I squeaked out, not ready to unpack how horrific my father had also been to my mother.

"Maybe we should wait to debrief this until you can sit up and keep your eyes open." Greer looked at me like I might float away in a slight breeze.

"I think I'm fine," I croaked out. She chuckled, and it made my heart grow in my chest.

"You are most certainly not. Waverly is here chatting with her sister on the phone. There is a lot to tell you, and we're trying to decide whether Lux and Sutton will join us. So, why don't we get you to a comfier bed instead?"

My mother and Greer scooped up my arms and moved me

to a wheelchair. They brought me to a new room with a huge, king-sized bed, and all the windows were already drawn with the blinds.

"I think I can take it from here, Verity. Thank you," Greer said, and my mom kissed my forehead.

"Rest up, Kyra, things are only going to get..." I could tell she wanted to say worse, but instead it came out as, "intense."

"Thanks, Mom."

She helped Greer move me to the bed before walking out.

"So, I probably can't make love to you, can I?" My speech was slurred from the effort of moving that small distance. Her green eyes twinkled.

"Kyra Valequay, absolutely not. We need to talk about some things first, anyway." Her eyes watered, and I knew she probably felt betrayed by me, again. But I didn't want to add to her already incredibly long list of burdens.

"Pleaseeee?" My eyes barely open.

"How about just a few kisses?" she offered, gently trailing her lips across my jaw.

"I think that's nice."

"How about this?" Her hair tickled my chest as her lips dusted over the aching skin there. Just like in my dream, her touch soothed me.

"You did this, in my dreams," I hummed, wishing I could return the favor.

"You dream of me?" Her voice whispered across my hip bones.

"Always."

She continued her path across my body, barely missing an inch of exposed skin on my torso, chest, and arms with her fingertips or her lips or the gentle swish of her hair.

"Sleep, my love, and dream of me again. Maybe in a day or two, you can return the favor." She finally placed her lips on mine, and it was the last bit of comfort I needed before I fell into a deep sleep full of hope for the future.

↤

I woke up to something warm beside me and the smell of vanilla and cinnamon spice. I opened my eyes with ease this time and gingerly sat up to see Greer sprawled next to me; her presence immediately made me smile.

My body felt better. Not as raw and achy, but rather on the upswing and over the worst of it. I still had no idea how many days had passed, or what Lux and Sutton were up to. I could only hope everyone was making steps in the right direction. My father had been furious, and I knew he would come with a vengeance for what he felt was his.

He wasn't one to simply roll over and give up. He would come for us, and he would have a price he wanted us to pay. I sighed. This game of cat and mouse was getting old, and we had just fucking started it.

"Hey." Greer was on her stomach and looking over at me, her face squished into the pillow.

"Hey, sleepyhead," I said, gently pushing her hair out of her eyes. She gave me a grin that made my heart sing.

"You're the one who's been sleeping," she said, getting up abruptly and looking at me accusingly.

"I was fighting off evil in my body, okay? I think I got a pass for this one."

She laughed and sat up to look at me. "I was really worried about you; you've been in and out of sleep for several days now." She chewed on her lip and looked at me with tear-filled eyes. "Why didn't you want me to know things were this bad?"

"Greer, you have already suffered so much. You have so many of your own wounds, and I didn't want to add to that.

We both ignored those things when we were in hell just to make it through, and I guess I was doing the same to protect you from more hurt," I confessed, and it was true. We hadn't talked about everything that had happened. One minute we were in hell, the next we were here, and somewhere along the way we forgot to fucking talk to one another.

"We can do better than this. I want to share your burdens. I love you. And I want to share mine with you when I'm ready. We can both take time and space, but eventually the truth needs to come out. Deal?" Greer asked, looking at me expectantly.

"Deal," I said, smiling, my heart feeling the lightest it had been in months. "Anything from Lux and Sutton?"

"They are still figuring it out with Raelyn. Waverly and I's task seemed easy to accomplish, but I would guess that many of the others will be hard." She hugged a pillow to her chest.

"We'll figure this out. You won the fucking Immortality Trials. I'm in love with a badass who can kick butt and save the world." I smiled lazily at her and rubbed the hair out of my face.

"I missed you a lot." She tentatively slid closer to me and placed a gentle kiss on my lips.

"I missed you," I whispered, letting my forehead rest against hers. "I feel much better now." I leaned back against the headboard.

"Ah, and how much better?" She slid onto my lap.

"Better enough for a little light physical activity?" I said it like a question, and she giggled.

"Okay, but I get to be in control, and first things first, you sit back and relax," she whispered in my ear, and it made my cock hard right away.

"I can obey orders." I sat back while she climbed off and gently pulled off her shirt, revealing her lovely breasts. Her nipples were already hard.

"You're stunning, Greer." I looked at her in amazement.

She smiled coyly and turned around, sliding off her shorts, showing off the curves of her ass. She turned around and sauntered over to me, trailed her fingertips up my arm, and placed a gentle kiss on my lips.

"Watch me, Ky."

She walked to the side of the bed and sat facing me, opening her legs so I could see her pretty pussy. She sucked on her fingers and gently started to slide them down her body, teasing her nipples and trailing down toward her wet folds. Greer dipped her fingers inside herself and gently started rubbing her clit in slow circles. She threw her head back, lifting her breasts higher in the air.

"Are you watching, Ky?" she breathed, sliding her other hand down. One worked inside her while the other teased her clit.

"I couldn't fucking look away if I wanted to."

I was transfixed, mesmerized by her lush body. The more she pleasured herself, the harder my cock got. I wanted to touch her. To devour her. To stick my face in her pussy and taste her on my lips all fucking day.

She started to writhe and moan, panting my name, and her legs shook on her release. She dipped her fingers back inside and came over to me, offering her fingers for me to suck. I licked them clean, and she hovered herself over me. I could feel the heat of her.

"How'd it taste?" She teased me while she rubbed the head of my cock along her wet center.

"Like I could die between your thighs as the happiest man alive." I ran my fingertips along her soft sides and cupped her breasts in my hand.

"May I?" I hovered my mouth over the rosy buds of her nipples, needing to feel her in my mouth and around my cock.

She nodded, and I began to gently nibble and suck along

her body while she continued to tease her entrance with my cock.

"Gods, Greer, I love you so fucking much." I could drown in the taste and smell of her. Then she slammed down on me; her wet heat was glorious.

We both moaned while she pushed me down, and I watched her ride my cock. I teased her clit even more. There wasn't anything gentle about the way we tangled our tongues and scraped our teeth against one another. We were starving for one another. She moved against me until I could feel my own orgasm coming. I cried out, clinging to her as she crashed over her own pleasure, again.

We sat there intertwined. I had to remind myself that this was real, and we were together.

"How was that for some light physical activity?" she whispered, and I laughed. Gods, it felt good to feel like me again.

"I think it felt good, but who knows if my witch doctors will think so." I snuggled deeper into her and held her tight.

"Maybe they don't need to know?"

"We already know," Nova said from the outside of our door. And we both froze and looked at each other before laughing hysterically.

"Guess it didn't matter anyway." She giggled.

"I wish we could just stay in this bed forever," I whispered against her skin.

"I know. Things are rough right now. It's like emotionally edging, waiting for the next move. A giant game of chess except I don't know where the other fucking players are or what powers or rules they have." She sighed as we untangled our limbs from one another, and she slipped on her clothes.

"Truly, we're going in mostly unprepared, so we're doing the best we can with what we've got." I gently got up and looked around to see a neat pile of clothes waiting for me.

"Hyacinth said I could see Xael's body today. Supposedly,

I may be able to connect her body and her soul. Which sounds fucking terrifying and exciting." Greer chewed on her lip and sat on the bed while I dressed slowly.

"You can do that?" I didn't exactly know how the power of time worked, but that seemed like necromancy shit.

"Apparently, because her body has just been here the whole time existing, and her power can't really die as an original immortal. If I give her my blood like the immortality spell I gave the others, it could be what she needs to make the physical connection back to herself. She said as much in my dreams." Her eyes looked far away, like she was thinking back to all the conversations she and Xael had shared.

"Well, I guess you won't know until you try. Who the hell knows, since magic likes to make up its own rules just like the fucking twelve do. It's like, as soon as we have one thing figured out, they find a way around it. It's maddening." I sat next to her, and she leaned against me.

"I'm glad we're together again. I want Lux and Sutton here, too." She slipped her arm around me, and I breathed her in deeply.

"I know we need the team back in one place so we can all stop having a heart attack anytime something scary happens to one of us."

"Exactly."

"Well, are you ready to do this? To keep doing our save the mortal realm shit?" I stood and offered my hand to her.

"If I have to." She grabbed it, and I pulled her in close.

"I mean, we don't have to." I squeezed her hard.

"Yeah, we do."

She was right. We didn't have much of a choice if we wanted to keep our home and loved ones safe.

THIRTY-TWO

LUX

"You want us to steal something?" Sutton was angry. He wanted this curse lifted, and Raelyn was being manipulative as shit.

"Technically, it was always mine, and it was stolen from me, but I do need someone to fetch it for me as they won't be giving it back anytime soon." She smiled wolfishly at us.

"Who are we retrieving your item from?" I wondered if this item truly belonged to her.

"Just an old friend-turned-enemy, you know. It's a heart-shaped locket with a purple diamond. Nearly impossible to miss. It was buried in her family's graveyard, and I am not permitted to go there because she has shunned me, so alas, I need someone to fetch it for me." She waved a hand dismissively, but I could tell this would be more complicated than grabbing a necklace.

"What's the catch here? Who are we taking this from?" I needed to know who we would be up against if things went awry.

"It doesn't matter, shifter. The important part is getting what I asked for so this curse can be lifted, and we can forget that this," she waved her hand at Sutton, "ever happened."

"My mother begged for your help, and you made a mistake. The least you could do is allow me to right your fucking wrong." Sutton's eyes were bottomless as he leered at her.

"Retrieve this, and I will do it, no problem." Her smile was exceptionally toothy.

"Where is it?"

"I'll draw you a map." With a snap of her fingers, an old scroll appeared with a crudely drawn map, and an X marking the spot.

"I will send you to the outskirts of her estate, and it's up to you to sneak in and get what I asked for and come back. Call my name, and I will return you. Simple, isn't it?" Raelyn clapped her hands excitedly.

"Fine. Here we go," Sutton grumbled. We stood, and I reached for his hand, intertwining our fingers.

"You ready?"

"Let's do it." Sutton sounded almost bored, but I knew he was fuming inside.

The world around us melted and molded like we were being thrown into a washing machine, and then we were spat out onto a grassy lawn, toppling into one another. Sutton landed on top of my chest, and I wrapped my arms around us, closing my eyes.

"Are you alright?" Sutton muffled into my chest.

Heat clenched at my core, and I tried not to think of what this would be like under different circumstances.

"I'm great." I tried to control the start of my erection.

"You sure?" Sutton teased, wiggling his hips against me.

"Don't start something you can't finish." I nipped at his ear, and he swatted me, pushing off my chest.

"Well, maybe we can finish *this* when we finish this." He

laughed, and it was such a rare, wonderful sound that I wished I could bottle it up and hold it in my pocket forever.

"Doesn't this seem suspicious to you?" I said, taking in our surroundings.

We were on top of a hill next to a tree, and down in the valley was a graveyard, and then further away was what looked like a small village. But no one was around. It was oddly empty.

"Very. But I'm sure whoever we steal from it will be fine." Sutton seemed unconcerned, but I had a gnawing feeling in my chest that this was going to be a problem later. We had enough looming things on the horizon; I didn't want to add another thing to the list.

"Okay, well, let's look at this fucking children's map."

We opened the scroll, and it revealed a layout of the graveyard, with a tall fountain of a woman in the middle. That was apparently where the heart would be.

"Is it underneath it?" I asked.

Sutton shrugged as we walked toward the grave site. Magic rippled in the air, thick and heavy like fog.

We slowed, making our way through the tombstones and up to the fountain. It was breathtaking and full of heartache. The woman looked as if she were in agony and pain. Her eyes screamed.

We walked around the white marble, and I didn't see any dazzling purple heart.

"We have to dig up and destroy this fountain, then?" This idea was getting increasingly worse.

"Possibly, let me try to call up someone from their grave and see if they can find it for us." Sutton walked around the fountain, speaking softly, and he quirked his head to the side.

"The bodies here, they do not want to speak to me. Almost like they were told not to?"

I didn't know a lot about necromancy, but he seemed to think it was odd.

"Okay, so we do have to dig it up," I said. "This is now the second time in the last seventy-two hours I've dug up a fucking grave," I grumbled, closing my eyes and breathing deeply.

"You're so good at your magic, Luxton," Sutton said sweetly, and I scowled at him.

"Okay, what small animal can burrow?" I said, wracking my brain for what would be most beneficial to turn into.

"A prairie dog?" Sutton perched himself on the edge of the fountain and ran his fingertips along the blue water. The tiles shimmered underneath him.

"That's a new one."

I called my magic and slid into the small form of a prairie dog.

"You're fucking adorable." Sutton's mouth opened in a little o.

I curled my head to the side and scowled. "Stop that face and go find our purple heart!"

He blew a kiss at me, and I rolled my eyes as I turned to burrow underneath the fountain.

The earth was densely packed, and I figured it was probably right in the middle. So, I went straight to the center. I found nothing but more dirt. However, I could go up. I wondered idly if the statue itself housed the heart, so I wiggled up through the bottom of the woman until I spotted a shiny piece of stone. I dug through it more and grasped it in my little paws.

Immediately, the earth started shaking, and the world exploded around us. The statue melted into dust as I scrambled to transform back into myself and not get sucked into the debris. The woman was absolutely destroyed, and the fountain was full of mud.

"Shit," Sutton said.

"It collapsed around me when I grabbed the heart." I brushed myself off the best I could, holding out the necklace.

A howl sounded in the distance. And then another. We looked at each other frantically.

"What was that?" I looked towards the village, and suddenly, the edge of it was full of giant wolves. "Holy shit. What is with these fucking beasts and the gods?! We should go." I grabbed Sutton.

"Raelyn," he shouted. Nothing happened. "We've got to get out of this magical boundary!"

We didn't have time to wait. I shoved him ahead of me, and we ran towards the hill. I spared only a moment to glance back and found the wolves were surging towards us at an alarming rate.

"Fuck."

We continued to sprint towards the tree. The wolves were snarling behind us as we continued up the hill.

"Lux!" Sutton seemed scared for the first time.

"Run! Keep going and wait until I meet you back at the tree!" Sutton looked like he wanted to argue, but I didn't wait for his response. I shifted into my leopard form, turned, and snarled at the wolves, racing back down the hill to face them.

I charged towards the snarling animals and roared. Gods, it had been a long time since I had been in this form, and I forgot how good it felt.

I rounded on the start of the pack and tore into the first wolf I came across. It let out a yelp as I swiped my claws across its snout and sent it sprawling. The next one was on me in an instant, and I closed my mouth around its neck and tossed it aside. They were big, but I was bigger.

More kept coming, and I clawed and snapped at as many as I could until I was piled underneath gnashing jaws and growling teeth. I changed into a cobra, and the pile fell on top of itself while I bit at heels and ankles, sending a few stumbling. Poison coursed through their veins. I shifted again to a falcon and took to the skies as they looked confused and disheveled, nursing wounds, and limping off back to where they had come.

I flew back to Sutton and changed to stand in front of him. His eyes were dancing side-to-side, scanning our surroundings. He was nervous. I winced as I changed and placed a hand on my ribs.

"They got you?" Sutton's nostrils flared, and he reached for my other hand.

"Just a scratch. Nothing big. Let's get out of here, though."

"Raelyn!" he snarled, and we warped back to her estate. We landed back in her living room, where she was sipping a glass of red wine lazily.

"You got it?" Her smile grew like she couldn't believe we had made it out alive.

"Thanks for the heads up about the wild wolf pack." Sutton gently sat me down and scowled at her.

"I mean, she does have a flair for the dramatics. The necklace, please? You had to destroy the statue for it, no?" She seemed delighted as Sutton handed her the necklace, and she gazed at it longingly.

"Gods, I can't believe you didn't get eaten alive!" Raelyn snicked and tossed it onto her dining room table like it didn't mean a damn thing.

"Lux got hurt." Sutton's shadows shuddered around him, and the air turned sharp like static electricity.

"He's fine, darling. Immortals can't die." She rolled her eyes. My injuries were seemingly inconsequential despite my ribs being skewered.

"But they can still get hurt." Sutton ground his teeth together.

"Do you have a first aid kit or something?" I groaned. The pain in my side was growing, and red was blooming on my hand. The healing would start eventually, but in the meantime, it hurt like a motherfucker.

"Gods, I wished I could just see Damari's fucking face!" Raelyn said, practically crackling.

She threw a first aid kit at us, and my mouth dropped open. Sutton and I froze while she cackled louder.

"Do you just say Damari?" Sutton grabbed the kit and ripped it open. He gently lifted my shirt away from my skin, and I winced. He looked at me apologetically.

"Oh, did I?" Like she didn't know exactly what she said. Her eyes looked positively bloodthirsty as she flicked her tongue over her sharp canines.

"Yes. Did you just make us steal from another goddess?" This was not good. Our goal was to enlist both of their aids. We probably couldn't do that when we had just stolen from her on behalf of Raelyn.

"I said it was mine in the first place." Her eyes narrowed like we had just made some sort of accusation.

"Do you two not get along?" Sutton's hand gently applied antiseptic, and I hissed at the pain. He grabbed a bandage and wrapped it around my whole torso.

"It's all in good fun, I suppose. Not sure Damari would agree, but she's always been a stick in the mud, you see." The corners of Raelyn's mouth tipped up slightly.

Sutton finished the bindings on my ribs and slid his fingers along my skin, making me want to shiver.

"Lift the loveless curse." Sutton was done with her games, and his posture was rigid and controlled.

"Done. Now, that was easy, wasn't it?" She blew a kiss at him, and a pop sounded that made his shadows shudder, and he dropped down to a knee.

"Are you alright?" I said, kneeling next to him, his breath coming in pants.

"He's fine. The curse is lifted. And I'll help you and your little timewraith. But I bet Damari won't, now that you stole from her." She giggled again, like this was all some hilarious joke.

"Is the mortal realm a game to you?" I hissed.

"Oh, darling, to us it's all a game. Good luck getting her on your side after you've aligned with us. Briar will, of course, do whatever I say, so don't worry about him. He'll be here tomorrow for breakfast before you go on your way, so you'll meet him then." She got up and swept out of the room, and my mouth dropped open.

Sutton shook behind me.

"FUCK!" he yelled, and his dark eyes appeared bottomless. "I need some air. Will you be okay by yourself?" His fingers were shaking.

"Yeah. I'll figure out where the hell we're supposed to stay and then I'll come find you." He nodded and left; his emotions barely contained.

I didn't know which part of our day had been worse: the fact that we had stolen from Damari, that I had been attacked by wolves, or that we were now inadvertently tied to a selfish goddess.

Gods, I hoped the others were having better luck than we were, because if they weren't, we were never going to win the fight ahead.

THIRTY-THREE
GREER

"We have good news and bad news."

Everyone was gathered in Hyacinth's house, and I was pressed up against Kyra. Things were not exactly back to normal, but I could feel that there was a way to get there. Even though so much was still unsaid, we had at least acknowledged the walls we had up. If we wanted to stop hurting one another, we would need to be more honest and open. Even if that, too, was painful, at least it was an investment in a better future, one I hoped the demons of our past wouldn't taint so heavily.

Kyra looked much better than he did when I first arrived. His color was returning to normal, and life was back in his eyes. He moved a bit more slowly as if his muscles and bones were trying to figure out how to work together once again, but for the most part, he was getting himself back.

We both were.

"What's the bad news?" Waverly was snuggled up next to Nova.

"Lux and Sutton stole something from Damari because Raelyn tricked them into it to lift Sutton's curse." Lux had sounded exasperated on the phone, like he was ready to punch Raelyn's face. Sutton had stormed off, and he hadn't seen him since, which wasn't a great sign.

"Well fuck." Hyacinth rubbed her forehead and pursed her lips.

"Damari won't like that at all." Farren paced behind her and tapped his fingertip to his bubblegum pink lips.

"I forgot the games Raelyn likes to play, especially with Damari. We should have seen this coming." Hyacinth crossed and uncrossed her legs.

"I mean, I don't think it's anyone's fault that Raelyn acted like a child, or that she and Damari haven't grown the fuck up in the last hundreds of years," I scoffed. If they were children, it wasn't our job to parent them. My patience for the original twelve was nonexistent. Not when they threw around violence so carelessly and didn't give a shit about the collateral damage it caused.

"Well put, Greer," Verity smirked. "Either way, this does cause a bit of a problem. It means that even though we now have Armello, Raelyn, Briar, Hyacinth, and Farren, we still need one more to fully tip the scales. It sounds like Damari might not be a great option."

"Who else would be on team mortal realm? Because it sure as fuck didn't seem like anybody was willing to help when we were in the infernal realm?" Kyra scowled and looked down at the ground as if speaking to hell itself.

"Great question. I would need to think about who we could pull over to this side and how we could approach each one," Farren said.

"It gets a bit tricky because technically the original twelve are now the original eleven, plus Greer. Which means even with five of the original gods and goddesses plus Greer, we are still at a bit of a disadvantage. We would be most secure in coming to peaceful terms of saving the mortal realm if we could have the majority and pressure the others. Phayre and Riordan won't budge unless they don't think they can win. They will make up an excuse to avoid embarrassment, but they have had years to plan. And then there's the extra complication of Kyra, as well." Hyacinth added.

"Why do I make things more complicated?" Kyra stiffened beside me.

"Riordan wants you on his side, and you would be a powerful ally. You have magic that is his and ancient. Under the right cultivation, you could have a power to rival his. Especially because of the way you have earned immortality and had it bestowed on you from the trials, which were through Xael's magic. You could make things harder or easier for him. Ideally, we would have years to prepare, but here we are," Verity said, tapping her fingers.

Gods, I was sick and tired of all this balance of powers. There were too many ways all of this could go wrong, and not nearly enough ways it could go right.

"You have powerful friends as well. But I would prefer to stack our team first and then see." Farren perched next to Hyacinth, and she laid a hand on his slim thigh.

"Great, well, I guess the first step is to see if we can get an audience with Damari, correct?" I needed an actionable step to take, and this seemed like what we needed to do next, even though she might spit in my face and turn me away, considering my friends had stolen from her for another goddess. But nothing would be as bad as my time in hell. I could at least take comfort in that thought, that no matter what, things could be better and that the worst was behind me.

"Well, it sounds like Sutton and Lux went to her estate so that we can try the same thing. I mean, the worst thing is she turns us away, and then we did our best?" Nova offered.

"Great, so let's go." I went to stand, and Kyra pulled on my hand.

"Greer." He looked at me with his scarlet eyes.

"Let's wait a few more days until I'm at my fullest strength. I want to go with you, and I just need a little more time," Kyra pleaded, and I couldn't say no to him. We had agreed to do this together. And fuck, I wanted that for us. I wanted to feel like I wasn't carrying the whole world on my shoulders, but that I could trust the people around me to help me with this impossible burden.

"Okay." I kissed his forehead and sat back down.

"In the meantime, I think we should go see Xael's body." Hyacinth stood and offered the crook of her arm to Farren.

"Okay, and then maybe we'll try the ritual?"

I was unsure of what would happen, but I wanted to give it a go. If I could have more of Xael's help, then I wouldn't refuse it, but there was no way to know how this magic would take. Magic often felt like a living, breathing entity that had its own agenda, and we were all doing our best to play along.

"Let's see her body first and then speak of the ritual," Hyacinth said, and she led the way. She took us to an elevator where we all stepped inside, and she planted her palm against the wall. It looked like she sent some magic through. In the blink of an eye, we were whisked down several floors.

Nobody said anything while the doors slid open, and she stepped out with Farren still attached to her arm. We entered a moodily lit hallway. It was stark and empty, with a few doors branching off from the corridor. Hyacinth walked swiftly, taking a right and then opening another door.

It was like she had a whole other life down here.

"I have more facilities for all of my needs."

I didn't ask what that meant, and instead, we all just nodded while we stepped into another room. Lights turned on as if motion-activated, and in the center of the room was a huge container where a body lay.

The room was lined with some machines and instruments

on the outskirts, but the tomb in the middle of the room was what drew you in. It was a tall white table with drawers on either side and Xael's body floating on top of it in a tube of greenish liquid. Her red hair floated around her, and her body seemed eerily suspended in space.

She looked peaceful. An unexpected pang of jealousy shot through me. What would it be like to finally rest? To feel nothing and just exist for years at a time?

Mentally, I chastised myself. It wasn't realistic, and it wasn't like I actually wanted to meet death. What I wanted was a fucking break. But that's what we were working towards —peace for us and for everyone else. We just had to get through some of this other shit first, and then we could actually enjoy whatever immortality had to offer.

"What is she in?" I asked, pulling myself out of my mental spiral. I didn't know much about medieval embalming, but this was not normal. It seemed viscous, almost like syrup; she moved slightly from the liquid being cycled in and out.

"It's a special type of magic necromancers came up with to keep her body alive. It sustains her physical abilities by constantly monitoring and feeding us information on what she needs," Hyacinth replied.

We all surrounded it, and Nova waved her hand over the tube.

"Her blood feels different. Unlike anything I've ever felt before. Not exactly dead, but almost without life, but with remnants of magic. I'm not sure how to describe it." She scowled, and Waverly leaned in close.

"She looks just like you, Greer," Waverly murmured as if the words might make me fall apart. The bruises I was accustomed to seeing on her wrists, ankles, and throat were gone, leaving untouched skin behind. I shivered and flexed my own palms, trying to resist the urge to touch my neck. We both had been shattered by cruel hands and forced to pick ourselves up again.

She was dressed in just a white wrap around her breasts and small shorts. Nothing like the casual outfits she donned in our dream state.

"And this liquid keeps her muscles and organs from atrophy?" Kyra said, sticking close to me. I was grateful for his presence because I didn't know what to think. My body had always been drawn to him. It was my head and my heart that had been the most battered by what had happened in the infernal realm. But those wounds were healing, too. We both had impossible circumstances to navigate, and at the end of the day, we were trying to do what was best for the people we loved. It was hard to hold onto the anger when I certainly couldn't fault him for doing what he thought would keep me safest in the end.

"It does. It was like an immediate suspension of her body's physical capabilities. Her organs and muscles are still working as if she were living life normally," Hyacinth said.

"Truly spectacular, my love." Farren wandered over to her face, looking at her with longing. "She deserved a better fate."

"Yes, she did," I responded. "Can we wait for the ritual? I want to talk to Xael one more time before I do this. Just to make sure I've got all the information I need."

"Of course. The only timeline we have is yours, Greer. Sleep on it and speak to Xael in your dreams." Hyacinth almost looked sad that she wouldn't be reunited with her friend right away, but she nodded in respect to me.

"Okay. Let's do that." I didn't know why I needed to speak to her one more time. We had been over everything several times. There were no surprises, but I just wanted one last moment in my dream world with her. I didn't know if that would go away when her physical body became suitable for her soul once again.

We didn't know anything for sure. I wondered if Sutton would have answers, and I realized that either way, I needed to speak to her to find out.

We all shuffled out of the space and back up to Hyacinth's house, where I peeled off from the group to take a walk outside.

"Can I join you?" Nova asked, and I nodded, leaving Ky behind with his mom and Waverly.

We hooked arms and walked the grounds.

"How are you doing in there?" Nova said, tapping her heart and then her head.

"Oh, what a loaded question," I replied, turning my attention to the beautiful gardens around us. How could I even begin to answer such a question?

"I can go first, if you want?" she offered.

"Please do. I would rather hear someone else's chaos right now." I squeezed in tighter to her, and her silver stars sparkled.

"Well, I'm glad to have you and Waverly back. I know going to see her sister and Armello was a lot for Wave. So, I'm glad to have her here safe and sound, where we can work through things together again."

I nodded. I was starting to feel that way about Kyra, too. But I still ached for Lux and Sutton to be here as well. It felt like part of my heart was gone when Lux wasn't around.

"And the world feels funny right now. I can feel the anticipation rising. We're a powder keg preparing to explode. There are many moving pieces to this game, and all the players have been playing much longer than we have. It makes me nervous, not to know what we're walking into, but we don't have much of a choice, do we?" She reached out and touched a white lily with her fingertips.

"Seriously, it's like we just joined the game and they have been playing this battle for hundreds of years, so things have happened that we weren't a part of, but we're just expected to understand and jump on board right away!" I was frustrated to be in this inherently disadvantaged position. It wasn't like I was given a choice for this fate. It was thrust upon me with aggressive hands.

"It's funny to be chatting with the original gods and goddesses. To see how the other side of the world lives. We have many rules and regulations we were told to follow our whole lives, most of which were laws made to serve some and not others."

"The world has not always been what it seems," I whispered, leaning into her strong shoulders.

"Exactly. And immortality feels interesting in my body. I have always felt strong, but I have played with the delicate balance of not scaring those around me and keeping true to myself. In truth, I'm excited to have the opportunity to use what I'm truly capable of. To push my boundaries and limitations of what is possible." She smiled, and I knew that whatever was at the end of Nova's full power would be nothing short of mesmerizing strength.

"Now it's your turn." She nudged me.

"That's it? Nothing else?" I wasn't ready to explain everything in my head. It was horrifying for me to think of, let alone share with Nova.

"I know you aren't great at confronting what's inside, Greer, but I'm asking you—as your friend, as someone who loves you—to not fight all of the battles that live inside your head by yourself." Nova squeezed my hand reassuringly.

"Well, it's a bit funny, now that I'm an immortal, those anxious and depressed thoughts don't have the same outlet they once did. I'm, in a way, cursed to live this life forever. It's a bit odd to come to terms with, so I don't often think about it. But my time in hell... it fucking haunts me like a ghost I can't get rid of." I closed my eyes and breathed deeply.

"I want to be normal again, or at least as close as I can be.

But my body was treated like a punching bag down there. Verity had to shatter my hands to remove the damn manacles that made my life miserable for us to escape. The collar and cuffs dehumanized me in a way I didn't know was possible. I thought I knew darkness before, but it grew tenfold down there in a different way." I stopped and touched a rose petal, trying to find the words to explain what I was dealing with.

"The physical pain was abhorrent, but the worst part was that I lost my fight. My will to live diminished to new levels, except this time, there was no other option but to live and endure. It's fucked up to know that I would have chosen death if I could time and time again, but I couldn't. And I would have been letting a whole realm of people down. And now I am trying to deal with life outside of those months, which is good. And safe for the time being. That includes people who love me and want to help me, but I am terrified to let them see how far I've fallen from the woman I was during the trials. The woman who could overcome anything and did. But that version of me just doesn't exist right now. Right now, I'm taking it day by day and trying to let myself be alright again... " I let the words trail off and bit my lip, nearly drawing blood. Tears pricked the backs of my eyes, but I was so tired of crying.

"And I just feel like this whole mess wasn't something I asked for, but now I'm a part of it. I do want to do better. I want this godsdamned world to be better. I have no idea what that looks like exactly, but I sure as hell know what it doesn't look like, and it's not being ruled under the likes of Phayre and Riordan."

"The whole immortality trials were just a farce, a distraction for them to get a means to an end, and now we're here waiting to start the beginning of the end! I feel like I'm losing my mind half the time because I don't know what the fuck I'm doing, and I feel so broken, but here I am doing it anyway." I couldn't stop the tears then. They ran freely down my cheeks, and I didn't have it in me to swipe them away.

"I'm so overwhelmed in a different way than I was before. I can barely keep track of all the nuances with gods and goddesses and the rules of magic, and all this other bullshit. And gods, I'm just tired. So tired," I whispered as I looked into Nova's empathetic eyes.

"Things have moved and changed rather rapidly in the last year. You have overcome so much and dealt with so many tragedies. There isn't a right way to heal from trauma, and you, my dear friend, have had more than most," she said, validating my feelings.

"And all I want is for us to be safe and happy now. Is that too much to ask for? Gods, and I just don't want to live forever. I don't feel like most people should, but who am I to make that decision, you know? It's supposed to be this desirable thing, and right now I just want to throw it all away and sleep for eternity." Words tumbled out of my mouth that I had no idea I was holding in.

"I feel the same about immortality, but here we are, both immortals." She sighed, wiping tears from my face with gentle fingertips.

"But not because we wanted to, but because it felt like a necessity." I didn't know if that made it different, but it felt like it should.

"True. There are a lot of heavy things to work through right now. And you are so young in the world of magic. I remembered how intense it all was in the beginning. I wish you had the time to be curious and joyous, celebrating everything in between, but you are being forced to be ready and powerful to defend and protect right away. It's not as much fun that way." We found a bench to sit on, and we leaned into each other.

"Can you tell me about what happened when you first learned to use your magic?" I asked quietly.

What would it be like to experience this as a child? Where everything was new and shiny and exciting, and you had the world ahead of you.

"Ah, okay, where to start?" Nova tapped her finger on her red lips. "I accidentally made my cat do a few ridiculous things before I realized I was forcing her to do it." She laughed, and I listened to her tales of a young blood witch learning the awe of magic.

By the time Nova and I had finished reliving her whole childhood, I was feeling lighter and ready to talk to Xael. The sun had already gone down, and I went to find Kyra in the room we shared.

"Hey." I closed the door behind me and snuggled up next to him, and he smiled, kissing my forehead.

"Did you have a good chat with Nova?"

"Yes, and I think I'm ready to start trusting you again. I want to tell you everything... I'm so tired of guarding my heart from you," I whispered, squeezing my eyes shut for just a moment and blinking back my own tears. Kyra's eyes turned watery, and he nodded, giving me the space to collect my thoughts.

I recounted everything I'd told Nova, and it was easier this time. Each time the words came out of my mouth, they held me in their claws less. Kyra listened as my tears came again, and this time, I didn't try to fight them. I let him hold me as I finally bared my soul to him.

"I'm so sorry, Greer," Kyra whispered into my hair, and I could feel his tears against my scalp.

"Me too," I said, and we sat there for what felt like an eternity, soaking up the feel of one another on our bodies. For the first time in a long time, my shoulders relaxed and my jaw loosened.

"I think I'm ready to talk to Xael now." I finally said. "How are you feeling now that I've dumped everything on you?"

"I wanted to know, Greer. But I'm doing okay. Better now that you're here." He tipped my chin and gave me a long, sweet kiss. I wiggled against him, and he chuckled against my lips. "We both need rest, so save that." He gestured to all of me. "For another time."

"You're right. I just can't resist you." I nipped at his chest, and he pulled me in tighter.

"Same." He started gently stroking my arms and scratching my head.

"This isn't fair, you know this makes me sleepy." My eyes were already starting to close.

"That's the point. Sleep, Greer."

I didn't need to be told twice. I slipped into my dreams with Kyra's touch.

↤

"Hi, Greer." It was always the same meeting for Xael and me. A reprieve from everything else and a moment of stillness. Of simple existence.

"Hi, Xael. I saw your body today." I didn't want to waste any time despite how uneasy I was feeling.

"Ah, and how did that go?"

"A little unnerving, honestly, you're floating in magic green goo." I made a face, and she laughed.

"Yes, I imagine it would be." She smiled almost regretfully.

"I wanted to talk to you one last time before we go through with the ritual. I just... I don't know why, but I'm scared. Will we still have our dream space, or only physical mortal realm space?" I twisted my fingers in my hand, and she sat back, tilting her head up to the dream sun.

"I really don't know. I am not sure what will happen. My soul is free-floating now and seems to only find its tether when you sleep. It might mean that our tether now translates to my physical body and only my physical body. I cannot say for sure."

"I will miss this, us, if it only ties to your physical body. I know that might be a bit selfish, but you bring me comfort in my dreams."

I hugged my arms around myself. Xael had been my saving grace during my time in the infernal realm. "And then what if it doesn't work, and then I end up fucking something up and you're gone forever?" My eyes went wide, and I tried to erase the words I had just spoken out loud.

Xael chuckled, "Greer, my dear. If several gods and goddesses couldn't wipe me from the face of the earth, I imagine you can't either. I don't know if that brings you comfort or not, but it does me. I am bound to live here as one of the originals in one way or another. I think the others did their best to get rid of me, and they simply couldn't."

I nodded, knowing that it made sense, but I was still scared. All of this was still so new.

"Okay, tomorrow morning I'll do it, and we will see what happens?" I asked, hoping I sounded more confident than I was feeling.

"Yes. Try my child, the worst that will happen is we will meet back here, which is not terrible at all." She reached out and grabbed my hands.

"I know things are starting to catch up to you. You have put on a face for quite some time since you got your powers. Let yourself feel and breathe and live. We are going to figure this out." She released my hands, and we spent the rest of the time just basking in the sun. No training today.

I tried to savor every bit until morning came, and I was pulled away from our world into another, ready to face Xael, in person, once and for all.

↤

"You ready?" Hyacinth said, and I nodded. Today it was just us in her funny laboratory. I had asked for some privacy, and I knew she and Xael were close, so it felt like the right people were in this room.

She gently inserted a needle in my arm and removed a couple of ounces of blood into a blood bag. She approached a machine, entered some information, and then placed the blood into a small metal drawer, closing it afterward. It had been a hard twist of fate that Xael's blood could still give immortality, but she couldn't have it for herself.

Some random beeps sounded, and all of a sudden, the green goo surrounding Xael had wisps of red until the whole thing was a soft pink.

"It will be absorbed into her body," Hyacinth informed me as we moved to either side of the tank. "The incantation, Greer."

I whispered the words that were Xael's own spell for immortality and placed my hands on the glass surrounding her, praying to someone that this would work. Several painful minutes went by as the goo around her started to return to its regular coloring.

A monitor beeped behind me.

"What was that?" I looked straight at Hyacinth.

"Her heart responded."

Another beep.

"And that?"

"Her brain and several other organs are functioning on their own."

Another beep.

"And that?"

"Her lungs."

There was a thump on the glass. We both looked down to see Xael's eyes wide open and her fist hitting the glass.

"Open it!" I panicked and screamed, and Hyacinth pressed her palm to the glass, and it melted all around her, and the goo evaporated into thin air.

Xael gasped for air and coughed as if trying to release all the gunk from her lungs.

"Xael?" Hyacinth said tentatively, kneeling as Xael rolled to the side and continued to cough, her hair hanging wet on the sides of her face.

"Hyacinth?" she hacked. Her voice sounded like it hadn't been used in decades.

"You're here." Hyacinth had tears rolling down her face as she helped Xael sit up.

"It's good to see you, my friend." Xael wrapped surprisingly sturdy arms around her, and they both cried into one another.

"It worked," I whispered. I couldn't believe she was here.

"Greer." She held out her hand, and I grasped onto it, kneeling beside her as well.

"Xael," I whispered. My heart felt like it could explode out of my chest.

"I don't know what to say." I sobbed.

"It's good to see you." She wiped the tears from my eyes.

"You too." And I meant it. My fairy godmother had finally come back to life.

Thirty-Four

Kyra

"They've been down there a long time." I paced the living room as Mom sat, drinking her coffee. Nova and Waverly were with Farren, going over information about the other original twelve, and I was forced to wait for Greer.

"You'll wear a hole in the carpet, dear. Give them time. Xael seemed like a very important person to Greer. It's intimate to have someone visit you in your dreams." She sighed into her drink.

I looked down, thinking of when my father had visited me in my dreams and how it felt like a violation of my innermost psyche. What was it like to have someone in your head who was kind and caring? I shuddered.

"I know, I just worry about her. Like all the fucking time."

I ran my hand through my hair and breathed out through my nose. My strength was almost back to what it was. Oddly, now that both of us had immortality, the worrying was worse. Was I doomed to feel like this forever? Worried about what would be done to Greer when her body was forced to regenerate again and again?

The longer this went on, the more it felt like a curse that we were destined to live forever.

"How about we work some of that energy out?" Verity stood and smiled at me.

"What do you mean?"

"You haven't trained since we took you through the detoxification. Let's see what your firepower can do." She winked and turned, gesturing for me to follow. I looked over to where Greer had disappeared with Hyacinth and groaned.

"She will be a while, Kyra. You might as well move through some of that energy. And you can spend some time then with your dear old mother."

She was right, I needed to blow off some steam, and it would be nice to spend some time with a parent who actually gave a shit about what I wanted and who I was.

"Sure, okay. Where do we go?"

"Hyacinth has an open field out back if you're okay to walk a bit."

I nodded and followed her outside. The sun was high, and there was a cool breeze. Perfect weather to throw some magic around. We walked in silence for a while before we arrived at a wide-open field behind Hyacinths' property.

Except the field wasn't empty. Someone was standing in the middle of it.

"Who is that?" I asked as we walked closer, and Verity stopped abruptly, reaching for my arm and pulling me back.

"Afton." She practically growled, and he spun around, his eyes lighting with mischief.

"Verity! It's so good to see you. How cute, a little mother and son bonding time?" He was practically giggling.

"What do you want?" I asked, wanting nothing more than to throw a fireball at his annoying face.

In the blink of an eye, he was right next to me.

"Oh, just checking up on our little runaway delinquents," he whispered in my ear. Before I could grab his neck, he flashed a few feet in front of me.

"You need to get off Hyacinth's property. She will not welcome you here, and you know how she deals with unpleasantries." Verity's voice was calm and cool.

My blood was roaring to rip him to shreds, but what would be the point? He was an immortal and a god. What the fuck could I do against him? What could any of us do to stop this horrible fate? Was there any future in this that we could win? How did you rid yourself of immortals who were part of the fabric of this earth and reality?

"Looking a little hopeless there, Kyra." Afton taunted, and my eyes went wide. Could he read my thoughts or something?

"You don't know anything," I hissed, and in the blink of an eye, Afton replicated himself. Again and again and again. Until the whole field was replicas of him. Hundreds of them, sneering at me.

"It is not real, Kyra, it's a trick." My mother's grip tightened on my arm as she slowly backed us away from him.

"Just because it's a trick doesn't mean it's not real," All the Aftons cooed, and it made my head swim. "Or perhaps you need another reminder of Riordan." In a flash, all of the Aftons morphed into Riordan, and it made me want to vomit.

"Don't you want to hurt me? I've been so horrible to you both," all the Riordans said, closing in on the two of them.

"Kyra, it's not worth it. We should leave." Verity pulled at my arm, but my control snapped. In a roar, I ripped from my mother's hands and ignited my hands, sending fire shooting out and around me, ripping through each vision of my father, only for it to shimmer and slide back into place.

"You can do better than that, son," they jested, and I tore through them again.

Rage clouded my vision as I shot power from my hands again and again. Explosions littered around me while I tried to find the one that was truly Afton. But I couldn't. Again and again, the Riordans poked and prodded and joked at me as my mother yelled for me to stop. I couldn't see anything except my father's smirk and the red filling my vision. Flames and heat filled the air around me, and my control continued to slip until everything was a fiery haze.

"Enough!" Verity screamed, and her hands shot out; my flames winked to nothing besides me, and Afton stood off to the side, laughing manically.

"Or you're just as bad as your father, look at the damage you've caused." Afton looked practically gleeful. I took in the area around me. I had destroyed everything near me. My stomach plummeted as I took in the scorched earth and ruined trees around me. Nausea rolled through me. I realized that I had been just as careless as my father was. Ruining everything in my path simply because I could not see further than my own fury. I sank to my knees and looked at my hands. I had rid myself of my father's curse and his hold on my heart, only to become just like him when my emotions bested me. The realization was like a punch to the gut. How could I let myself be like this?

"Kyra, it's okay... Don't let him get to you." Verity waved her hands about, and the trees bloomed green again, and the earth returned to its originally grassy state.

"Like father, like son. I do have an actual message for you." Afton clapped his hands together while I sat cemented on the ground.

"Your father says surrender now, and he won't torture Greer and Verity. Instead, Verity can go back to her cage, and Greer can join her. But the longer you let this little tantrum play out, the more years get added to them being at the mercy of Phayre."

"Fuck you, Afton, and go tell Riordan the same," Verity seethed. She reached down and pulled me to my feet.

He would never let us go. Ever. The only way to defeat him was to contain him, and how the hell were we supposed to do that?

"Very well, just know the longer this goes on, the more torturous ideas Phayre will have about what to do when your reunion comes." Afton winked, and then he was gone.

"Are you alright?" Verity's hands landed on my arms, her gaze scanning my face.

"No," I said truthfully, and she nodded. What else was there to say?

"I know things feel hopeless right now. But you are not your father, Kyra. Afton likes his tricks, and you simply fell into one."

Verity continued to fix the foliage around me. The irony was not lost on me that she probably had fixed much of my father's destruction, too.

"I don't want to be like him, and I just proved I'm exactly the same," I whispered.

"You are not. I have grown more accustomed to Afton's ways of antagonizing people. This was your first real go. He doesn't stop until his trick is played out, once you're ensnared in his game. Now you know, and you can be more prepared next time."

I didn't know what else to say, so I simply nodded while we made our way back to Hyacinth's house. I barely knew what any of the original immortals were capable of, and if that showed me anything, it was just how unprepared we really were. My sense of hopelessness only grew the closer we got to the house.

Greer was right through the glass doors of Hyacinth's

patio, and next to her was a woman who looked so similar. Wine-red hair, pale skin, and a similar build. If you looked too quickly, they could be twins.

Greer was solid and took up space with her whole being. But the other sat differently. A delicate regalness about her. It could only have been Xael. Beside her, Hyacinth was snuggled in close, as if she couldn't bear to be far from her long-lost friend for a second longer.

"You're back!" Greer's voice was music to my ears.

"I was getting anxious waiting for you, so we took a little walk and had a run-in with Afton," I said, not wanting to hide anything else from her.

"Oh my gods, are you alright?"

I couldn't hide the sorrow in my eyes.

"Yes, I will be. Nothing new to report except he's an asshole and so is my father."

I didn't want to pull this moment away from her. Greer had looked ecstatic seconds ago.

"Okay..." She searched my face, her eyes narrowing.

"Afton was using his usual tricks. Being an annoying prick and poking all our sore spots with his normal threats," Verity added, sitting next to Hyacinth, who just rolled her eyes.

Maybe I was overreacting to Afton's words, but I knew the lengths Phayre and Riordan would go to get their way. And I would be lying if I said I wasn't afraid.

"Okay, well... If you're sure. This is Xael." Greer sat, and I sat next to her, so we were facing Xael.

"Hi, Kyra. I've heard much about you." She bowed her head and smiled. She sounded like a queen.

"Hi, Xael, I could say the same for you. You brought Greer comfort and guidance when she needed it most. I cannot thank you enough for that."

"We are linked spirits, as they say." They beamed at each

other, and there was an energy in the air that didn't exist before.

"Farren is here, is he not?" Xael asked, turning to Hyacinth.

"Yes, as well as Nova and Waverly, but I believe they went out for some food. They should be back shortly so you can meet most of the team."

"Lux and Sutton aren't here yet. We have run into a bit of a dilemma. Maybe you'll have some insight. I haven't told you much about what we've found in terms of the others residing on earth."

Xael frowned. "Time has a funny way of changing what we know to be true."

Hyacinth pulled her aside, and they started chatting about something else, and I took that opportunity to check in with Greer.

"How are you feeling after resurrecting Xael? I imagine that was probably a bit intense."

"It was. I imagine it would be strange to wake up in your body once more after so many years and then not to have your powers. It was a surreal moment for all of us. I feel like I'm still in shock that she's in front of my face, and her face is my face, which is also strange." She was rambling now, and I threw my arm around her.

"You do look a lot alike, but there are differences," I replied, smoothing a strand of hair behind her ear.

"Gods, I just want to be back home for a second and leave this mess behind and breathe for one fucking minute."

"So, let's take a break. Lux and Sutton still have to meet Briar, so let them do that, and we can wait it out at your place. There isn't anything to be done until we hear from them again. We should probably wait to talk to them in person anyway. We can give Hyacinth her place back and give Xael some time to rest."

She chewed on her lip. "Okay, a little break wouldn't hurt anyone, probably?"

"Exactly. Just a few moments to breathe. Let's finish today here and then go home for a minute to relax."

"Home. I like the sound of it. Okay. Let's do it."

The rest of the day, we finished up what we could there and said our goodbyes. Hyacinth seemed excited to have her home back, and Xael was yearning for some rest. We portaled back to the apartment, where the four of us collapsed on the couch.

"Gods, I'm fucking tired." Nova threw her hand over her eyes.

"I would just like to say that I've made up a pretty serious case with the FEC to cover for our mission of saving the world, so I don't get fired, and it's exhausting to keep that crap up." Waverly lay fully down on the sofa.

Greer laughed loudly. "You made up a mission?"

"I mean, is it really made up when it's actually the truth, but no one will believe you?" she inquired.

"Everyone's life has taken a giant pause button with all of this. What a chaotic ride," I grumbled as Greer rested her head in my lap.

"I just want Lux and Sutton back and everyone to be on our side and for no one to try to take over the world. And to live my life drinking wine and eating chocolate and having sex with you." Greer looked up at me, and it was my turn to laugh.

"And I just want to have sex with you!" Waverly responded by throwing her hands at Nova, who also chuckled.

"Well, I'm pretty sure we can all still have sex with whoever we want to. Lux and Sutton will be back soon. I just hope that Briar and Raelyn don't fuck it up even more. If one immortal could be less of a piece of shit, that would be fabulous," Nova huffed beside her.

"Speaking of that, we'll see you two later." Waverly grabbed Nova's hand, and she giggled as she dragged her into the spare bedroom that was basically theirs for how often they stayed here the past month.

"That was unexpected," I mused.

"Was it actually, though?" Greer winked at me and dragged her hand across my chest.

I grabbed her wrist and kissed her palm.

"I mean, why not? We could be whisked away at any moment in time to go mess with these immortals. I want you to be inside of me now."

I planted a long, lingering kiss on her lips.

"How long do you think those two will be?" I stood and ran my hands up and down Greer's legs, and her eyes darkened.

"Long enough." Her voice turned huskier, and I threaded my hands through her hair and tilted her head back. Her lips were on mine in an instant, nipping, teasing, and prodding while I groaned into her.

"Let me taste you," I whispered in her ear.

"Ky, are you sure you're alright from earlier?" Greer brought her hands to my face and forced her eyes to connect with mine.

"Yes, it's nothing new. I just felt out of control with my powers and my emotions, amongst Afton's taunting," I confessed.

"Ah, well, take the control back. It's yours," she whispered, and I gave her a bruising kiss before moving down her body.

"Fuck, Ky," she breathed, and I slid her leggings and panties off.

I kissed along the inside of her thighs, and her head fell back on the couch. I scooped her generous ass into my hands and pulled her wet pussy right up to me.

"Gods, I've missed this." I ran my nose along the wet seam

of her and inhaled the scent of Greer. I took one long swipe along her folds, and she shuddered.

"Ky," she whimpered, and my control snapped while I devoured her. I sucked at her clit and teased her with my fingertips until her hips were bucking up and her legs were shaking. Gods, I could drown in the essence of her.

She started to writhe while she came apart on my mouth and my fingers. Her inner muscles tightened around me. Greer's thighs around my ears, and she yelled out my name.

"Ky!" It was like a prayer on her lips.

"Inside me, please, now." She pulled me up and sloppily kissed me. "I like the way I taste on you." She smiled against me, and I pressed my mouth to hers, claiming it.

I threw off my own clothes and peeled off her shirt.

"I could die a happy man between your thighs and these breasts." I cupped them in my hands, and she eyed me greedily.

"Your turn."

She pushed me away and sat me down on the couch, where she slid in between my thighs, my erection right next to her face.

"Greer, you don't have to...ahh—" Her mouth latched on and moved its way along my shaft, and pleasure started tickling at my spine while she worked her mouth and tongue along my cock and played with my balls.

"Godsdamnit," I pressed into her mouth, and she smiled at me, her one hand digging into my thigh. She released my cock with a pop, and I lunged for her. She laughed while I caught her around the waist and threw her on the couch, looking down at her.

"I love you, Greer Roberts." I lost myself in her eyes.

"I love you too, Kyra Valequay."

I drove myself into her, and godsdamnit, she felt good, hugging my dick like a glove. We moved together like we were made for each other. She clawed at my back, and my pleasure rose hard and fast. I pounded into her and reached in between us to play with her clit.

We catapulted into our climaxes together, and all that was left in the world was Greer and me. There was no beginning or end of our bodies, or our magic or our love. We were one.

THIRTY-FIVE

LUX

"Knock knock," Sutton called while he entered the room.

I stirred awake in a fog.

"Hey." My voice was stiff, and my body wasn't much better off.

Sutton came and sat next to me on the bed. His eyes traveled to my chest, and his tongue darted out, licking his bottom lip. I swear to gods, my cock stiffened at the sight of it. He cleared his throat and took his time drawing his dark eyes to meet mine.

"I assume you contacted Greer." He tilted his head to the side.

"I did. I think after we meet Briar, we should go back and see what can be done about the meeting with Damari. I don't know what exactly that amulet stood for, but obviously, it has a lot more history than we realized, and we just made it that much worse."

Sutton nodded and chewed his lips. "I'm curious about the curse being lifted." His voice deepened as his eyes traveled along my naked chest again. His shadows curled around me and whispered against my skin.

"I would very much like to put that to the test, but perhaps we can wait until we're out of this place and hopefully out of danger. As there is nothing, I wouldn't like more than to throw you on the bed and devour you." I leaned close so our lips were only inches apart.

"Is that a promise?" He moved to meet me, his cherry red mouth nearly brushing against mine.

I pushed through the rest of the distance, wrapped my hand around the back of his neck, and pulled him in for a long kiss. He tasted like smoke and amber. He moaned into my mouth, and I almost lost it then and there.

"Does that answer your question?" He panted while I pulled away, and a blush crept up on his cheeks.

"It sure does." He got up and looked at me one more time, longingly. "If you wake up looking like that every day, I don't know how either of us will get out of bed."

I slapped his ass, and he cackled, leaving me to get ready to face the breakfast ahead with Briar. I didn't know much about Briar except that he was a sibling to Raelyn. She acted as if he would follow along with whatever she said. Raelyn had been a menace to work with so far, so I couldn't imagine that her brother would be any more pleasant. My expectations were rather low for how this would go between the two of them.

We walked into the dining area to find Raelyn chatting with someone at the table, who presumably was Briar. She laughed loudly at something he said, and he beamed at her.

Briar was petite, his skin a light purple, and green faerie wings sprouted from his back. He looked at us with crystal blue eyes as we walked in.

"You must be Luxton and Sutton. What a pair you two are." He waggled his dark purple brows at us.

"You must be Briar." Sutton sat and pursed his lips.

"I am!" He held out his hands, and glitter sprouted from his fingertips.

"The necromancer and the shifter." He tilted his head to the side.

"And they have a blood witch, a siren, a warlock, and the timewraith as well. Quite the band of people if I do say so myself." Raelyn flashed her pointed teeth and went back to her toast.

"And you all are seeking my assistance as well as my sister Raelyn's?" Briar took a sip of a bright pink liquid in front of him.

"We're looking to form an alliance." I pressed my elbows on the table and leaned forward.

"An alliance?" Briar muttered.

"Yes. The original immortals who reign off Earth will make a power play for the mortal realm. We would like to stop them, so we're just making sure everyone who is already on earth wants to keep things the way they are." I chose my words carefully.

"Well, I certainly don't want Riordan coming in and throwing a tantrum. Gods knows the West is already a shit show because of those folks. They played a little too hard with the society they made. They should have just picked smaller things to mess with, much more satisfying and much less fuss." Briar giggled.

I ground my teeth together. These two were disconnected from the world, besides their own bubble. They weren't my favorite allies, but we needed them to stand against the others.

"Right, so we want to make sure that you will fight for the mortal realm the way it is with Hyacinth, Farren, Armello, Xael, and the rest of us if it comes to it."

Hopefully, the threat of all of us banding together would be enough for Riordan to stay in his place.

"Sure, sure. Why not? We haven't had a good row in

years!" Raelyn clapped her hands like the idea was delightful. Sutton rolled his eyes beside me.

"Great. We'll contact you if it comes to that, then." I nodded and went to stand, wanting to leave this place as soon as fucking possible and get home.

"Oh, don't worry, dear, you won't need to call us; we will know if they all step foot in the mortal realms. Strong magic calls to strong magic. If the others show up, you bet it will be a reunion for the ages." Briar smiled sweetly at us.

"Right. Okay." Sutton grabbed my hand, and we hauled ass out of there. As soon as we set foot outside the mansion, I wrapped my fingertips in his.

"That was suspicious, right?" I kissed his fingertips one by one.

"Extremely. Raelyn was already on my shit list, and with Briar, those two screamed mischievous antics."

I nodded, grabbed his hand, and pulled him against my chest.

"Can we leave now?"

"Yes." He licked his lips, and we warped and molded through the darkness until we were standing right in the middle of my living room.

"Godsdamnit, Lux, you scared the shit out of me!" Kyra stood in a wide stance, his eyes wide, fireballs at the ready. I laughed and went to hug him, his flames extinguishing.

"I'm sorry, we literally ran out of Raelyn's house."

He clasped me strongly, and Waverly let out a sigh.

"We were about ready to kick your ass." Kyra grabbed Sutton and pulled him for a reluctant hug.

"Doubtful." He cracked a small smile.

"What's going on in here?" Nova rounded the corner, and her stars lit up. "You're back!" She ran over and squeezed both of us aggressively.

"It sounds like you're wrestling in here." Greer followed shortly and smiled widely, running into my open arms.

"Gods, it's good to see you all," I said, smothering her with my frame.

"You too," she mumbled and let go, giving me a once-over and then looking past me at Sutton, raising her brows. I shook my head no. Gods, nothing got past her.

"I'm so glad we're all together. I truly cannot handle the childishness of the immortals." I sat next to Kyra.

"It's like a bunch of children fighting over the same toy— the toy being us, Earth, or Greer, minus Hyacinth, maybe." Kyra sighed.

"Briar and Raelyn were nearly intolerable. But my curse is gone. Even if it did fuck us over with Damari." Sutton smiled quickly, and then it faded as he scowled.

"Well, she hasn't answered Hyacinth's call from what I understand, so I guess we're just waiting until someone makes their next move." Greer fiddled with the end of her braid and tapped her fingertips on her thigh.

"I don't like this waiting game. It feels like a trap." Nova stood and paced.

"I know. Maybe we should be doing something else?" Waverly added.

"What else is there to do right now?" Greer asked.

"We could prepare some more. Learn how to work more effectively as a team. Right now, we all use our magic in a very everyday way. If it comes to a fight, we should know how to do this together, and if weapons are involved, we should come ready," Kyra said, uncrossing his legs.

"Against immortals, we will need to be smarter and more creative. Our brute magic strength and physical prowess won't do it. We need to be more." Nova stopped and looked around at us.

"How do you propose we do that?" I wasn't sure how we would all learn how to move and operate as a team.

"We could take a field trip?" Waverly looked at Greer.

Greer stopped messing with her hair, and her eyes lit up. "You want to go back to your island? They did have the most impressive training facility I had ever seen. Your sister, I think, would be happy to have us."

"I mean, until we have something better to do, we could start there?" I nodded, liking the idea of at least being more prepared.

"I need to take care of a few things first, and then I can. Let's take a break for a few days, and then we can go do Camp Waverly-and-Greer." Kyra smiled and stood, placing a kiss on Greer's cheek.

"Great. Then it's settled!" Waverly clapped her hands, looking delighted.

"I need to see where my team is at with the serum. We need that as another tool in our arsenal." I got up and went to my room, leaving the group behind to call my offices.

Merritt picked up on the second ring.

"Hey, where are we with the serum?" I thrummed my fingers on my desk.

"I think we may have got it!" She sounded excited.

"How positive are you?" I challenged. I needed her to be sure.

"Pretty positive. But the only way is to try it out on someone. But I don't know who would voluntarily give up their immorality to just be a part of an experiment? This one shouldn't kill the immortal right away like the other one did, but rather render them back to their original state. And uh, the other one, well, if you try it on someone, they will most likely die immediately."

True. There was no way to know if it worked without giving it a go on someone. But I didn't know how we would go about that. Who would want to test it? Greer could techni-cally give the immortality back to them, but that process could be excruciating. We had no idea what the body or mind would do going back and forth between immortality and not. It had never been done before.

"Let me think about it and I'll get back to you. Keep it a secret and keep it safe. No one is dying for this serum this time around." I hung up and walked out of my room, nearly running into Ky.

"You good?" he asked, leaning against the wall.

"I think we got the formula for the serum."

"That's good, right? So, why do you look unhappy?" He frowned at me.

"It was loosely based on the research my parents had, but we didn't get the exact formula, so we had to fill in the blanks and make a non-lethal version. We need to try it out on some-one, but who would give up their immortality?"

Kyra furrowed his brows.

"We also don't know what it will do to someone if they take it. Can they be turned back? Will their body and mind be able to handle switching through those states? I don't know how to make sure it works without hurting someone."

This serum should have probably never been invented in the first place, considering it was just another tool the original immortals were using to control people.

"Good point. Not sure there is a humane way to go about checking the validity of the product." Kyra crossed his arms.

"I don't know, I'm going to have to think on this one." I sighed.

"Are you and Sutton...?" Kyra raised his eyebrow while changing the subject.

"You're just as bad as Greer! Calm your tits. You'll know when there's an update." I laughed and shoved him. His eyes went wide, and he feigned innocence.

"I simply care about your relational well-being and was just curious if anything had occurred."

I laughed, and it felt good to be with my friends again.

"Whatever." I shoved him out of the way, and we walked back to the living room to join the rest of the group.

Nova looked pissed, and the vibe was immediately different since we left.

"What's wrong?" Kyra asked right away.

"We have a problem; the President called," Greer hissed.

"And?"

"He wants to meet to show off Kyra and me as winners. We couldn't have one goddamn moment of peace." She threw her hands in the air.

"Wait, this gives me an idea." I smiled mischievously at Kyra. The President had already fucked with us enough, so who's to say we couldn't fuck with him?

"The President, really?" Kyra lifted his brow.

"What's going on here?" Waverly waved her hand between us.

"The President is going to be our test subject," I said, smiling.

"A test subject for what?" Sutton asked, looking at me quizzically.

"For the serum my team just put together. We're going to take the President's immortality."

Nova laughed loudly. "Please tell me more."

THIRTY-SIX
GREER

"F ucking hell."

I stood next to Kyra. He looked immaculate in his deep red suit, and his long hair had been pulled back in a little half-up, half-down moment. I fidgeted in my skin-tight black dress and messed with the braid down my back.

"Are you okay?" Ky's scarlet eyes danced as his gaze roved over me.

I wasn't, but I was trying to be.

"This dress is just fucking tight, and I don't want to be here, and these shoes are pinching my toes." It was all true, but mostly I didn't want to do this.

My senses were on overload, and I was so tired. How the President knew that we were back was beyond me, but he had eyes and ears everywhere. How were we supposed to do this on top of everything else going on?

"I'll happily take all of this off for you if you'd like, my love." Kyra kissed right under my ear, and I shivered. His words and touch brought me back to the moment.

"Please, I'm begging you," I moaned, wanting nothing more to be anywhere but here.

We walked to the President's secretary, who ushered us into a conference room where we were supposedly meeting him to discuss our press tour. They were apparently excited to use our relationship as a fun way to spin the story.

Gross.

"You have it, though, right?" I chewed on my lip.

The plan we had hatched with the others was that, at some point, we would have to slip the serum into the President's drink.

"Of course," Ky whispered, slipping his fingertips into mine and sending heat through my palm.

We took our seats and faced the floor-to-ceiling windows of the President's conference room. We were the only ones in here now, and nothing was offered to us in terms of comfort, so we were just forced to sit.

"Why does the whole godsdamn world want us to wait on them?" I grumbled, and Kyra chuckled.

"But seriously."

"I'm tired of this anticipatory time. I just want to get all of this over with. I want Riordan to make his fucking move and everyone to move on with their lives outside of this because right now I feel like I've made the whole thing up in my fucking head because no one else besides us knows what's going on." I dug my fingernails into my palms.

"I know it feels like we're losing our minds. But we aren't. My dad is biding his time. He's been waiting years for you. For this, it's just a matter of time before he reveals his hand. I'm just worried about when and where and what it will be." Kyra's gaze went out to the window, and his shoulders tensed.

"It's like waiting for a bomb to go off."

"Hello, Greer and Kyra." President Adonia swept in with only one other person.

My stomach plummeted as I locked eyes with someone

who had been haunting my nightmares since I had left hell. Someone who I wanted dead even more than Riordan.

Phayre.

"Oh, look at my little puppet!" She clapped her hands, and my mind fractured.

Suddenly, I was back in that room. My manacles on, shaking uncontrollably while she threw her power at me, shouting at me to act, to do something, anything to show her what I knew about the power of time. My own screams echoed throughout my brain as I relived the pain of her blows. My power had been like water then. Too slippery for me to hold on to and use in those moments where all I could feel was physical torture. I couldn't find the strength then, when all I wanted was to fall apart into a million little pieces.

"Dissociating, little one? I thought you were all big and bad from breaking out with Kyra's mommy's help." Phayre sat across from us with a sinister smile. Her teeth were too white, and her skin was the ghostly pale I knew all too well, dusted with gold patterns.

"Don't speak to her like that," Kyra snapped.

I shook my head, trying to formulate a way to get out of here. There was no way we could do this now. Not with her here.

"I'm here to ensure you behave," Phayre folded her hands in front of her and smiled, showing all her teeth.

"How are you even here right now?" I asked, finally able to find my words.

"I made a special trip just for you," she purred, and I fought the urge to shudder.

"What do you want?" Kyra asked, gripping the table in front of him so hard I thought he would break it.

"Oh, many things. But today I will settle for you reading this paper on camera and giving us that little dose of immortality serum, Luxton has cooked up in his lab. Your time to come back to us is near, but it's not right now."

I choked on my air as I fought to get control of my emotions. I reached out in my mind for the time current, but it was like a rushing river barreling through my control while I fought to focus on what I needed to do. I had asked for this moment where they would make a move, and I realized, in horror, that I wasn't ready. My power and strength were so depleted from my inability to regulate what I was going through.

"You'll let us go, if we comply?" I asked in a whisper, and Kyra's attention whipped to mine. His scarlet eyes were blazing as he looked at me with a frown.

"Today? Yes, I will," Phayre replied. The President continued to look at us like we were a bug to be crushed underneath his boot.

"And if we don't?"

"I will shove you out of this building window and say that a lover's spat turned deadly between the two of you. Your bodies, of course, will recover, but it will hurt you immensely. Ambassador Kyra will be imprisoned for his behavior, and you will be forced to do a marketing tour of your lover-turned-enemy story."

"What the hell is wrong with you? Who even comes up with shit like that?" I gasped.

"Oh, darling, I have had centuries to think of delicious ways to break things. Hand over the serum, please." She held out her hand expectantly, and I nodded at Kyra, who practically snarled, flinging it at her.

"Thank you, that wasn't so hard, was it?" Phayre snatched it out of the air, and she leaned back.

"Now, onto the interview. Make it convincing, you two. This is practically a winning marketing strategy written perfectly by you two." President Adonia called in a camera person, and we said nothing. They got a teleprompter set up, and camera people fluttered around.

I could feel Kyra stiffening beside me, but I didn't know what to say. We weren't ready for this fight with Phayre when it was just the two of us. This was supposed to be an easy setup with the President, and we were fools to think that this would work out in our favor. Things were escalating, and I didn't understand why Phayre didn't try to take us now, but I wouldn't question it.

"Make sure to look like a couple in love. Let's start rolling and do a couple of takes." President Adonia clapped his hands, and I winced at the sound, clearing my throat.

The words on the screen rolled by, and I fought the urge to scream and slam my powers out, but I didn't know what good that would do. I didn't have a plan for this, except to go through with it.

"Hi, I'm Greer Roberts. You may recognize me as the latest Immortality Trials winner."

"And I am Kyra Valequay, a winner from a few years ago." Kyra chimed in, his smile dazzling despite his body language screaming discomfort.

"We are so excited for this year's trials. We would have never met and fallen in love without the trials." I hated every word that was coming out of my mouth. "Not only did it bestow immortality and great power on me, but it also gave me the man of my dreams. The trials are an incredible gift from the Republic. If you work hard and fight smart, you can win, just like I did. A human's chance of winning is higher than ever, and I can't wait to see you all compete this year! Remember the deadlines to sign up are..." the rest of the words spilled out, and I could barely remember what I said. Soon, we wrapped up, and the camera crew left.

My body felt hollow. Void of everything that made me

who I was. My goal was to get rid of this heinous game, not encourage people to join. How did I ever think that I could conquer this monstrosity of a thing?

"That wasn't too bad, was it?" Phayre stood and walked over to where I was sitting and clasped my shoulders. My body seized up, and I lurched away, but her fingertips clawed into my skin.

"Soon we will be together again, wraith. I can't wait." Phayre whispered in my ear, and then she was gone in a swirl of smoke, the imprints of her fingers still fresh on my flesh.

"Are we free to go then?" Kyra growled next to me, and the President looked at us with a lazy smile.

"By all means. Enjoy your day." He waved us off, and I practically ran out of there.

"Greer, wait!" Kyra called out, but I was sprinting down the stairs two at a time, desperate to get outside. I reached for my powers again, and it was again hard for me to find my footing.

"What is happening to me?" I screamed, bursting through the exit door at the bottom of the stairs. Kyra was seconds behind me.

"Greer," he reached for me, and I collapsed into his arms, sobbing uncontrollably at the memories of Phayre's hands on me and the lack of control I felt with my powers when my emotions got the best of me.

"I couldn't do anything. I froze," I choked on those words and shook in Kyra's arms.

"You don't have to be strong all the time, Greer," he whispered into my hair.

But I did. If I wanted this to end, I needed to be able to control myself better. If I froze next time, it could very well be someone's life at risk.

Instead of saying any of that out loud, I let Kyra hold me and tried to pull myself together. That would need to be the last time. I could no longer fall apart in the presence of Phayre or anyone else, for that matter. Time needed to be held by me on a tight leash. There was no other way.

We made our way back to the apartment, and by the time we arrived, I had pulled myself together. My emotional armor was back in place, and I refused to let anyone get the best of me anymore.

The others thought that we had no choice but to accept Phayre's demands, but I couldn't shake the feeling that I could have done more. That I should have been able to stop her from taking the damn serum right out of our hands. They all continued to speculate on what would happen next, but my body was exhausted from the tears and mental gymnastics I was going through, so I excused myself to bed and vowed to destroy anyone who tried to come for me and my friends ever again.

↤

"Damari replied to Hyacinth," Nova announced at breakfast the next morning.

"Shit, what did she say?" Luxton looked nervous, and honestly, he should. He and Sutton stole from her, and that would not go over well.

"She wants Greer to come alone," Nova scowled.

"Absolutely not," Kyra proclaimed.

"Anything else?" I rolled my eyes at him.

"Tonight, she wants to meet you. Then other things will be discussed later." Nova tapped her fingers on the table and took a sip of her coffee.

"That's vague as hell. What does that mean?" Waverly rubbed the sleep out of her eyes.

"Nothing good. She knows it was Lux and me. This is

going to get messy." Sutton hadn't touched his food at all and was, instead, working on his second cup of coffee.

"Okay, so let's go meet her," I stated.

"I'm going with you." Kyra wouldn't take no for an answer.

"Okay."

"You won't argue with me?"

"No, I want you there. And what is she going to do to us? We'll see what she has to say, and then we'll go from there. Things are already messy, so why not make it that much worse, you know?" I stabbed my pancakes and chewed on the bite thoughtfully.

"It's true. We're already in over our heads with this, and we don't even know how it will play out." Lux snacked on some eggs.

"Alright, what should we come prepared with? Anything?" Kyra looked relieved.

"We should go talk to Xael and Hyacinth now before we meet. Farren might have some knowledge, too."

"Man, we were going to go to Waverly's Island today to train, too." Lux pouted.

"You all go, and we will do this and then come back. It shouldn't take all day, right? I assume she wants to set some terms or something, and then we will reconvene. I don't know, my negotiations with the twelve have all been very different person-to-person," I grumbled.

We all got ourselves together and called for them to portal us to Hyacinth's.

"Who knew my house would be such a gathering place?" She smiled and looked pleased.

"It's good to see you all again." Farren greeted us as Verity walked in with Xael.

"Greer!" Xael reached out with her hand and grabbed on.

We had still been able to communicate via dreams, so it wasn't like too much connection was lost. We had been training consistently at night, and it was starting to wear on me. But I didn't want to be ill-prepared for what was to come. I was already nervous about not knowing what we would be up against.

"We're supposed to meet Damari soon, and I wanted all the information you can give Ky and me. I know she said to come alone, but I'm not going to do this without Ky. Especially since she must know that Lux and Sutton are the ones who stole from her because of Raelyn."

"Oh, she definitely knows." Farren raised his brow.

"Fucking great," Kyra groused next to me.

"Okay, well, what can you tell us?" I nervously tapped my foot.

"Well, she is the goddess of power and strength. And she has an army of wolves at her disposal. They say that anyone who betrays her gets put into her pack to defend her for eternity," Hyacinth said it nonchalantly.

"Is that really true?" Waverly's mouth dropped open.

"Not sure." Hyacinth narrowed her eyes.

"I knew her to be someone who wasn't so filled with hate and hurt." Xael looked sadly at us.

"The mortal realm wasn't the kindest to her, from my understanding. She isolated rather quickly and tried to garner support with populations already here. They didn't take to her, so she threw a fit and has been picking fights with random populations and Raelyn since. I think she is bored and without purpose. She originally sided with Xael because she believed in her power, but her belief in it has slowly faded." Hyacinth crossed and uncrossed her legs.

"So, you haven't seen her since everything went down?" Lux leaned forward on his knees.

"No, I mean she wasn't my biggest fan, but Xael was always our equalizer, the balm to the fiery nature in both of us.

Without Xael, we crashed and collided in gods awful ways. We didn't initiate things after we took to the Eastern Hemisphere."

"So, she has a temper. I wonder if this is even worth it. I mean, could we convince someone else to join our side?" I wondered out loud.

"I mean, Afton was a possible ally, but he seems to want to just go with the side that will win or that has the path of least resistance for them."

"A lot of them want it to just happen because they feel entitled to the mortal realm," Verity added while taking a sip of coffee.

"Gross." Sutton scrunched his nose.

"Okay, so what do we think she'll want then?" I didn't know how we would win her over.

"She will most likely want you to complete a series of tests to know your strength and power. That will win her over even if she doesn't like you. She respects and loves power, so that will be the way you can get to her," Hyacinth speculated.

"Great, more fucking trials." I wanted to be done with these obsolete tests. Ky reached over and squeezed my knee.

"We'll figure it out together."

We spent the rest of the time catching them up on everything that had happened with the President, Afton, and our own training agenda.

"It's time, Greer," Xael announced, looking concerned at us.

"Okay, portal us?" Hyacinth nodded. Nova and Verity joined hands while Kyra and I held onto one another.

"Three...two...one..." Time and space warped around us, and I shut my eyes until we landed in front of what I assumed was Damari's place. We were on the outskirts of a graveyard with a crumbling statue nearby. My mouth dropped open.

"That has to be the statue they destroyed, right?" Kyra threw his head back in a cackle.

"It's not funny! This shit is going to make everything harder for us." I swatted him with my hand, but couldn't contain the giggles.

"So, it's funny that your friends destroyed my property?" A voice said behind us, and we both stilled, closing our mouths and turning slowly.

Damari looked pissed. She was a tall woman with mostly human-looking features, minus her cat-like eyes. She was muscular and wore a cape that covered nearly all of her form. Her black hair was braided down her back, and her skin was a light orange color.

"You must be Damari." I tried to sound confident, but it didn't feel very strong.

"And you were supposed to come alone." She scowled at Kyra next to me.

"We're a team." He sounded much more confident than I did.

"I see. Do you need another to feel strong?" she asked innocently, but I could feel the test on her tongue.

"There is almost always strength in numbers," I replied coolly.

"Not this time, timewraith." Damari's lips turned up as she pushed Kyra aside with such force that there was an audible crack. Claws ripped from her fingertips, and she sliced into Kyra's flesh like paper, grabbing at his spine and yanking hard, letting him soar.

His body flew and broke even more, bone shards sticking out of his muddled, bloody skin. He sprawled in a heap of flesh and screams. I didn't have time to process Kyra's massacred form before she wrapped her fingers around my throat, and in a sickening crunch and pain like I have never felt before, my trachea snapped.

The air disappeared from my lungs, and I choked on nothing but my own torture.

"Remember that you did this, wraith. You killed them all." Spit flew from her mouth, and she slammed me down to the ground. It was the last thing I could remember before darkness and agony swallowed me whole.

THIRTY-SEVEN

LUX

We didn't hang out long at Hyacinth's and instead went back to the apartment. Nova and Waverly left shortly after to run some errands, leaving Sutton and me alone to wait until Greer and Kyra returned.

"We're alone." Sutton looked at me seductively.

My chest warmed at his words. This moment had felt like it would never come. Now it was here, and I didn't even know what to do. I froze in place. My heart was nearly beating out of my chest.

"Yes, we are," I whispered.

My eyes took a slow perusal of his entire body, and I groaned. He always looked good enough to eat.

"You look like you're ready to devour me." He scooted to where I was perched on the couch. He ran his hand up and down my leg, and I shivered at his touch. His fingertips left little lightning sparks across my skin, and something in me snapped. As if his touch ignited me into action, and there was nothing else I could do except take more.

"I am." I leaned in and captured his red lips and threaded my hand through his brassy hair.

He pressed into me, and I wrapped my other arm around him and pulled him, so he was in my lap. Sutton ground against me, and my erection grew with each wave of his hips.

"Sutton," I whimpered into him, and he moved his lips down my jaw and to my throat, where he nipped at me. I ran my hands down his back towards his ass, grabbing him and pulling him into me. He made a little sound of surprise, and I pulled his chin back up so I could taste him more.

I had been waiting to taste and touch him for so long. I had thought about his lips everywhere on my body for months now. All I wanted was to take my time learning all there was to learn about Sutton.

I stood, taking him with me.

"Lux!" He squirmed in my hands, but his legs and arms wrapped around me.

"We're moving to the bedroom," I growled into his neck, and he chuckled softly.

"If you insist."

I closed the door behind me with a kick and set him down in front of me.

"Are you sure?" I whispered against Sutton's lips. Gods, I was sure. I had been thinking about this for so long. Dreams of Sutton had haunted me for gods knows how long.

"I'm sure. I'm a little nervous, honestly, but I know I want this with you, Lux. I've wanted this for a long time." Sutton's eyes turned watery, and I held him close.

"I want this too," I said, wanting to erase the anxiety plaguing Sutton because of his damn curse. He deserved to be loved and cared for exactly as he was, without fear or repercussions.

He pressed his mouth to mine, and my control snapped.

I lifted him up, and he wrapped his long legs around me. He felt so good underneath me, and I wanted to touch and taste him everywhere. My whole body was on fucking fire for him. He smelled like whiskey and smoke, and I devoured the skin at his neck.

His long fingers raked against my back, and I gently pressed him onto the bed.

"Less clothes," he whispered against my mouth, and I smiled, standing up and whipping everything off.

"Gods, Lux." He licked his lips, and his shadows almost purred around him. His eyes left heat in their wake as he stared at my eyes and traveled down, snagging on my tattoos, chest, torso, and finally to my cock, which was more than happy to see him.

"Your turn," I said, waiting to see all of Sutton's beautiful skin.

"Help me?" he asked, standing and lifting his arms.

I gently brushed his skin and discarded his shirt. I rained kisses on his chest and then sucked gently on his nipples. He arched into me, and I sucked harder. Gods, he was so responsive to me.

"Lux," he breathed, and I wanted to throw him down and bury myself inside him.

"More. Please, I need you," he demanded.

I reached my hands down to cup his ass and gently removed his pants, sucking at his hip bones and leaving bite marks on the insides of his thighs.

"You're breathtaking," I breathed, looking him up and down, feeling myself fall even deeper into love with the man in front of me. It didn't scare me, like I thought it would. I knew Sutton was mine, and I was his, even if we had taken our time to get to one another.

"So are you."

Sutton got down on his knees and licked the head of my cock. Pleasure raced through me. His red lips wrapped around me, and stars dotted my vision. His mouth was glorious, and my hands found their way back to his hair.

Pleasure built in my spine and threatened to take me over, but I wanted this to last. I wanted to feel every part of Sutton with my hands, my fingers, and my mouth. I pulled away from him, and my cock left his pretty pout with a loud pop.

I pulled Sutton's chin up and pressed my lips against his. He smiled seductively, and he turned around and got on the bed with his perky ass up in the air and a smile on his face.

"I need you, Lux. Please, show me I'm yours and you're mine."

My entire body responded to those words. They washed over me like a warm caress, and all I wanted was to show Sutton again and again how much he meant to me. I grabbed some lube and set it on the bed next to me, desperately wanting our bodies to be as close as possible.

"Fucking hell, Sutton," I hissed as I slid underneath his legs and positioned his cock right over my face. I started to suck and lick him, letting his moans and hips do the talking as he shuddered around my mouth. I could have stayed there all night, but I wanted to taste all of him.

I slipped out from under him and palmed his ass, kissing and biting my way along his cheeks.

"Don't stop, Lux. More, please," Sutton whined.

"Don't rush me. I've been thinking about this for days."

I slapped his ass playfully. He yelped, and I rubbed the spot gently. I took some lube onto my fingers and started to tease his tight hole, which had him pressing even closer to me. Grinning, I worked my finger slowly into him. I wanted him to remember every touch of me and think about it for days to come.

I kissed against his spine and leaned over him, whispering in his ear. "How does that feel?"

"So good."

He shuddered, and I added another, gently stretching him,

and finding that special place that had him moaning and shivering around me.

"Will you come for me just like this, Sutton?" I said, kissing his back and pumping in and out of him with my fingers while he wiggled around on the bed. My fingers wrapped around his cock and stroked.

"Yes," he breathed, and his back arched even more as he moaned out my name.

"More, Lux. You can give me more."

I smiled, pulled him to the edge of the bed, and lined up my cock at his hole. I put a generous amount of lube on both of us and squeezed his hips.

"Tell me if it's too much, okay?" I gently nudged inside him and took it slow as I slid in inch by inch to let him accommodate me, until I was fully sheathed.

"It's perfect," he purred, and I pulled him up, so his upper body was flush with mine. I wrapped my one arm around his chest, and the other was still wrapped around his cock, my hips grinding into him.

"How about this?" I nipped at his ear.

"Even better," he said, moving his hips with me.

"Fuck," I said and started to lose control while we both moved in tandem together, finding a rhythm that would nearly kill me.

"Lux," he moaned, pushing harder against me.

My own release was imminent. I stilled my cock and continued to rub his shaft.

"Come for me this way, and I'll finish in your ass," I said, moving up and down with my hand.

"Lux," he whined, and he started to shudder around me until he was moaning my name and tightening around me once more.

He orgasmed while screaming my name, his release shooting all over my hands. Sutton sagged against me, and I took that as my cue to start pumping in and out, both my hands scraping against his nipples.

"Such a good boy," I hissed in his ears as I tried to push off my own release, but it was building, and Sutton felt so gods-damned good that I was having a hard time stalling the pleasures that built inside me.

"Ahh," he moaned, and I couldn't hold it off any longer. With a grunt, I pumped my own release into him and buried my head into his neck. We collapsed on the bed with me wrapped around Sutton.

He turned to face me, his hair disheveled and his lips nice and swollen.

"You're quite the lover, Luxton. I think I could get used to this..." He ran his fingertips across my lips.

"You're delicious, Sutton. I could ruin you every fucking day... that is, if you'll let me." I kissed his fingertips.

"So, does that mean we're together?" he asked, his eyes widening and his gaze searching my face.

"I knew a long time ago I didn't want to be with anyone else. You stole my heart from the first moment I met you. So yes, we're dating, and I would very much like you to not be with or date anyone else," I confessed, and it was true.

I wasn't good at juggling multiple partners. My need for Sutton was like a bone-deep ache. There was no one else who had made me feel this way.

"Me either," he whispered against my neck, and we held each other tight until sleep took both of us and we were just a tangle of arms and legs.

THIRTY-EIGHT
GREER

D arkness rushed around me while I stumbled through time and space. I flailed my arms and legs, trying to stop the world around me from moving too fast, but it was impossible. I was caught up in a current like a tornado. It flung my body around, disorienting my sense of direction.

My screams were swallowed whole. The wind tore at my hair and thrashed against my cheeks. Suddenly, my body crashed into solid ground, and I face-planted with a loud smack.

Gasping for air, I coughed and choked, trying to understand where the hell I was and why I was so out of control. Feeling the ground beneath me, I shoved myself to a seat, trembling and heart pounding.

Where was I?

What was this?

I could see a light in the distance and squinted at it, trying to get a better understanding of what it was. The darkness swallowed everything else and beckoned me forward. Pushing me to go see what this random illumination was.

Gingerly, I stood and took a deep breath. My body was finally acclimating to this rollercoaster ride. I started walking *towards the glow and happened upon a scene that was all too familiar.*

It was like a movie being played out in front of me. Lux held my sobbing body while I screamed and thrashed. This was the night I found out about my mom. The night she had died. The pain rolled off me in waves as I clawed at my skin, and Lux's hold on me became like irons around my torso. He mumbled incoherent things into my hair. I rocked back and forth, Lux keeping my fingernails away from my skin so I couldn't scratch the pain away.

A lump formed in my throat, and I didn't know what to do. It was like I could see what was happening in front of me, but I couldn't touch it. When I reached my hand out to investigate further, my fingertips caused a ripple in the air around me. Almost like a wall of water separating me from the memory in front of me.

Why was I being shown this? Was this another dream?

It didn't feel like what Xael and I had experienced together. We were in control there, or at least she was. This felt like I was simply an observer unable to do anything but watch helplessly as the younger me broke into a million pieces and my friend tried to hold them all in his hands.

The hair on the back of my neck started to rise, and I swept my head side to side.

"Who's there?" I asked, trying to sound brave, but my voice cracked. "Xael?"

The scene in front of me was moving away from where I stood. My feet moved before I realized what was happening. I ran towards the disappearing light. The feeling of someone or something else started to creep into my bones.

Goosebumps erupted, and my stomach dropped. I pounded my feet against the darkness and chased after the memory that was fading away to nothing. A hand shoved into my back, hard and fast, and I went flying, cracking my knees against the unforgiving ground. Crying out, I nearly busted my nose for what would be the fourth time, but I rolled and landed on my shoulder instead. White hot pain laced up against my joints.

"Who the fuck are you?!" I screamed, wanting answers, but then another light flashed in the distance.

I didn't have any idea where else to go, so I picked my battered body off the ground and made my way over to the other source of light.

It was another memory. It was me fighting off the guy who tried to come at me when I walked home from the Shadow Lounge by myself. In the moments before me, I looked fierce and strong. A snarl ripped through me while I charged at him with my switchblade.

I remembered feeling terrified, but I wouldn't allow myself to become a victim. My strike was true. I took a slice out of his skin, and it sent him skittering away. My breathing was labored, and my hand shook as I watched him disappear around the corner. Tears rolled down my cheeks, and I aggressively swiped them away. Past Greer took out her phone and called Lux.

The same thing occurred, where it was as if the memory was being torn away from me, and that same feeling of being watched breathed down my neck. This time, I didn't run; I waited as something caressed my spine. I refused to look back and stood my ground.

Another source of light started moving towards me, and suddenly, I was watching the last year of my life play out. When Riddley attacked me, all the trials, my confrontations with Edward and the President, the murders, it was all flashing past me like a movie I couldn't look away from.

Terror wracked my body every time I was kicked, dragged, and targeted on screen. It was one thing to live it and tuck it away in the recesses of your mind and another to watch it like a movie play out in front of you.

"I don't want to watch this. Why am I being forced to do this again?" All the pain and anguish that I had experienced was being brought to me like entertainment.

At some point, I sank to my knees because the nightmare was not done. The moment I turned immortal was forced in front of my eyes, then my time in hell, Ky's betrayal, our narrow escape... Choking back sobs, I forced myself to get through it.

Surely there would be an end to this monstrosity? But when I tried to remember the last thing that happened to me outside of this endless night, I couldn't find it.

It was like sand through my fingertips. I tried to think of the last thing Ky said to me, or Lux, or Nova, but I couldn't exactly get my brain to find what I was looking for.

"Damari," I whispered. The pain reverberated through my body, and I brought my hand up to my throat.

"Ky!"

The way his body had been tossed like a rag doll was the most unnatural thing I had ever seen in the world.

I tried to remember what happened afterward, but the picture wasn't there. Frantically, I looked for another source of light. There was a shadow off to my right, and I got up to make my way over to it. The picture wasn't like the others, though. It flickered in and out with pieces missing.

But the pictures I did see made me vomit on the spot. Phayre and Riordan were there with Damari. There were moments where I saw their version of the immortal death serum being shoved down Sutton's throat. Each of my friends were being hurt again and again by Damari's hand. Nova was yelling and cradling a broken Waverly in her arms, surrounded by immeasurable amounts of blood. Ky was bound and gagged at Riordan's feet. Lux was losing his mind, rattling the cage everyone was in.

My body spasmed, and I collapsed to the ground, watching my worst nightmare unfold in front of me. I desperately looked *for any sign of myself, but couldn't see anything or hear anything except Damari's cackling and the screams of my loved ones.*

I reached out to the image and was suddenly being sucked in by an invisible force.

"No!" I screamed while I was dragged forward and through the atrocious scene in front of me.

I kicked and clawed at the energy around me, and it did nothing. I was continually pulled forward and then flung in front of another.

It was the mortal realm, but not as I knew it. Riordan's fire roared through the streets, and Phayre had humans leashed around her like the pets she wanted. It flashed to another where Kyra was slumped in a cage with blood pouring out of his nose and mouth. Then it flashed to me being in another dark space, my eyes feral and my clothing ripped. I looked like when I first met Xael. Bruised and beaten from chains dragging at my hands, feet, and throat.

The scene moved again to where Xael, Hyacinth, and Farren were in pods full of red liquid. They didn't move, simply floated, and were contained in whatever liquid preserved them. I was forced to watch Phayre come into my darkened cell and drag me out, and strapping me to a chair. Needles and ports were stuck in me while I screamed, and my blood was drained out of me. It went on far too long, and I could physically see my body deflating.

"Don't worry, your blood always comes back, immortal timewraith. You're like a never-ending bloodbath despite how often you throw tantrums about this part."

My eyes closed eventually, and the fight went out of me. Phayre continued to drain my blood.

I was helpless. In the scene in front of me, and wherever the fuck I was now.

"How do I make this stop?!" I screamed and pounded my hands on the ground. Sobbing, my body shook uncontrollably.

I reached for my power. Time swirled around me, and I sniffled as it became corporeal between my fingers.

"None of this makes sense," I whispered to no one. The horrible scene in front of me slowly faded away.

This time, there was nothing else that greeted me. The monster that had chased me was gone, and there was no light to be had. I didn't know which was worse, being alone in the dark with nothing or having light with a monster at my back.

I took a deep breath and tried to manipulate the time current around me. I found what felt like a string leading straight from my chest to somewhere else. My fingertips wrapped around the cord, and I pulled. The sensation of falling greeted me. I screamed again, so tired of being out of control and in pain. This time when I fell, I opened my eyes to a familiar face.

THIRTY-NINE
GREER

"Xael!" I exclaimed.

Gods, I was so relieved to see her in front of me. She looked so whole. Her red hair was shining and her eyes were bright. But the expression she wore was one of confusion.

"Human? How are you here?" she whispered as she whipped her head back and forth.

I realized then that the room we were in was not one I recognized. It was an ethereal-looking bedroom. Rich tapestries hung from the ceilings and walls, decorating an enormous bedroom with a large canopy bed and golden fixtures, releasing a warm glow.

"Xael. This isn't funny. Where the hell are we?"

Sweat started to slide down my back, and I looked down at myself. There were splashes of blood on my clothes, and for some reason, I couldn't remember where they came from. Was this my blood? Or someone else's? Mentally, I scanned my body and didn't feel a specific source of pain.

"Are you alright, my dear? I do not understand how you came to be here, but I will help you. We mustn't make too much noise and alert the others," Xael said quietly. She rushed over to grab my hands and guide me into an opulent bathroom.

It was all white marble and large mirrors. A huge ground tub snuggled into one side of the room, and an open shower covered another area.

"Where are we?" I asked, standing in awe at the luxury around me. My head felt heavy, and my thoughts were foggy. Xael was safe. Maybe this was another one of her dream realms.

"My washroom. What is your name, mortal?" She sat me down on a bench and slowly started to wash red off my arms and face.

"Xael, it's me, Greer. Did something happen?"

An uneasiness started to take root in my belly and claw at my throat. I thought this was real and right, but I couldn't remember where I was before this. With Kyra? I shook my head, trying to clear my muddled mind, and couldn't hold onto anything solid. Where were my friends?

"It does look like something happened, Greer. But I do not know what. One minute I was brushing my hair in my bedroom, and then the next, you simply appeared. I am not sure how a mortal came to be in the celestial realm, but it is very odd indeed."

My eyes whipped to hers, and I swallowed.

"The celestial realm?!" My voice grew high and tight.

"Of course, my dear. Perhaps the others are playing tricks on me, as they know my fondness for you humans. The mortal realm has nasty business since the others started using it like a damn game. But I can only do so much right now." Her eyes shifted across the room as if looking for someone.

"Xael..." I started, but I didn't know how to end my sentence. "Um, do you still wield power?"

She laughed then and gave me a small grin. "Of course,

dear. I am the goddess of time after all, and power overflows in all of us through our god and goddess lineage. We are the originals." Xael left the room, and my mouth fell open.

Was this a dream? Or some alternate reality? I watched while Xael came back in and offered me a change of clothes into a gauzy pair of dark trousers and a sleeveless tunic. The blood had not been from any wounds on me personally, so I must have been in some other altercation.

"Feel free to get changed, dear, and then I will look for some sustenance. I know you mortals have different needs than we do, and we can talk more about how to get you home."

No words came out of my mouth. I stood on shaky legs and began to change out of the messy clothes I was in. Holding the blood-worn fabric up, I tried to remember why there were slashes of gore on me. My hands started to tremble. Why could I not remember?

My heart was racing, and I tried to take a few deep breaths. I clearly had been a part of something very, very bad. What if my friends had been caught up in the mess? Were they simply bleeding out somewhere while I was now in the celestial realm with Xael, who didn't even know who I was?

I called forth my own power of time. It sizzled underneath my skin, and I closed my eyes, reaching for the current flowing around me. It was still there, but it was changed. As if some small piece was out of place, but I couldn't place it. Perhaps Xael would know.

"Are you alright, dear?" Xael called from her room, and I quickly came out to her, sitting at a small table with a pot of tea. She gestured for me to sit.

My spine was stiff while I settled myself. "Xael, I don't know why I'm here. And I know you. You taught me how to wield time."

Xael's eyes widened, and the tea she had just been pouring came to an abrupt stop.

"What? No one..." She cleared her throat. "No one else has the power of time. I have given none of my gift to anyone."

I could feel the lingering word of yet on the tip of her tongue.

"I think something bad happened in my present time, and for some reason, time sent me here. To you." I carefully grabbed the teapot from her and continued to pour into our cups. Xael closed her eyes, and a muscle in her jaw feathered.

"Would that be possible? I don't know if I would have done it, but my power has been wielded in strange ways before when my emotions get out of control." An image of me in the throne room came to mind. I screamed and cried for hours while holding time in a vice grip around me.

"Where in time have you come from, Greer?" Xael asked carefully.

I frowned. I didn't know how to answer that question.

"I think thousands of years from now. There's a war and the gods fight, and you give your power to mortals, but it's cursed, and I... break that curse. Except now the gods are coming to fight again." How much was I allowed to say? Would I be breaking time itself by telling her what would come to pass?

Xael's hand reached out to mine. "As the goddess of time, I have a clear path ahead of me for what I must do right now. Words from you will not change that. It seems as if time will always have its way, no matter those of us who are simply conduits of its power."

That gave me a small sense of comfort. I took a sip of the warm liquid and let it slide down my throat. "I don't remember how I got here, or why I was bloody. I'm worried that something terrible has happened in the mortal realm because of this," I said again.

"Ah, so a time puzzle to figure out. It is strange indeed to see you here, Greer. Wielding power I have not given. We need to pull from your memories, as it seems your time traveling has meddled with your mind."

I bit my lip and tears sprang to my eyes. None of this sounded good. The sense of gloom and dread hung heavy on my skin. I looked desperately at Xael for answers.

"What is the last thing you remember, child? Perhaps we can try a trick of mine to help you get there." She took the teacup from my hands and pulled me up, leading me to a chair close to a roaring fire.

"Lie back, Greer. We will get to the bottom of this."

I did as I was told, my breath coming in shallow pants while I thrashed against my own mind, commanding myself to find something to latch on to. But it was as if my whole brain had turned into spaghetti. Everything was wrapped and intertwined in ways I didn't understand, and it was a miracle that I could even remember my friends' names at this point.

There were gaping holes in my consciousness. How could someone simply have blank spaces in their mind? I don't think this had ever happened to me before, but time was a powerful thing.

"It could be that your mind is trying to protect you. That your power manifested in a way to help you find a way to survive." Xael's words wrapped around me like they were supposed to offer comfort, but they did the complete opposite.

I had been through many terrible things. That much I could remember. The feelings of hopelessness and pain were an old friend. Grief and rage. But I had never once had something like this happen where only bits and fragments of those painful pieces filled my brain, and ones from what felt like long ago.

"That doesn't make me feel better about why I'm here," I whispered, clutching the soft sheets of fabric underneath me.

"We will figure this out soon enough." Xael produced a pendant and held it at eye level. "Watch the pendant go back and forth. We will start to go through your psyche together."

I did as I was told and breathed as she commanded, in soft whispers for me to relax and close my eyes. My body felt heavy and sleepy while I slipped into my memories and relived my own day of reckoning.

FORTY
GREER

Everything around me fractured and broke into a starburst of light, and then I was gasping for air. Thrust back into my body, into my memory, where everything went wrong. I clawed at my throat, my airway completely cut off while I blinked in and out of consciousness, my body desperately trying to heal what Damari had so viciously broken.

I tried to remind myself that this wasn't happening in real time, but it didn't matter. It had happened, and I needed to remember. I needed to feel and see what was done to me and my friends; otherwise, I would never be able to recover.

Damari stood tall and victorious over me while I gasped and flopped about like a fish trying to find breath that would not come. I blinked back tears. My chest barely inflated, my lungs screaming for air. The immortality in me worked slowly, too slowly. Damari reached down and grabbed my ankle before she lifted my body up so I was dangling upside down. My head spun, and I couldn't find any semblance of control over my emotions or my power. My head just kept chanting, breathe, breathe, breathe. She slammed my body down in a big swinging arc so I landed on my back. My mouth flew open, but no sound escaped. The little air that I had gathered was thrown out of my body in a puff.

"Stop this, Damari!" Kyra called out, his body in pieces too.

My eyes became fuzzy. His form crawled over to me. His back looked wrong. Bones shoved out of the skin, too much blood running on the surrounding grass.

"Oh, Prince of Hell, I am the only one who can. You weren't supposed to be here, but I am sure your father will understand I did what I had to do," Damari snickered, watching Kyra slowly make his way over to me. Flickers of flame touched his fingertips, but nothing pushed through.

"Did no one tell you it is very difficult to call upon magnitudes of your power when your body is working to heal life-ending wounds? Of course, your immortality will stop you from dying, but when your body is in its baseline survival mode, your power comes with... certain blocks," Damari sneered.

I finally was able to get a full gasp of air. My trachea knitted itself together. She was right, though. I never put it together. My power was so far away when my body was practically lifeless from the wounds inflicted by others.

"Greer..." Kyra was almost to me now, but I couldn't move. Air was just starting to circulate through my system, and my throat felt like a million needles were stabbing me simultaneously with every ragged inhale and exhale.

There was an audible pop and crack. A huge portal appeared behind Damari's smug face. People flew through like a bag of laundry being tossed. Several bodies landed with sickening thuds and crunches. I was cemented in place, so I could only watch as my friends gasped and writhed in pain while they connected with the ground.

Sutton, Waverly, Nova, and Lux were all heaped together, groaning in various states of agony. Sutton was out cold. Lux tried to talk him into waking up. Waverly had a black eye, and

Nova seethed with rage. Afton stepped out of the portal after them, looking equally as mistreated.

How had they taken all of them at once? Where were Xael, Farren, and Hyacinth? My mind whirled. I tried to roll over to my side to face them, but the movement made bile rise in my throat, and nausea swept through me.

Ropes flew out of Damari's outstretched hands and encircled my friends. The coils brightened and sang with her power, digging into their flesh.

"You can thank your mother for these. Her spells and inventions have been quite helpful for me to find new ways to manipulate my magic," Damari said, watching in glee as the ropes dug into the soft flesh of my friends.

"Phayre and Riordan are on their way. They needed to take care of a few things first," Afton said, looking at the pile of my friends while Kyra moaned next to me. A crunch sounded, and he screamed, rolling into the fetal position.

Time stood still while Damari and Afton engaged in a conversation that I couldn't hear, or rather, I couldn't focus on their words as I clawed and fought to access the time current around me. But it was no use. My body was healing too slowly, and I couldn't find my connection to my gifts. So, I simply had to bear witness to my friends writhing in pain and Kyra breaking apart next to me. My soul was shattering because I did this. These people, who I loved, the version of me that existed at this time, couldn't focus on their words. Instead, I was fighting the searing pain in my body while watching our friends fight in their roped cages.

"Greer, can't speak. My back is mending itself, but my spine snapped in half," Kyra heaved to the others.

We hadn't expected such immediate violence from Damari. We should have. It was absolutely naive and ignorant of us to think that she wouldn't come in this way when she was the goddess of power and strength. It was idiotic to believe that Lux and Sutton stealing from her wouldn't cause irreparable harm and be deserving of her own special brand of punishment.

I wasn't the only one who couldn't find words. We were all fighting our own painful battles, and there was nothing we could do except endure.

"Take them to my dungeon so they don't bleed all over the lawn," Damari said, her tone clipped. Afton made another portal, and we were all thrown into what looked like a medieval torture chamber. It was all stone with a disgustingly musty smell puncturing my senses.

It was the last thing I saw before darkness welcomed me, and I fell into my own oblivion.

↔

Coughing aggressively, I gasped for air and blinked my eyes.

"Greer, what happened? What did you see?" Xael leaned over me, searching my face.

Tears ran down my face. The echoes of agony rang through my body, and my hands flew to my throat. I curled my knees to my chest and rocked back and forth, trying to convince myself that I was here, with Xael. The out-of-control feeling in my memory wasn't happening... now.

It didn't make me feel better because it *had* happened. I could remember it clearly, now. That had been my reality, and now I was here, back with Xael in another timeline, but one that I was now a part of as well as my own.

But I still didn't know exactly how I ended up here.

"Greer, stay with me," Xael cooed, and I nodded, breathing deeply and wiping my face.

"I didn't get to the point where I time-jumped. It's bad, Xael. Like really, really bad. I've been through some shit, but I just know that's just the beginning of what happened."

I didn't explain the things I had seen; I could barely voice them out loud, so I just wrapped my arms around myself and continued to shake.

"I know this is painful. Your mind was trying to protect you and make you forget, and we are shoving it through this heinous moment again. But remember, you survived. You are here, and you escaped. We need to get to that moment, Greer. We need to understand it. The past will help us even if it's painful."

I knew she was right, but I didn't want to go back. Damari's plight had just begun, and I couldn't fathom where it would go for me to lose control and time jump so drastically.

"Okay, let's do it again. I can do this. I survived, and the only way through this is to live it once again," I whispered, and Xael nodded.

We began the process again, and I was thrust back into the pains of my past.

FORTY-ONE
GREER

I woke up again like I was drowning. Kyra was right there, looking less broken but equally as disheveled. Ropes had been fastened around all of us. We were trapped like feral animals locked in a cage. I thrashed and squirmed.

"Greer! You're going to hurt yourself. Take a breath," Kyra soothed from next to me.

It was dark in our cage. Iron bars kept us in, and they hummed and glowed with the same magic that had enchanted the ropes. It was hard to explain except that they simply felt like the same thrum of power.

"How did you all get here?" I asked, looking to where Lux and Sutton leaned up against one another in the corner. Nova sat next to me with Waverly on her other side.

"We were ambushed.... They snatched me and Waverly first, and then came for Sutton and Lux. We were not ready. Afton knocked both Waverly and me out in a surprise burst of light and power. Then we were being thrown onto Damari's lawn. We got too comfortable. We should have been more ready." Nova sighed and closed her eyes.

"Lux, you all too?" I asked, wanting desperately to free my

hands from these binds. But ropes wrapped around my wrists, ankles, and then around my whole body like I was a piece of meat encased. I tried not to focus on how immobilized I was; otherwise, I knew I would spiral. This was like hell all over again. And I had walked right into this one. How foolish could I be?

"Yes, Sutton and I had our guard down. He came in and stunned us basically, then threw us here. Obviously, he was not very gentle." Lux grumbled, trying to wipe some dried blood off his face with his shoulder.

We were all tied up the same, and as I reached for my time power, it again fell through my fingers. The urge to scream bubbled up into my throat, but I kept it in. I was sick and tired of feeling powerless here. Why was my power nowhere to be seen when I needed it most?

"How do we get out?" I whispered, afraid of the answer.

"I don't know..." Waverly said, looking at me with watery eyes.

"Does anyone have access to their powers?" Sutton questioned. The bruise on his cheek was lessening, but the yellow-purple mark was still there.

"No." Kyra wiggled next to me, and the others shook their heads.

"How long was I out? Has anyone come down here?" I asked, whipping my head around to see what was going on.

Our cage was in the middle of a room. Stone encased the walls, and there were random pieces of equipment around the outskirts of the room. Little lightning flickered throughout, and there was a door on one side of the rectangular room and a few chairs that looked like what they would put you in at the dentist.

"Maybe an hour? No one else has come down here, but I would guess we could expect company soon," Nova responded, and we all sat in silence.

I didn't know what to say. There was no way out of this. No one had access to their powers with these bars and ropes around us.

The door slammed open, and Phayre practically skipped in. "Oh, lookie here, all our favorite pets are ready to play!"

Damari was right behind her with Afton and Riordan at their heels.

"Tell us where Hyacinth, Xael, and Verity are," Riordan commanded, looking at all of us. Nobody said a fucking word.

"Fine, you only need the wraith and your son, correct?" Damari asked, eyeing us all closely.

"I think the others could be useful, but I want the wraith and my son to sign a blood contract for me." Riordan purred, walking around our cage.

"Blood contracts have to be consensual," Nova spat, and Damari laughed.

"Yes, but consent is a loose term. We can persuade or coerce the other party, and the blood contract has no idea as long as the person signs willingly despite whatever odds are stacked against them." Damari crossed her arms and looked smugly at us.

"Why do you need a blood contract?" I hissed, finding my voice.

"Because I want in writing and blood binding your loyalty and power to me and only me and my causes. You got away before little wraith, and I won't let it happen again. I do not like to bind my blood to others, but for you two, I will make an exception." Riordan smiled sinisterly at us, and Kyra and I exchanged glances.

"I won't do it. So, you can fucking forget about it," I challenged, and Damari raised her eyebrow.

"Oh, I was so hoping you would say that. Let's get to work, shall we?" Damari moved through the open metal grate of our cage and dragged Lux and Sutton out.

"Let them go!" I screamed as the others yelled their own protests. Sutton and Lux thrashed and snarled.

"I don't think I will." She shrugged, and Afton helped get them settled into chairs and strapped in.

"It's such a waste to destroy these powers. You all could really be something if you simply would listen and not steal things not meant for you!" Damari growled while Phayre and Riordan grabbed Waverly and Nova.

Fear gripped my heart. Yelling and screaming filled the space. I watched all my friends get forcibly shoved and strapped into chairs.

"You get to watch too," Riordan said, walking in and grabbing Kyra by the collar and shoving him into his own chair.

The metal gate swung closed and rattled with a thunk. I was the only one left in the cage. Alone and cursing, I watched all my friends fight for their own release.

"What are you going to do?" I whispered.

Damari moved to stand with Phayre in this horrible, dungeon-like place. Phayre had shoved some potion down the throats of Sutton and Lux, who were in a drunken-like state. Nausea rolled in my gut, and I shifted my weary gaze to where Riordan was roughly shoving Waverly and Nova around to get them to settle next to the others.

"Well, you did give us your handy-dandy little serum that would turn them all back into mortals without the immediate side effect of death. I thought we could play with them as immortals for a while and then turn them into humans. More torture, kill them again, and then make their corpses a permanent fixture in hell. Or... you could sign the contract, come to hell willingly, give up the location of the other gods and goddesses, and we could all go on with our lives." Damari acted like the choice should have been easy. But I hadn't made it this far to fucking give in to her demands now. I just needed another way out.

"Don't do it, Greer," Nova spat.

"Kill me, if that's what you need to do. We aren't letting

you destroy everything this world is made of just for fucking fun," Sutton added.

"Suit yourselves. Shall we begin?" Phayre asked, skipping to Lux's side and stroking his face lovingly.

"You are very pretty. Tragic that we will need to break you."

And so, the torture began.

It was tame at first. Well, as tame as torture could be. I tried to remind myself that I was changing the course of this timeline. This wouldn't have actually happened once I got back to my own timeline and out of Xael's thousands-of-years-ago, but that thought didn't bring me comfort.

I watched in horror while each of the original immortals took time breaking my friends. They started with Sutton. Slamming power into him, beating him black and blue as the rest of us screamed and begged for them to stop. Sutton never said a word. He was forced into a husk of himself, and unconsciousness finally dragged him under. Blood caked his face; his eyes were swollen shut.

"He didn't last very long, did he?" Phayre pouted.

My throat was raw from yelling. The others had to watch and wait for their torture to come.

"You ready to stop this?" Damari asked.

"No," Sutton croaked out, and she back-handed him so hard his cheek split open.

"Sutton!!" I yelled, unable to move with my bindings around me. I could only sit and watch.

"The siren next?" Afton offered, and Waverly's pink eyes turned fuchsia.

"Do your fucking worst," she seethed, and they did.

Each blow to her body sent Nova into a frenzy. Eventually, Riordan stuffed gags into all our mouths because he was tired of hearing all the fuss.

Waverly met unconsciousness, too, and it kept going from there. Nova. Then Lux. Again and again, I watched in horror as my friends were pummeled by the immortals' gifts. Only stopping when they passed out, because Phayre claimed it wasn't as fun.

"Your son is next?" Damari walked over to Kyra, and Riordan stepped in front of him.

"He is our last resort. Let's move to the serum next." Riordan said, stepping in front of Ky and Damari, rolled her eyes.

"He makes you weak," she challenged, and Riordan narrowed his eyes. "Careful of your tongue, Damari, before I turn my wrath on you instead."

"So touchy..." Damari stepped away, and Phayre walked right up to the bars, reaching through and grabbing my face to pull it to hers.

"Ready to sign things now?" she asked, and I shook my head, the gag preventing me from saying anything.

What was I supposed to do? All of them had told me not to do it, but I was running out of options and time. My resolve was crumbling with each blow, and my body was so tired.

"Well, since you handed over your little immortal serum. I made a few different options. See these three bottles here?" She pointed to a small counter. I didn't say anything. Phayre didn't like that and slammed my face into the bars.

"Answer the question, wraith!" she hissed, and I nodded my head.

"One of the serums is immediate mortality and then straight to death, one is mortality without death, and one is like a slow-acting poison stripping the immortality and sending you to death anyway. We are going to play a little roulette game. You choose the vial, wraith, and I think we shall start with the necromancer first."

Tears started streaming down my face. I shook my head and began to shake. No, no, no, no. This could not be happening. I had run out of time while I had watched my friends be destroyed by my enemies.

"Pick wraith, they could survive it, it's a thirty-three percent chance. But if you don't pick one, I will choose for you!" Phayre snatched the gag out of my mouth, and I choked and spluttered on my dry tongue and lips.

"The first vial," I said, knowing that either way I would lose.

I looked at Kyra helplessly. The rest of my friends were still lost to unconsciousness. He shook his head, tears streaming down his face. Everyone else would just wake up to Sutton dead.

"Should we rouse everyone else to bear witness?" Phayre asked.

Damari smirked. "Yes, let's." She walked around with a jar of salts, forcing everyone awake.

"No, no, no, no...." I started chanting frantically, looking to where the others were as Phayre advanced with the glass vial.

"Please, stop," I begged.

Tears clouded my vision as my fear grew and grew. It was a gnawing creature in my chest that wanted to consume me and leave me breathless and immobile. But I wouldn't let it.

"You know what you have to do to stop it." Phayre hissed.

Sutton woke up, then. Looking at me and shaking his head.

"Sutton, please," I said, my whole body aching from being tied up and my face throbbing from where I met the metal bars.

"Bottom's up." Phayre ripped the gag from Sutton's mouth, and Damari held open his mouth.

"It's okay, Greer," Sutton managed to get out before the contents of the vial slipped past his lips and the whole world exploded in light.

Forty-Two
Greer

There was a scream like a siren, and I realized it was me. The sound was so high-pitched and loud that it pierced my ears and fractured the space around me. Cracks formed in the space like shattering glass.

Voices ricocheted around me, but I could barely hear them while I channeled my feelings into just doing something. Anything to help the people I loved. The cracks pulsed and flashed, with light disoriented me. But I did not stop. I couldn't. The power of what I could do swelled within me, and all I knew was that it needed to get out. It needed to be released, damn the consequences.

Sutton coughed and spluttered while I continued to shriek. All I could think was that I couldn't let him die. He couldn't die because of me, because of these shitty circumstances. I would not sacrifice any more of my friends or myself for these immortals.

My body was about to implode with all the pent-up rage and sorrow threatening to drown me. Instead, it sharpened. Like blades ready for battle, it sliced the ropes around me. My time power thrust forth in a forceful wave. Clawing to get out, triggered by my desire to save the ones I loved.

My scream continued to reverberate through the space. The air swirled and mixed around me. My heart ached for Sutton's imminent death, for my friends' pain, and my own. I fell to my hands and knees and pushed out with all my might the power that was building and budding in my soul. It engulfed the space around us from a white light into a starless night as my world tipped and turned around me. Air whipped my hair, and I was thrown into what felt like a tornado, and the room fell away. Pops and cracks sounded in my ears, and I pushed harder, wanting something, anything to happen so my friends would not die by my hands.

I continued to bellow, my throat aching and my heart pulsing in my head. I was battered and rammed around in this container of air, unable to escape. The cage and room falling away like pieces of a broken picture. Where was I going? Was I simply leaving my friends behind? The thought sent me spiraling deeper and deeper into this need to release what I could at my hands. My mind flashed to Xael and what she would do if she were in this situation, and then my body slammed into a wall, and I crumpled, heaving air in and out.

My mind emptied, and I could not remember what had happened only moments before. Only this darkness and this explosion of force. Everything else had faded away, and I was alone. So, I crawled, not knowing where I was going until I collapsed from exhaustion and let myself rest for the first time in months.

I awoke with a shriek back in Xael's presence, and my vision swam in front of me. My mind was trying to puzzle out what was real, what was a memory, and how to recover the pieces I could no longer remember or what I was simply meant to forget.

It was starting to give me a headache, but I took a deep breath and told myself those details could be sorted out later.

What was most important was to tell Xael what I saw in my last moments with Damari.

"I know what happened."

Xael didn't say anything while I explained how I thought I got here.

"You must have altered the stream of time immeasurably, and somehow you ended up here," Xael said, tapping her finger to her lip.

"How do I get back? How do I stop what happened from happening again?"

Panic flooded my voice. I saw my friends' bodies destroyed beyond measure. The gods were cruel, and they would do it again if given the chance. Not just to us but to all those who disobeyed them. Those who threatened their new regime.

Xael didn't say anything for a few moments. She looked into the fire and squinted her eyes. I could see her brain working to puzzle out exactly what could be done.

"How is it even possible that I jumped here? Thousands of years ago?" I sagged against the chair. I was desperate for answers we didn't have.

"Time-jumping is a fickle thing. You have never done this before?"

"Never."

"In my many lifetimes, I have only ever done it a few times, with a clear destination of where I was going and the intention of going back to the exact time I jumped. Since you didn't set a course but simply lashed out emotionally, I think you got swept up in the time current and it deposited you here."

"However, time is not without reason, so there must be an explanation of why it was this moment. Perhaps it was because I am alone and will be alone for the rest of the evening, and my love for mortals has grown exponentially over the past few months. Either way, this means something, Greer." Xael grabbed my hand and squeezed.

"Can I go back to a time before that whole mess started? Not very far, but maybe we never left to go see Damari? Maybe it was earlier in the day or the night before?"

"Hm, yes, we need to decide on a clear destination for you to land and figure out how to get you there down to just a few seconds," Xael replied.

She stood quickly and made her way over to a large bookcase, where she pulled down some dusty tomes to rifle through.

"What are you looking for?" I asked. She began to flip through some pages.

"A very specific time spell. One I did not memorize because it is quite lengthy, but I knew that it would come in handy one day."

"I didn't even know we could cast time spells," I said in awe.

"It's a finicky space to occupy. It's more like we are commanding time a little differently than we normally would. We are making an acute demand as opposed to an overarching push or pull. Greer, I do not know if this will work, but we realistically only have one chance to get this right and save your friends."

"Okay." I swallowed, nodding at her.

The two of us spent the next several hours pouring over this book, preparing for my time jump of thousands of years. Something that had never been done before.

FORTY-THREE
GREER

"You will also need to be aware of the time ghouls," Xael said after we had talked at length about how this would even be possible.

"I'm sorry, what?" I asked.

"The greater your time jump, the greater the risk of encountering the monsters of time. They lurk in the in-between spaces of the time current, and if you spend too much time in that stream, they can cause irreparable harm." Xael's pale face suddenly went ashen.

"But I'm immortal. They can hurt me, but it's not like they can inflict permanent damage, right?"

My palms started sweating. Great, another enemy out to get me, but this one was purely because I was trying to get back to my friends and my timeline. It wasn't like I asked my powers to thrust me here. I didn't even know this was possible.

"In theory, they cannot kill you. But the wounds they cause can last for much longer than others, if not for all of eternity. They defy time logic like an ever-present poison. And if you start to gather too many of them in one place where you are already tampering with the time current, then you could release them onto this world. They cannot die. They can only be trapped back into the fabrics of time."

"Fuck me," I whispered.

Xael frowned. "I do not wish to do that, but I am assuming it's a human colloquialism."

That made me giggle.

"I think... I may have encountered one actually, before I landed here," I said quietly.

I grabbed onto the memory of the place that felt like eternal night. There had been a presence looming. I could feel its hot breath on my neck and fingertips reaching for me while I was forced to revisit the tragedies of my past. But it had not attacked.

"And you walked away relatively unscathed, so perhaps they will not bother you. It is only when we start to really interact with the time current across many years that they appear. It is the natural consequence of having such power. A way to keep us in check from not leaping from year to year carelessly." Xael gave me a reassuring smile.

"It felt bad, though. I was scared, and I ran from it. What do I do to defend myself? Is it corporeal? Or is it like smoke? I couldn't see it; I could just feel it."

"That, I do not know. I have never encountered one because I have never jumped this far before. It's what I know from these tomes given to me, but that is all."

She opened the book she was pawing through to a page where the time ghouls were mentioned. Not in great length, but there was a picture. It was like a ghost from a bad horror movie.

"*The power of time can help scatter them among the years, so it takes years for them to reform... But once one is created, there is no way to permanently kill it. It must be ensnared once again with no way out.*" I read out loud the little information that accompanied the drawing. "Gods, I'm really fucking tired of all this magical bullshit and random rules and monsters who are out to get me."

Tears started to leak down my cheeks, and I angrily swiped away. My head was full of horrors, and my heart was heavy with the burden of keeping them to myself. I was exhausted with all that was happening, and adding this to the long list of dangers was about to tip me over the edge.

"Greer," Xael scooted over to me and wrapped her arms around my body.

"Why are you not more freaked out by this? I invaded your space, your timeline, and told you that you knew me, that you practically created me, and you have been as cool as a cucumber."

My tears were turning into snotty sobs at this. Xael had been my reprieve when I was trapped down in the infernal realm. A calm to my raging power and emotional storm.

Now, here she was doing the same thing again, but she didn't even know who I was.

"You're my mirror, child. I have known that things were brewing to a tipping point of some kind. I am not a future seer, but I do have the sense that this tension in the celestial realm will break. In what ways, I still do not know, and I won't ask. But you look like me reincarnated, and I sense the time power within you. It is not within me to question what the universe has so clearly decided must be done. You were sent here to connect with me for a reason."

"So, you're simply accepting this because it's too serendipitous not to be true?" I asked, wiping the snot from my nose. Xael handed me a tissue and sat back.

"You could say that. It is not within me to question the time magic when clearly whatever occurs, this is what was meant to be."

I blew my nose loudly and nodded my head. Xael's gentle demeanor started to ooze into my own until my breathing became less ragged and my heart didn't feel like it was going to beat out of my chest.

"Okay, so we know how I can time jump and that I need to be aware of these ghouls, but I don't know when or where. When I jump, will the other me in that time current just disappear, or will I become that Greer and she will become me?"

The whole thing made my head fuzzy.

"You will become one and the same, but your memories might not be the same. You might lose bits and pieces. I cannot say. It is not uncommon for the mind to hide what hurts us most in times of great distress, and then you add in your time power, and things get muddled quite fast."

"Sure, just add permanent memory loss to my list of other things," I joked, but it fell flat, and Xael did not look as amused.

"As to when you should go to, I do not know because I have not yet lived the reality you are speaking of. I don't know when you could make the most impact on your cause. It sounds like you are fighting many fronts from the time you are coming from?"

"Yes."

I couldn't tell her all the details, because that felt like a breach of this time magic, anyway. I didn't want to lose any more memories or any more time. Which meant I needed to make the decision by myself. When would be the best time to thwart this plan?

We had talked about going and training with Waverly's sister. Perhaps instead of visiting Damari, we could go straight there. Surely with the help of Evanya and Armello, we could go there instead and avoid the harrowing events with Damari. She was even more unhinged than Riordan. At least Riordan had a clear take-over-the-world plan, where it seemed like Damari didn't care who she hurt; she just wanted to hurt us and anyone who stood in her way.

Sutton and Lux stole from her, which was personal, and her anger most closely aligned with Riordan, but she seemed ready to go rogue at any moment.

I couldn't let what happened originally happen again. My friends and I would not survive it. There was no way I could fail this; otherwise, it could be the end for all of us.

"Can I ask you a question about one of the other goddesses?" I asked.

Xael had been quietly staring into the fire, her lips pursed together as if in deep thought.

"Of course."

"Damari, is she your friend?" That wasn't the question I really wanted to ask, but it felt like a good place to start.

"Hm, I do not think we are friends in the way you humans think of friends. We do not spend time together as I do with someone like Hyacinth, but we seem to have a mutual understanding. She likes that I stand up for what I believe in, maybe not in the violent way that she demands what she wants, but in a different way. In that, I believe, she thinks there is strength. But she is also the most volatile of us. She and Phayre spend a lot of time bickering, but I think they enjoy it. Riordan thinks himself in charge, but really, those two just appease him because they don't want to deal with his tantrums. The reality is the people who are most likely to rip the world in two would be Phayre and Damari. Perhaps together or perhaps to go at one another's throats."

My stomach dropped at that. This whole time, we thought Riordan was the most dangerous, but he could sort of be controlled by his delusional love for Kyra and Verity. Even though it wasn't a true kind of love, it was more like *I want to control and possess these things that are mine*. In reality, Damari and Phayre were the ones we should have been watching more closely. We had no way to reason with them. No way to defeat them, really.

The moments I had with Phayre in the infernal realm were grim. She seemed excited when I inflicted violence on her, as if she were excited to see my teeth. And Damari had invited us in under the guise of just wanting to chat, only to break our bodies over and over again with the intention of death.

Riordan wanted to take over the mortal realm and make it his. That much was clear. But what did Phayre and Damari want? What would they be willing to do to get it?

A full-body shiver ran through me. This wasn't good. We had been playing this game, thinking our enemy was one person, only to find out that some of the other players were actually much more dangerous.

"You must be careful of her, Greer. I already know she has caused you great pain. But she has a wrath unlike any of the others. It could rip the fabric of time apart if she wanted it to."

"How would that even be possible?" I whispered, my whole body nearly shaking.

"I do not know. I just know that if anyone could do it, it would be you. It could be her."

Swallowing, I tried not to think of how horrifying that could be. "What about Estoria and Cerena?" They were the two I knew the least about.

"Ah, well, they are great lovers, you see, and they have what I call quiet power. Similar to me, but you can tell they are more cunning, smarter than the others, but lethal in their grace. I would argue they play a longer game than the rest of us. Many of the gods and goddesses can only see what lies an inch in front of them, while both Estoria and Cerena seem to think lightyears ahead in terms of how the world works out." Xael had admiration for them, even though they had barely said any words to me in the infernal realm. They were just there. I shouldn't underestimate their desires either.

"I think I need to go to a very specific moment right before we leave for Damari's. I will gather everyone together, and we will decline her invitation and head to Waverly's sister's place instead."

"I'm guessing Damari cannot leave her place. If something happened for the gods and goddesses to be in the mortal realm permanently, I would guess they are sequestered by my strong magic to be contained in one place or the other. It would be the only way to make it work," Xael commented.

"Now, I know exactly when I want to go back to where I was. How do I make that happen?"

"You must hold and keep that vision of the exact moment you want in your head and your heart. We will create a rip in the time current, and you must be quick. The ghouls will feel you as soon as you enter and may start to come from you. They will most likely be tentative and slow at first, but as soon as they start to find one another and you, they will become emboldened. Do not stop until you see the vision of your time crystal clear. Then you can jump through and seal the time current behind you. You must be careful, Greer, as if one of the ghouls escapes, only you or someone powerful enough to rip the time current open can do it. Gods speed." She kissed my forehead, and we stood.

"We're good friends in my time. I owe you so many things. Thank you for being my friend in this time, as well." I gave her one big hug before I stepped back. I could do this. I had won the Immortality Trials; this would be a piece of cake, right?

"Whatever destiny lies ahead, you are certainly one of its most profound weavers. I am grateful to have helped you in this time. Remember that time jumping is jarring, and you can get lost easily. The universe will make a decision for you if you do not hold your own goal steadfast in your mind."

"I understand. Thank you, Xael. Until next time." I kissed her cheeks, and she nodded at me solemnly.

"Here goes nothing."

Xael handed me a dagger, and I thought about feeling

time ripple around me. The soft caress of the watery power. My hands rose in front of me, and just like I would rip something in two, I sliced open the void of time. It oozed and flowed out of the rip I created, beckoning me into the inky haze.

"Go, Greer, be brave," Xael whispered.

I didn't need any more encouragement before I leaped into the rip and tumbled through time once again.

FORTY-FOUR
GREER

This time was only marginally better than the last. At least I knew I was in the time stream now, as opposed to before I had woken up and been scared shitless. The rip behind me stitched itself closed. Xael gave me a reassuring nod before darkness enclosed me fully.

This time, there wasn't a light anywhere. I simply stood in a darkness so vast and wide that it could swallow me whole, if I let it.

"Should I just wait?" I asked myself, not knowing what direction I should go, but knowing that the ghouls would be stirring already.

Xael said to keep the vision of where I was going strong and clear in my mind. Perhaps there wasn't a correct direction, but rather a certain amount of time I must traverse to get there. Anything was better than staying still and waiting for those shadow monsters to come and get me.

I couldn't even see my hand in front of my face, but I began to walk quickly in the direction I decided would be the right way to go. I pictured the moment before we chose to go to Damari's. Kyra had thought I would argue about him going with me, but I hadn't. I don't know how Damari had rounded us all up with such efficiency, but she did.

There was no way the horrors of before could happen again. If I failed, it would be the end of us. And then what would become of the world as we knew it? The original immortals were restless and tired of the agreements made thousands of years ago. They were hungry for more. More power, more control, more of everything.

I didn't want to live in a world where they were the kings and queens of the land. And I certainly didn't want to live in a world where all I knew was pain and where my friends were gone. Where Kyra and I didn't exist.

Those last few moments before I jumped would be forever branded in my mind and in my blood. I could not let those events come to pass.

Shaking my head, I decided I couldn't dwell on that, in case time itself presented that memory to me instead of the one I needed. So, I was laser-focused on everything from that moment before we decided to go. That's where I would need to land, or at least as close as possible. I had no idea how long this would take, but it already felt like I had been walking for quite some time. My knees started to ache, and sweat dripped down my brow. Xael had said to go until the image was crystal clear.

A small twinkling light appeared far, far away like a small speck of glitter. That had to be where I needed to go. I picked up my pace and moved towards it. Relief flooded my body only momentarily while I held that memory in my head. I tried to recall the words that were spoken, the smells, the feelings, the lights. Everything.

Then I heard what sounded almost like a wail. Like a sad song being sung in one screeching note. I whipped my head back and forth, which was absolutely useless in this abyss of time.

"Ghouls," I whispered.

There was another wail and then another. It sent chills down my spine. I started to jog towards my little piece of glitter. It was getting closer, but not very quickly. The air around me started to change. A phantom wind whipped and swirled in the darkness.

"Fuck."

That was when the first one made its way over to me. It had a haunting aura, almost eating the air around it. One moment, it looked like a large person, and the next, it morphed and swirled into a smoky cloud. Its movements were smooth and watery at first, easily flowing from forms close to me or Lux and then back into vapor.

I burst into a full-on sprint towards my little speck of light in the distance, and the ghoul snapped into a new form. Hands and claws appeared, and a snapping mouth. It had an elongated snout and horns swirling and stabbing straight up. Its broad shoulders and bulging muscles rippled as it moved, and its legs were long and powerful.

Its eyes were like endless pools of murky water, rippling and shifting. Its long, grey tongue flicked out and licked its sharp teeth. It watched me as I ran. As if it were just bidding its time to catch its prey.

Fear gripped my heart, but I couldn't stop. I desperately clung to the image in my head as I sprinted past a few more ghouls becoming corporeal. None looked the same. Some looked like skeletons with sharp bones and gaunt faces. Others looked like individuals I would see on the street in Odessa every day. Others were more animal-like than the original one. Maybe they took the form of whatever poor creature encountered them last.

They were moving slowly, coming together in a crowd

while I ran. My anxiety skyrocketed as dozens of eyes followed me, hauling ass toward my glitter. Why were they just standing there? It was like waiting for a bomb to go off. I knew they would come for me, so what were they waiting for? It didn't matter. Maybe, if I kept running, I would make it before they got their wits about them.

The wails grew louder and more aggressive, turning into screeches that set my ears on fire and made my skin crawl. Then they started to move. Morphing from their corporeal forms to floating balls of smoke, eating up the space between me and them by simply switching forms in rapid succession. My heart pounded in my ears, and I still ran towards my little light of hope that was growing almost to the size of my chest now.

"Keep moving, Greer. Don't stop," I chanted to myself.

I pumped my arms and legs as fast as they would go. In a harrowing screech, everything changed. The ghouls started to fly at me then. Jumping from place to place. Occupying where I had just been moments ago. They were getting close enough to touch, but not quite—almost like they were waiting for something, but they were hot at my heels.

One launched itself right at my face, and I screamed, slashing out with my dagger. The ghoul howled, and I ripped through what felt like fabric. The claws it had nearly bruised my arm, and it was singing with heat, like it knew the destruction it could have faced. If I let it break my skin, I would be infected with time poisoning.

I looked back and saw that they were swarming together now, and I pumped all my fear into my legs and propelled myself forward. My memory was starting to expand; it was almost the size and shape of my body, but it felt like no matter how much I ran, it stayed the same distance away, only growing larger.

The ghouls were working themselves into a frenzy now,

pulsing and rushing towards me. I couldn't even slow them down with my own magic because I was so fucking focused on getting this damn memory to crystallize.

"Damn it!" I yelled. Another nearly nicked my ankle, and I screamed again. They were gnashing and howling at my back, and I didn't know how long I could keep up this pace. My lungs were on fire. My body berated me to slow down, but they were too close. They were getting too bold. They lunged and tripped over one another to try to get a piece of me.

What would happen if they devoured me whole? Would I reform again to only be killed again and again in this time current?

I would not allow myself to fall victim to that eternal damnation.

Finally, the memory started to form. Instead of remaining a white light in a glowing oval, it came into picture with fuzzy shapes.

"*Don't go through it until it is a full crystallized image. If you go too soon, you won't jump to that point. It will send you somewhere else. It has to be as clear as a picture, Greer.*" Xael's words echoed in my head. I continued to dodge the flying ghouls, still swiping and hollering at me.

I was in a windstorm of shrieking entities, slashing and throwing themselves at me. My dagger slashed at the air again and again to keep them away. They were getting closer and closer. I could feel their breath and their limbs nearly touching me to deliver a devastating blow.

This was by far one of the most terrifying things that I had encountered thus far, which was saying something considering the last year I had. One clawed at me, and I was too slow. It caught the skin on my upper back. I screamed as searing pain ripped through me, and I stumbled forward. It was like a hot iron had ripped and flayed open my skin. Tentatively, I reached back, and my fingers came away sticky with blood.

I swore the creature laughed at me and licked its hands.

My whole body shuddered. The pain was nothing. Inconsequential. I knew pain. It was a friend, one I had turned to for a long time. I could do this. I could fucking make it.

My back continued to ooze blood, but I couldn't stop. There was no other option. I refused to entertain any other way.

My feet carried me forward while I tried to keep up my speed and stamina. Dodging the morphing visions of the ghouls as they threw themselves at me, my breath sawing in and out of me, my stamina starting to fade.

The image in front of me was becoming crisp, but it wasn't quite clear yet—like a bad pixelated TV or computer. Fatigue weighed on me. The ghouls were landing little nicks and scratches on me. I shrieked every time they got me, but refused to let it slow me down. My blood heated, and fever struck me while waves of hot and cold slammed into my body. My muscles ached, and my bones grew heavier with each step.

"I have to fucking make it!" I screeched.

The wails were like a wave of sound crashing into me. It felt like the entire horde of them was at my heels, and I was quickly succumbing to their attacks.

The image in front of me was almost there. I could feel that it was close, but the monsters were growing closer. My impending death was right at my doorstep, and I just needed this memory to fucking clear up so I could launch myself through.

Blinking heavily, the picture snapped into place, and before I could think about it anymore. I dove through. Something attached itself to my ankle, and we tumbled through the time photo. Heat seared across the skin of my leg. Moaning, I kicked at it while we fell through a tunnel, and then I hit the ground. My body groaned, and I knew I was a bloody mess.

The cuts and scrapes were all over me, and I could feel each one slowly oozing blood.

At least the weight on my ankle had gone. Without a second thought, the rip in time yawned open at me and snapped it closed with my power, heaving to the floor. Coughing and spluttering, I pushed myself up to see I was in mine and Lux's living room. I meant to jump back to the moment we were together, right before Hyacinth portaled us, but this would do instead. The morning of.

"Greer?" Kyra's voice was stunned. He stood in the kitchen, a pancake nearly to his mouth. The others gaped at me.

"Watch out!" Lux said, barreling into Kyra, sending him sprawling as a time ghoul took a lunge at him. This one looked like a skeleton with pieces of flesh hanging off it in ugly chunks.

"What is that?!" Nova yelled. The ghoul prowled around us.

Sutton's eyes narrowed, and Waverly stood ready to fight.

"You were right there. Then you weren't." Sutton motioned from an empty seat at the counter to where I was now. Then his eyes tracked the beast, and he sent his own shadows out to investigate it.

"Don't let it touch you. We have to send it back to the time current. I can't... I'm so tired... We can't go to Damari... We should go to Evanya."

"Greer, slow down." It was Waverly who rushed to my side while Sutton toyed with the ghoul, taunting it with his shadows.

Black started to seep into my vision, and my brain turned fuzzy in my skull.

"I'm going to pass out. You can't kill the time ghoul. It must be trapped and sent back. Warn Hyacinth and the others. Damari will kill us if we go..."

Then my whole world tilted again. I passed out on the floor, leaving my friends to deal with an enemy they knew nothing about.

And didn't have the power to defeat.

FORTY-FIVE
LUX

Chaos ensued when I landed on top of Kyra to avoid the hellish-looking creature who nearly gutted him.

Greer was bloody and haggard-looking on the floor where Waverly was speaking with her. It didn't last long, though, because in the blink of an eye, Greer's body sagged into Waverly, and she wrapped her in her arms.

"We need some help over here!" Nova called. She and Sutton were barely fending off what I heard Greer call a time ghoul. It changed shape and molded in odd ways, becoming a gnashing monster with claws and teeth one minute, then floating like smoke in the next. It was more skeletal than anything else, and its bones clacked together while it moved from one spot to the next, frantic in its pursuit.

"She said it can't be killed, it has to be sent back to where it came from," Waverly called from where she cradled Greer in her arms.

"I don't understand, one minute she was sitting there with us and the next she was bloody in the living room," Kyra muttered.

I nodded. None of this made sense. But we had more

important matters to deal with, like this abominable creature wreaking havoc in our apartment.

Kyra threw a small, contained fireball at the creature, but all it did was hiss again and absorb his flames. It sucked up the heat and dispersed it almost immediately across its skin.

"How the hell did it do that?"

His mouth hung agape. The creature got angrier and angrier.

"Maybe don't do that again. Less firepower, more shadows," I said, clapping Kyra on the back. We tried to move out of the way for Sutton to wield his power.

"Stand down, creature!" Waverly yelled, her voice singing.

The creature cocked its head and grinned, showing long white teeth and snapping at her once.

It seemed like the people best suited to defend us were Sutton, Nova, and Greer. One of whom was unconscious on the floor. We needed backup. Fast.

"Get your mom, Hyacinth, and Xael on the phone," I ordered. Kyra nodded, reaching for his phone. "I'll help deal with the creepy ghost."

The creature was prowling around the kitchen where Nova and Sutton had it cornered. It hissed and wailed, the sound piercing my eardrums and making me flinch. Its eyes kept flitting back to Greer's crumpled form. A grey tongue flickered out and licked its bony lips before turning endless eyes back to Sutton and Nova.

"It's a time ghoul. We need to open a rip in space and shove it back into a pocket of time," Sutton hissed. His shadows took swipes at the creature.

Sweat beaded down his forehead, and he narrowed his eyes. His fingertips moved while he controlled his shadows. They swirled and corralled it, keeping it in place while it made slashes and attacks. The shadows did an excellent job at keeping it contained, but how long could Sutton keep this up against a creature that we knew little about?

"Why do you know that?" I asked, welcoming my claws for an attack.

"I know many of the universe's creatures that the world would try and forget," Sutton murmured. One of his shadow creatures met the claws of the beast. He winced as if feeling the slash himself. His shadows scattered and reformed.

"Hyacinth and Xael say Nova can do it!" Kyra yelled, looking over at Waverly, who was trying to rouse Greer.

"Tell me how." Nova nodded at Kyra, her stars glowing. Kyra shoved the phone to her, and I could hear Hyacinth barking orders on the other end. Nova nodded and then handed the phone back to Kyra.

"Only a powerful witch or time wielder can do it. Nova is everything we've got right now, unless Greer can do it," Kyra said. We all took a moment to look at Greer's floppy form. Blood was still steadily oozing out of her cuts. I couldn't understand why her immortality hadn't at least fixed a few of them. Some were not that large and not that deep. What exactly was in this creature's claws and mouth that prevented healing from happening?

"She can't. She's too weak. Even if I siren sang her, it would be at her own expense, and I can't do that to her. I don't know why her wounds aren't closing, but clearly that thing needs to be avoided at all costs," Waverly said. She continued to hold Greer, inspecting her wounds.

"I can do this. Just everyone shut up!" Nova's fire eyes seemed to blaze. "Sutton, keep that thing busy until I can rip open the time portal, and then see if you can shove him in with your pets."

Sutton grunted. The time ghoul continued to stalk towards him, and his shadows came to his defense. The monster sucked all the light from the room as it molded and moved to evade the shadows of Sutton. But Sutton was relentless. Fatigue showed on his face, but he continued to chase the ghoul around and bully it with his power.

The ghoul couldn't escape his shadows, no matter how often he got rid of one, another slipped into its place. Sutton's eyes moved back and forth rapidly, trying to keep it contained, but his power could only do so much.

"I can't do this forever, Nova. Get it done," Sutton said, nearly breathless.

I ran over to him, wanting to help but not knowing what to do. This battle was all his. Nothing that I could do would have the same impact as his shadows. Getting too close would mean letting that thing touch me, which is exactly what Greer said we shouldn't do.

Nova was chanting and moving her hands in shapes that I didn't understand. A current of air started to swirl around her, and a spark of light erupted in the middle of the room.

"Everyone, get back!" she demanded. The bright light cracked and thundered, turning to living lightning. She bellowed out her spell, continuing the incantation despite the chaos around us.

The ghoul screeched at the sight and started moving faster and faster around the room.

"Nova!" Sutton screamed. The air went staticky, and the ghoul became frenzied.

"Almost there," she yelled back. The lightning strike went black and started to ooze until it pulled back to what looked like inky darkness.

Heat sizzled across my skin, and Sutton collapsed into a lunge, blood trickling down from his nose in a small, red river.

"Now!" Nova commanded, and in one huge rush of shadow power, Sutton sent beast after shadow beast at the ghoul and corralled it into the crack in time Nova had created.

He walked it into the portal, while it slashed and threw

blows out. Sutton screamed, the creature took a final lunge at him, and its claws raked across his chest.

"No!" I bellowed, shifting into my tiger form and throwing myself at the ghoul.

Its claws were still red from hitting Sutton's chest. The creature screeched as we made contact. I grabbed its arm with my jaws and flung it into the portal, but not before it took another swipe at me and sank its nails into my side.

Stars danced in front of my eyes, and pain like hot needles pierced through me. I collapsed on the ground, gasping for air. My blood turned boiling and then icy cool while I shifted back and groaned into the fetal position.

Sutton lay beside me, his eyelids fluttering. His hands were gripping his chest, coming away bloody. He flinched and twitched through the pain.

As soon as it slipped through, Nova's hands dropped, and the rip sealed. The air stilled like nothing had happened at all. Silence filled the room.

"That was an annoying little fucker," Sutton whispered after a beat.

"You two, I swear to the gods," Nova grumbled, coming next to us to examine our wounds.

"These hurt... really bad. Greer has so many. It feels like something is poisoning my blood," I heaved out the words, shuddering as pain wracked my body.

"Her wounds aren't healing right," Waverly muttered from where she still knelt at Greer's side.

"This time ghoul, what else do you know about it? Is it venomous?" Nova asked Sutton, who still hadn't opened his eyes. He gave a small nod.

"Lore says that a strike by its hands or teeth gives you time poisoning. A wound that will never heal and never stop causing you pain. The power of time is a fickle bitch, and the costs are heavy when you start to throw that power around," Sutton whispered, and silence followed once more.

What had happened to Greer for this thing to chase her?

"Fuck!" Nova sat down hard. Kyra helped Waverly bring Greer closer to where Sutton and I lay.

"You need to rest, Nova." Waverly laid a hand on Nova's arm. Her eyes were wary, and her shoulders were slumping forward.

"Let me see if I can do a little more, my love," she said quietly. She waved her hands around our bodies, eyes closed.

"What if I try to sing the wounds closed and you help? Maybe we can coax the poison out together?" Waverly sat next to Nova, and Kyra looked horrified at the bloody mess that was us on the ground.

Gasping, Greer choked on her own breath and tried to sit up, but collapsed, her eyes scanning the room frantically. Kyra was right by her side in an instant.

"Calm down, Greer," Waverly sang to her.

Greer's wide pupils went back to normal, and her breathing calmed. Nodding, she smiled weakly at Waverly and lay still.

"Damari will torture and kill us if we go see her," Greer said, her voice scratchy and hoarse.

"What?" I whispered.

"All of you need to shut up and lie down so Waverly and I can try and heal you!" Nova snapped. We obeyed.

"Them first. Please," Greer begged.

"Your wounds are worse," Nova countered.

"I made it this far, heal them first. Please, Nova." Something in Greer's voice made Nova oblige.

"Okay, Sutton," she whispered. She and Wavelry spent the next several minutes working together to seal and close his wound.

The poison danced out, an inky tendril slithering its way from his bloody scratch. He gasped and writhed; the tendril continued to pull out of him. Finally, there was no more. The wound closed, and Nova pushed the poison into one of her glass jars.

"We most likely did not get it all. It hit your bloodstream quickly. You may suffer from pain there regularly. Which we can help manage, but it will probably never be the same."

"I am so sorry, everyone. I have brought so much suffering to you all," Greer croaked out, tears running down her face.

"No, you haven't, Greer," Kyra whispered into her hair, and she shook her head.

"You don't even know the half of it," she said, closing her eyes.

I gasped as another wave of icy-hot sensation shot through my side.

"Lux," Nova rushed over and began the process on me.

Waverly sang the poison out with Nova's help. There was a sense of relief. My own wound began to heal, and the poison leeched out of me. Pain hummed at my side, but it was now localized as opposed to my entire body feeling like ice and fire from within.

"Thank you," I coughed.

Nova nodded, smiling weakly, and Waverly gave my hand a squeeze.

"Okay, Greer. How many have you got?" Nova asked. Waverly and Kyra helped remove her clothes, which were barely tatters at this point, to reveal at least a dozen or so scratches covering her skin.

"My gods," I said.

"Just heal the big ones, and the rest I can handle." Greer looked into Nova's eyes with tears running down her cheeks.

"She's lying. It hurts like nothing else I've ever experi-enced. Like a knife wound of fire and the worst fever experience you've ever had," Sutton groaned from next to me, sitting up and scooting closer to me.

"I'm fine," Greer gritted her teeth. Nova and Waverly went to work.

They worked on her wounds for at least an hour before both of them were swaying on their feet, and Greer commanded them to stop.

"We can do more another time. Thank you, both of you. But we need to leave. Right now. I'll explain later, but we need to go to Evanya's. It's the only safe place I can think of right now," Greer said.

I gave her a quizzical look. She was hiding things from us. But I wouldn't press. Right now, it seemed like the most important thing was to get moving. She had clearly been through something, and we didn't know what.

Her brave face certainly wasn't fooling me or anyone else.

Sutton's hand reached for mine, and I intertwined our fingertips together. We shared a look. We both knew none of this was good.

"Damari will torture and kill us if we go see her," Greer said again, quietly.

We hadn't even talked about our plan on how to handle her now that she said she wanted to meet.

"How do you know that?" I asked.

"Trust me. We need to leave. We aren't safe here. Waverly, we will be protected at Evanya's, right? Will we be shielded by what your sister has put in place?" she asked, the words tumbling out.

"Yes, it should protect against the gods and goddesses or at least hide us from them."

"Now, we must leave now. Please. I'll explain everything once we are out of here," Greer begged, looking at all of us. Everyone was confused, but considering she had just appeared in the middle of the room, beaten and bloody, with a ghoul on her ass, it seemed like maybe we should get moving.

"Okay, give us ten minutes and then we will go. I'll make the arrangements," Kyra said.

"I would offer a portal, but I can't do it right now..." Nova looked disappointed in herself.

"You've done so much, Nova." I gave her arm a reassuring squeeze.

"We can't portal there. It has to be by mortal ways. Flying or boating in." Waverly said.

Waverly talked to Greer in soothing tones while the rest of us quickly grabbed the necessities.

"I got a car waiting for us and a boat," Kyra said. We all stood ready to go.

Sutton was cradled in my arms. Greer was wobbling next to Kyra, and Nova was leaning heavily on Waverly.

"We look in rough shape," I commented as we went down the elevator.

Greer let out a breathy laugh. "Just trust me."

We did. When we finally made it onto the boat, I asked Greer for the whole story.

FORTY-SIX
KYRA

W e all waited patiently for Greer to explain to us what the hell was going on. She winced and fidgeted in her seat while Waverly's home island came into view.

"I don't think Riordan is our worst threat anymore. I think it's Damari and maybe Phayre," Greer whispered. "I can't tell you everything that happened. I won't. It's too gruesome. And I won't make any of you carry that."

"But that means you are carrying it alone," I said, reaching for her hand, and her shoulders slumped forward.

"It's better this way, trust me. Trust that if we had visited Damari, we would cease to exist. I-I pulled at time so hard so the events of the past wouldn't happen, that I time jumped thousands of years and got stuck in the time current to get back to you. It caused too much movement in the time current, which made those ghouls form and come after me. Everything is a little fuzzy for me; my memories don't all make sense, but we can't go see Damari. This is the only way."

Greer stared each of us down like a challenge, but whatever she had seen and experienced had rocked her. I would try to get her to tell me more, but I wouldn't push it right now.

"Let's just get to the island. Get with Evanya, and then we can discuss all of this later." I stroked her hair and she closed her eyes, leaning into me.

Evanya was already on shore. Waverly had sent her a water message before we got there.

"Hurry, let's get back into the city's protection," Evanya said, forgoing the pleasantries. She helped us out, and a few of her people guided us to what looked like an untamed jungle.

The image broke and fractured as we entered, and we were met with large metal doors. Evanya guided us through, and we walked through steel tunnels before breaking into a larger cityscape. Greer had described her travels to me last time she was here, but it was completely different seeing it in person.

"Wow, this is beautiful, Evanya," Lux said. He and Sutton were clinging to each other.

"Thank you." She smiled tightly.

"Can I use one of your medical facilities? Greer's wounds still need attention," Nova asked while we continued to walk deeper into the city.

The sun was dipping low in the sky as Evanya led us to her home.

"I have a space in my house you can use. Do you need anything? It's stocked with all the standard supplies."

"No, that should be alright. Can the rest of you get settled, and I'll get Greer sorted out? Waverly, want to come with?" Nova asked.

"I'll come," I offered, but Greer shook her head.

"It's okay, I will come find you later."

The three of them took off. I tried not to take it personally that Greer had brushed me off. But clearly, she needed some time to sort out all that had happened.

"Come on, Ky," Lux pulled me with him while we were shown around.

"She's hiding a lot," I said. The three of us were shown our rooms, and I settled myself into Lux's and Sutton's shared space.

"Major shifts had to happen in the time current for ghouls to appear. I don't know how far she jumped... but it must have been very significant to create not just one but many." Sutton frowned and paced the room.

"I wonder what happened with Damari. Why was she so afraid?" I asked.

It was hard to imagine how things could get worse for us. Many terrible things had already happened. Phayre stealing our serum, the President forcing us into lip service for the trials we hated, the torture of hell... the impending doom of mortal entrapment.

"I don't know. She needs time to sort it out. She will tell us when she is ready," Lux offered, and I nodded.

"I'm going to go wait for her in our room. See you all later," I said, excusing myself.

I needed some of my own time to sort through my emotions. Greer had been through so much, and I was afraid she was retreating back into protecting herself and the ones around her by being distant.

It didn't bode well for any of us if she tried to sacrifice herself for the greater good. We were stronger together if we shared the burden. We all were involved partly because of her, but we all had our own reasons. I was involved in this mess long before she was because of my father, and I would be damned if I let her shoulder all that now.

A knock sounded lightly at my door, and Greer appeared, looking like a shell of herself. Pale cheeks and hunched shoulders greeted me. I wanted nothing more than to take every burden off her shoulders.

"Ky," she groaned, her hand reaching for me.

I guided her to the bed and sat her down.

"I'm right here. What do you need?" I asked, getting on my knees so I was eye level with her on the bed.

"Will you just hold me, please?"

Tears showed in her eyes, and I lay down beside her, wrapping her up in my arms and pressing her body into mine.

"You're safe now, I've got you," I whispered into her skin. Sobs wracked her body. She shook in my arms, and I stroked her hair.

I wished I could do more. She was safe now, but what about later? What could I do to guarantee her safety? We were immortal for gods' sake, and that was causing us more harm than good, considering we could be fucking tortured for centuries.

She finally fell asleep, the day heavy on her skin.

"I'll do whatever it takes to keep you safe, Greer. I promise." I kissed her forehead and hoped to gods I would be able to stay true to those words.

FORTY-SEVEN
GREER

I dreamed of pain and pleasure. My subconscious mind trying to simultaneously comfort me while making me live everything in excruciating detail. Dreams of Kyra and I would flit in and out of the horrifying memories that made up my life. Flashes of Lux and I, or our whole group, would intertwine with the horrors of the trial, my time in the infernal realm, or my newest hellacious ordeal would rear their ugly heads. But there were pieces missing. Slips of time that I couldn't quite make sense of, or small jumps that went too quickly from one thing to the other.

Was I truly losing time and forgetting, or was this just my own dream mind playing tricks on me?

When I finally woke up, Kyra was right beside me. His body entangled with mine. He had whispered that he would keep me safe last night.

But what if the biggest risk to them all wasn't Damari or Riordan or even Phayre?

But me.

The girl who, at one time, almost succumbed to her own darkness, yet somehow managed to claw her way to the top of the trials, ready to fight the world. Only to be broken again and again. No matter how many times I fought my way out of terror, it always came for me again. Was this the life I was destined to live? One filled with heartbreak again and again for myself and others?

That wasn't a life that I wanted, but what choice did I have? I was the biggest threat to us all. Uncontrollable, in the most desperate of times; unreliable, in the safety I could hold for others.

My existence as the timewraith had monumentally fucked everything up. My existence was a threat to the world as we knew it, and so many people were trying to abuse me and my power so they could set things the way they wanted. And who was I to know better? To do better, when I couldn't even save myself?

But I couldn't say those words out loud. So instead, I stayed in Kyra's embrace and pretended like nothing else existed, savoring this moment of peace while the rest of the world slept.

FORTY-EIGHT
DAMARI

"Why didn't they come?" Riordan demanded, while I paced the living room.

"How am I supposed to know?!" I snarled at him. He didn't even flinch.

"No need to get testy, Damari, darling," Phayre purred.

The image of punching her in her smug little nose floated through my mind, but I refrained. The time for violence would come.

Neither one of them had agreed to my original plan, which was to kill Kyra and everyone else, then enslave the timewraith. Riordan was too attached to his abomination of a son and, for some reason, Phayre agreed with them. They thought we could leverage the others. I thought they were a waste of space, especially the ones who stole from me.

Afton popped into the room with a frown, already turning his face. "I can't find them."

"What do you mean?" Riordan demanded again. Glowering.

"They aren't in any of their usual locations, and I can't

pick up on any magical trail that leads anywhere," he responded.

"Keep fucking looking!" I snapped. He threw me the finger.

"Don't worry, Damari, you will get your revenge. Patience, darling." Phayre repeated.

I was so close to ripping her apart. They had all been plotting and planning for too long. I had reached my tipping point when Raelyn had them steal from me, and now I wanted nothing more than to rip the timewraith's little friends to shreds and watch her pay for the consequences of disrespecting me. The mortal realm needed a strong hand, and I was the only one prepared to do it.

"We will need to find another way to fulfill our plan," Riordan murmured.

"Then what are we doing sitting around? Let's get to fucking work," I snapped and stormed out of the room.

These little magical beings were nothing compared to the godly powers I wielded. I just needed to set a better trap. One that the others couldn't interfere with, one the timewraith would not be able to escape.

Tangled Encounters

A Sapphic Circus Romance

Book one in the Cirque Callisto series.

CHAPTER 1
OZZIE

"How did you hear about this show again?" Trevor asked. At this point, I had dragged him to attend several performances, all with varying levels of skill and professionalism. Some were extraordinary, while others were... not so much. But this one? This one felt different.

"It's another one of the circus companies I reached out to. I'm thinking about auditioning for them depending on how this goes, and it's their spring show." I flipped through the pamphlet in my hand and scanned the acts. It was an aerial cabaret show, and my skin was already buzzing. The auditorium was U shaped, so the audience hugged the stage. Soft red lights wrapped around us, and the backdrop dazzled and sparkled across the audience in the dimly lit room.

The seats slowly started to fill up, and I tried not to keep checking my watch for the official start time. This was always my favorite part of a show: the blossoming energy of the room, the frisson of anticipation that skittered across my skin and left me smiling in its wake. Cracking my neck from left to right, I tried to file away every small detail that brought this experience to life.

"Well, it's giving Christina Aguilera *Burlesque* vibes, and I'm here for it. Want me to go grab another round before the show starts?"

I looked over to where our empty drinks sat. I sure as hell wasn't going to get up; the pre-show atmosphere fueled me and warmed my chest. My brain was fully rooted in waiting mode and incapable of doing anything else but sit my jittery ass down.

"Sure, I'll take whatever their specialty cocktail is."

Trevor nodded and made his way through the red velvet seats and over the legs of everyone in our row with only ten minutes until showtime. My knee bounced erratically as I tried to read more of what the pamphlet said. My eyes scanned the page, hungry for more information about Cirque Callisto, the company putting on the show tonight. There was a slight blurb about inquiring artists and my heart sang. I had already reached out to them, but I couldn't wait to see their work firsthand.

Trevor and I had just settled into a rental house, and I wanted a circus space to call home. My skin tingled with excitement at the thought of training and performing again; it hadn't even been that long since I left my last company, but my body ached to create movement art. Even a little time away made me anxious.

It was hard not to listen to a song these days and immediately put together an act. The creativity inside me was fucking desperate for a release, despite the hellish ordeal my last company had put me through.

Glancing at the pamphlet nearly crumpled in my hands, the words on the pages blurred together, so I tried to focus on the pictures instead. They had pronouns included with the artists' bios, which was a great indicator that they would be queer friendly, and the roles in the production seemed to give the middle finger to gendered stereotypes. My smile grew bigger and my shoulders relaxed at the thought of having a community that would be safe and supportive of who I was. Coming out every time you met someone new as an adult got old, especially when you didn't know what their reaction would be. My job wasn't to manage anybody's emotions about my identity. They could fuck the fuck right off if it bothered them, but alas, sometimes it could not be avoided.

"Okay, it's some sort of dressed up Cosmo. It's good, but I couldn't tell you the name of it." Trevor's eyes danced as he handed me the bright pink liquid. He looked gorgeous in his black sequined tuxedo jacket and floral print button-down. He wore perfectly tailored slacks that hit just above his ankles, and the whole look was tied together with a pair of sparkling loafers. He fit right in with the sultry vibe of the evening.

All around us, people were dressed up to various degrees. The show had encouraged audience participation in their sexy aerial cabaret, so there was everything from full-on latex kink gear to suburban khakis and sweaters. It was a glorious mix, a beautiful reminder of how art could bring otherwise contrasting people together into a melting pot of appreciation and respect.

The lights dimmed, and my stomach did a flip. A hush fell over the audience, and I tried not to hold my breath as I death-gripped the arms of my chair. My eyes bounced around the room, waiting to see what would happen and how the spectators would react.

The emcee came out dripping in leather and chains. She was a beautiful Black woman who introduced us to the show with a megawatt smile and the crack of a small crop against her palm. The audience roared as she began to sing and dance in her dominatrix style outfit. She high-kicked and shimmied across the stage, belting out notes only Broadway stars hit, and finished in a jump split to the ground.

What a fucking star.

The crowd yelled and hollered while she blew kisses, and then, with a bow and a wide sweep of her arms, she welcomed the next act. Fog started to pour out, and the music changed from an upbeat jazz interlude to a deep sexy pulse. My heart seemed to thump in time to the bass, and I scooted closer to the edge of my seat.

I watched in awe as a white woman strutted on stage in a two-piece set that was made entirely of rhinestones and left little to the imagination. Her dark brown hair cascaded down her back and showed off the cords of muscles in her shoulders and arms. I swallowed as my eyes took in her athletic form.

There was a fluttering deep in my belly as I watched her command the stage. The stage lights turned to deep purples and blues, and the ensuing reflections from the rhinestones covering her body danced across the audience's faces. Her limbs flowed effortlessly on the ground until a hoop was lowered down, and she grabbed it with both hands. Floating up, she hooked a leg and blew a kiss to the audience.

People whistled and cried out all around me as she began her dance on the hoop as it was lifted, higher and higher. She moved like she was making love to it, and I tried to still my queer little heart.

Circus and aerial weren't inherently sexual. It was an athletic feat like any other professional sport mixed with performance art that could be a beautiful narrative of all kinds of stories.

But tonight, the things that woman was doing with her body felt practically carnal. My stupid imagination was running off in a million different directions, and I scolded myself for not keeping my weirdly horny ass in check.

Focus, Ozzie.

Her eyes were bright as she committed to her confident character and art in the air. It felt like she was looking into my soul each time her eyes swept across the crowd. Splits and spins were thrown out one after the other; audible gasps rang out from the crowd as she dropped from the top to the bottom of the hoop. Emotion that I couldn't place swelled inside me and had me breathing hard while heat crept up on my cheeks.

I wondered idly if I had ever made anyone feel like this when I performed. How was it possible to inspire such a visceral reaction in someone? Swallowing, I tried my best not to objectify her like some dumb man—I was literally no better than a horny fourteen-year-old boy by the way my body was reacting—and to focus instead on her creativity and talent. Performance artists worked hard to have their skill and strength recognized. Circus could be sexy and strong; I knew that firsthand.

My body was just reacting to a beautiful person, that was all. It was normal and natural. Nothing to be ashamed of, just something I needed to monitor. Probably just needed to get laid, honestly. Mentally, I put it on my to do list.

The audience continued to be enthralled by her as she wrapped and weaved her final moments in the air. She finished her act by spinning so fast she was practically a blur and then stopping on a dime, so that her hair fanned down and her chest heaved dramatically. She winked at the audience as she was lowered down slowly and gave us all a little wave as she exited the stage.

Who was she? My mouth was nearly dry as I sucked down the rest of my cocktail.

How could I create a mesmerizing experience like that, one where the audience was eating out of the palm of my hand? Every drop and spin had been met with gasps, claps, and whistles. I had never seen someone move like that on the hoop; it was practically mouthwatering. A spell had been cast over every single person here, and I wondered how she seemed to bewitch all of us so easily.

Trevor lightly coughed, and I whipped my head around to him.

"What?" I hissed.

"You just drooled all over that performance." He took a sip of his drink and lifted his dark brows.

"It was a beautiful display of athleticism." I narrowed my eyes as he rolled his.

"*Right*, had nothing to do with the performer?" he teased.

"Everyone was enraptured by her. She was extraordinary!" My voice was getting higher as I shifted uncomfortably in my seat, trying to ease some of the weird tension that had built in my belly.

"Yeah, but the hunger coming off of you is palpable, Ozzie." Trevor cackled, and I scowled. The lights were shifting, and our gorgeous emcee was back. I waved him off and took a deep breath.

Turning my attention back to the show, I exhaled loudly. The show flowed beautifully from silk performers, contortionists, dancers, singers, and acrobatics; all of which had the crowd singing and cheering. However, nothing had captured me quite like the first aerialist in the hoop. Maybe Trevor was right. I did have a little crush on the performer, but it was harmless. Nothing to be concerned about. I had lots of crushes on lots of different performers, and it literally meant nothing.

My mind wandered to the way her bright red lips cracked open, a smile that looked like she was holding on to a secret. Her eyes seemed to be glued to everyone in the crowd, like she could see the most intimate parts of my soul.

Before I knew it, the show was over, and I had half my mind on the first performer and had only been half watching the rest of the show.

Goddamnit, Ozzie.

"That was fantastic. I can see why you would be interested in joining them. Also, a very diverse cast. I think you'd fit right in," Trevor commented. Slowly we oozed out of the auditorium, where a happy buzz infiltrated every corner of the building. The performers were out in the lobby by the bar, greeting the spectators and taking photos with anyone who wanted them.

I scanned the lobby for the hoop artist and came up short. Why was I looking for her? I didn't even know her and how weird would it be for me to go up to her and be like, "Hey I was obsessed with your act and you're really fucking hot. Are you into women and are you single?" That would be a guarantee that I would never work with this company and that they would call me a weirdo.

"Ozzie Nelson?" someone said from behind me, and I turned around to see the director of the show in a pink feather boa and a hot pink lingerie set.

"Hi, Logan Beaumont?"

"Yes! I'm so glad you could make it tonight. What did you think of the show?" she asked happily. Logan's long, light pink hair was piled high on the crown of her head, and she grinned, showing off straight white teeth. Tattoos snaked along most of her body and she practically glowed from all the glitter on her skin. Logan had been walking around the aisles, teasing people with her feathers and flirting with the guests during the show.

"Thank you so much for the tickets! It was amazing. The first hoop artist was magnificent. Truly one of the best lyra acts I've ever seen." I blushed slightly, thinking of her hard muscles and the way her body moved around the apparatus.

"Jess is truly a star. You should come take her class sometime. I'll send you the schedule. You should come hang out this next week and see what you're interested in. Obviously, I'm biased, but we have amazing coaches and contacts here.

And we're always looking for people to help diversify our acts." She beamed at me.

I had already sent her my videos on lyra, as well as juggling, and I knew I was good. I had been training in a circus for several years now, but I wasn't captivating like Jess was. She moved in ways that felt impossible and magical all at the same time. Not that it was a competition, but it was hard for my mind not to wander there, to feel like an imposter in my art sometimes.

"I would love that." Tension prickled across my shoulders. I had been in my hometown for so long, but I needed a city with more connections and more action. This seemed like the perfect place to go, despite my own anxious energy.

"Oh, there she is! Jess!" Logan waved her boa frantically, and Jess seemed to pop out of nowhere. She still wore her dazzling rhinestone two-piece, but she donned a pair of black circular glasses. Oddly, she was even more endearing with the dark frames surrounding her light blue eyes. She was more petite than I realized, but all the muscles in her body seemed to ripple as she moved. Jess's dark brown hair looked even shinier up close. She had chunky teal pieces framing her face that I hadn't noticed while she was on stage. I had the urge to reach out and run my fingers through the silky strands.

Ugh, I needed to get it together.

"Jess, this is Ozzie. Ozzie, Jess! She just moved here and is looking for somewhere to train. I'll have to show you her videos. The juggling you do is truly phenomenal. We don't have anyone who object manipulates right now, and she's also a lyra artist!"

My cheeks grew hot again. Juggling was my main trick, and I was really fucking good at it when I actually gave myself due credit. I loved to blend it with dance, clowning and other apparatus work. It was like a puzzle to solve every time. People didn't often brag about me, though.

Jess's eyes crinkled as she beamed broadly, and a dipping sensation happened in my stomach. It was like her whole face lit up. She reached out a hand, and I stared at it a second too long before grabbing it and folding my sweaty palm against hers.

"Nice to meet you, Ozzie. Can't wait to see you in the studio sometime."

"You too! Your piece was enthralling, truly could not stop thinking about it the whole show. I would love to take a class from you sometime." I realized I still had a hold of her hand and let it go quickly, wiping my hand on my leather leggings.

Jesus, why were my hands so fucking wet?

Jess gave me a funny look, and I realized she probably thought I was wiping her touch off. My eyes widened, and a knot formed in my belly, but before I could explain myself, someone interrupted us and took the two performers away. Logan gave an apologetic grin, and Jess grimaced.

"Fuck."

"What happened? It looked like it was going well!" Trevor sidled up next to me with a new drink in hand from where he had been eavesdropping.

"I wiped my sweaty ass hand on my thigh, and I think Jess, the girl who performed on the hoop, thought I was wiping her touch off. Christ, I'm just stressed because I have an insta-crush on her. Pretty women are my weakness. My little queer heart can't help it." I bit my lip and sighed.

"Well, I'm sure it wasn't that bad. You'll just have to be extra nice when you see her next. You're visiting their studio this next week, right?"

I nodded. Butterflies erupted in my belly. I wanted to dazzle Logan, and I really wanted to impress Jess. She was breathtaking up close, and I had royally screwed it up.

"Come on, let's go drink some of your embarrassment away." Trevor dragged me to the bar with a knowing smirk. He was all too familiar with my embarrassing ways. Hopefully she would forget that I had been a total asshat and did that. Maybe she hadn't even noticed at all.

Acknowledgments

A huge ginormous thank you to my editor K.F. Starfell. This story transformed because of you. I am so thankful for your love, dedication and thoughtfulness.

As always thank you to Amanda at Eternal Geekery for the fantastic cover. You always make my dreams come true.

Thank you to Ciara for the sensitivity read. Your feedback was so incredibly kind and necessary.

Thank you to my friends, family and loved ones for hanging in there as this book slowly took the life out of me and then injected it back into my veins.

Thank you to my fellow indie authors, book besties and every single bookish friend who supports and follows me on threads, booktok, and bookstagram.

Finally, thank you to my readers who waited for this book for so long. For those who read my first book when I barely knew what I was doing. Thank you for sticking around for this story. I will be eternally grateful for your love of the first book and your excitement for this one. You are the reason I can do this.

Thank you. Thank you. Thank you!

AUTHOR'S NOTE

This was by far the hardest book I ever had to write. Very ambitious of past Madi to make her debut novel a fantasy romance trilogy as someone who is not a plotter. This book had more variations than any other book I have written and it took a long time to get right. I wrote The Immortality Trials from a very dark place inside myself. It was a way to process my grief, depression and heartache. When I sat down to write Timewraith many years later, I was in a very different place. I had healed and grown but the story I had started years ago started right where I left off. Navigating that was quite the roller coaster ride. But we did it!

It has been an incredibly intense, exhausting and rewarding experience to get to the end here. Thank you for being patient with me as I worked to get it exactly the way I wanted it. You all have been so kind as I have moved at my own pace.

This trilogy holds such a special place in my soul and I can't wait to finish it soon.

Xoxo,
Madi

Social Media

If you would like to stay updated on all the new book things, you can see my shenanigans here:

TikTok | Instagram | Threads
@madisonnicolebooks

Or get signed copies here:

Website: www.madisonnicolebooks.com

About the Author

Madison Nicole is a 29-year-old queer author who currently resides in Kansas where she teaches dance, fitness, and circus arts. You can catch Madi playing video games, reading dark romance books, and juggling when she is not writing. She is excited to continue to explore her writing career and bring more stories your way!

www.ingramcontent.com/pod-product-compliance
Lightning Source LLC
Chambersburg PA
CBHW072018020726
47501CB00006B/1860